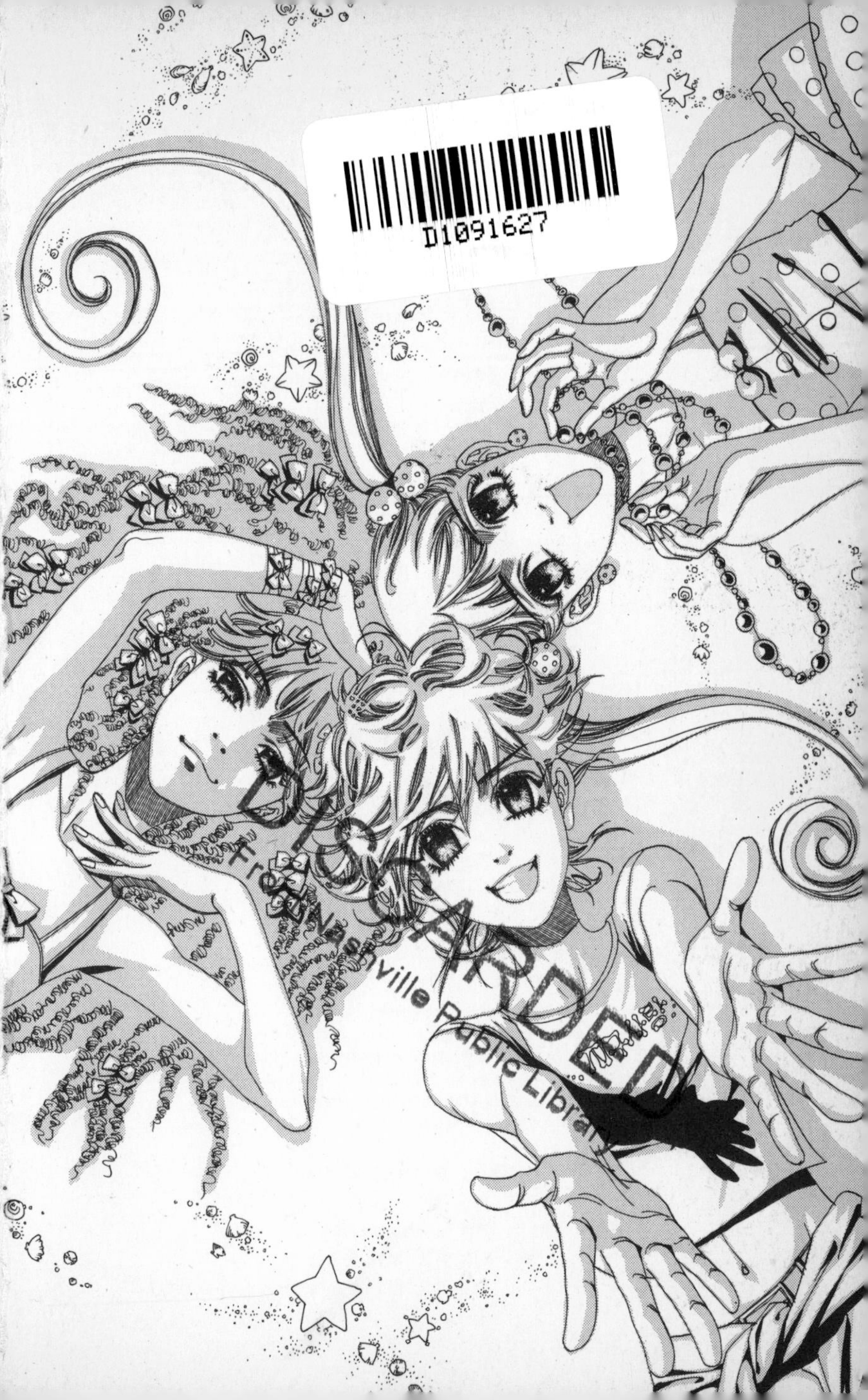

Ark Angels vol. 1
created by Sang-Sun Park

Translation - Monica Seya
English Adaptation - Jamie S. Rich
Retouch and Lettering - Lucas Rivera
Production Artist - James Dashiell
Cover Design - Seth Cable

Editors - Shun Nakazawa and Rob Valois
Digital Imaging Manager - Chris Buford
Production Managers - Jennifer Miller and Mutsumi Miyazaki
Managing Editor - Lindsey Johnston
Editorial Director - Jeremy Ross
VP of Production - Ron Klamert
Publisher and E.I.C. - Mike Kiley
President and C.O.O. - John Parker
C.E.O. - Stuart Levy

A  Manga

TOKYOPOP Inc.
5900 Wilshire Blvd. Suite 2000
Los Angeles, CA 90036

E-mail: info@TOKYOPOP.com
Come visit us online at www.TOKYOPOP.com

ISBN: 1-59816-262-4

First TOKYOPOP printing: December 2005
10 9 8 7 6 5 4 3 2
Printed in the USA

VOLUME ONE

Sang-Sun Park

HAMBURG // LONDON // LOS ANGELES // TOKYO

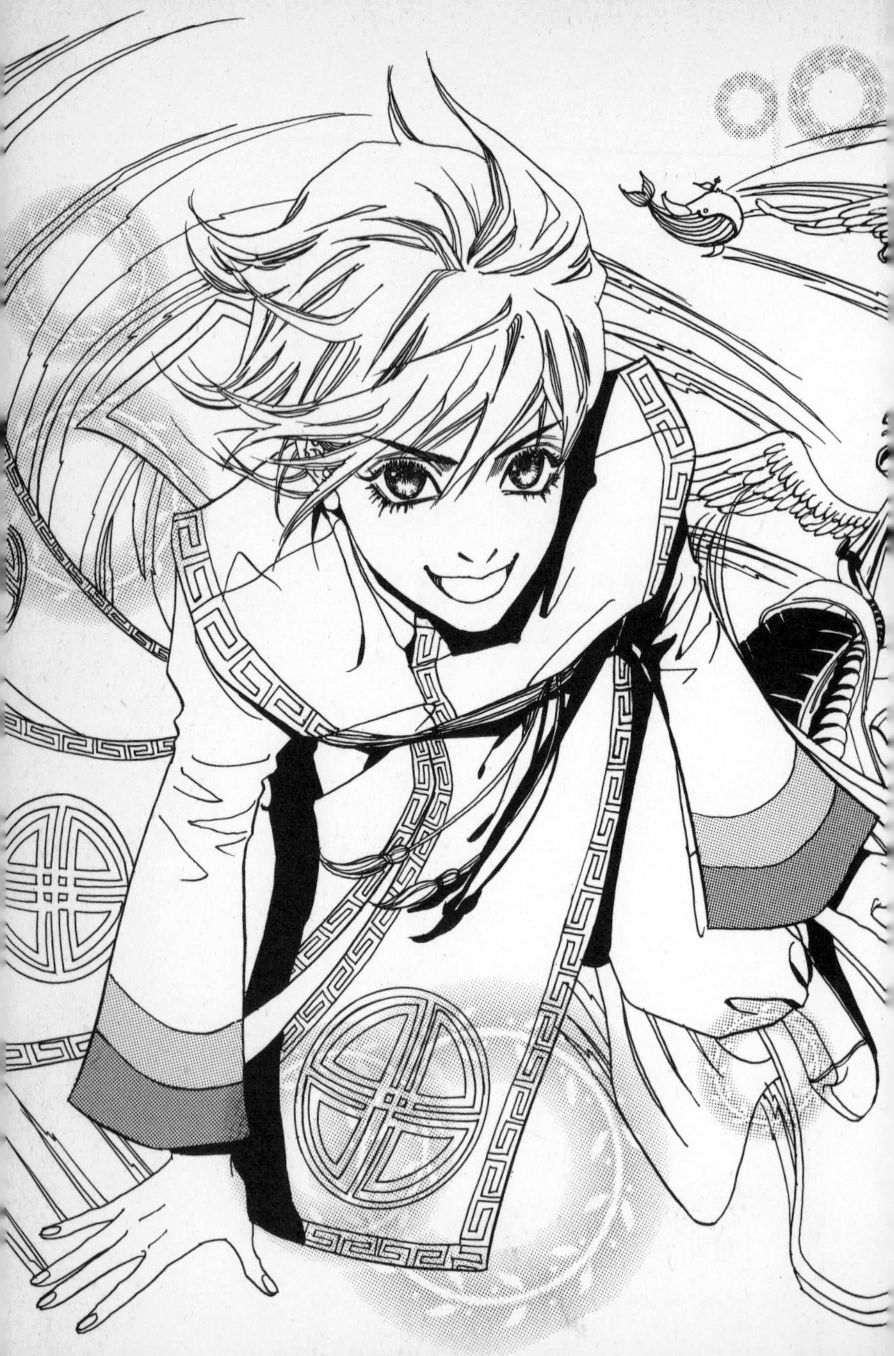

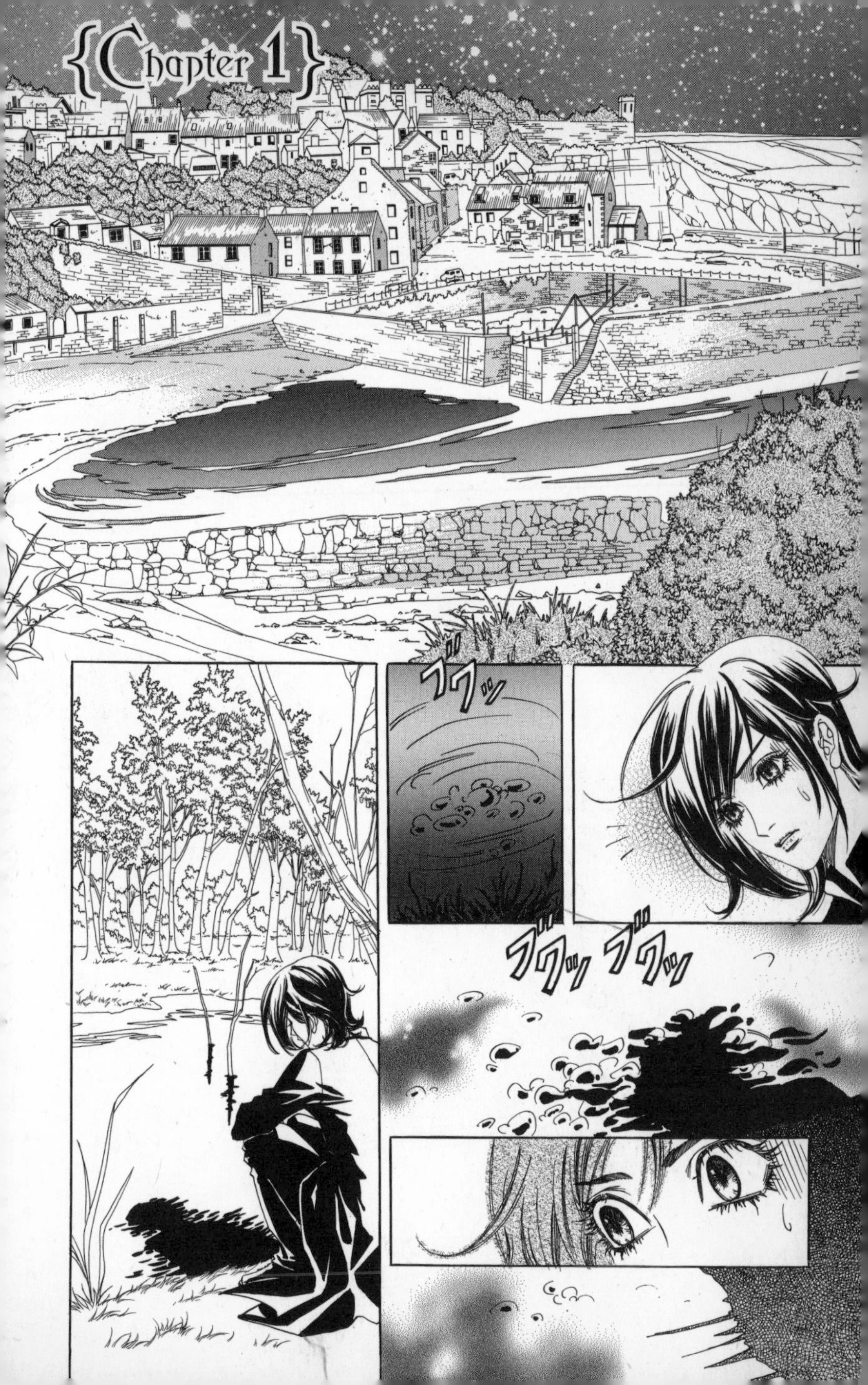
{Chapter 1}
ブワッ
ブワッ ブワッ

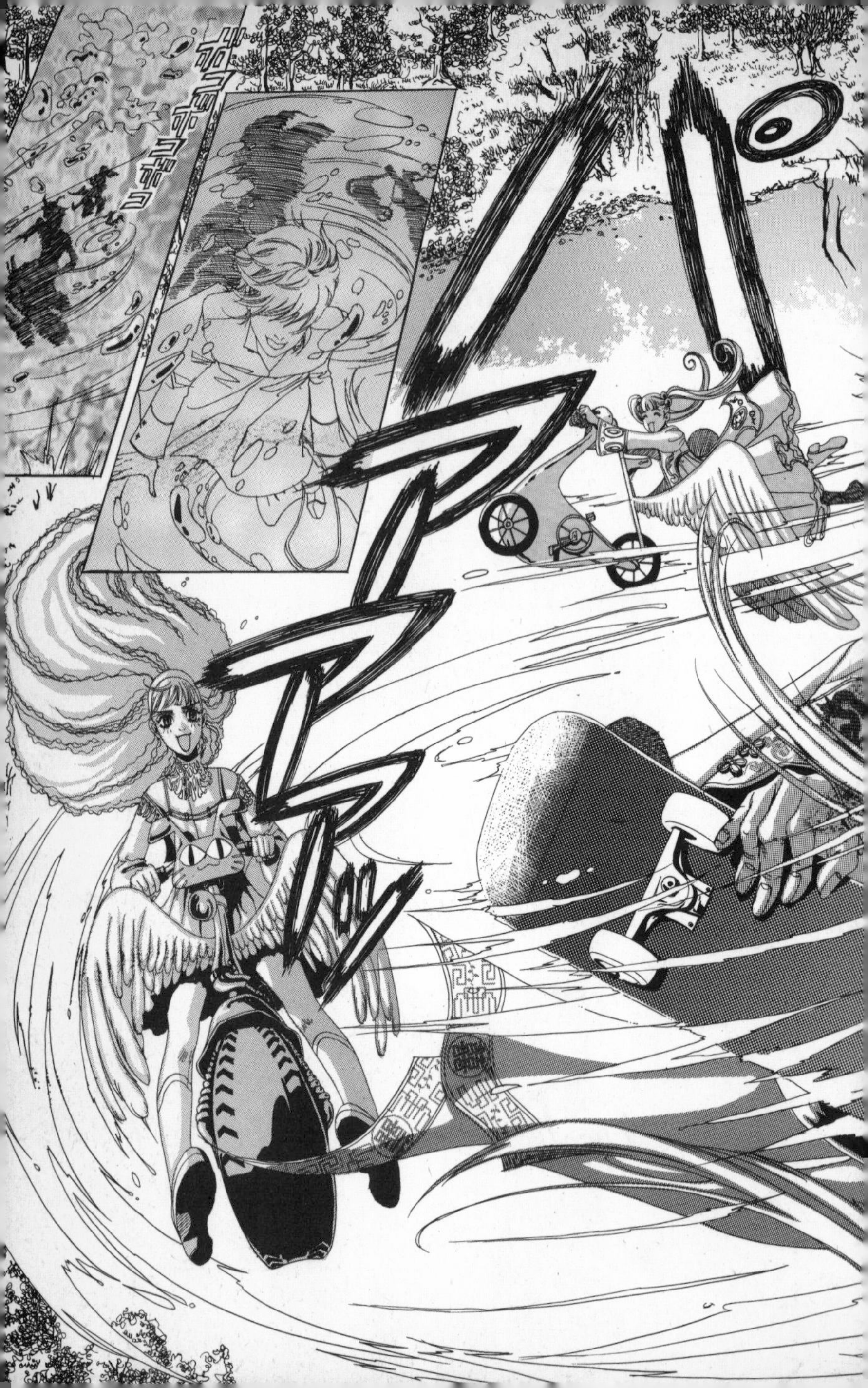
パァァァッ
ボコボコボコ

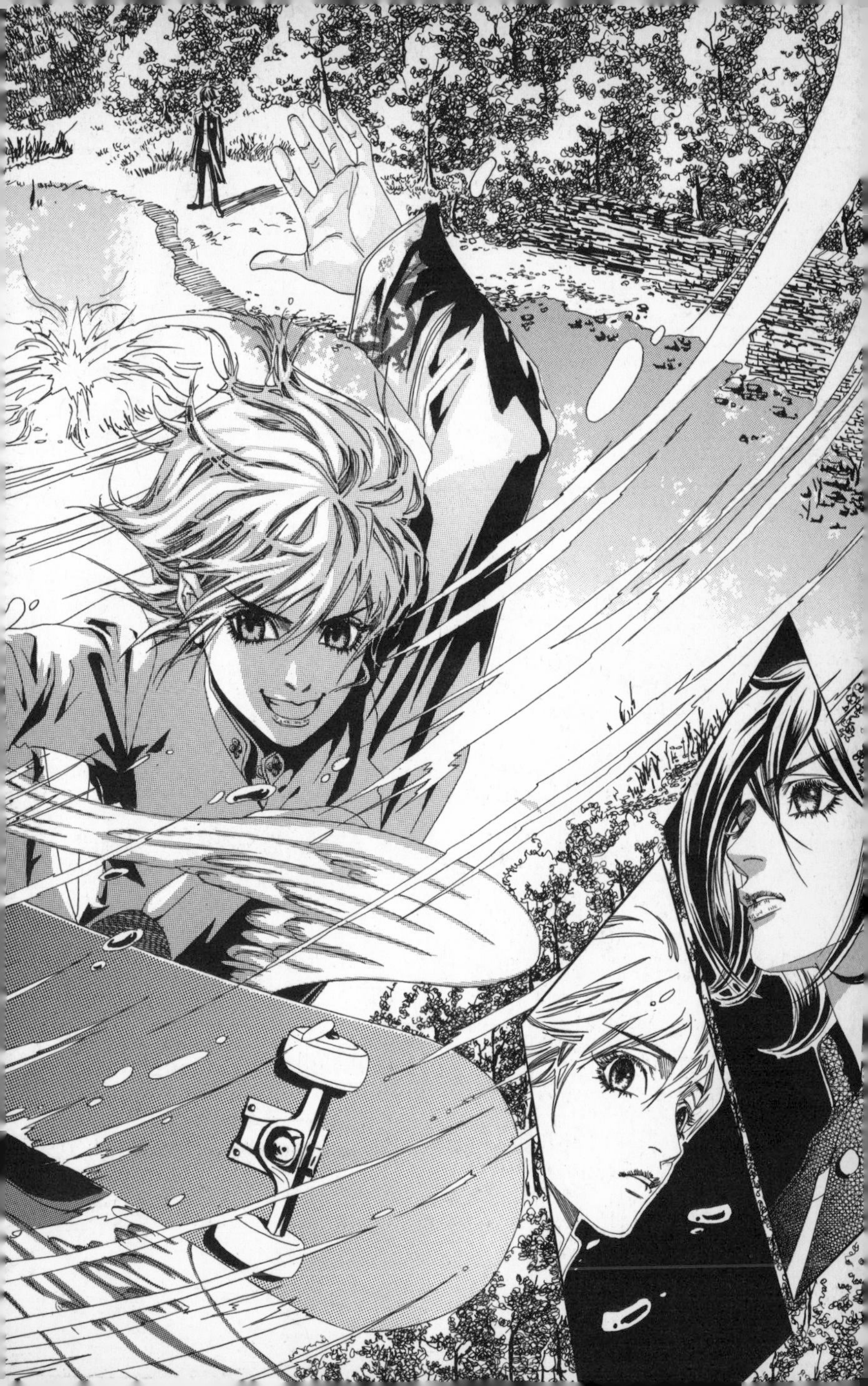

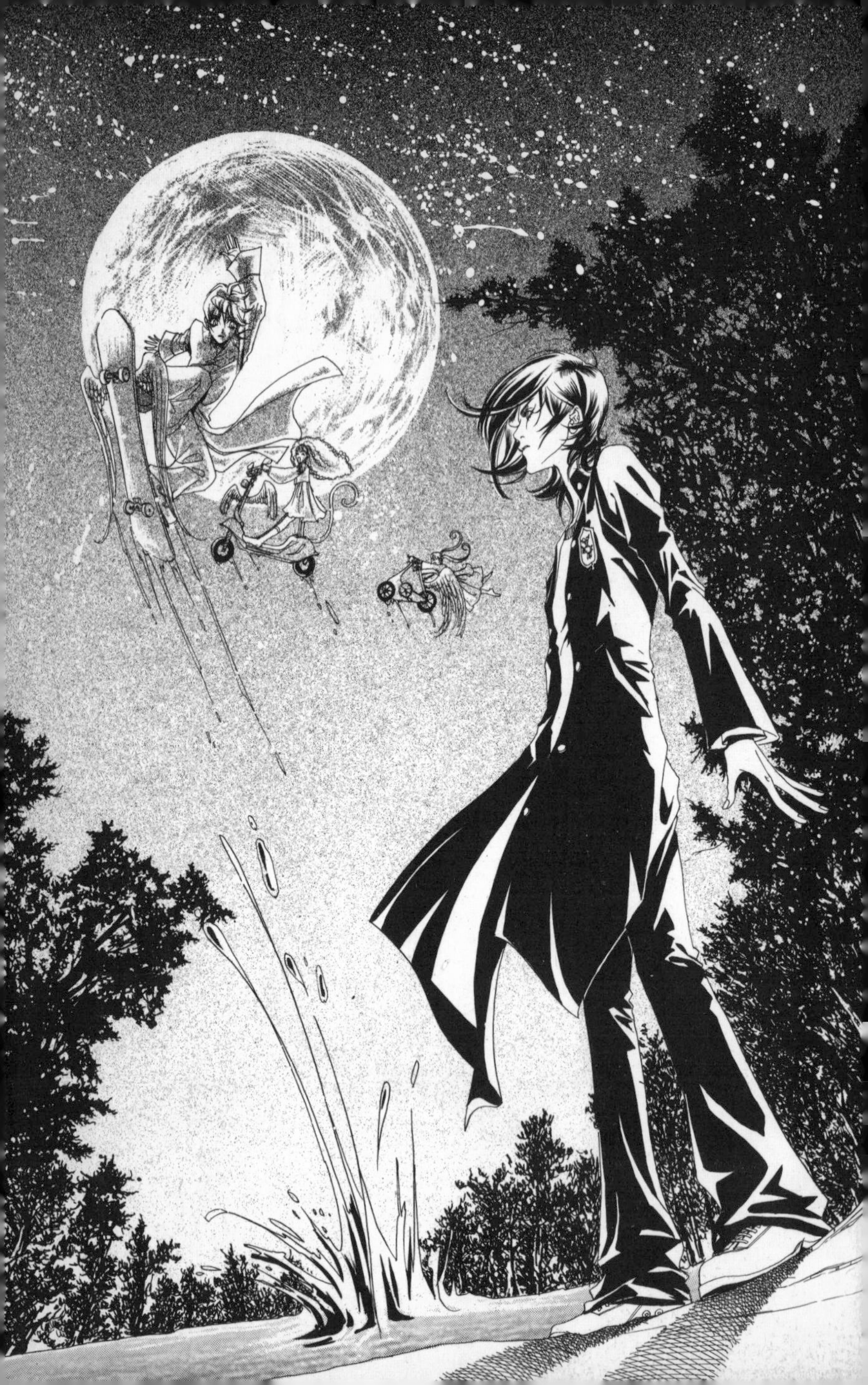

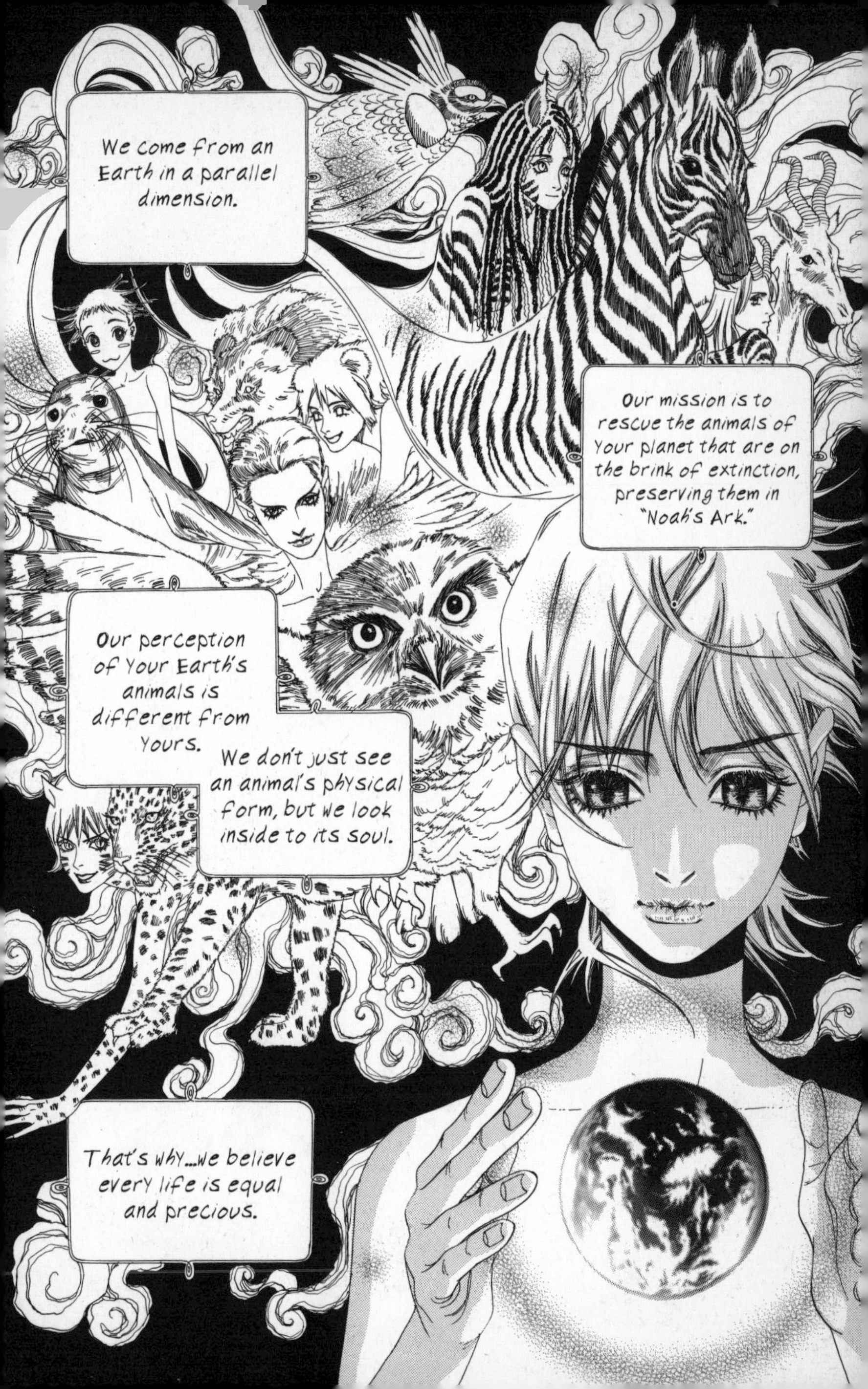
We come from an Earth in a parallel dimension.
Our mission is to rescue the animals of your planet that are on the brink of extinction, preserving them in "Noah's Ark."
Our perception of your Earth's animals is different from yours.
We don't just see an animal's physical form, but we look inside to its soul.
That's why...we believe every life is equal and precious.

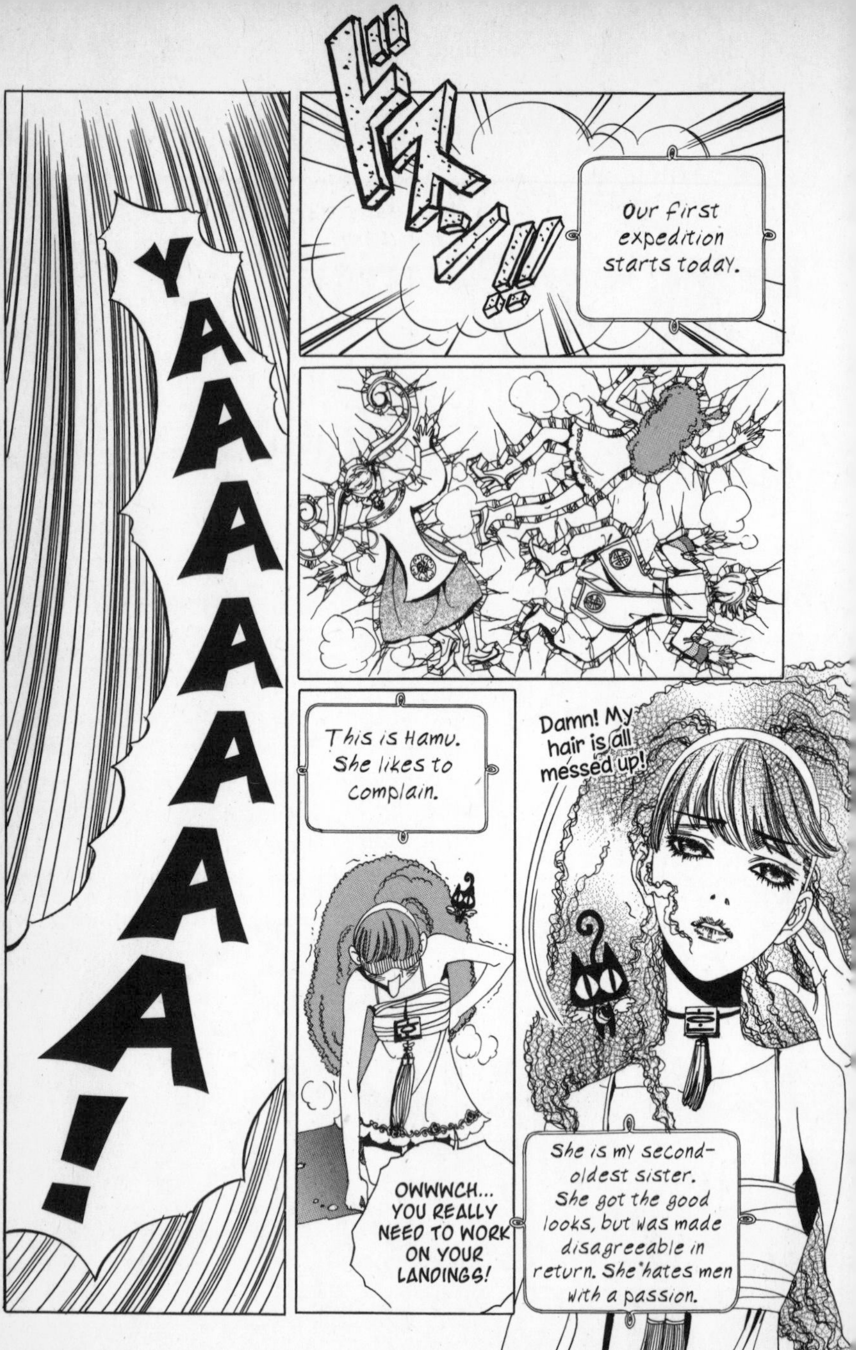
ドスッ!!
Our first expedition starts today.
Damn! My hair is all messed up!
This is Hamu. She likes to complain.
She is my second-oldest sister. She got the good looks, but was made disagreeable in return. She hates men with a passion.
OWWWCH... YOU REALLY NEED TO WORK ON YOUR LANDINGS!
YAAAAAAA!

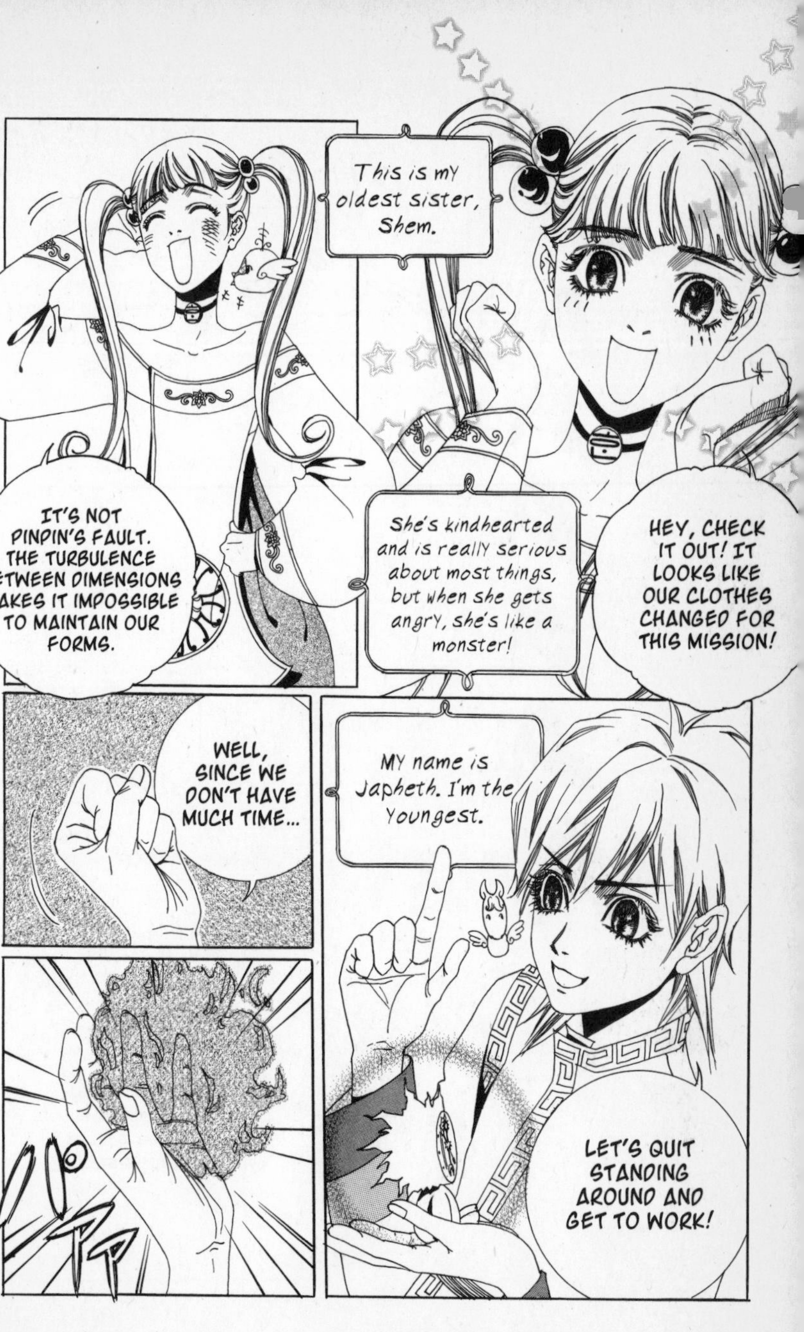

This is my oldest sister, Shem.
HEY, CHECK IT OUT! IT LOOKS LIKE OUR CLOTHES CHANGED FOR THIS MISSION!
She's kindhearted and is really serious about most things, but when she gets angry, she's like a monster!
IT'S NOT PINPIN'S FAULT. THE TURBULENCE BETWEEN DIMENSIONS MAKES IT IMPOSSIBLE TO MAINTAIN OUR FORMS.
MY name is Japheth. I'm the Youngest.
LET'S QUIT STANDING AROUND AND GET TO WORK!
WELL, SINCE WE DON'T HAVE MUCH TIME...

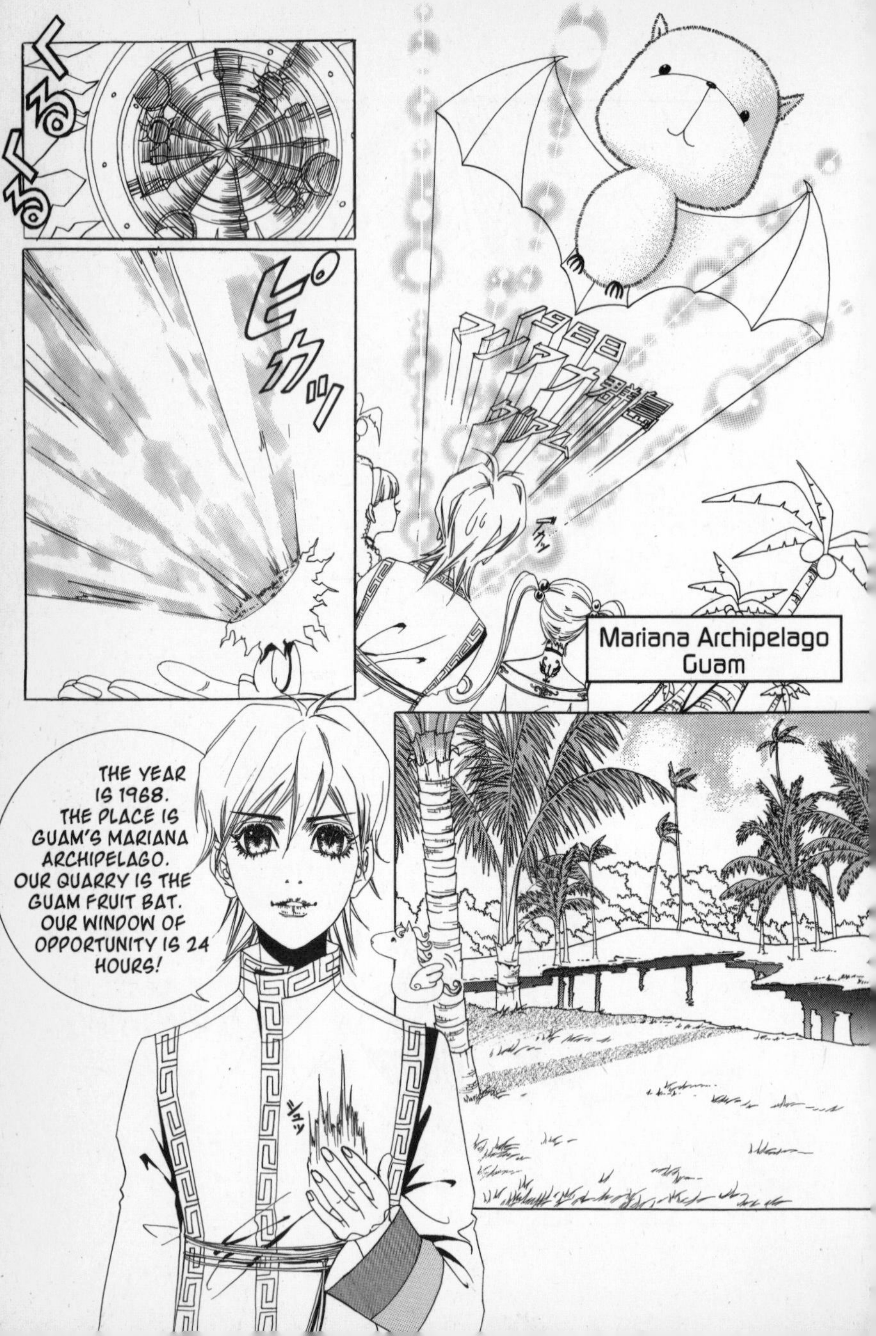
1968 マリアナ諸島 グアム
Mariana Archipelago Guam
ピカッ
THE YEAR IS 1968. THE PLACE IS GUAM'S MARIANA ARCHIPELAGO. OUR QUARRY IS THE GUAM FRUIT BAT. OUR WINDOW OF OPPORTUNITY IS 24 HOURS!

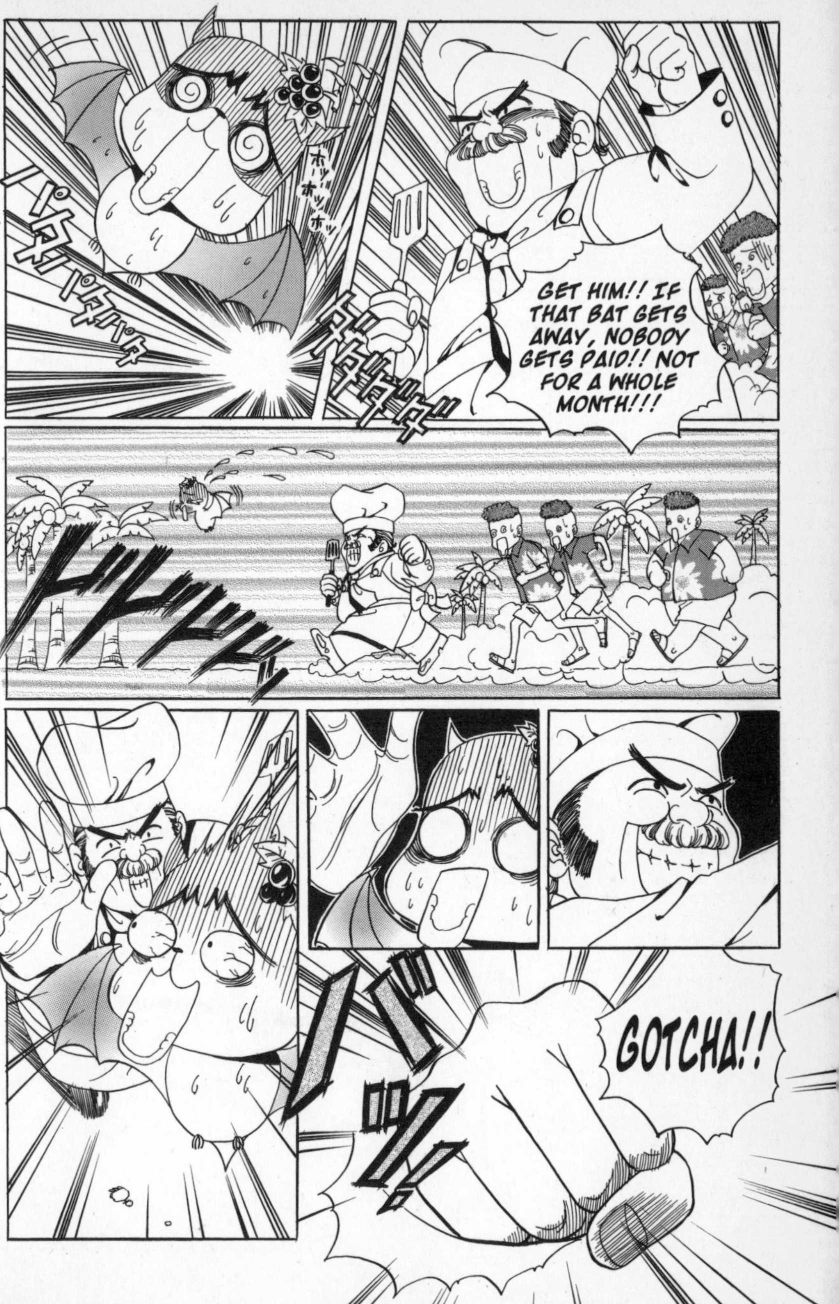
GET HIM!! IF THAT BAT GETS AWAY, NOBODY GETS PAID!! NOT FOR A WHOLE MONTH!!!
GOTCHA!!

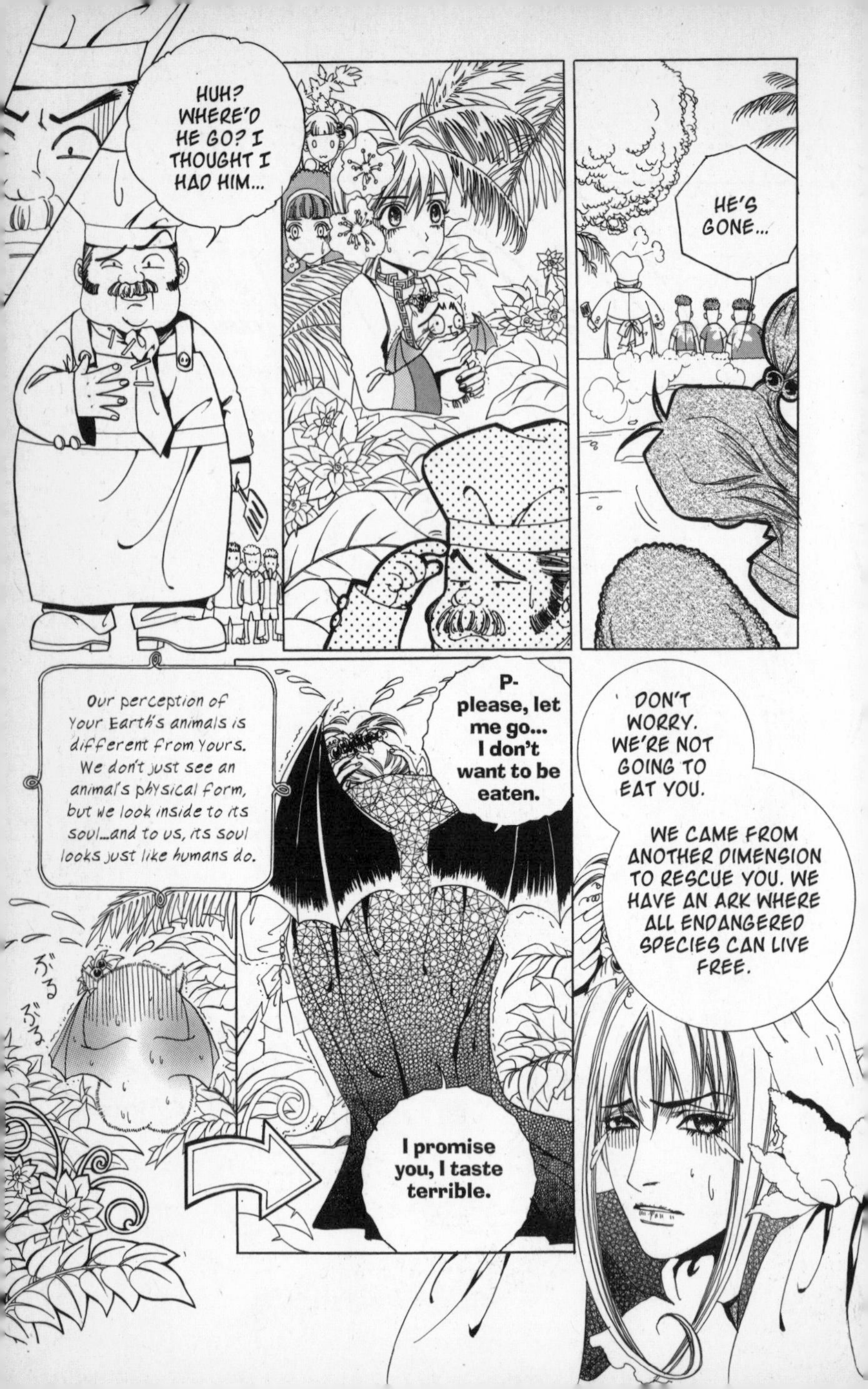
HUH? WHERE'D HE GO? I THOUGHT I HAD HIM...
HE'S GONE...
Our perception of Your Earth's animals is different from Yours. We don't just see an animal's physical form, but we look inside to its soul...and to us, its soul looks just like humans do.
ぶるぶる
P-please, let me go... I don't want to be eaten.
I promise you, I taste terrible.
DON'T WORRY. WE'RE NOT GOING TO EAT YOU.
WE CAME FROM ANOTHER DIMENSION TO RESCUE YOU. WE HAVE AN ARK WHERE ALL ENDANGERED SPECIES CAN LIVE FREE.

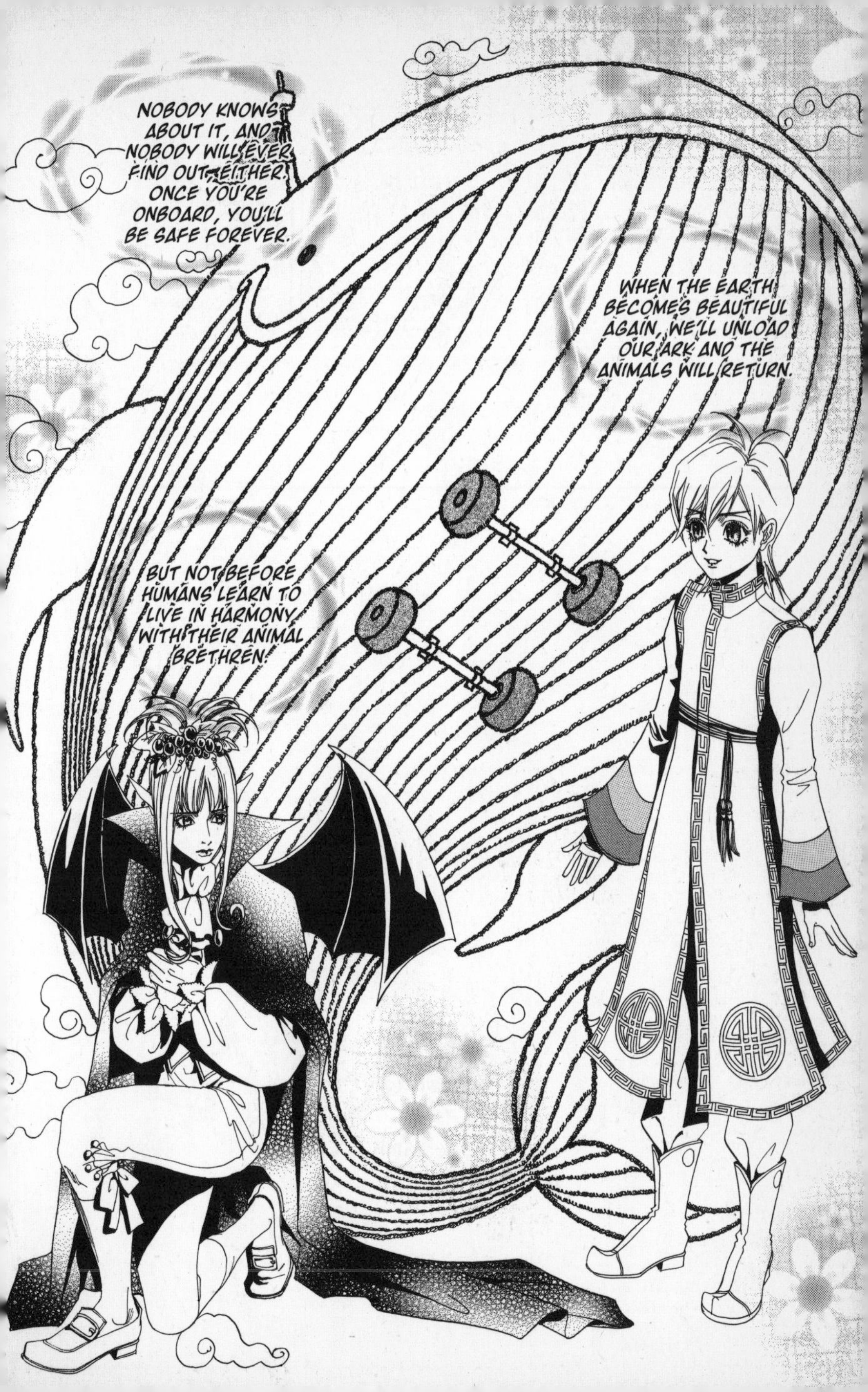
WHEN THE EARTH BECOMES BEAUTIFUL AGAIN, WE'LL UNLOAD OUR ARK AND THE ANIMALS WILL RETURN.
NOBODY KNOWS ABOUT IT, AND NOBODY WILL EVER FIND OUT, EITHER. ONCE YOU'RE ONBOARD, YOU'LL BE SAFE FOREVER.
BUT NOT BEFORE HUMANS LEARN TO LIVE IN HARMONY WITH THEIR ANIMAL BRETHREN.

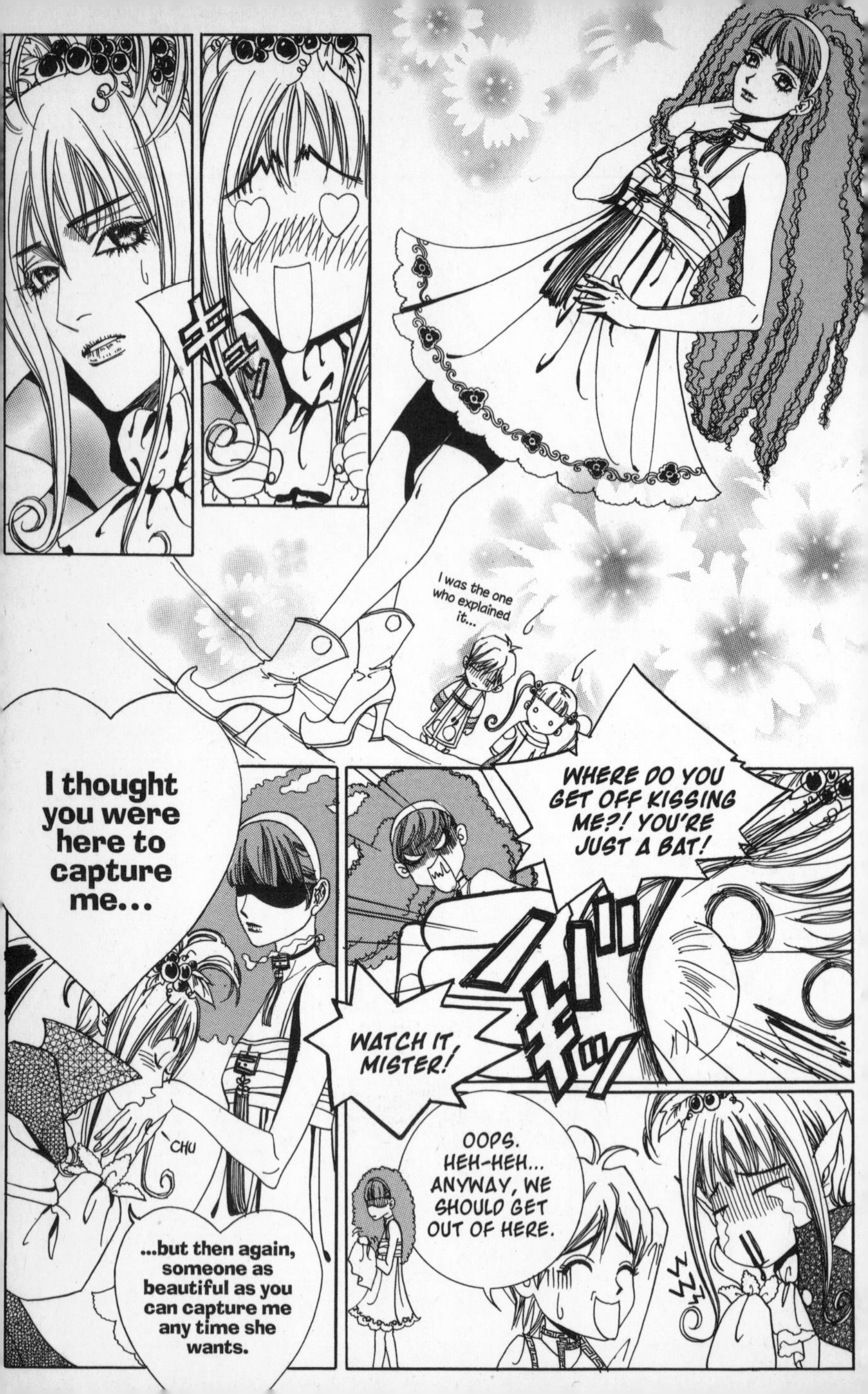
I was the one who explained it...
I thought you were here to capture me...
CHU
...but then again, someone as beautiful as you can capture me any time she wants.
WHERE DO YOU GET OFF KISSING ME?! YOU'RE JUST A BAT!
WATCH IT, MISTER!
OOPS. HEH-HEH... ANYWAY, WE SHOULD GET OUT OF HERE.

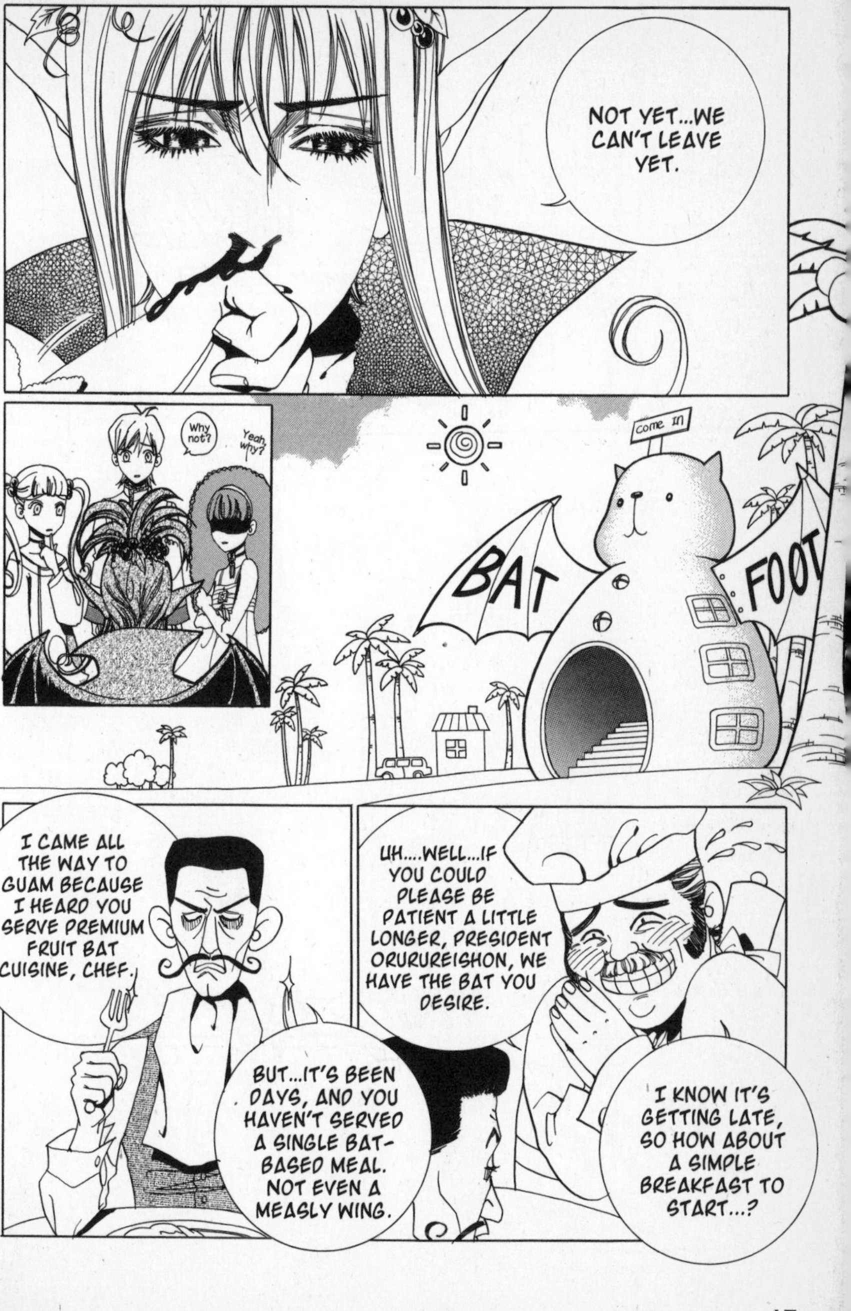
NOT YET...WE CAN'T LEAVE YET.
Why not?
Yeah, why?
come in
BAT
FOOT
I CAME ALL THE WAY TO GUAM BECAUSE I HEARD YOU SERVE PREMIUM FRUIT BAT CUISINE, CHEF.
BUT...IT'S BEEN DAYS, AND YOU HAVEN'T SERVED A SINGLE BAT-BASED MEAL. NOT EVEN A MEASLY WING.
UH....WELL...IF YOU COULD PLEASE BE PATIENT A LITTLE LONGER, PRESIDENT ORURUREISHON, WE HAVE THE BAT YOU DESIRE.
I KNOW IT'S GETTING LATE, SO HOW ABOUT A SIMPLE BREAKFAST TO START...?

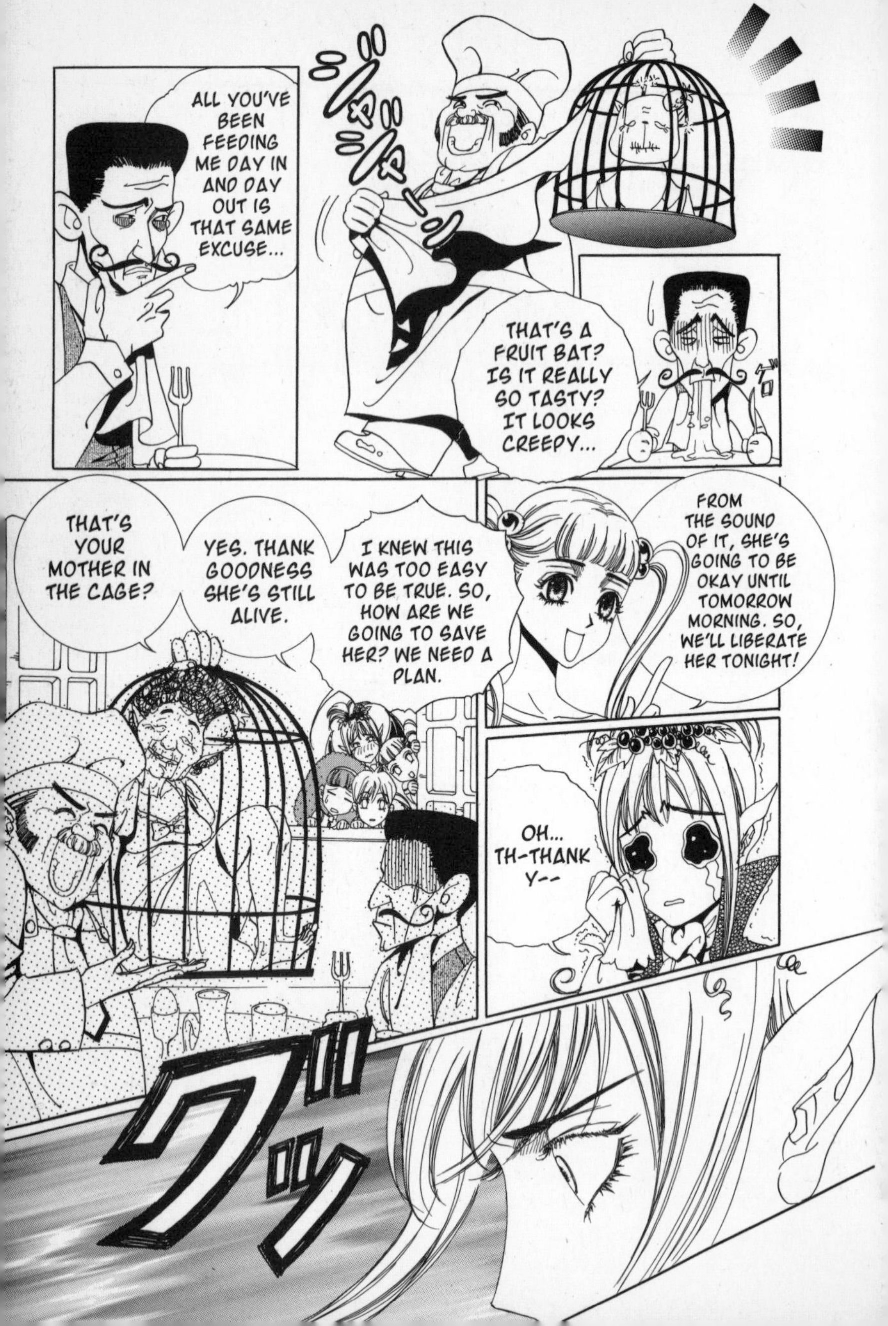
ALL YOU'VE BEEN FEEDING ME DAY IN AND DAY OUT IS THAT SAME EXCUSE...
THAT'S A FRUIT BAT? IS IT REALLY SO TASTY? IT LOOKS CREEPY...
THAT'S YOUR MOTHER IN THE CAGE?
YES. THANK GOODNESS SHE'S STILL ALIVE.
I KNEW THIS WAS TOO EASY TO BE TRUE. SO, HOW ARE WE GOING TO SAVE HER? WE NEED A PLAN.
FROM THE SOUND OF IT, SHE'S GOING TO BE OKAY UNTIL TOMORROW MORNING. SO, WE'LL LIBERATE HER TONIGHT!
OH... TH-THANK Y--

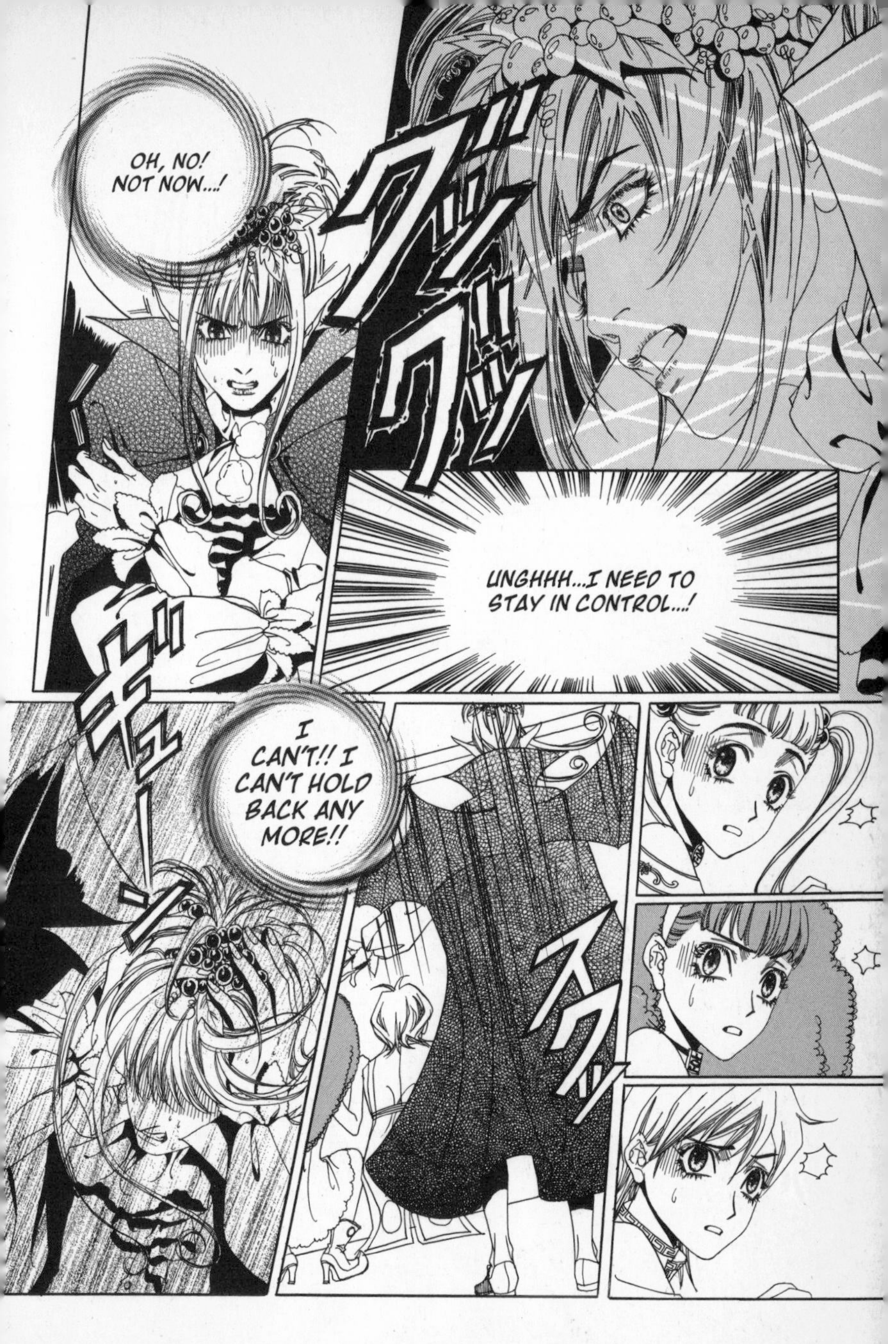
OH, NO! NOT NOW...!
UNGHHH...I NEED TO STAY IN CONTROL...!
I CAN'T!! I CAN'T HOLD BACK ANY MORE!!

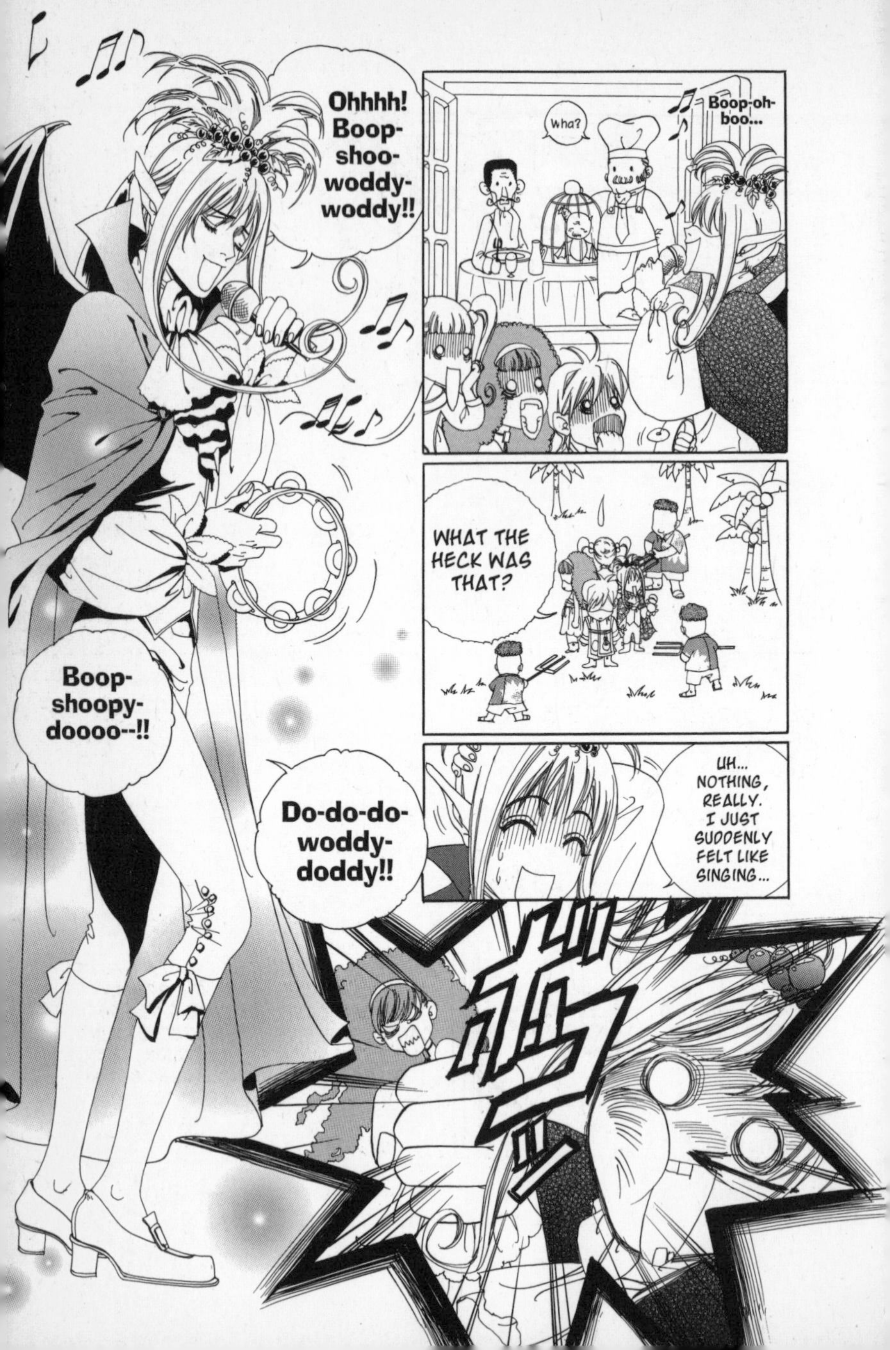
Ohhhh! Boop-shoo-woddy-woddy!!
Boop-shoopy-doooo--!!
Do-do-do-woddy-doddy!!
Wha?
Boop-oh-boo...
WHAT THE HECK WAS THAT?
UH... NOTHING, REALLY. I JUST SUDDENLY FELT LIKE SINGING...

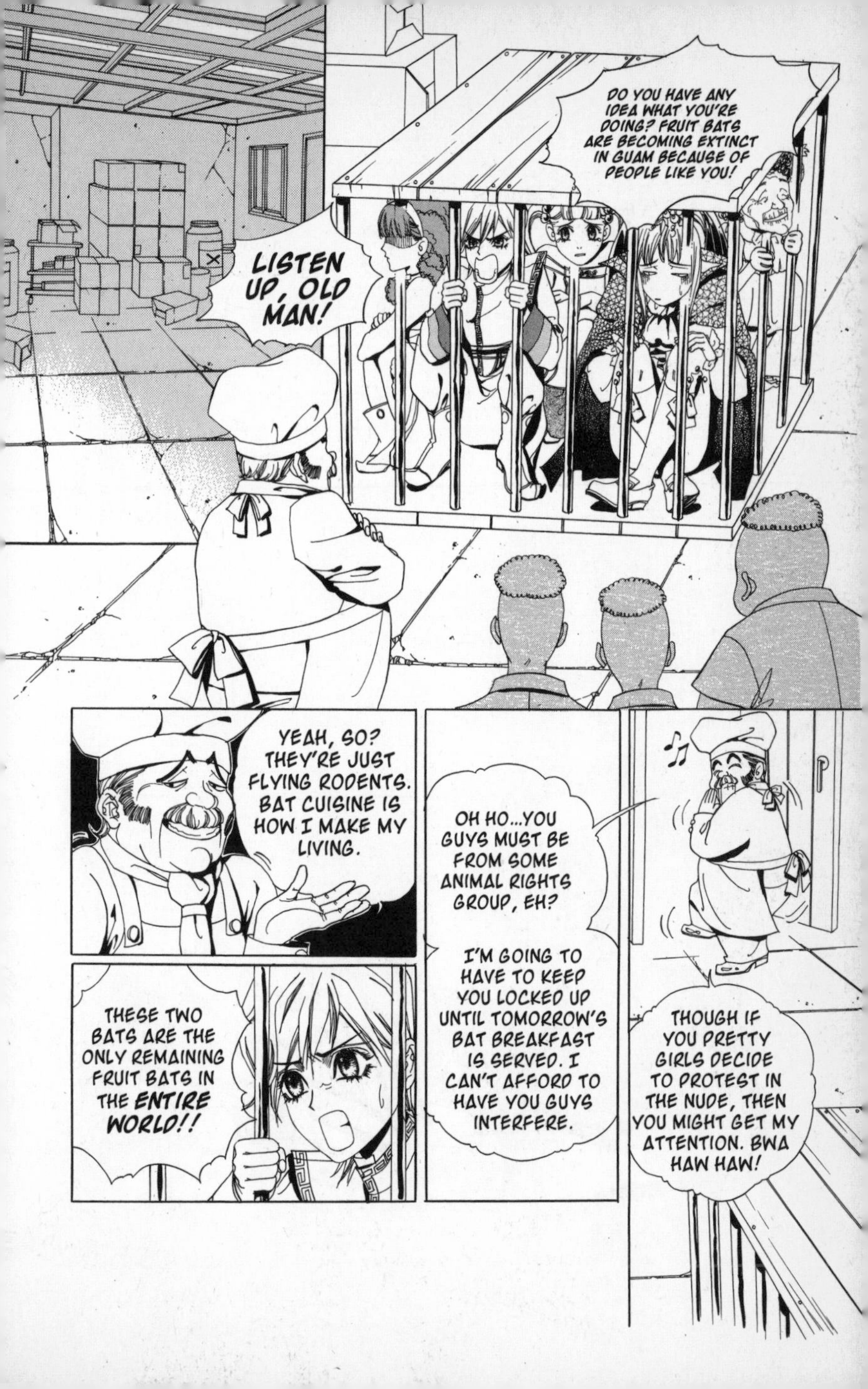
LISTEN UP, OLD MAN!
DO YOU HAVE ANY IDEA WHAT YOU'RE DOING? FRUIT BATS ARE BECOMING EXTINCT IN GUAM BECAUSE OF PEOPLE LIKE YOU!
YEAH, SO? THEY'RE JUST FLYING RODENTS. BAT CUISINE IS HOW I MAKE MY LIVING.
THESE TWO BATS ARE THE ONLY REMAINING FRUIT BATS IN THE *ENTIRE WORLD!!*
OH HO...YOU GUYS MUST BE FROM SOME ANIMAL RIGHTS GROUP, EH?
I'M GOING TO HAVE TO KEEP YOU LOCKED UP UNTIL TOMORROW'S BAT BREAKFAST IS SERVED. I CAN'T AFFORD TO HAVE YOU GUYS INTERFERE.
THOUGH IF YOU PRETTY GIRLS DECIDE TO PROTEST IN THE NUDE, THEN YOU MIGHT GET MY ATTENTION. BWA HAW HAW!

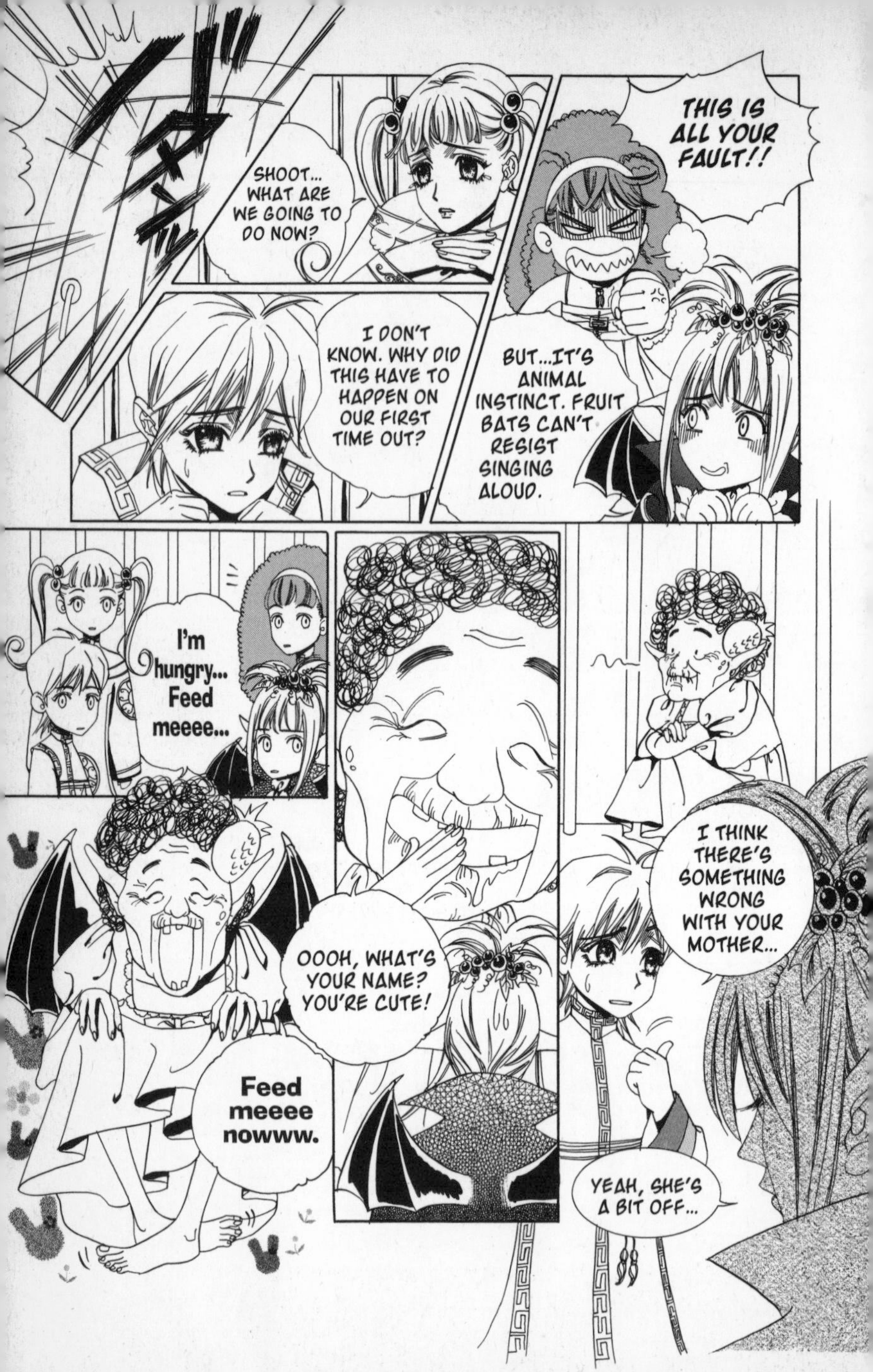
THIS IS ALL YOUR FAULT!!
SHOOT... WHAT ARE WE GOING TO DO NOW?
BUT...IT'S ANIMAL INSTINCT. FRUIT BATS CAN'T RESIST SINGING ALOUD.
I DON'T KNOW. WHY DID THIS HAVE TO HAPPEN ON OUR FIRST TIME OUT?
I'm hungry... Feed meeee...
OOOH, WHAT'S YOUR NAME? YOU'RE CUTE!
Feed meeee nowww.
I THINK THERE'S SOMETHING WRONG WITH YOUR MOTHER...
YEAH, SHE'S A BIT OFF...

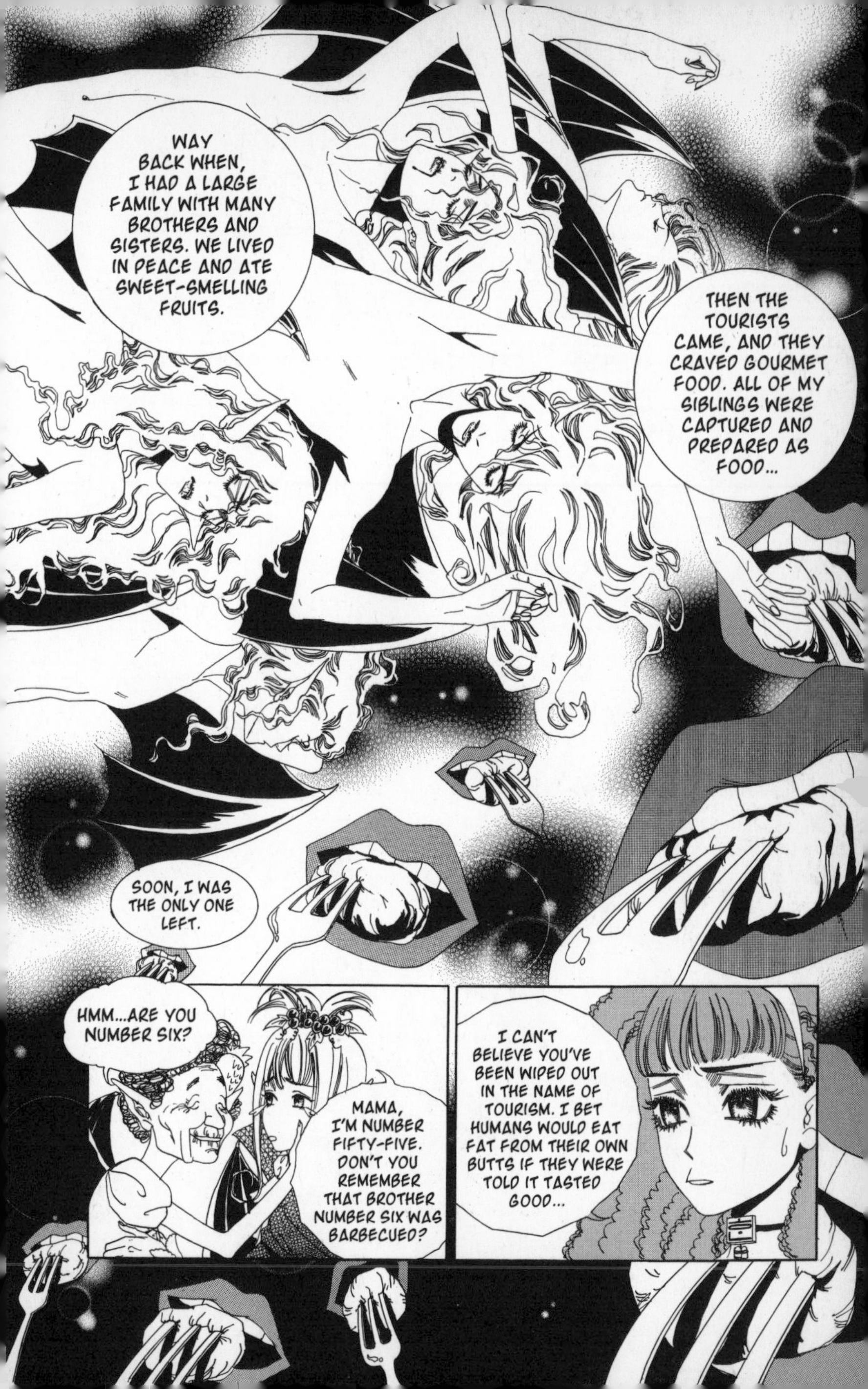
WAY BACK WHEN, I HAD A LARGE FAMILY WITH MANY BROTHERS AND SISTERS. WE LIVED IN PEACE AND ATE SWEET-SMELLING FRUITS.
THEN THE TOURISTS CAME, AND THEY CRAVED GOURMET FOOD. ALL OF MY SIBLINGS WERE CAPTURED AND PREPARED AS FOOD...
SOON, I WAS THE ONLY ONE LEFT.
I CAN'T BELIEVE YOU'VE BEEN WIPED OUT IN THE NAME OF TOURISM. I BET HUMANS WOULD EAT FAT FROM THEIR OWN BUTTS IF THEY WERE TOLD IT TASTED GOOD...
HMM...ARE YOU NUMBER SIX?
MAMA, I'M NUMBER FIFTY-FIVE. DON'T YOU REMEMBER THAT BROTHER NUMBER SIX WAS BARBECUED?

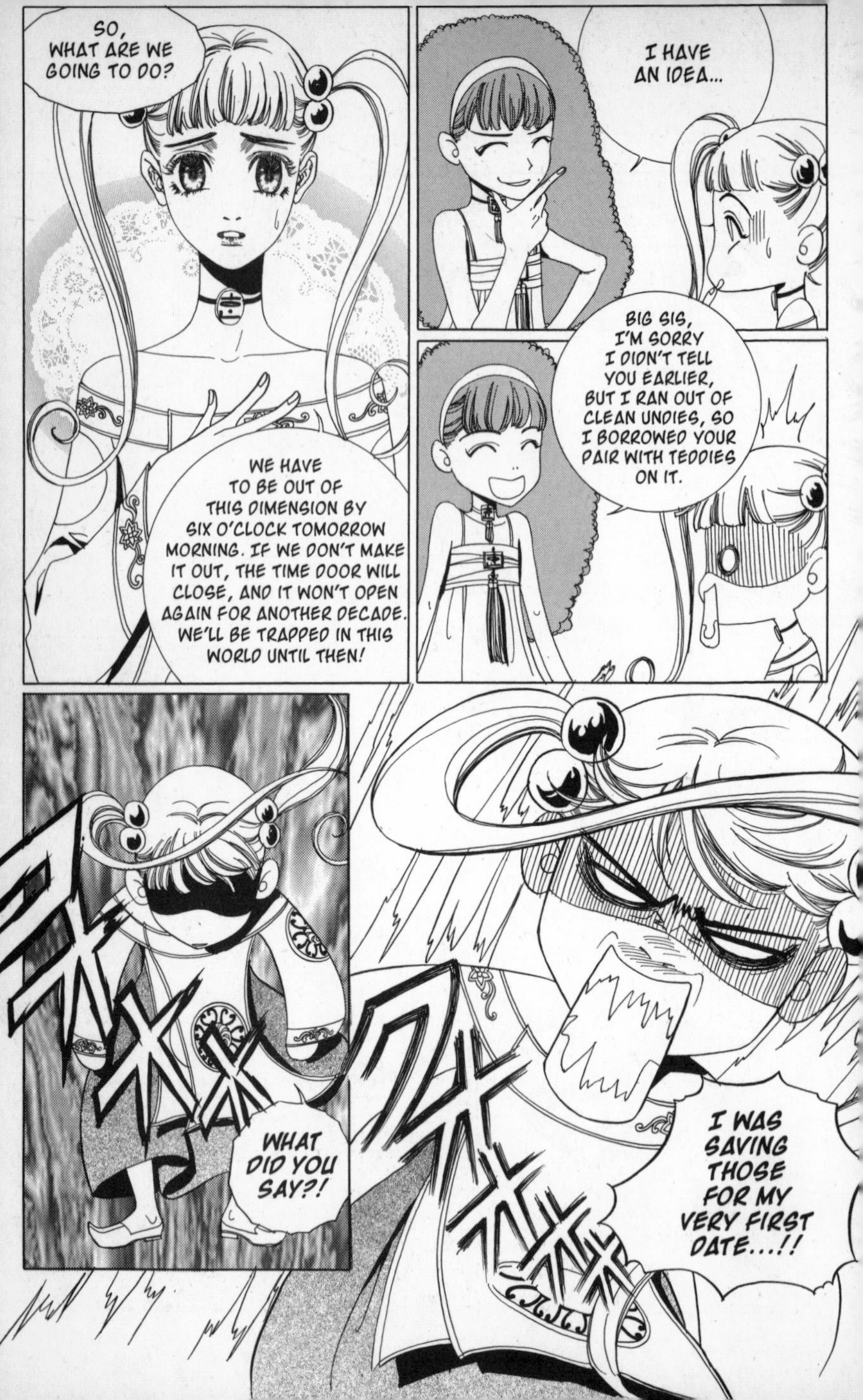
SO, WHAT ARE WE GOING TO DO?
WE HAVE TO BE OUT OF THIS DIMENSION BY SIX O'CLOCK TOMORROW MORNING. IF WE DON'T MAKE IT OUT, THE TIME DOOR WILL CLOSE, AND IT WON'T OPEN AGAIN FOR ANOTHER DECADE. WE'LL BE TRAPPED IN THIS WORLD UNTIL THEN!
I HAVE AN IDEA...
BIG SIS, I'M SORRY I DIDN'T TELL YOU EARLIER, BUT I RAN OUT OF CLEAN UNDIES, SO I BORROWED YOUR PAIR WITH TEDDIES ON IT.
WHAT DID YOU SAY?!
I WAS SAVING THOSE FOR MY VERY FIRST DATE...!!

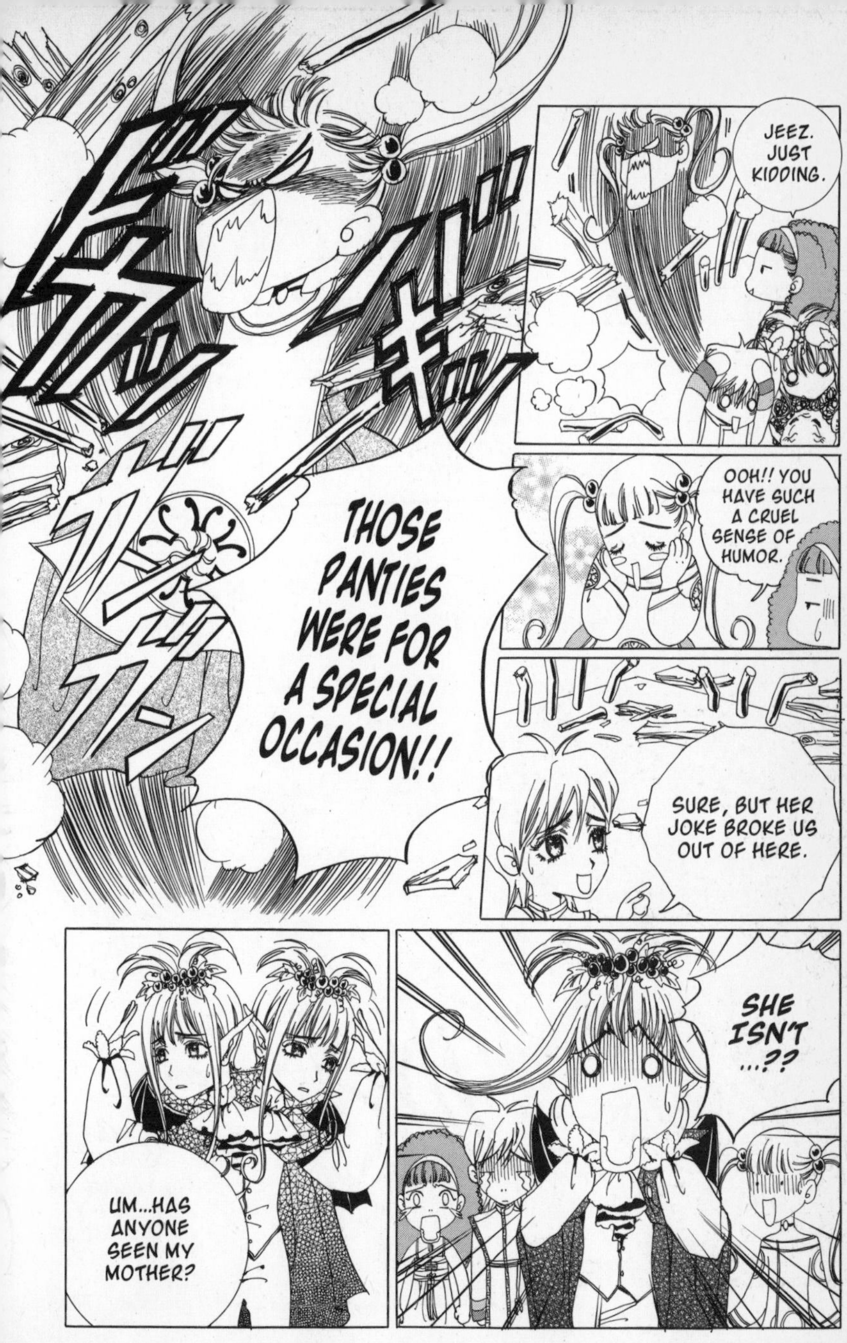
THOSE PANTIES WERE FOR A SPECIAL OCCASION!!
JEEZ. JUST KIDDING.
OOH!! YOU HAVE SUCH A CRUEL SENSE OF HUMOR.
SURE, BUT HER JOKE BROKE US OUT OF HERE.
UM...HAS ANYONE SEEN MY MOTHER?
SHE ISN'T ...??

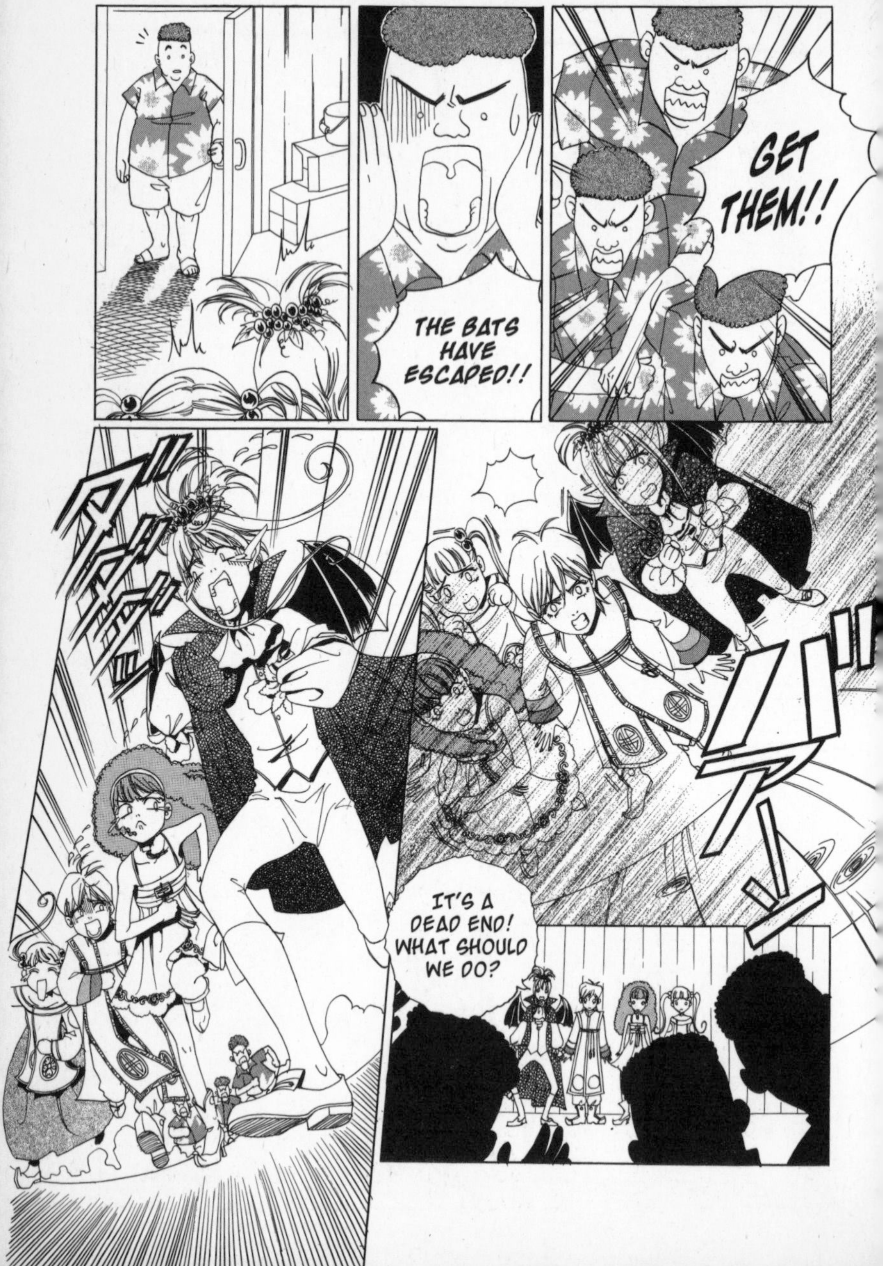
THE BATS HAVE ESCAPED!!
GET THEM!!
IT'S A DEAD END! WHAT SHOULD WE DO?

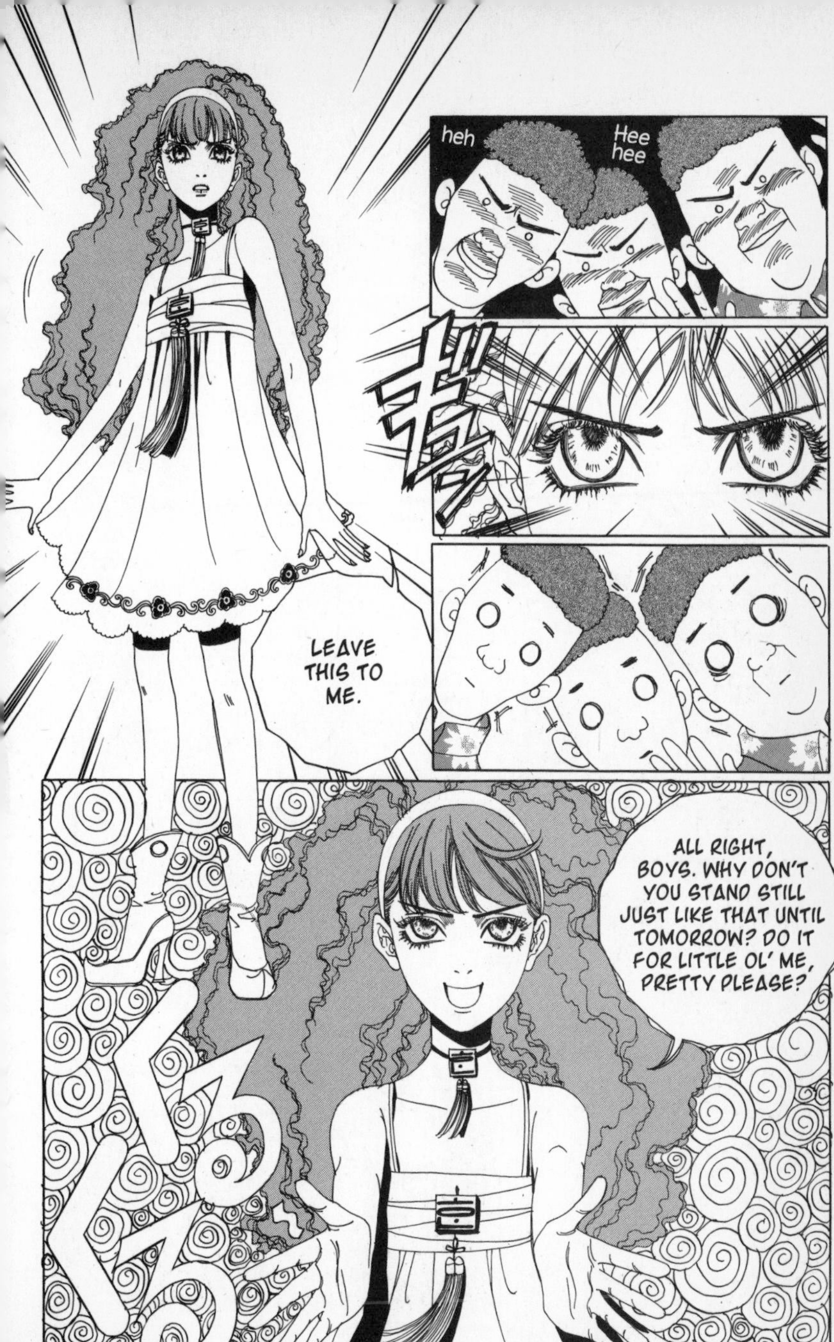
Hee
hee
heh
LEAVE THIS TO ME.
ALL RIGHT, BOYS. WHY DON'T YOU STAND STILL JUST LIKE THAT UNTIL TOMORROW? DO IT FOR LITTLE OL' ME, PRETTY PLEASE?

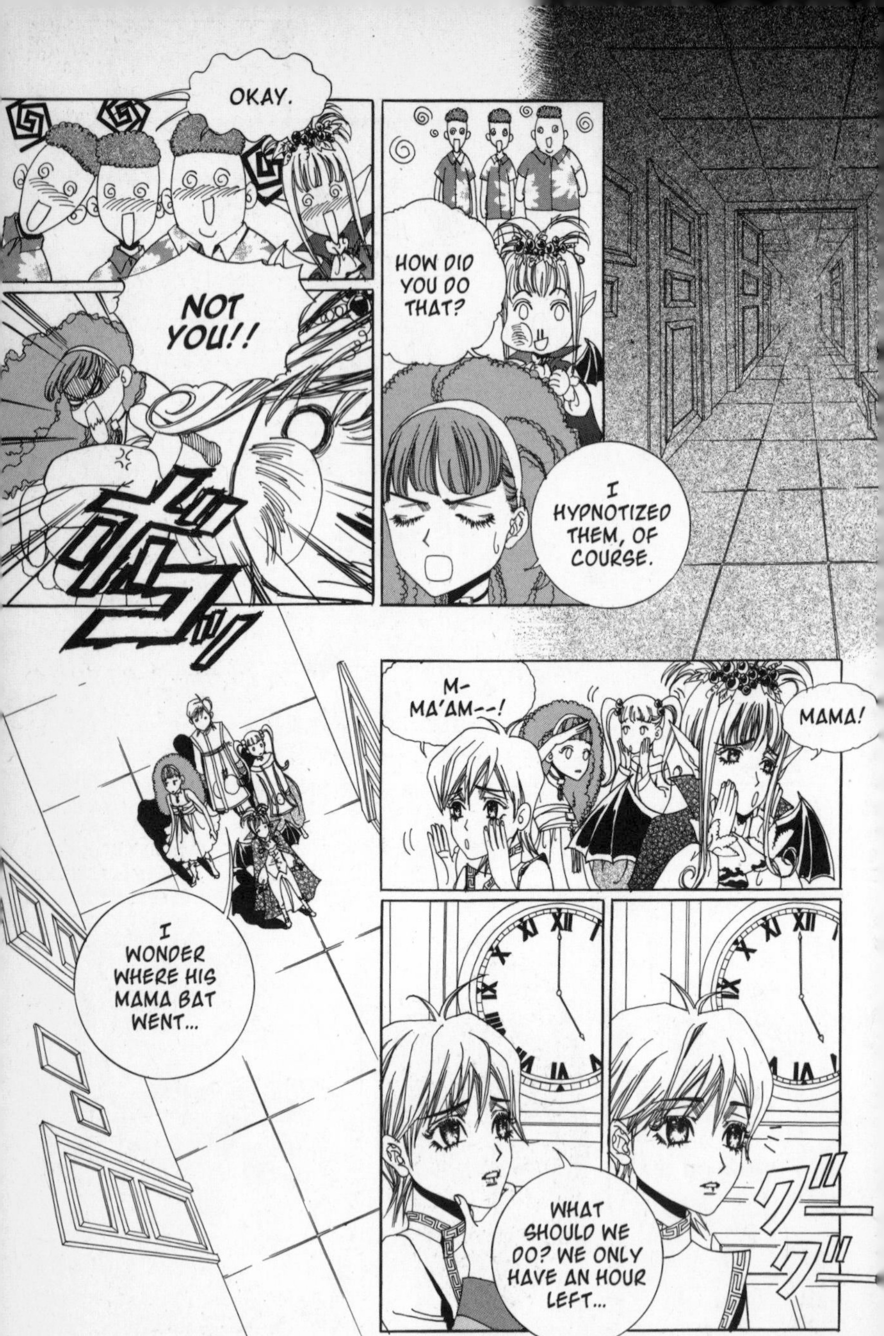
OKAY.
NOT YOU!!
HOW DID YOU DO THAT?
I HYPNOTIZED THEM, OF COURSE.
I WONDER WHERE HIS MAMA BAT WENT...
M-MA'AM--!
MAMA!
WHAT SHOULD WE DO? WE ONLY HAVE AN HOUR LEFT...

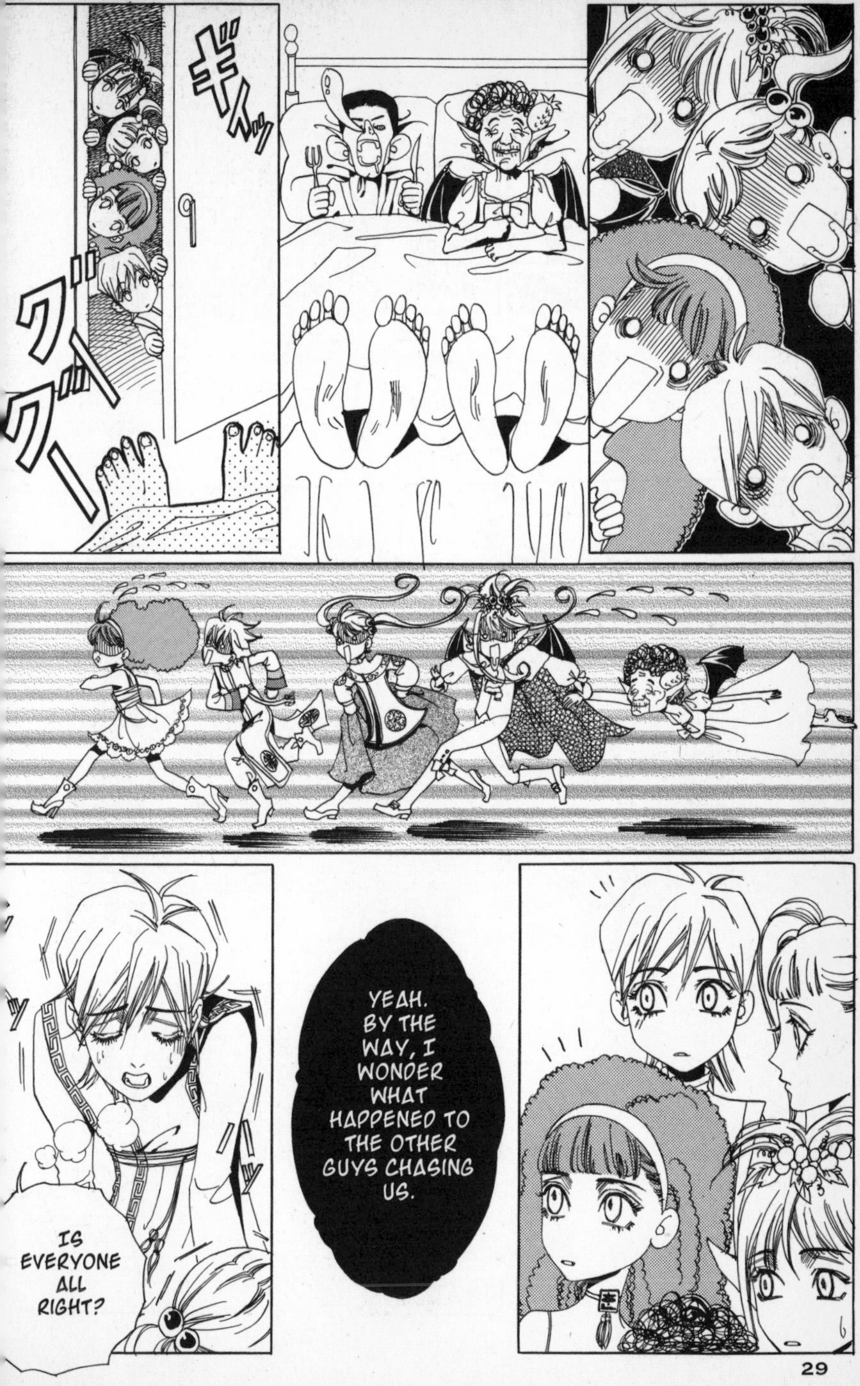
ギィッ
IS EVERYONE ALL RIGHT?
YEAH. BY THE WAY, I WONDER WHAT HAPPENED TO THE OTHER GUYS CHASING US.

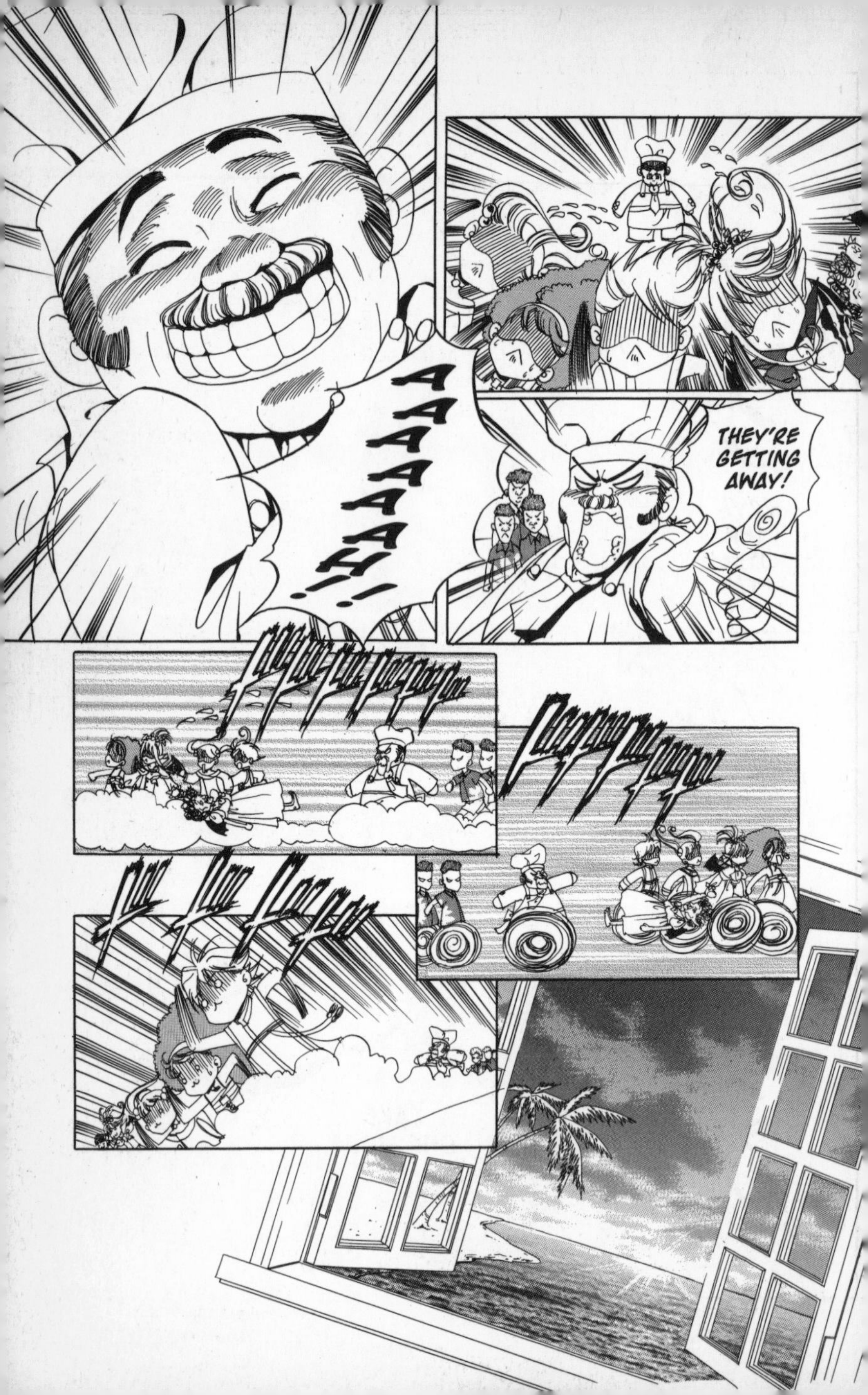
AAAAAAAH!!!
THEY'RE GETTING AWAY!

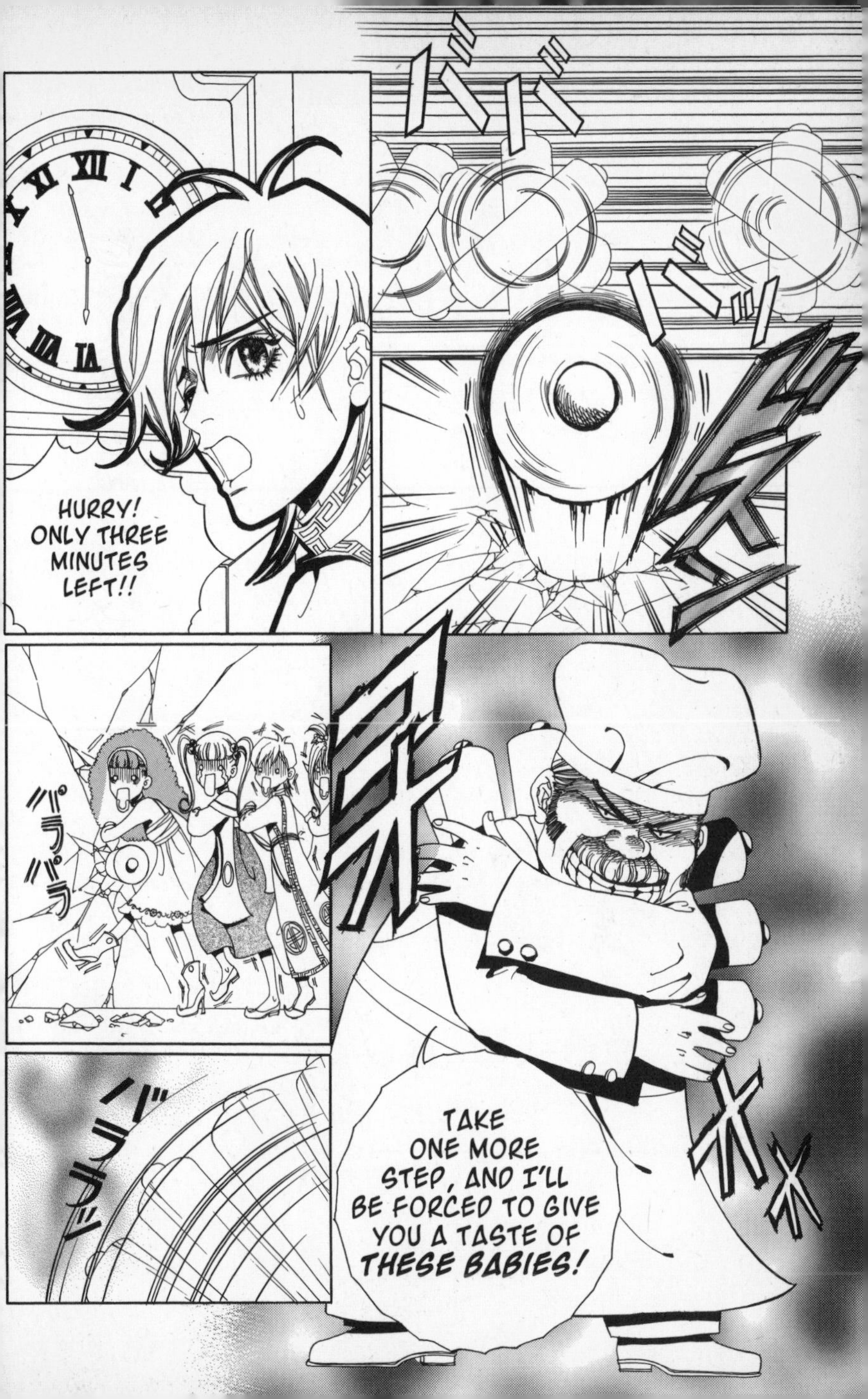
HURRY! ONLY THREE MINUTES LEFT!!
TAKE ONE MORE STEP, AND I'LL BE FORCED TO GIVE YOU A TASTE OF THESE BABIES!
パラパラ

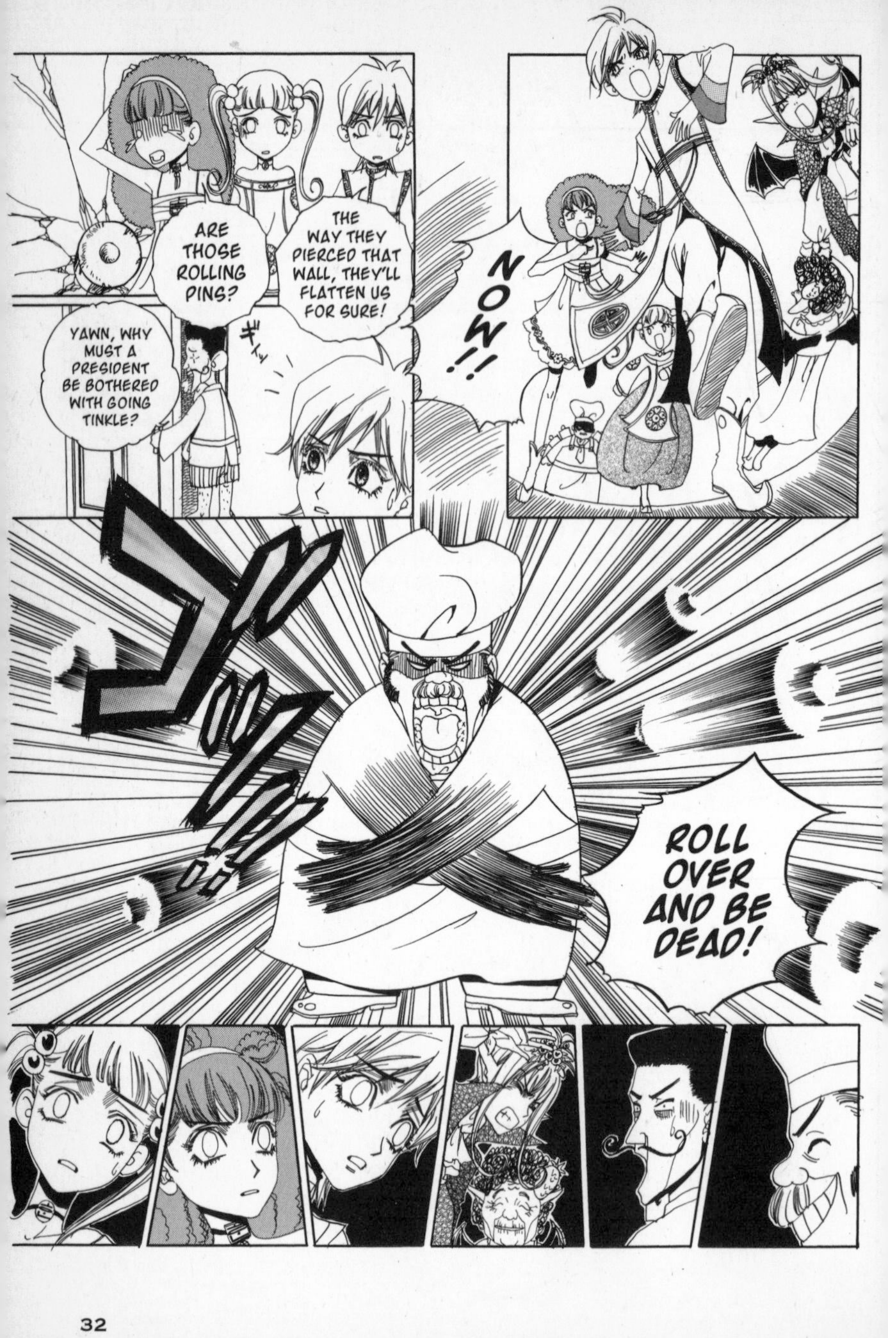
ARE THOSE ROLLING PINS?
THE WAY THEY PIERCED THAT WALL, THEY'LL FLATTEN US FOR SURE!
YAWN, WHY MUST A PRESIDENT BE BOTHERED WITH GOING TINKLE?
ギィッ
NOW!!
ROLL OVER AND BE DEAD!

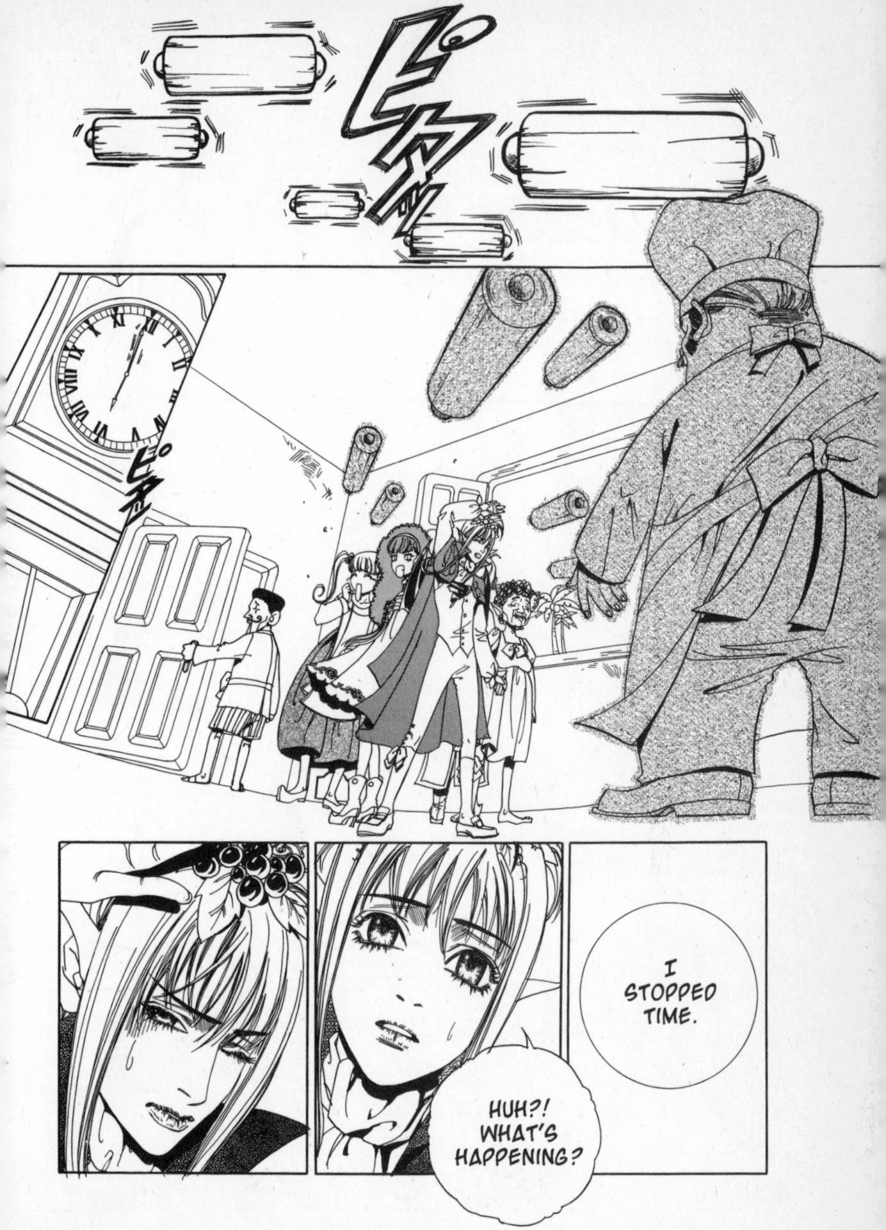
ピタッ
ピ
I STOPPED TIME.
HUH?! WHAT'S HAPPENING?

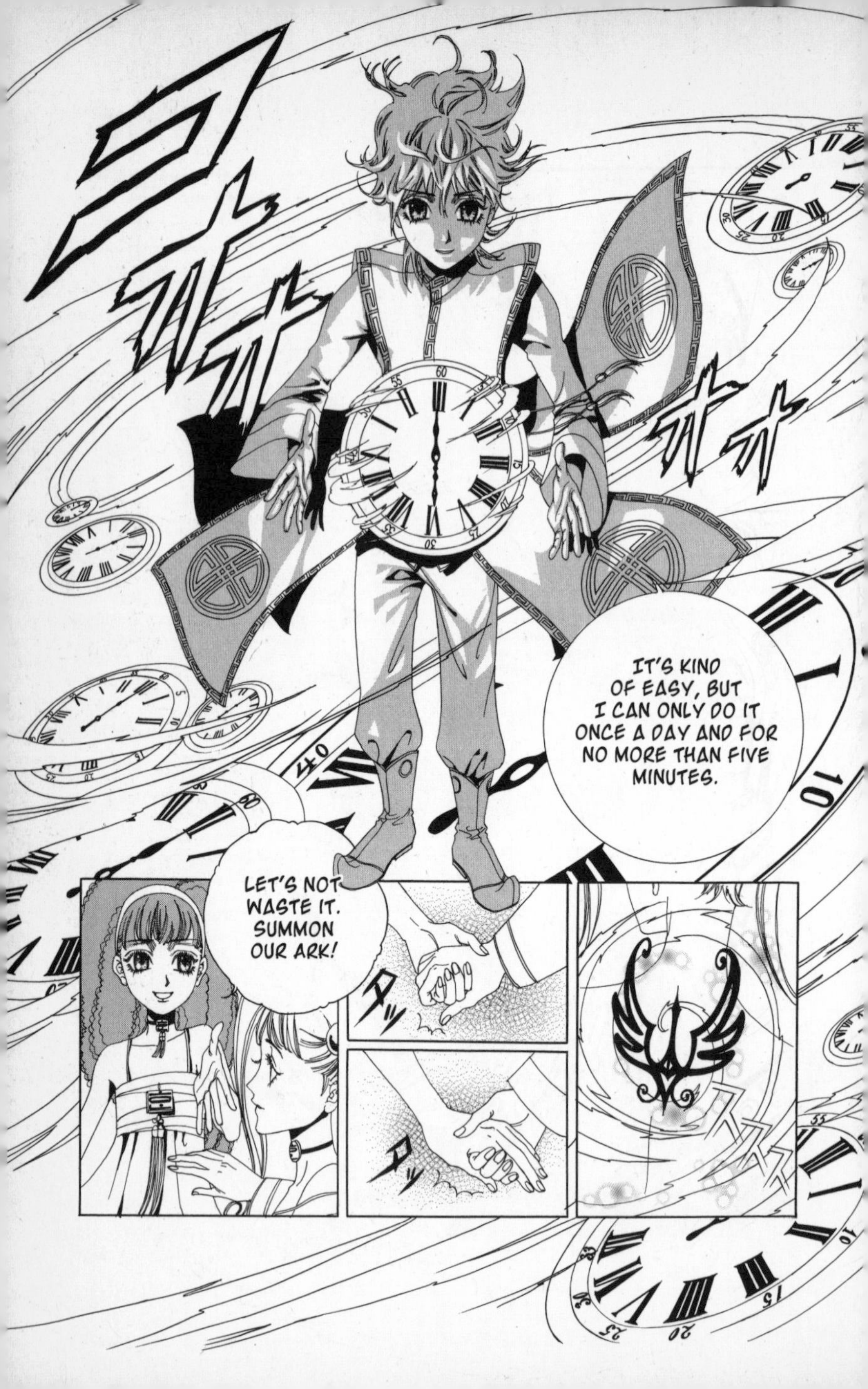
IT'S KIND OF EASY, BUT I CAN ONLY DO IT ONCE A DAY AND FOR NO MORE THAN FIVE MINUTES.
LET'S NOT WASTE IT. SUMMON OUR ARK!

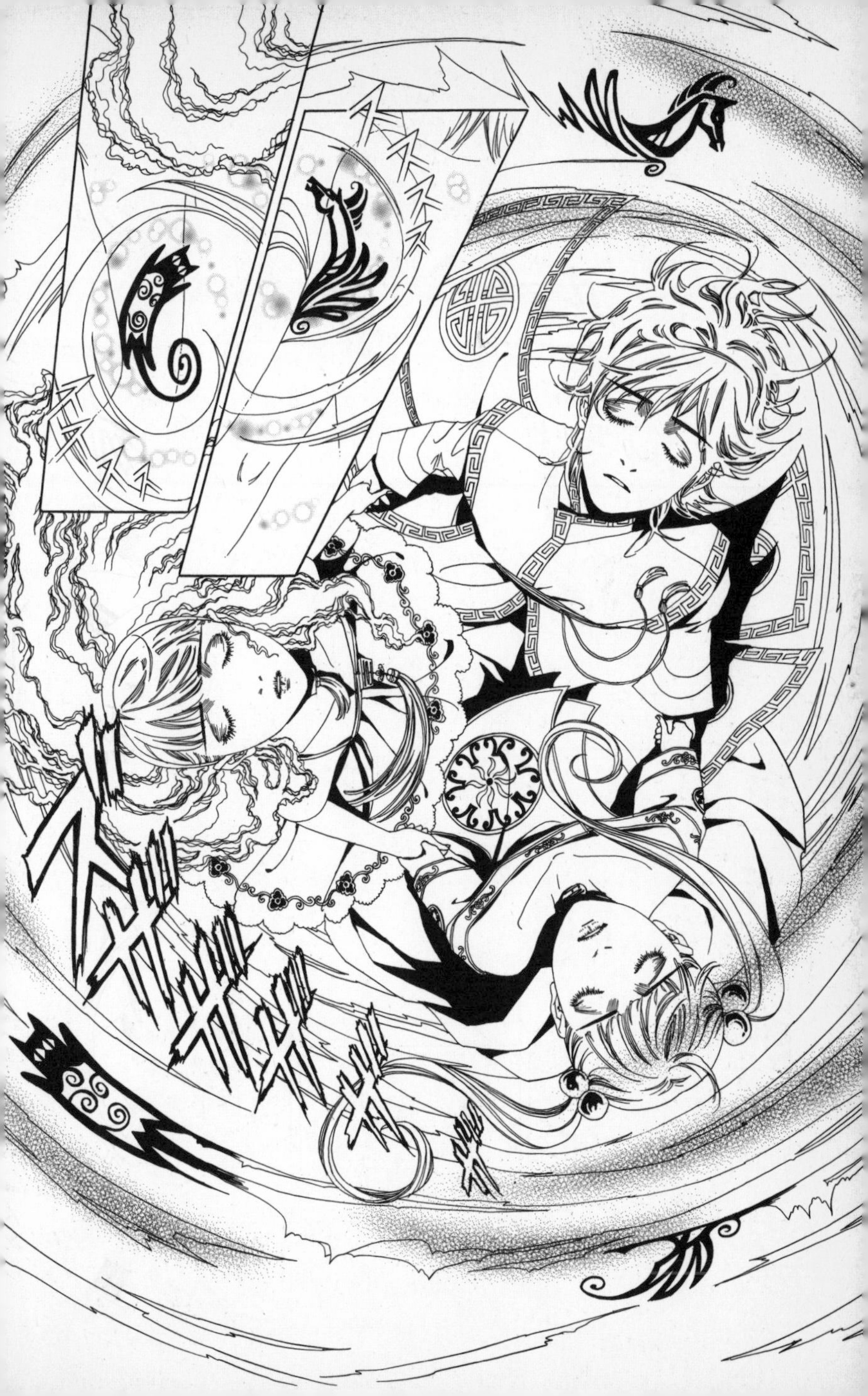

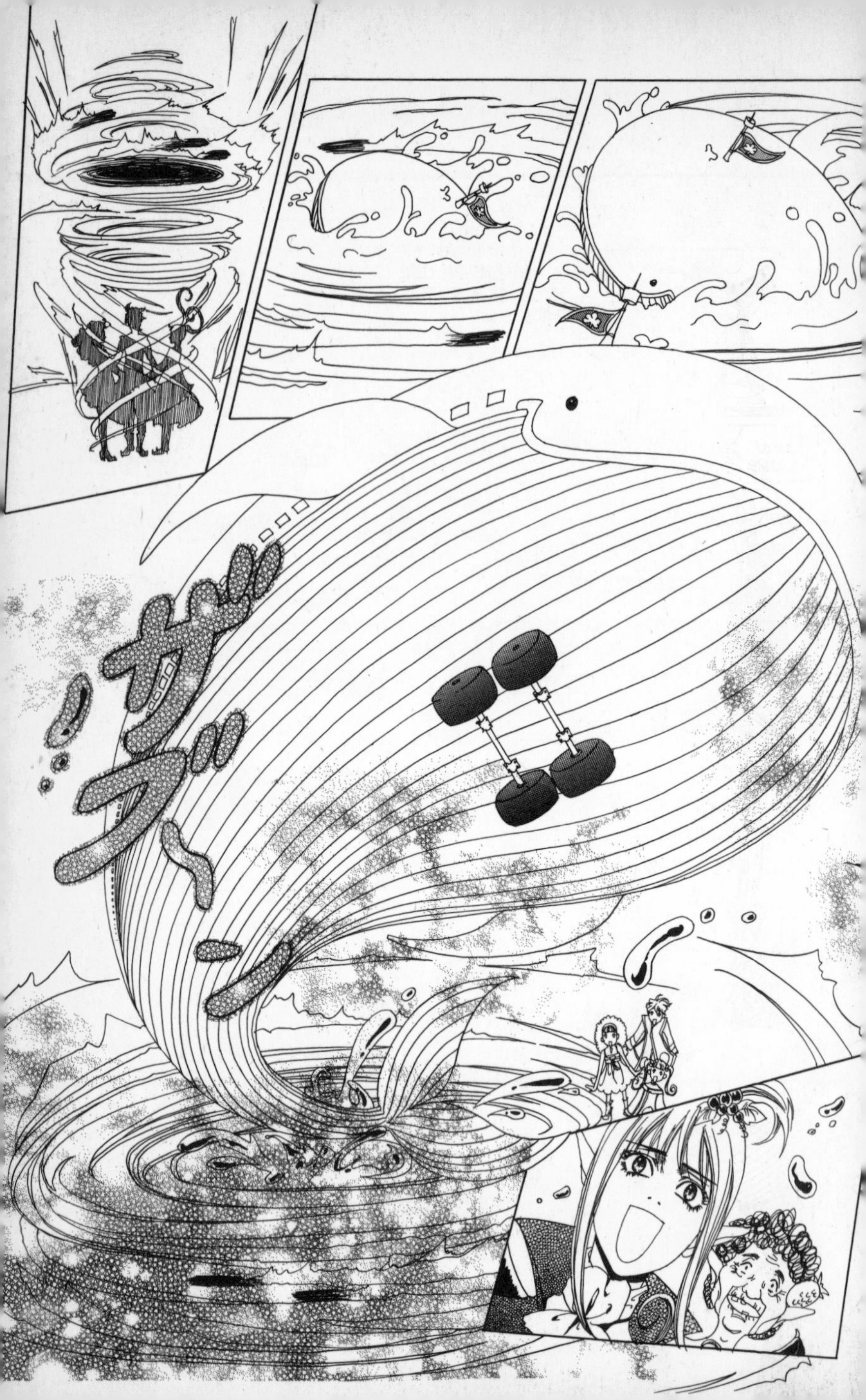
ザブ～ン

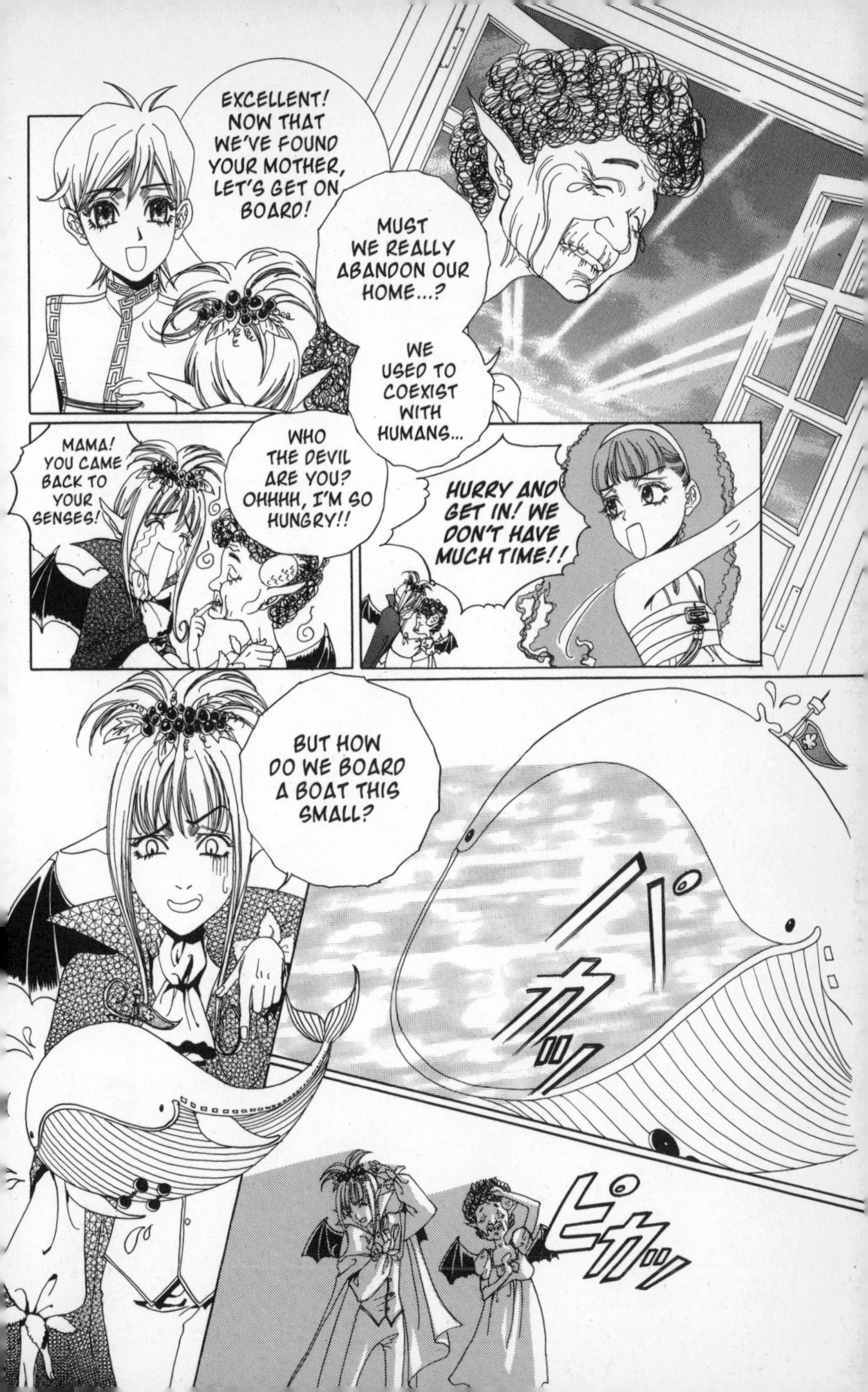
EXCELLENT! NOW THAT WE'VE FOUND YOUR MOTHER, LET'S GET ON BOARD!
MUST WE REALLY ABANDON OUR HOME...?
WE USED TO COEXIST WITH HUMANS...
HURRY AND GET IN! WE DON'T HAVE MUCH TIME!!
MAMA! YOU CAME BACK TO YOUR SENSES!
WHO THE DEVIL ARE YOU? OHHHH, I'M SO HUNGRY!!
BUT HOW DO WE BOARD A BOAT THIS SMALL?
パカッ
ピカッ

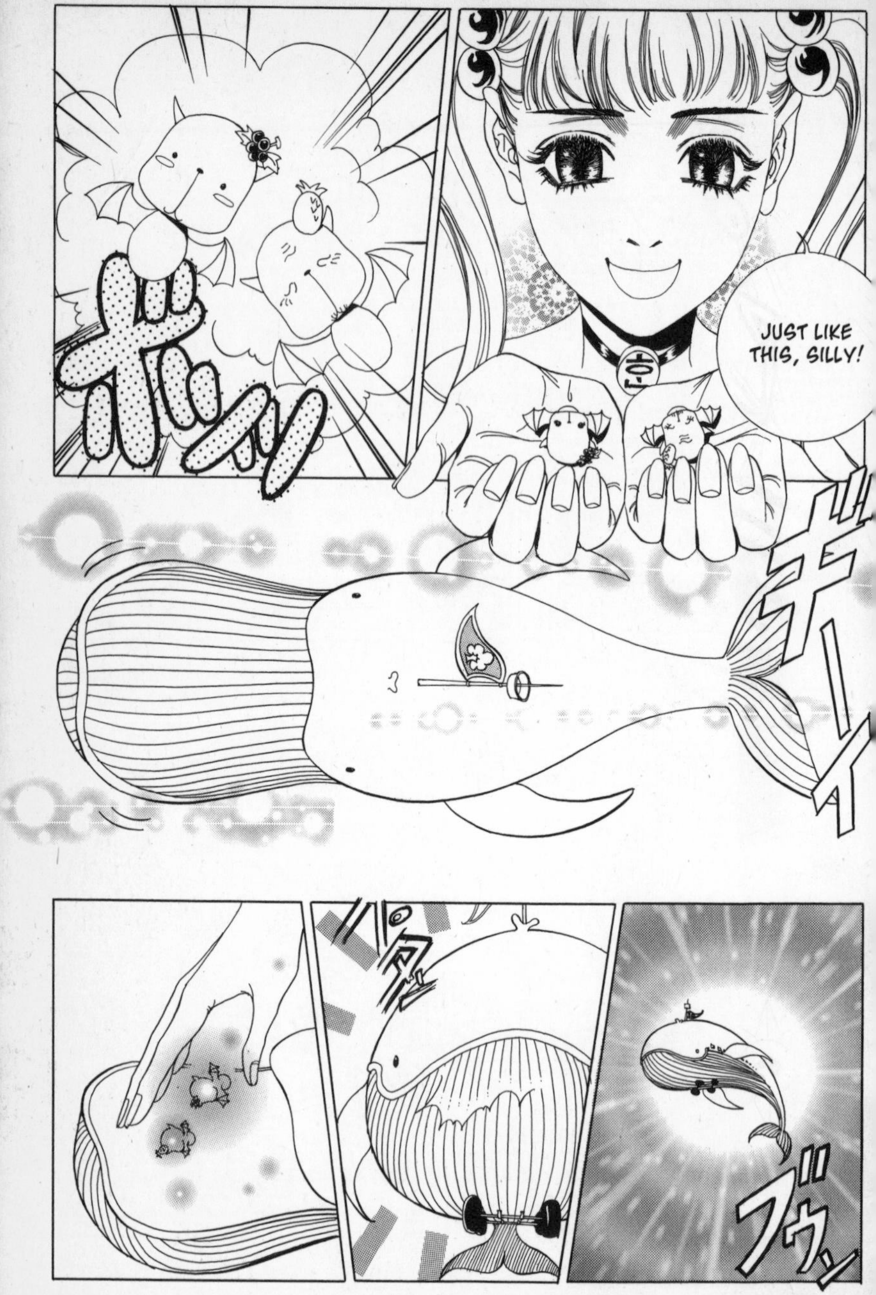
ボン
JUST LIKE THIS, SILLY!
ギーィ
パタ
ブウン

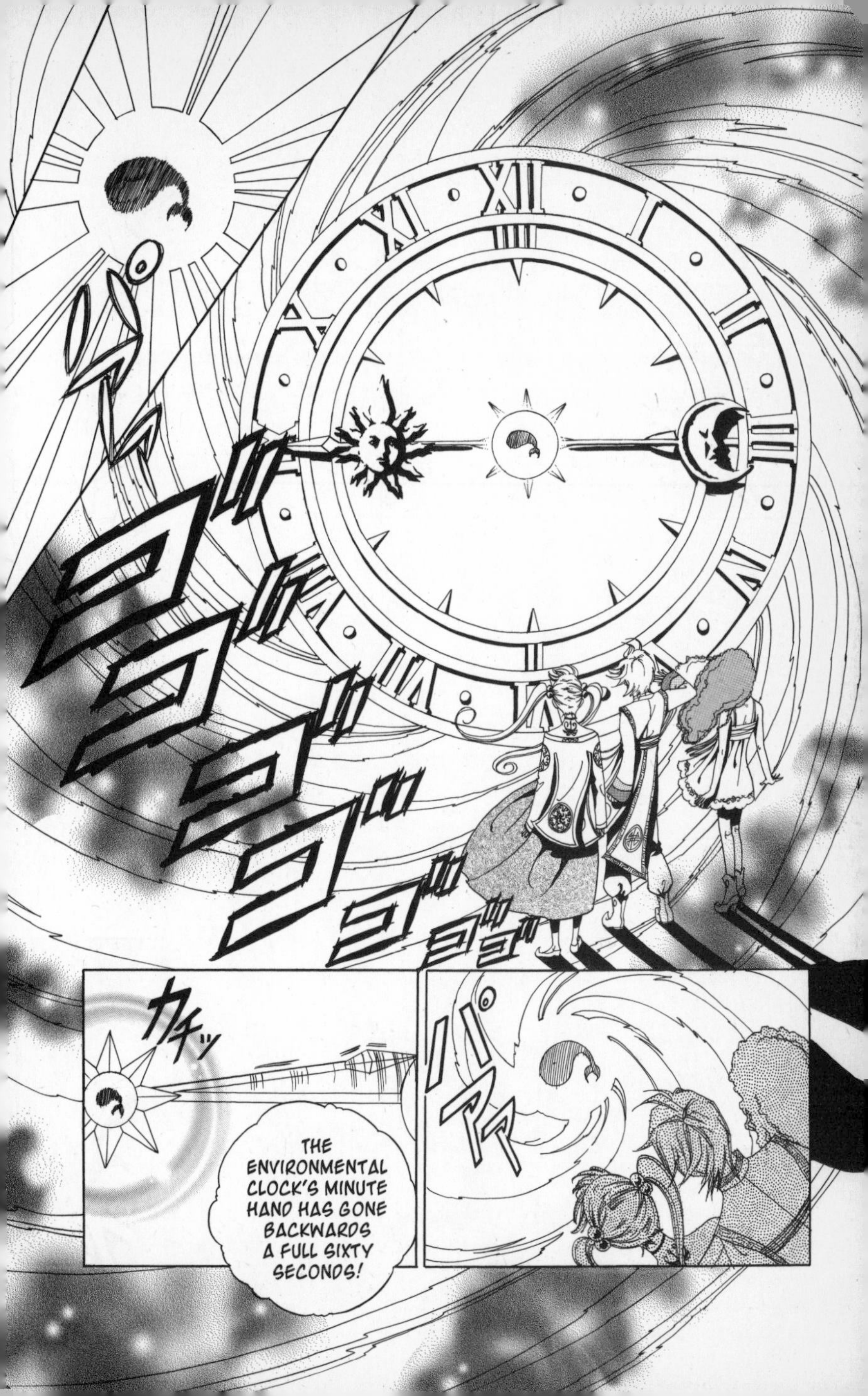
パァァ
カチッ
THE ENVIRONMENTAL CLOCK'S MINUTE HAND HAS GONE BACKWARDS A FULL SIXTY SECONDS!

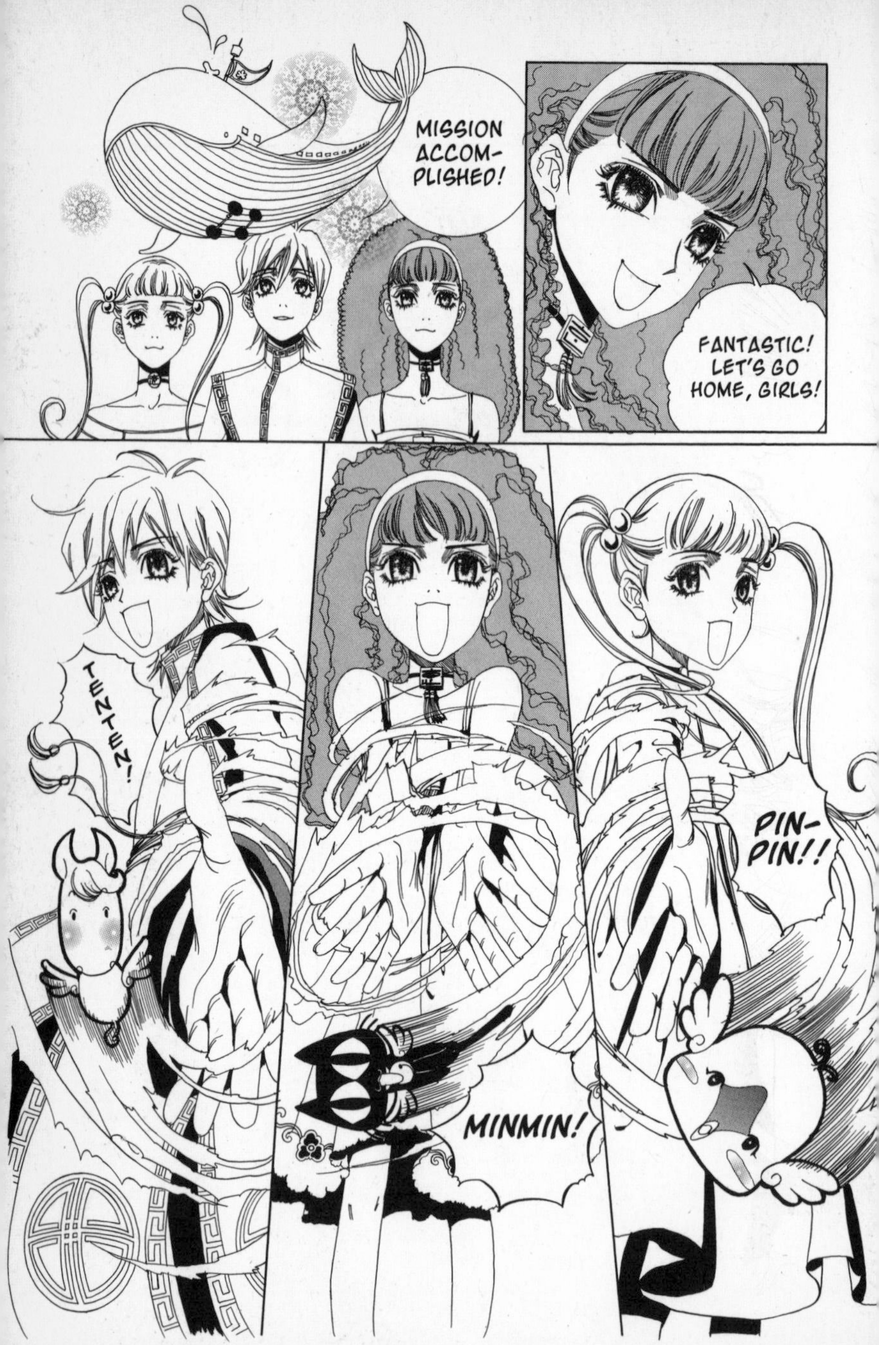
MISSION ACCOM-PLISHED!
FANTASTIC! LET'S GO HOME, GIRLS!
TENTEN!
MINMIN!
PIN-PIN!!

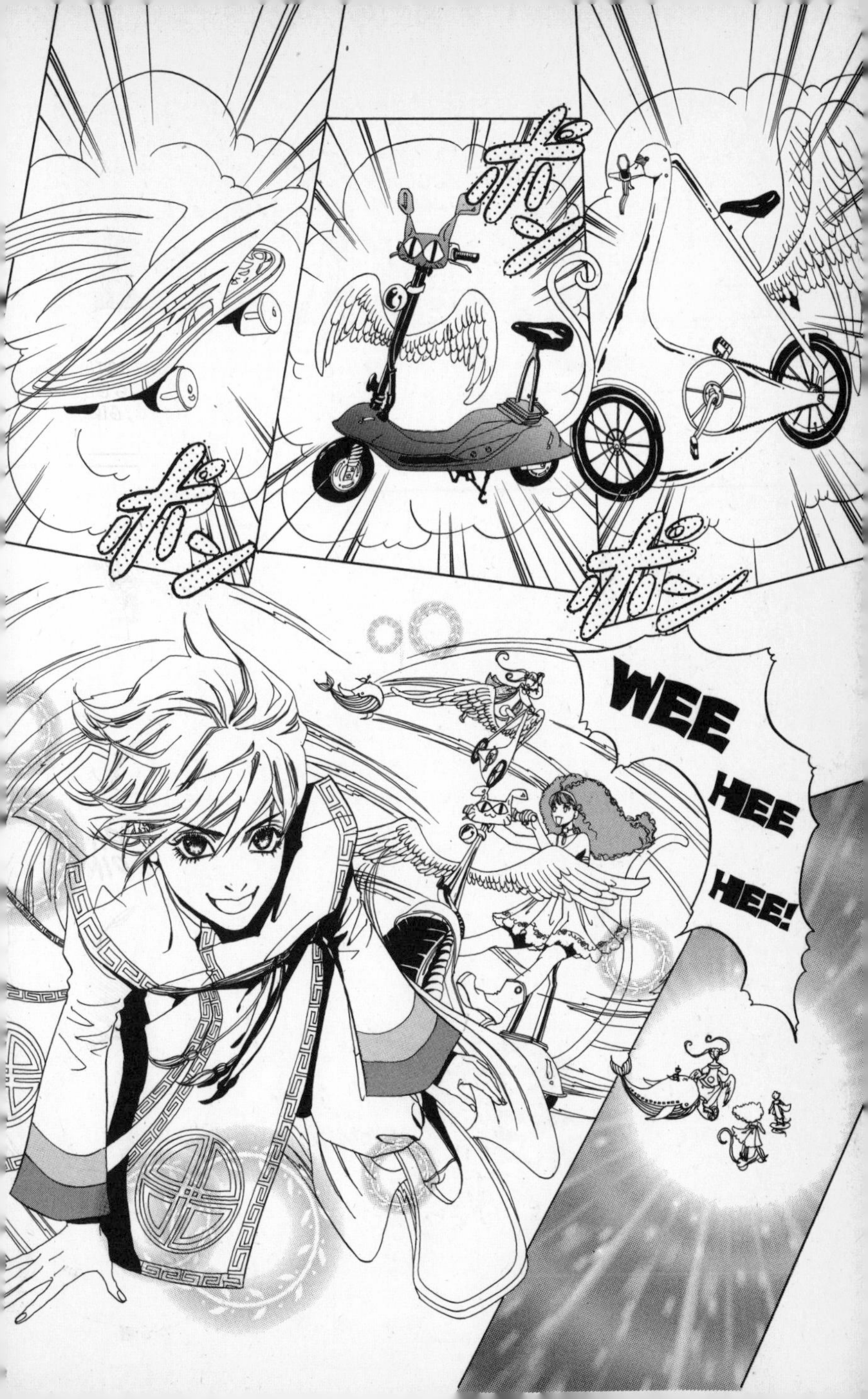
WEE HEE HEE!

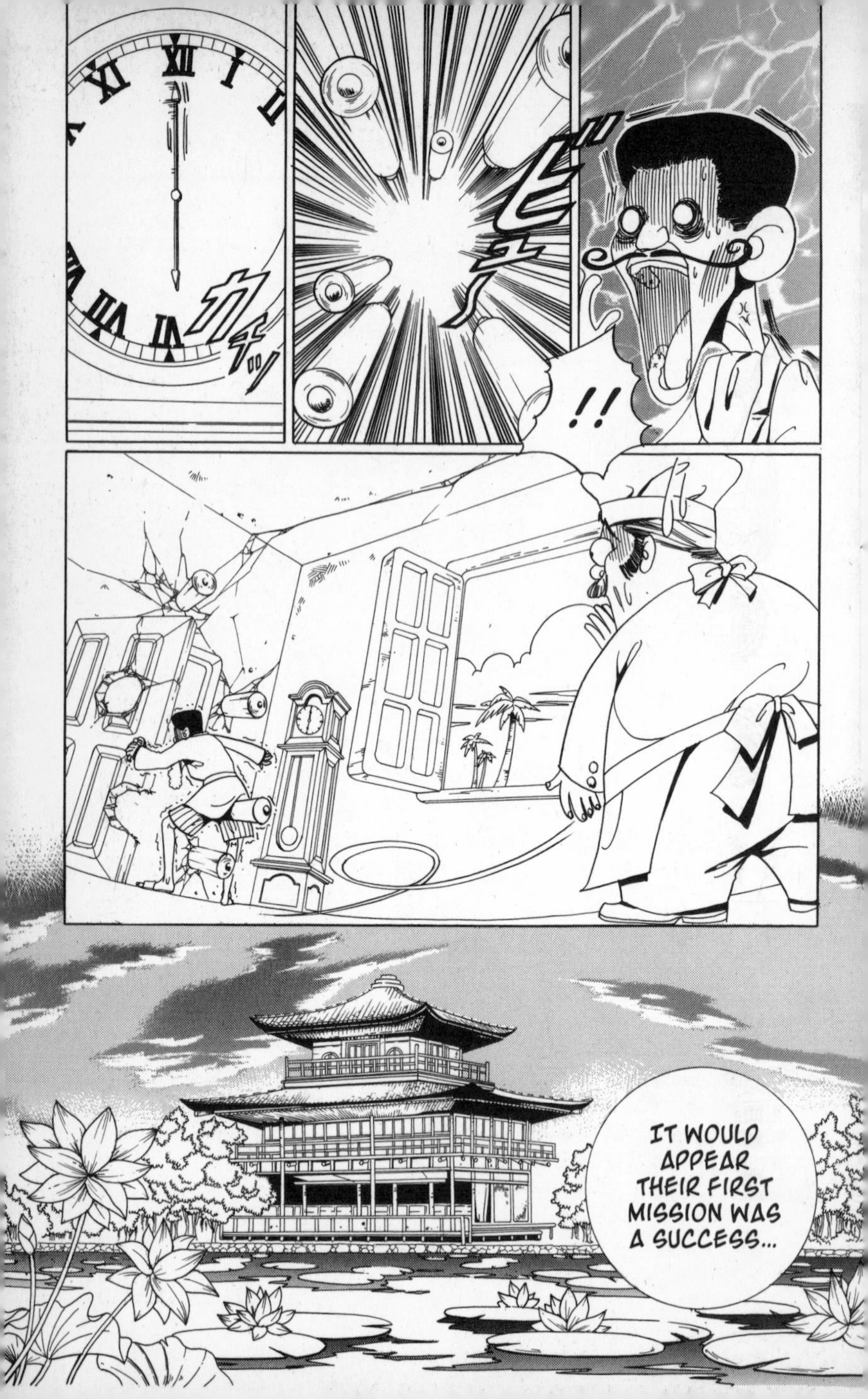
!!
カチッ
IT WOULD APPEAR THEIR FIRST MISSION WAS A SUCCESS...

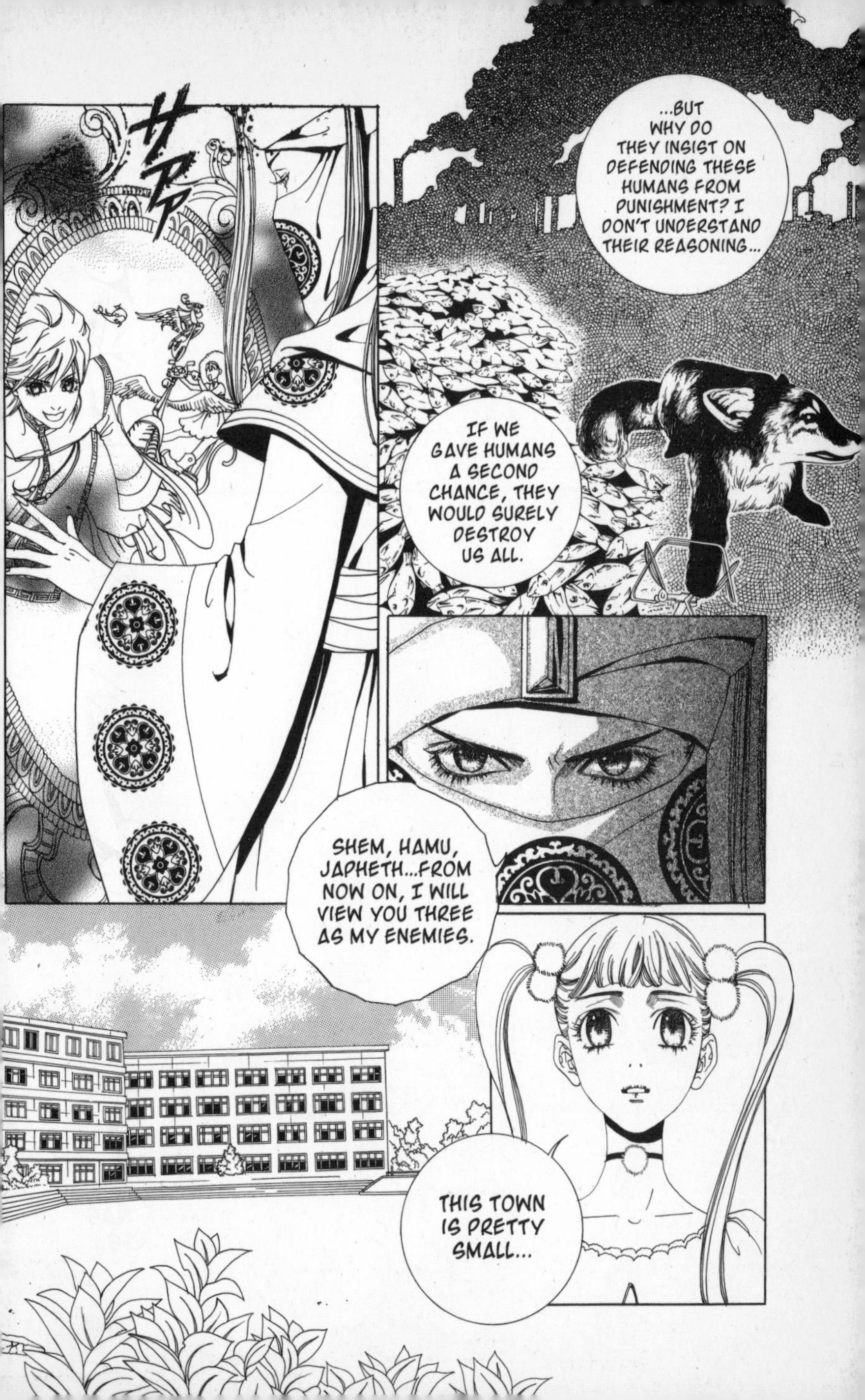
...BUT WHY DO THEY INSIST ON DEFENDING THESE HUMANS FROM PUNISHMENT? I DON'T UNDERSTAND THEIR REASONING...
IF WE GAVE HUMANS A SECOND CHANCE, THEY WOULD SURELY DESTROY US ALL.
SHEM, HAMU, JAPHETH...FROM NOW ON, I WILL VIEW YOU THREE AS MY ENEMIES.
THIS TOWN IS PRETTY SMALL...

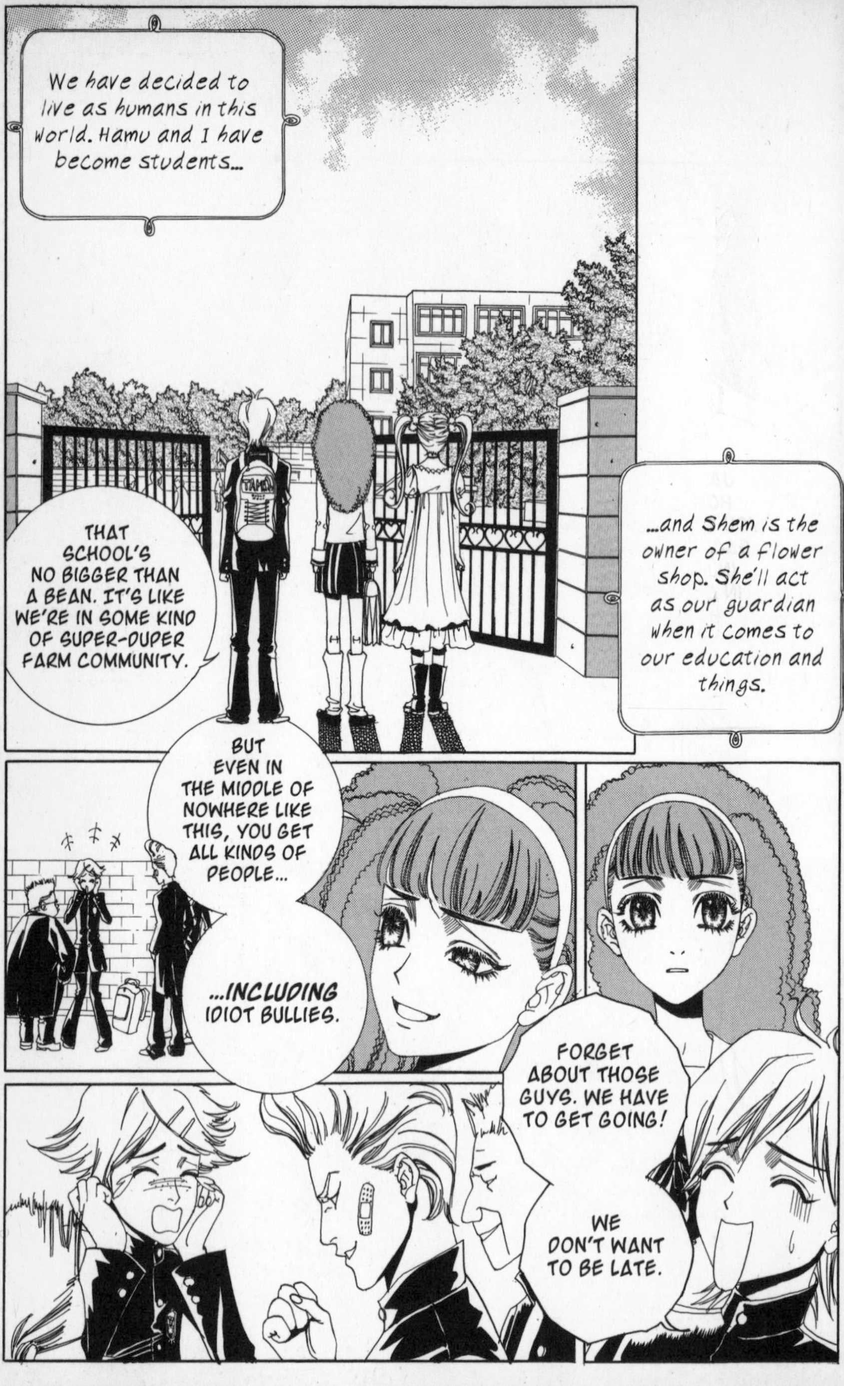
We have decided to live as humans in this world. Hamu and I have become students...
...and Shem is the owner of a flower shop. She'll act as our guardian when it comes to our education and things.
THAT SCHOOL'S NO BIGGER THAN A BEAN. IT'S LIKE WE'RE IN SOME KIND OF SUPER-DUPER FARM COMMUNITY.
BUT EVEN IN THE MIDDLE OF NOWHERE LIKE THIS, YOU GET ALL KINDS OF PEOPLE...
...INCLUDING IDIOT BULLIES.
FORGET ABOUT THOSE GUYS. WE HAVE TO GET GOING!
WE DON'T WANT TO BE LATE.

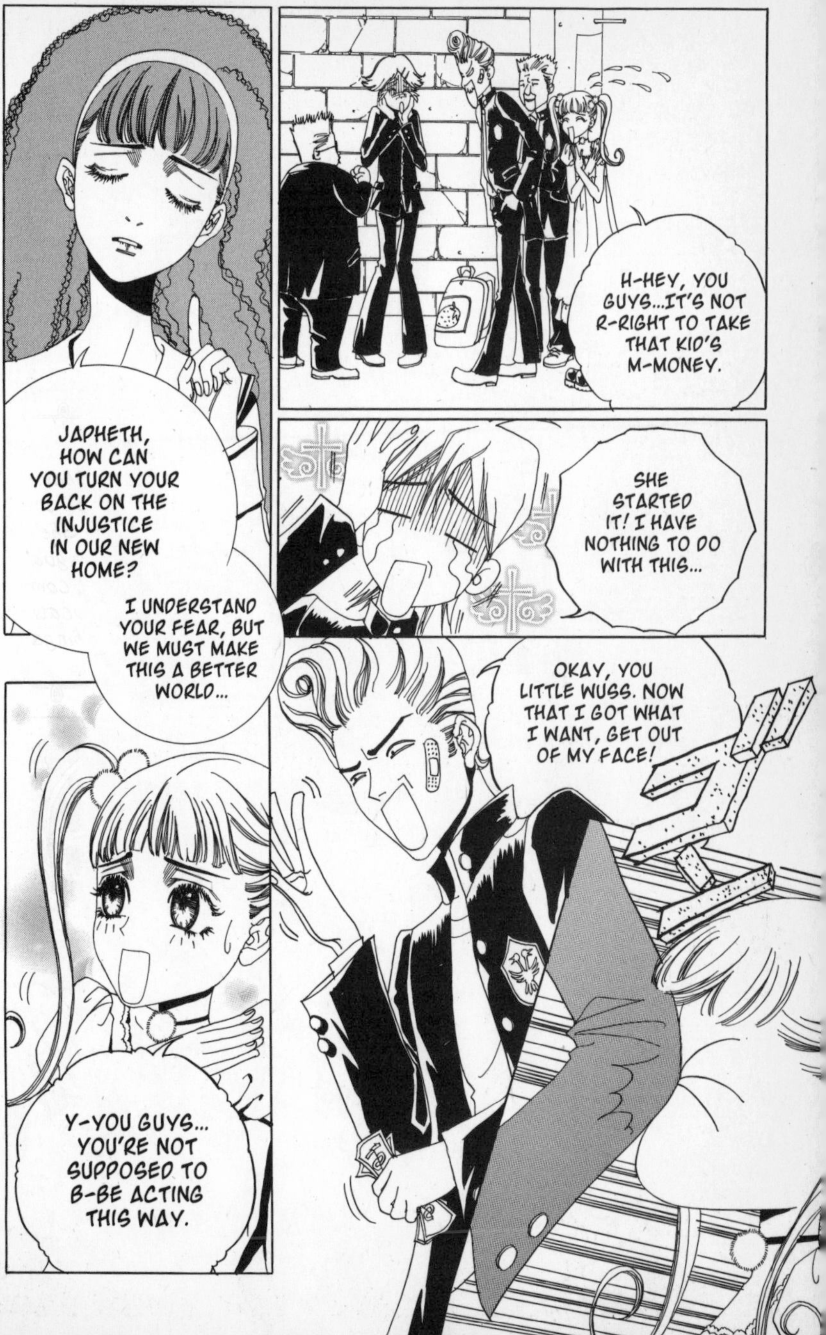
H-HEY, YOU GUYS...IT'S NOT R-RIGHT TO TAKE THAT KID'S M-MONEY.
SHE STARTED IT! I HAVE NOTHING TO DO WITH THIS...
JAPHETH, HOW CAN YOU TURN YOUR BACK ON THE INJUSTICE IN OUR NEW HOME?
I UNDERSTAND YOUR FEAR, BUT WE MUST MAKE THIS A BETTER WORLD...
OKAY, YOU LITTLE WUSS. NOW THAT I GOT WHAT I WANT, GET OUT OF MY FACE!
Y-YOU GUYS... YOU'RE NOT SUPPOSED TO B-BE ACTING THIS WAY.

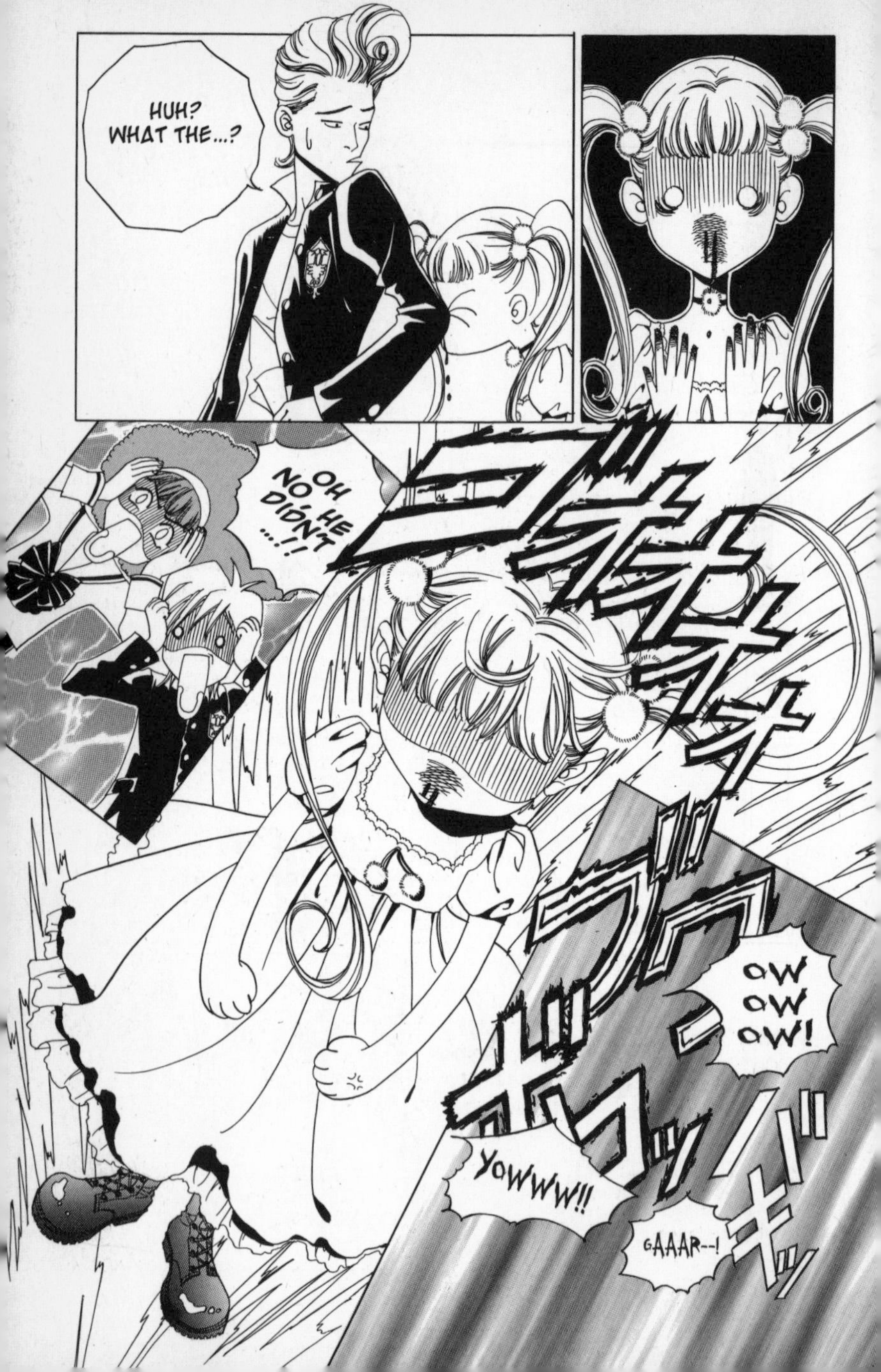
HUH? WHAT THE...?
OH NO, HE DIDN'T ...!!
AW AW AW!
YOWWW!!
GAAAR--!

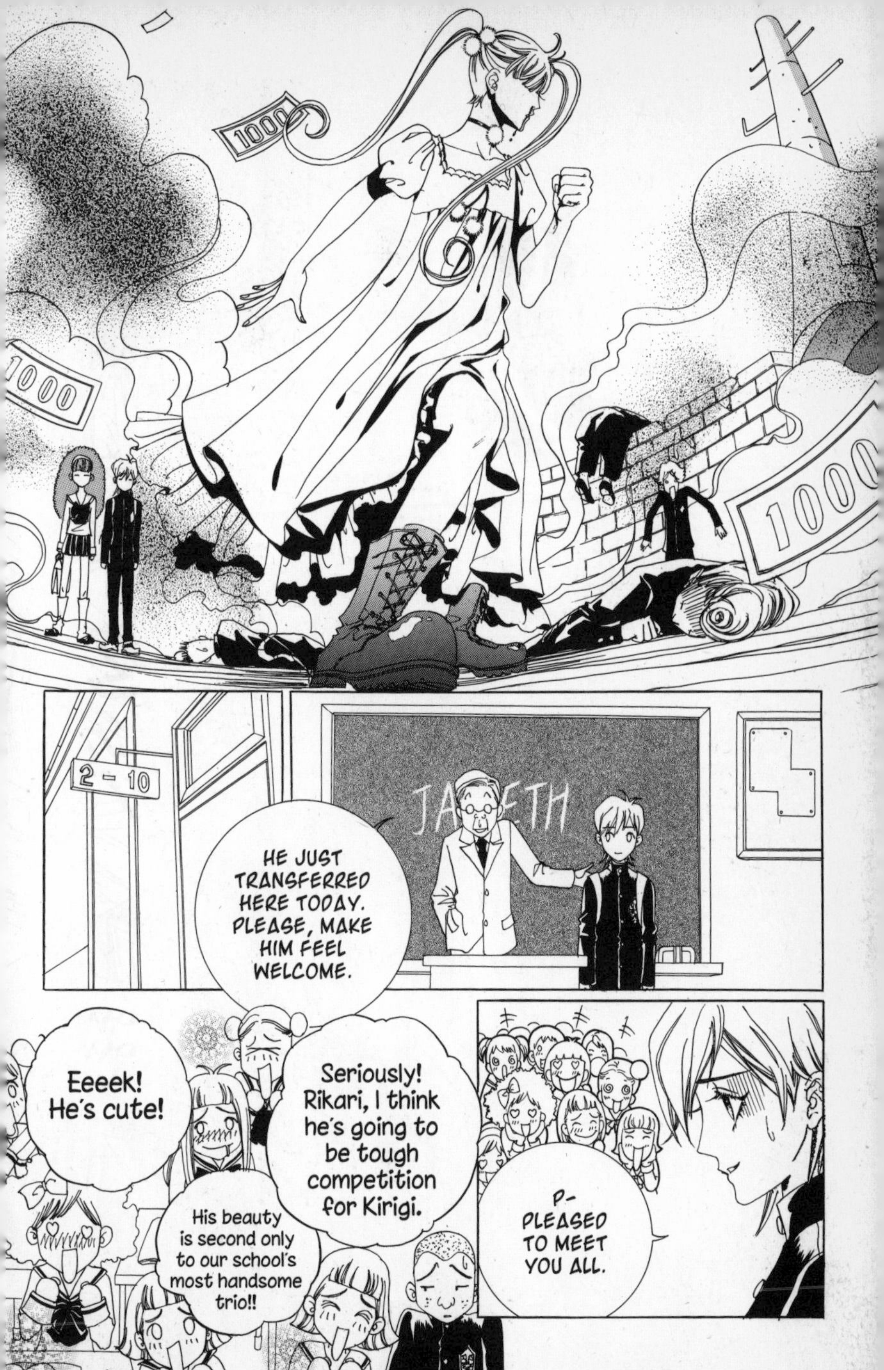
1000
1000
1000
1000
2 - 10
HE JUST TRANSFERRED HERE TODAY. PLEASE, MAKE HIM FEEL WELCOME.
P- PLEASED TO MEET YOU ALL.
Seriously! Rikari, I think he's going to be tough competition for Kirigi.
Eeeek! He's cute!
His beauty is second only to our school's most handsome trio!!

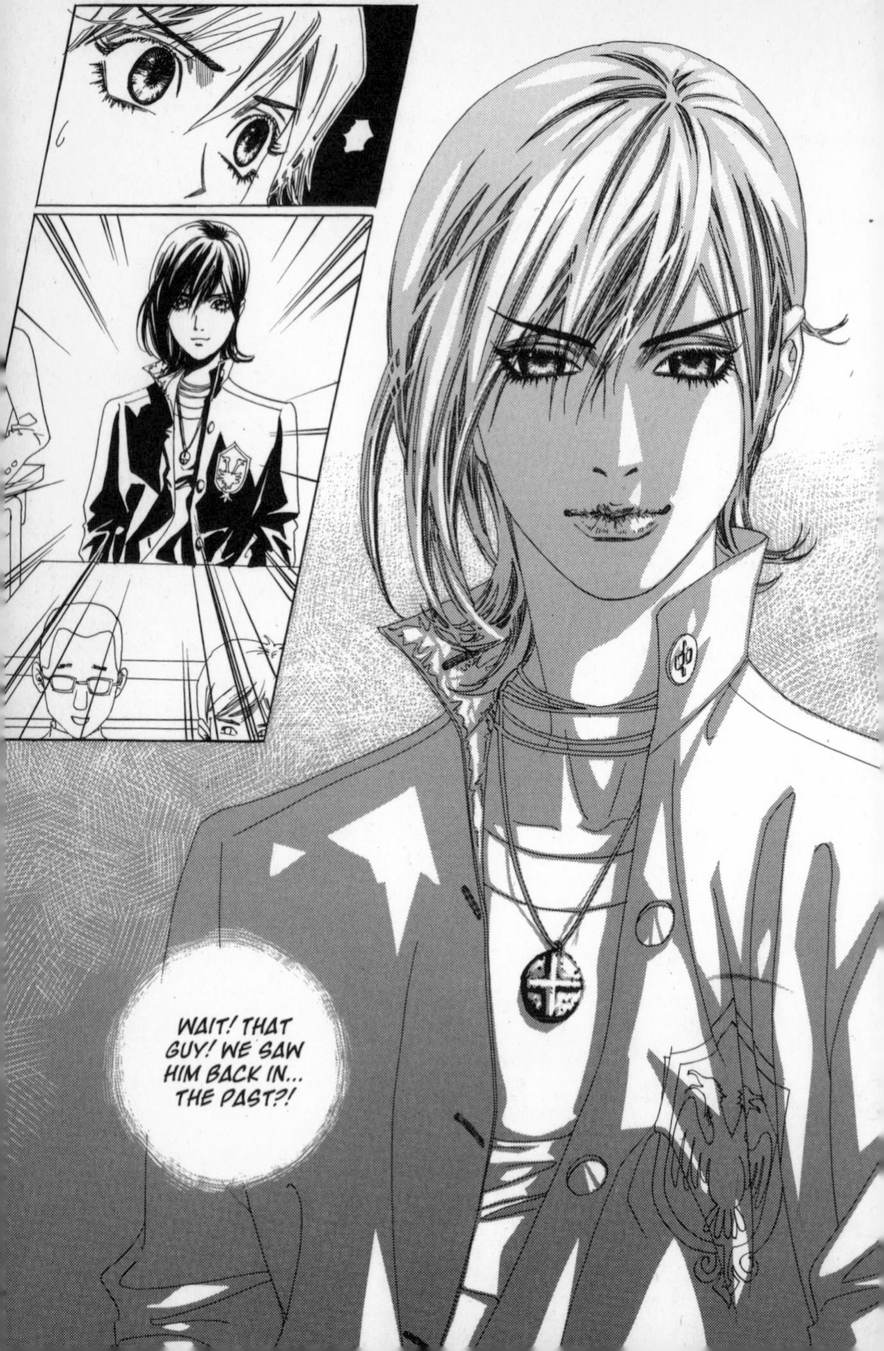
WAIT! THAT GUY! WE SAW HIM BACK IN... THE PAST?!

{Chapter 2}

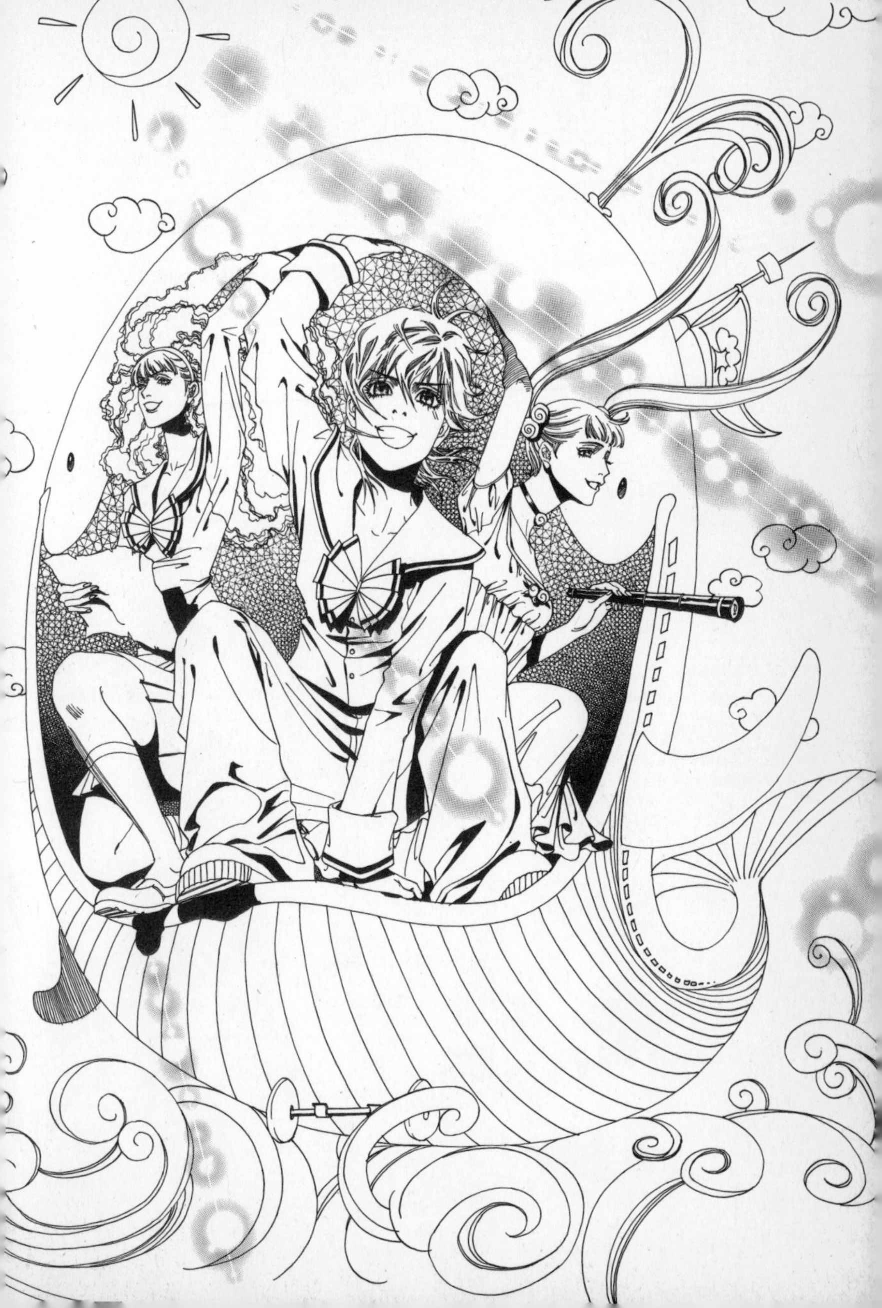

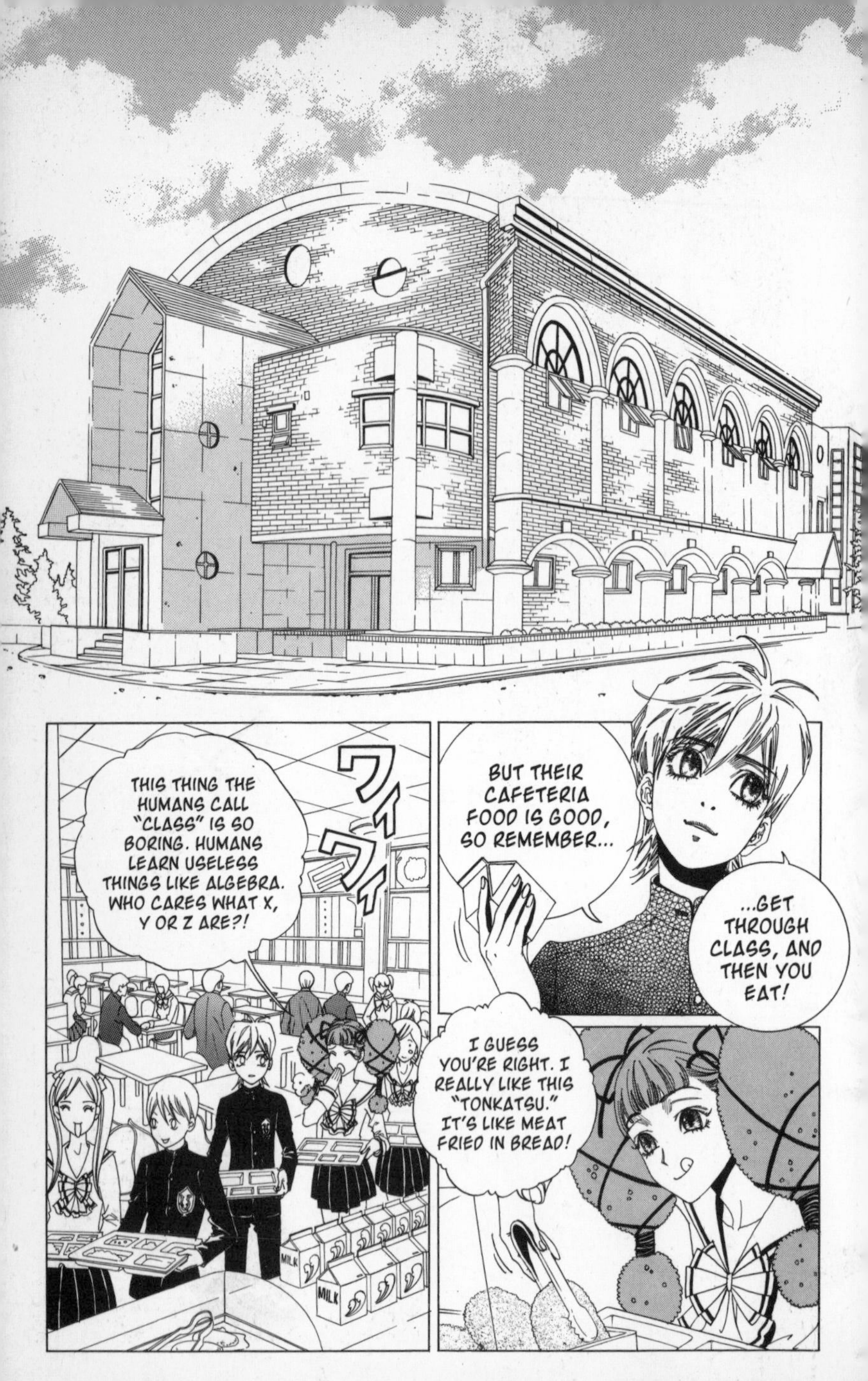
THIS THING THE HUMANS CALL "CLASS" IS SO BORING. HUMANS LEARN USELESS THINGS LIKE ALGEBRA. WHO CARES WHAT X, Y OR Z ARE?!
ワイワイ
BUT THEIR CAFETERIA FOOD IS GOOD, SO REMEMBER...
...GET THROUGH CLASS, AND THEN YOU EAT!
I GUESS YOU'RE RIGHT. I REALLY LIKE THIS "TONKATSU." IT'S LIKE MEAT FRIED IN BREAD!

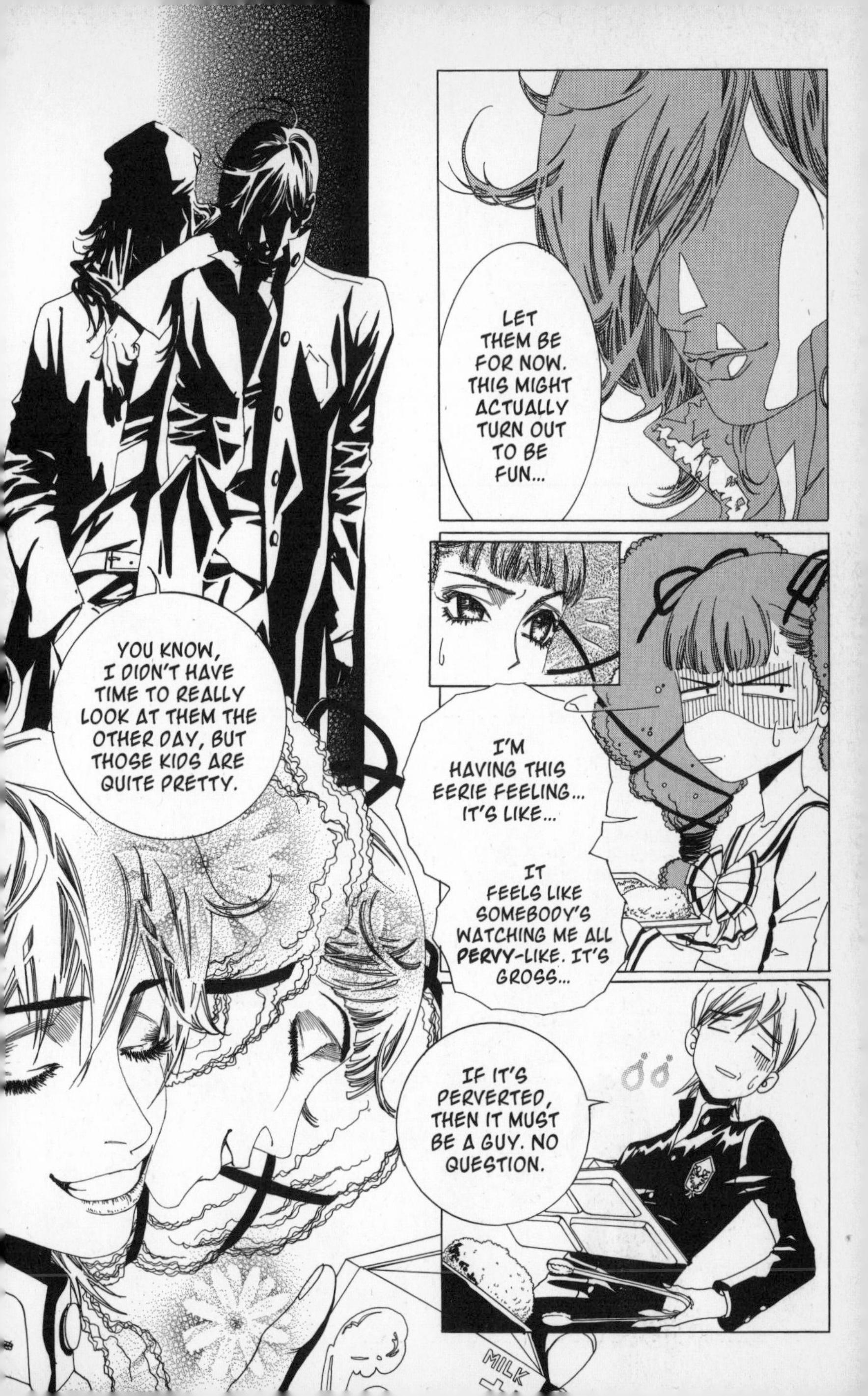
LET THEM BE FOR NOW. THIS MIGHT ACTUALLY TURN OUT TO BE FUN...
I'M HAVING THIS EERIE FEELING... IT'S LIKE...
IT FEELS LIKE SOMEBODY'S WATCHING ME ALL PERVY-LIKE. IT'S GROSS...
IF IT'S PERVERTED, THEN IT MUST BE A GUY. NO QUESTION.
YOU KNOW, I DIDN'T HAVE TIME TO REALLY LOOK AT THEM THE OTHER DAY, BUT THOSE KIDS ARE QUITE PRETTY.
MILK

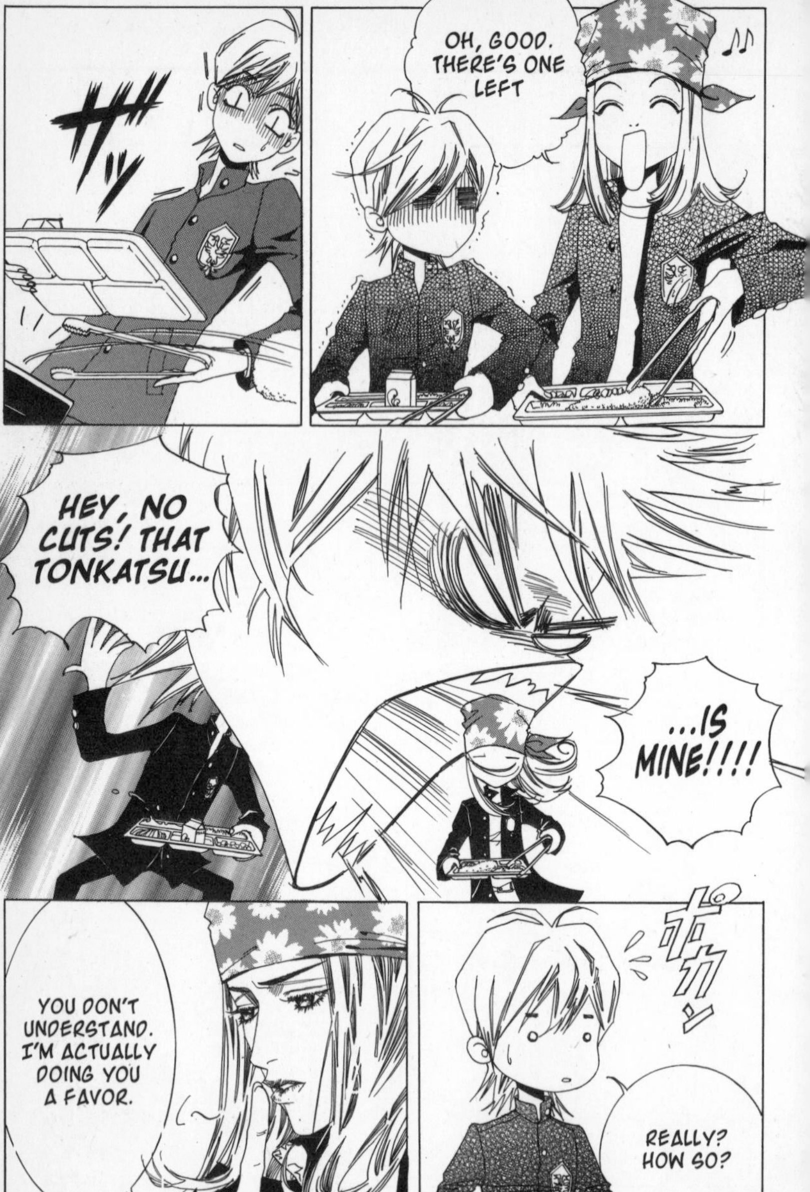
ザッ
OH, GOOD. THERE'S ONE LEFT
♪♪
HEY, NO CUTS! THAT TONKATSU...
...IS MINE!!!!
YOU DON'T UNDERSTAND. I'M ACTUALLY DOING YOU A FAVOR.
ポカン
REALLY? HOW SO?

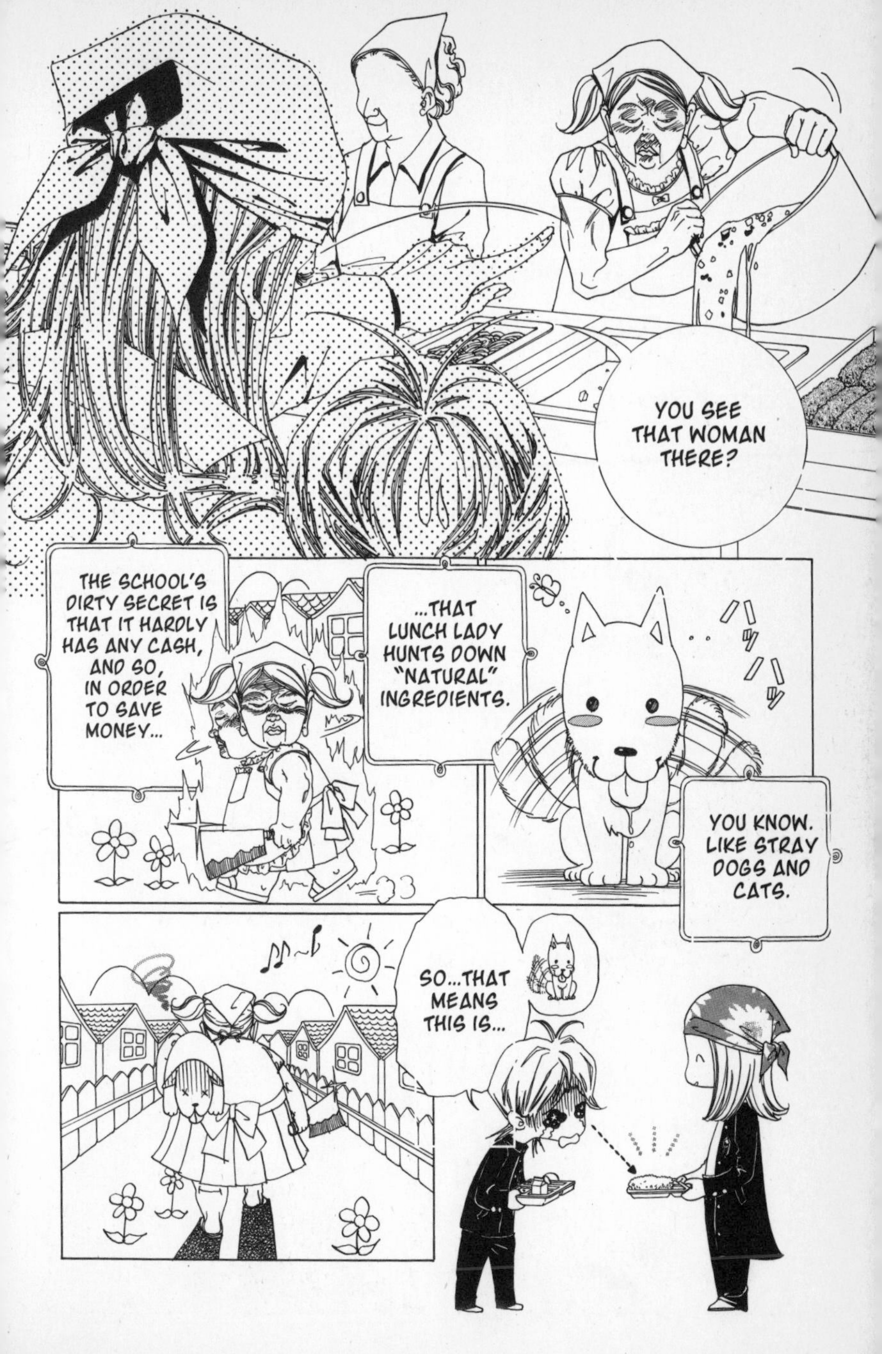
YOU SEE THAT WOMAN THERE?
THE SCHOOL'S DIRTY SECRET IS THAT IT HARDLY HAS ANY CASH, AND SO, IN ORDER TO SAVE MONEY...
...THAT LUNCH LADY HUNTS DOWN "NATURAL" INGREDIENTS.
ハッハッ
YOU KNOW. LIKE STRAY DOGS AND CATS.
SO...THAT MEANS THIS IS...

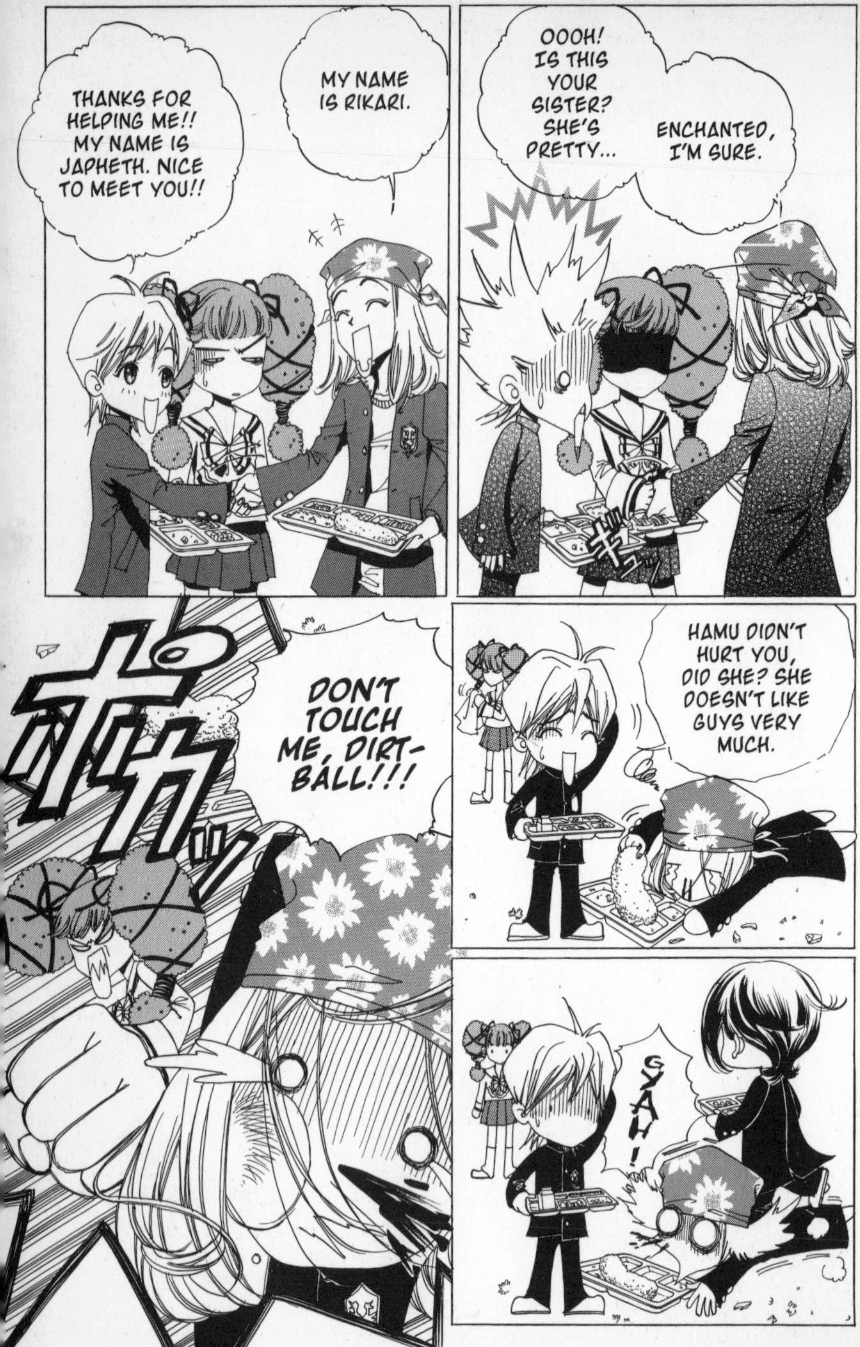
THANKS FOR HELPING ME!! MY NAME IS JAPHETH. NICE TO MEET YOU!!
MY NAME IS RIKARI.
OOOH! IS THIS YOUR SISTER? SHE'S PRETTY...
ENCHANTED, I'M SURE.
DON'T TOUCH ME, DIRT-BALL!!!
HAMU DIDN'T HURT YOU, DID SHE? SHE DOESN'T LIKE GUYS VERY MUCH.
GYAH!

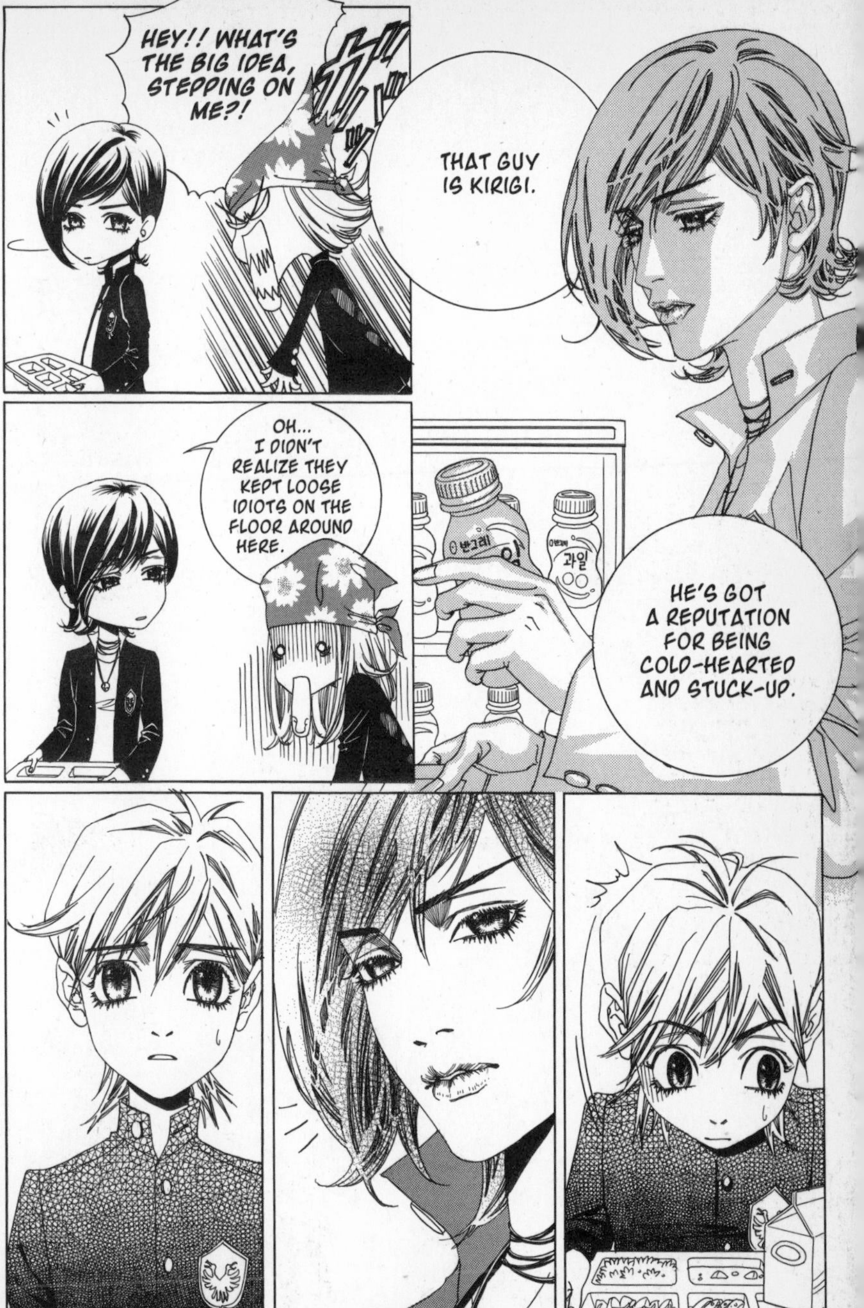
HEY!! WHAT'S THE BIG IDEA, STEPPING ON ME?!
THAT GUY IS KIRIGI.
OH... I DIDN'T REALIZE THEY KEPT LOOSE IDIOTS ON THE FLOOR AROUND HERE.
HE'S GOT A REPUTATION FOR BEING COLD-HEARTED AND STUCK-UP.

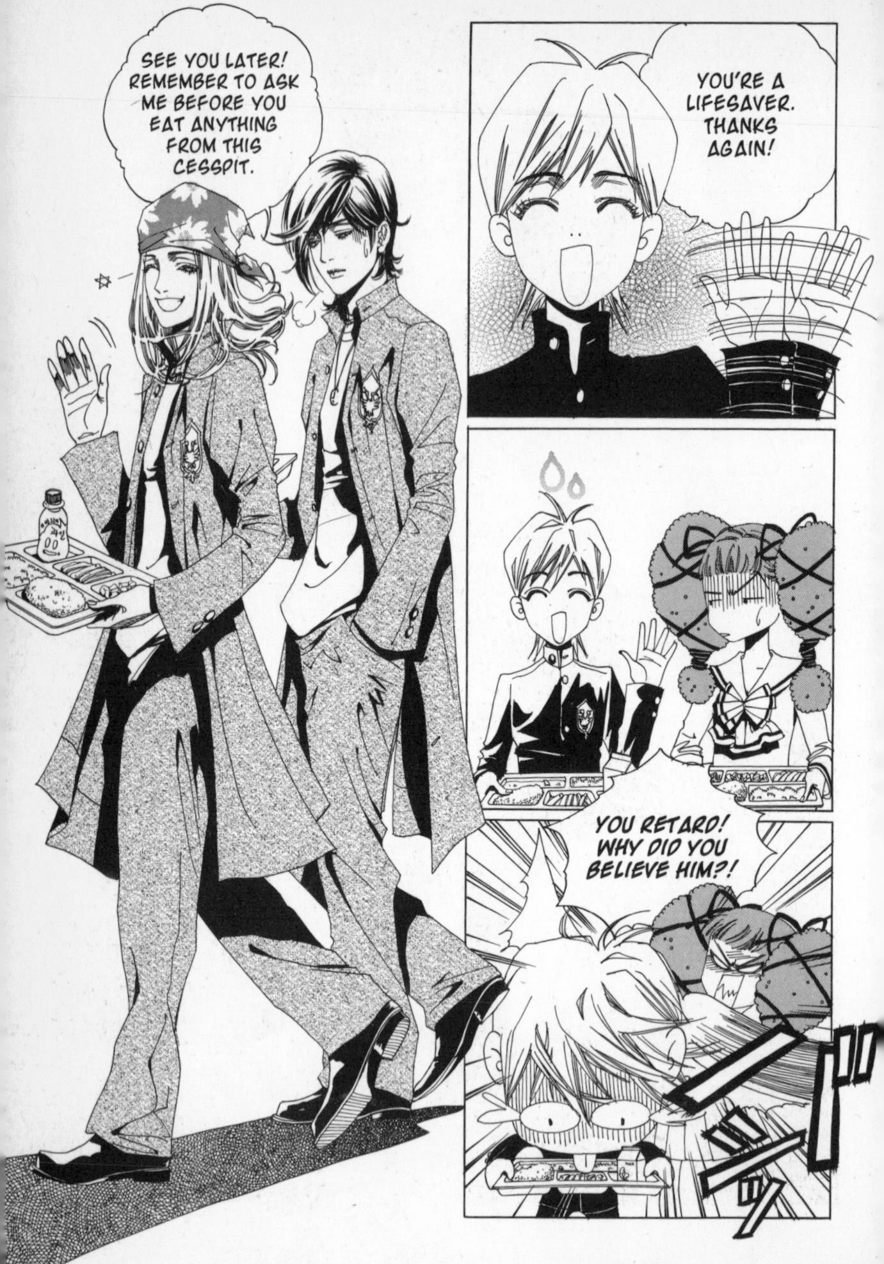
YOU'RE A LIFESAVER. THANKS AGAIN!
YOU RETARD! WHY DID YOU BELIEVE HIM?!
SEE YOU LATER! REMEMBER TO ASK ME BEFORE YOU EAT ANYTHING FROM THIS CESSPIT.

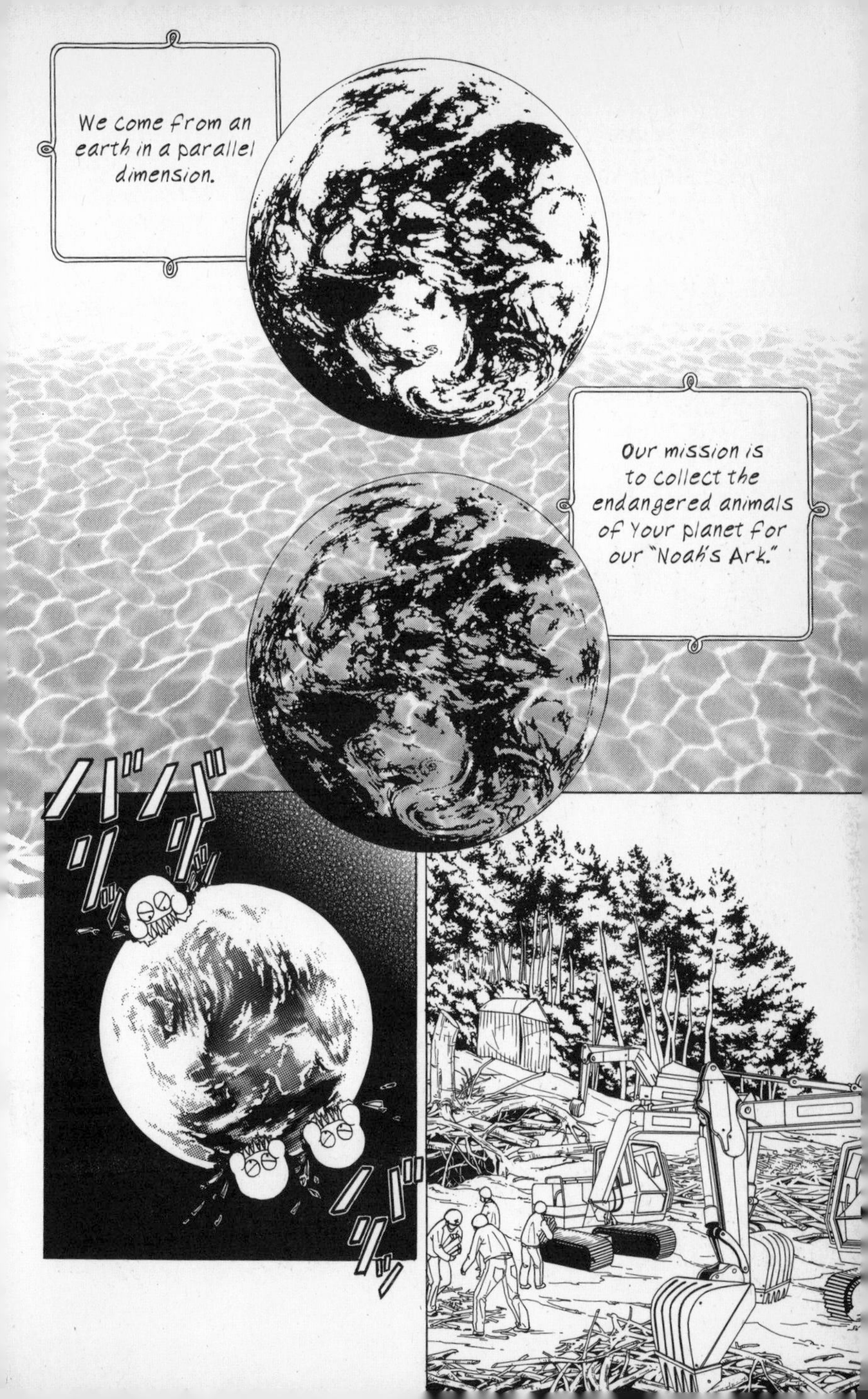
We come from an earth in a parallel dimension.
Our mission is to collect the endangered animals of your planet for our "Noah's Ark."

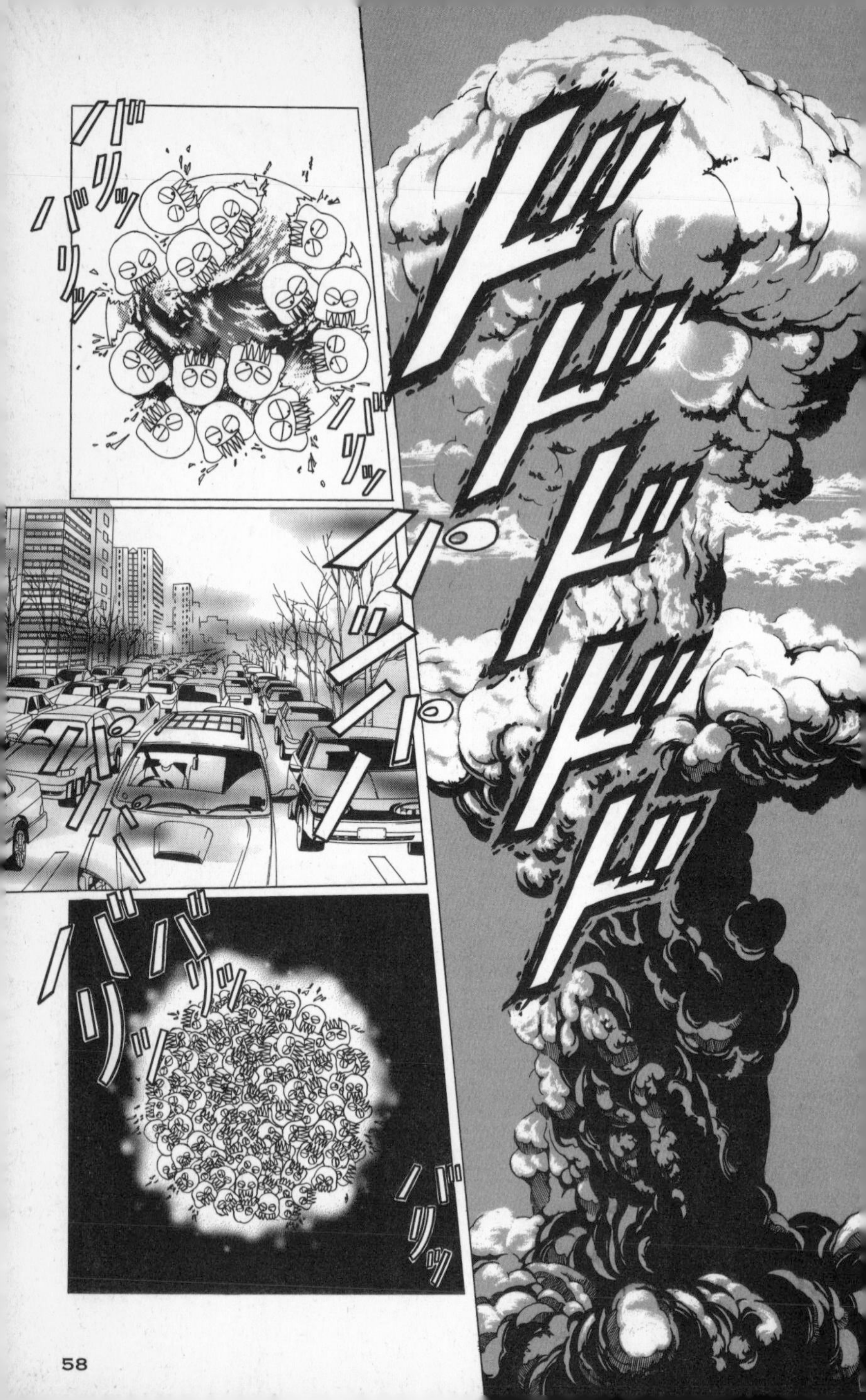
ドドドドド
バリッバリッ
バリッ
パンパン
バリバリバリッ
バリッ

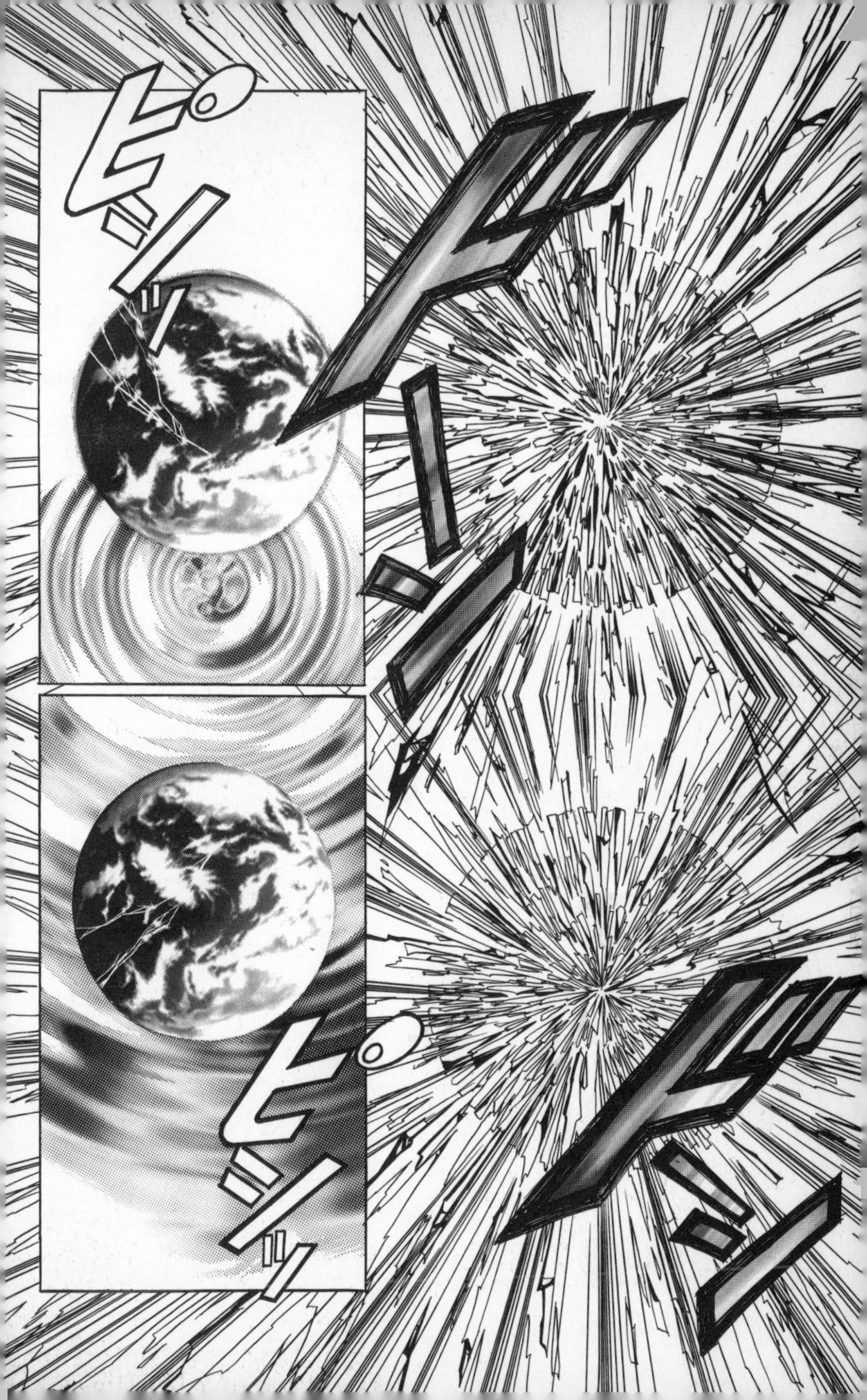
ピシッ
ピシッ

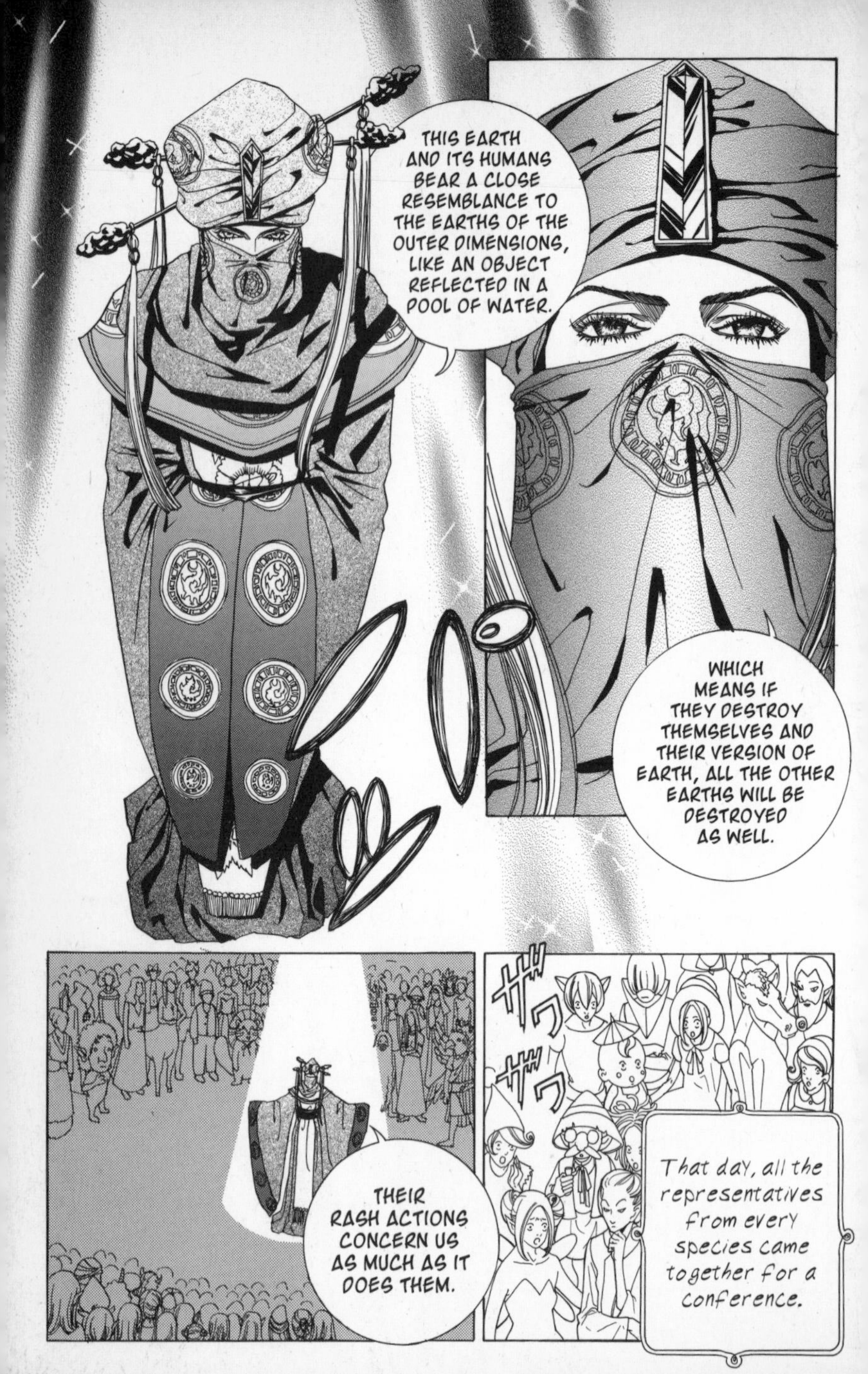
THIS EARTH AND ITS HUMANS BEAR A CLOSE RESEMBLANCE TO THE EARTHS OF THE OUTER DIMENSIONS, LIKE AN OBJECT REFLECTED IN A POOL OF WATER.
WHICH MEANS IF THEY DESTROY THEMSELVES AND THEIR VERSION OF EARTH, ALL THE OTHER EARTHS WILL BE DESTROYED AS WELL.
THEIR RASH ACTIONS CONCERN US AS MUCH AS IT DOES THEM.
That day, all the representatives from every species came together for a conference.

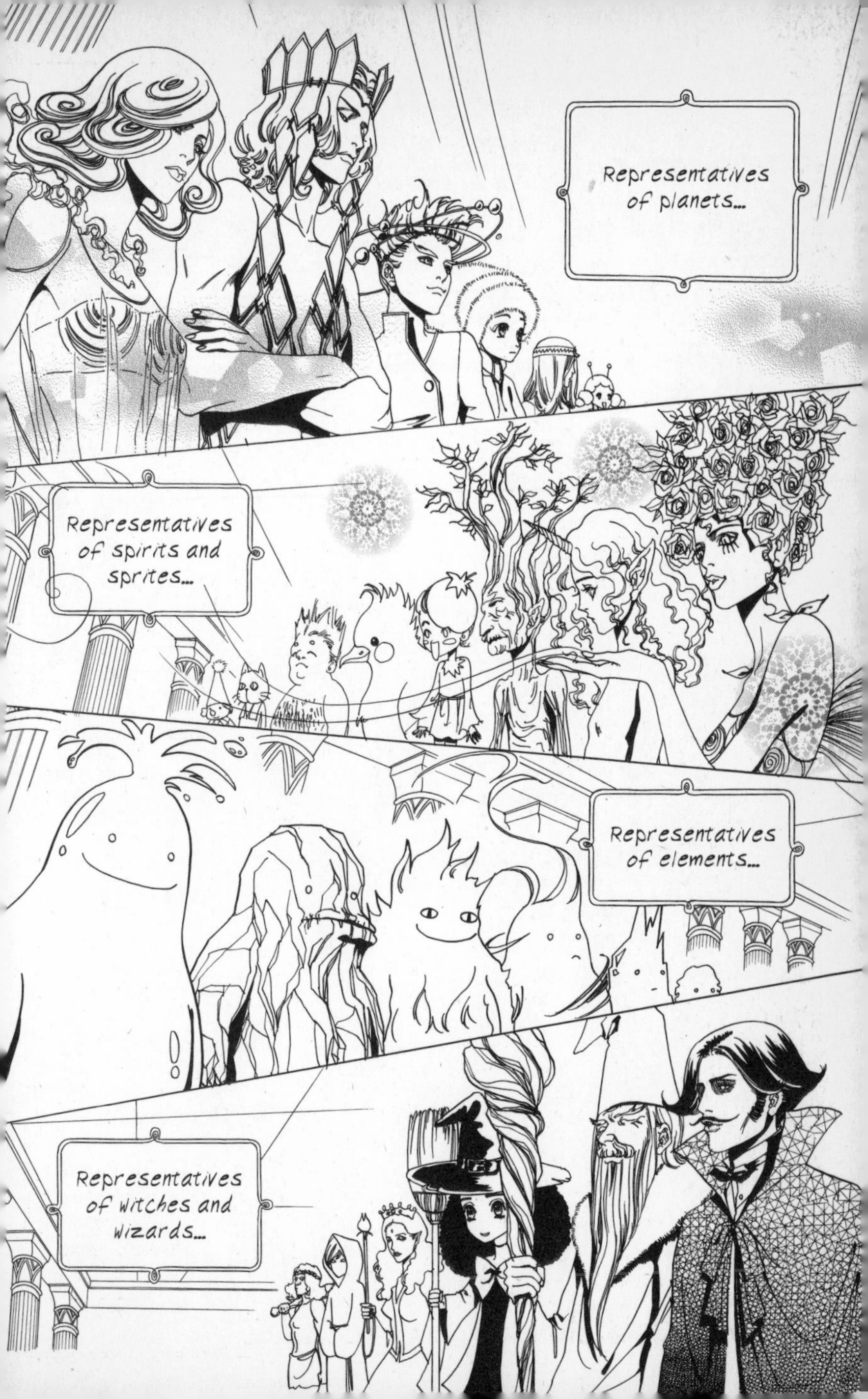
Representatives of planets...
Representatives of spirits and sprites...
Representatives of elements...
Representatives of witches and wizards...

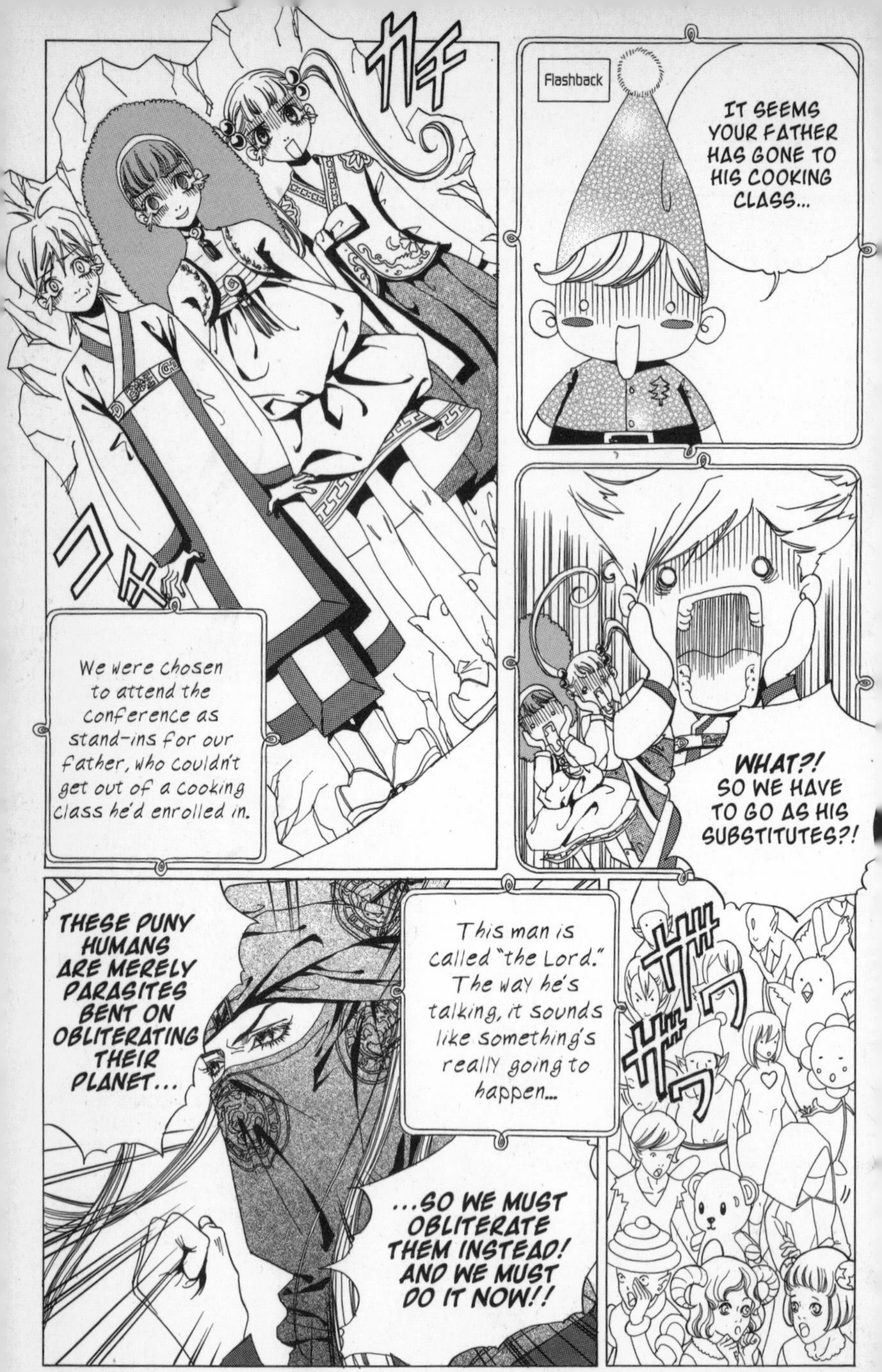
Flashback
IT SEEMS YOUR FATHER HAS GONE TO HIS COOKING CLASS...
WHAT?! SO WE HAVE TO GO AS HIS SUBSTITUTES?!
カチ
We were chosen to attend the conference as stand-ins for our father, who couldn't get out of a cooking class he'd enrolled in.
ザワッ ザワッ
This man is called "the Lord." The way he's talking, it sounds like something's really going to happen...
THESE PUNY HUMANS ARE MERELY PARASITES BENT ON OBLITERATING THEIR PLANET...
...SO WE MUST OBLITERATE THEM INSTEAD! AND WE MUST DO IT NOW!!

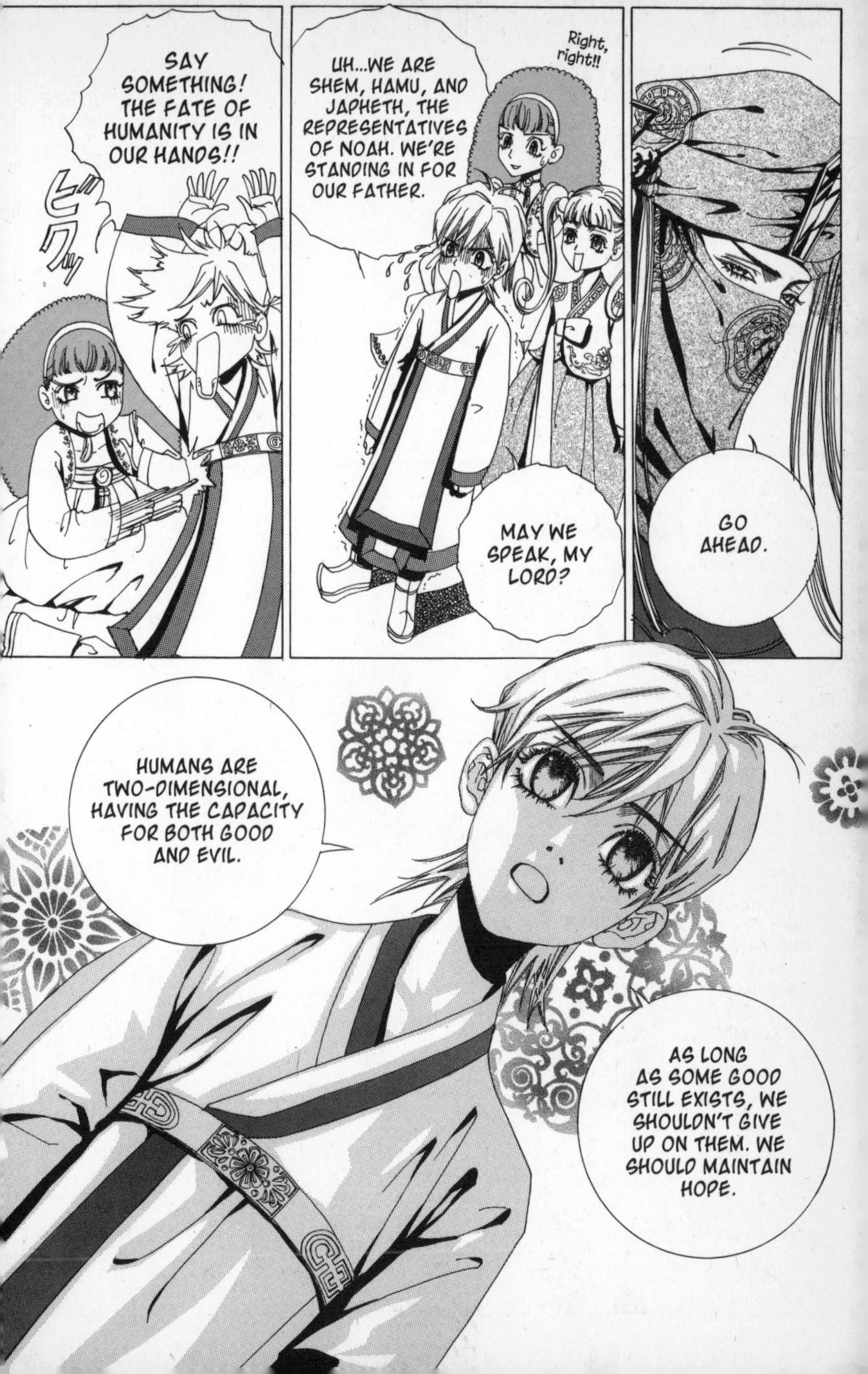
SAY SOMETHING! THE FATE OF HUMANITY IS IN OUR HANDS!!
ビクッ
UH...WE ARE SHEM, HAMU, AND JAPHETH, THE REPRESENTATIVES OF NOAH. WE'RE STANDING IN FOR OUR FATHER.
Right, right!!
MAY WE SPEAK, MY LORD?
GO AHEAD.
HUMANS ARE TWO-DIMENSIONAL, HAVING THE CAPACITY FOR BOTH GOOD AND EVIL.
AS LONG AS SOME GOOD STILL EXISTS, WE SHOULDN'T GIVE UP ON THEM. WE SHOULD MAINTAIN HOPE.

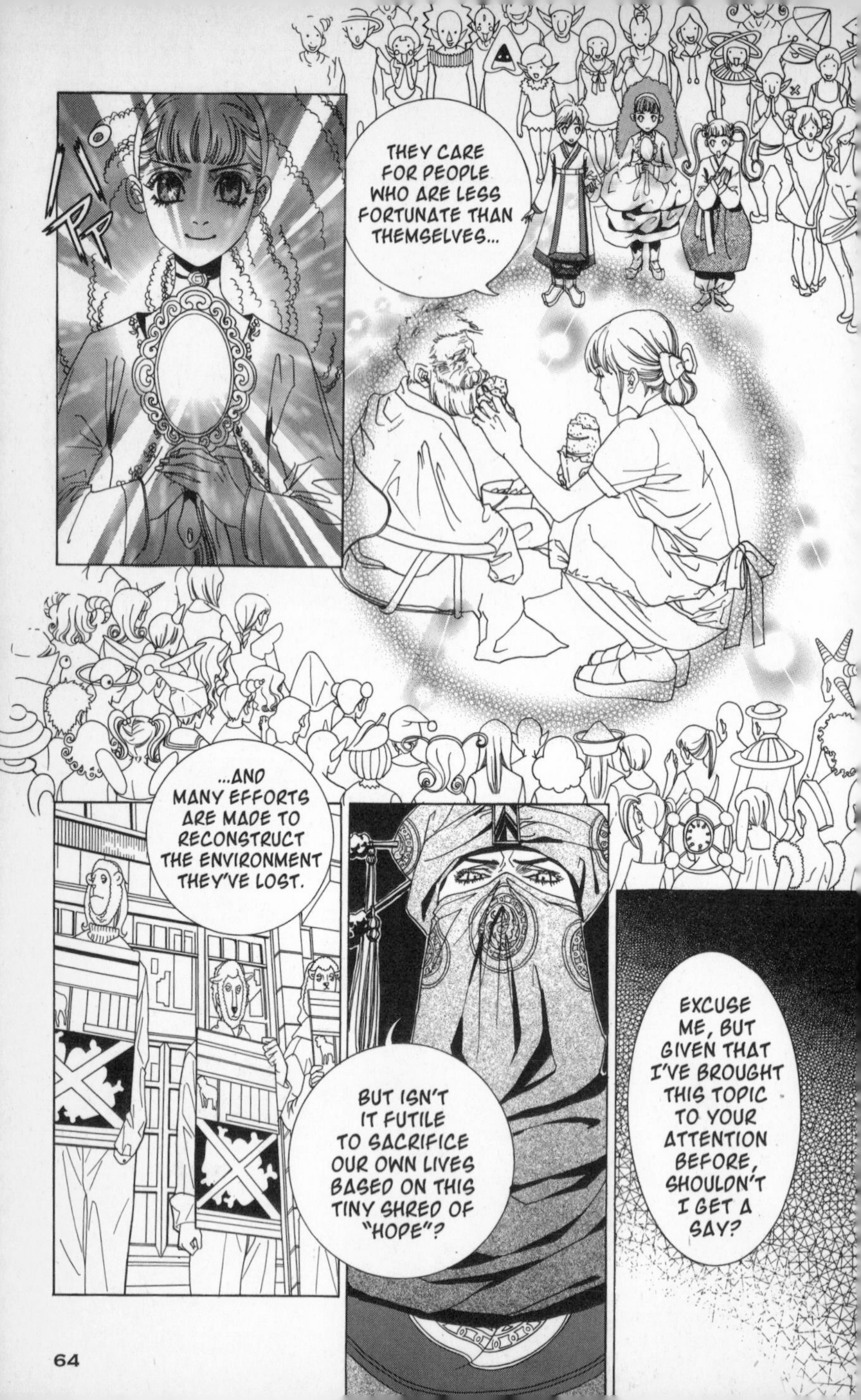
THEY CARE FOR PEOPLE WHO ARE LESS FORTUNATE THAN THEMSELVES...
...AND MANY EFFORTS ARE MADE TO RECONSTRUCT THE ENVIRONMENT THEY'VE LOST.
BUT ISN'T IT FUTILE TO SACRIFICE OUR OWN LIVES BASED ON THIS TINY SHRED OF "HOPE"?
EXCUSE ME, BUT GIVEN THAT I'VE BROUGHT THIS TOPIC TO YOUR ATTENTION BEFORE, SHOULDN'T I GET A SAY?

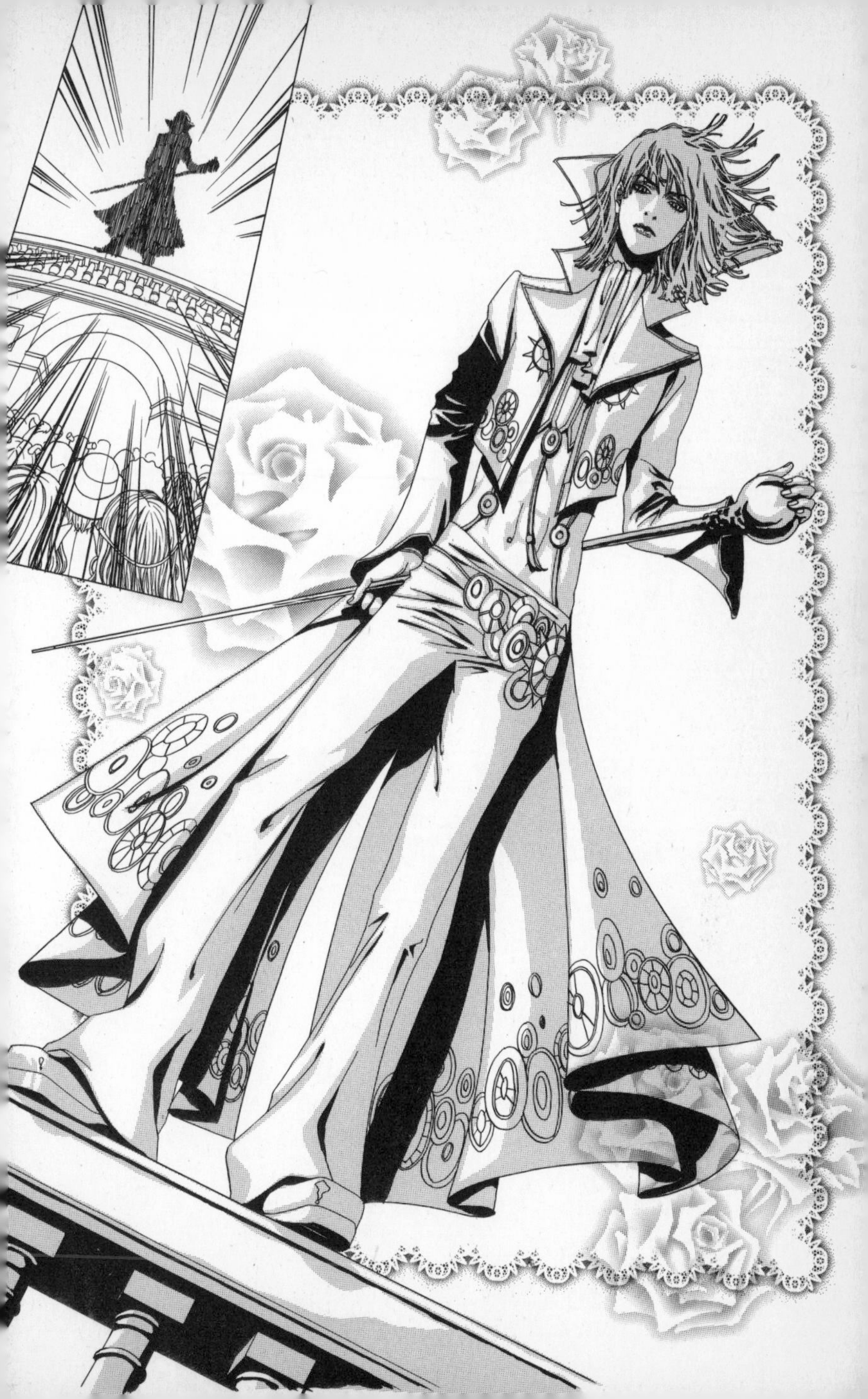

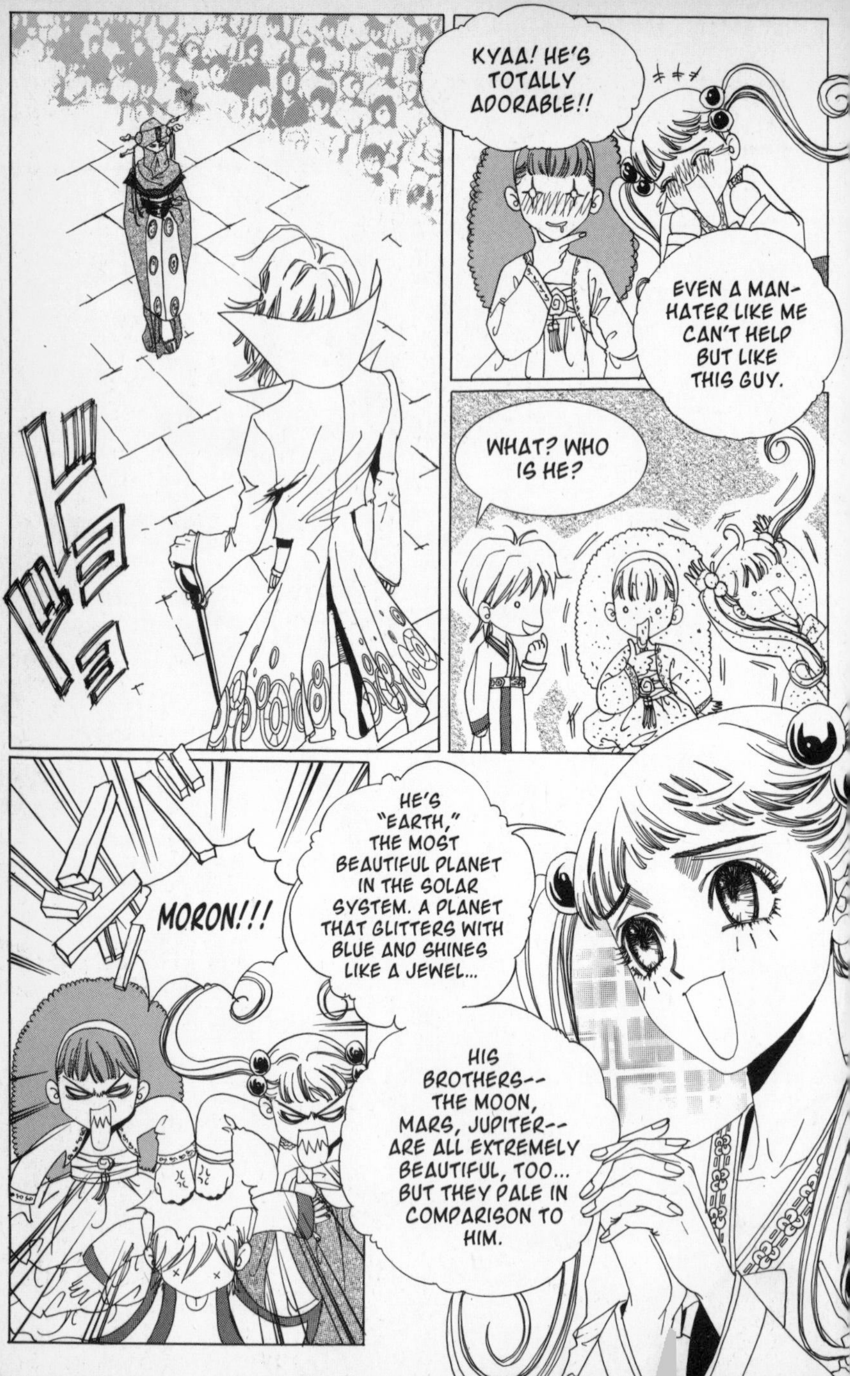
KYAA! HE'S TOTALLY ADORABLE!!
EVEN A MAN-HATER LIKE ME CAN'T HELP BUT LIKE THIS GUY.
WHAT? WHO IS HE?
MORON!!!
HE'S "EARTH," THE MOST BEAUTIFUL PLANET IN THE SOLAR SYSTEM. A PLANET THAT GLITTERS WITH BLUE AND SHINES LIKE A JEWEL...
HIS BROTHERS--THE MOON, MARS, JUPITER--ARE ALL EXTREMELY BEAUTIFUL, TOO... BUT THEY PALE IN COMPARISON TO HIM.

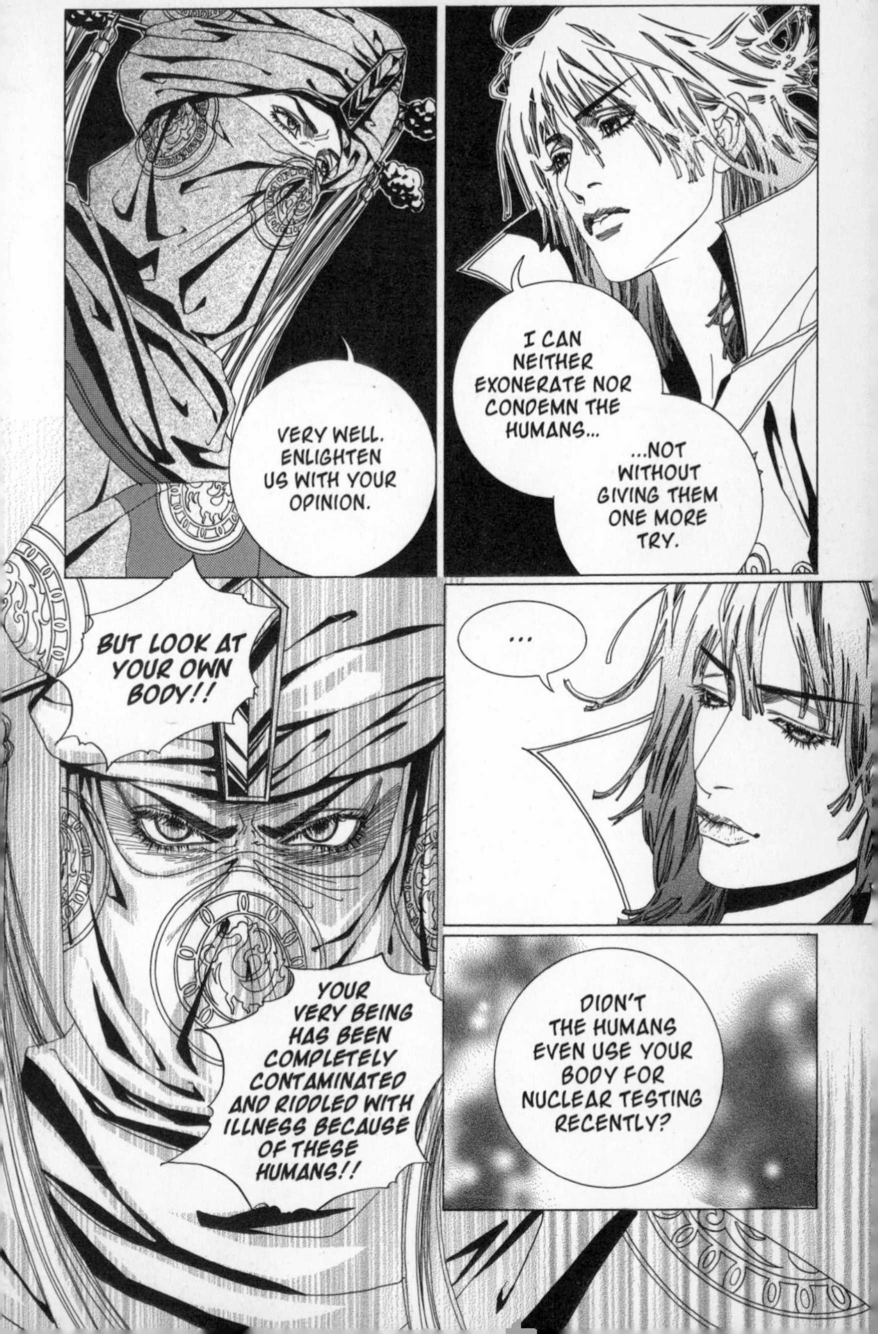
I CAN NEITHER EXONERATE NOR CONDEMN THE HUMANS...
...NOT WITHOUT GIVING THEM ONE MORE TRY.
VERY WELL. ENLIGHTEN US WITH YOUR OPINION.
...
DIDN'T THE HUMANS EVEN USE YOUR BODY FOR NUCLEAR TESTING RECENTLY?
BUT LOOK AT YOUR OWN BODY!!
YOUR VERY BEING HAS BEEN COMPLETELY CONTAMINATED AND RIDDLED WITH ILLNESS BECAUSE OF THESE HUMANS!!

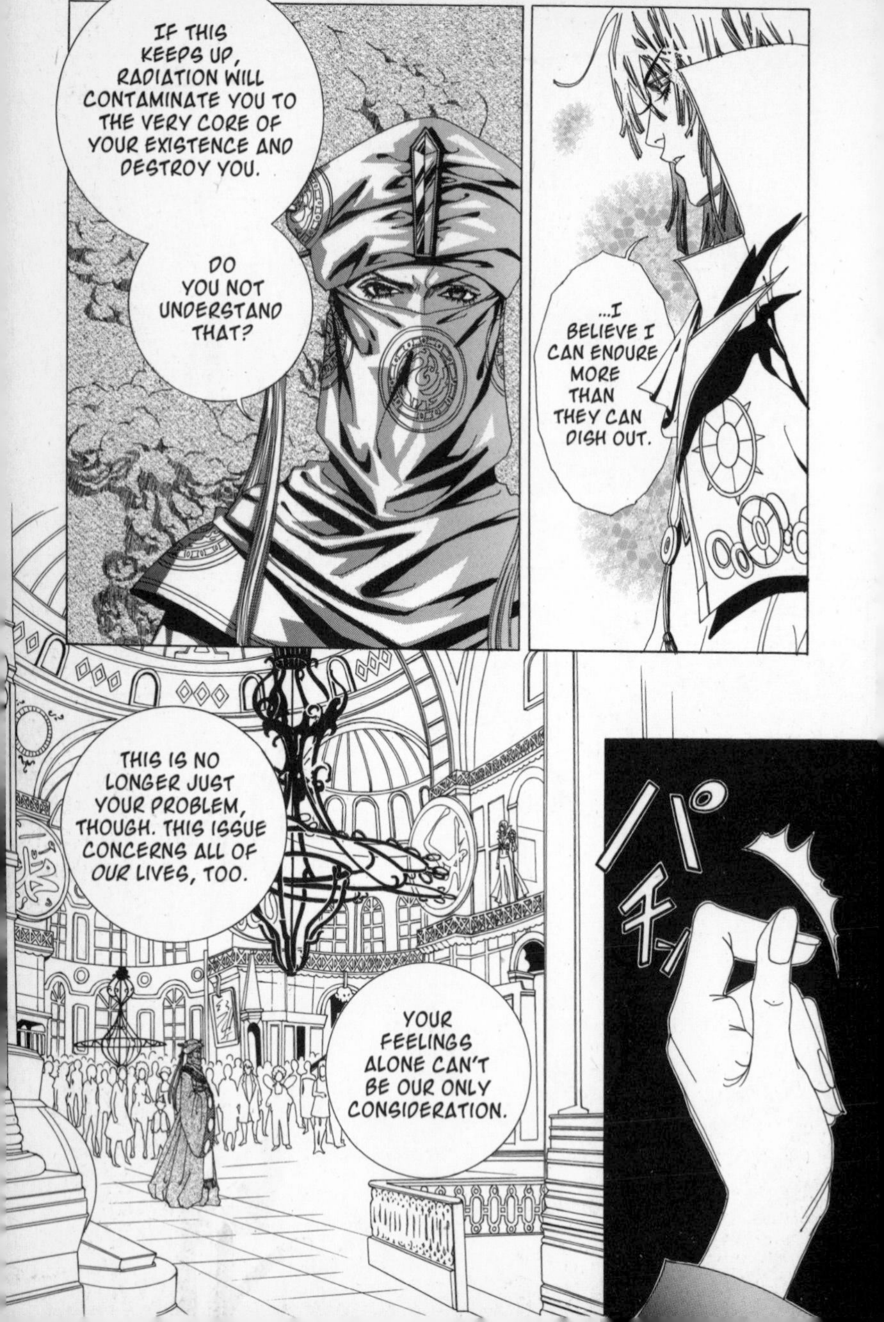
IF THIS KEEPS UP, RADIATION WILL CONTAMINATE YOU TO THE VERY CORE OF YOUR EXISTENCE AND DESTROY YOU.
DO YOU NOT UNDERSTAND THAT?
...I BELIEVE I CAN ENDURE MORE THAN THEY CAN DISH OUT.
THIS IS NO LONGER JUST YOUR PROBLEM, THOUGH. THIS ISSUE CONCERNS ALL OF OUR LIVES, TOO.
YOUR FEELINGS ALONE CAN'T BE OUR ONLY CONSIDERATION.
パチッ

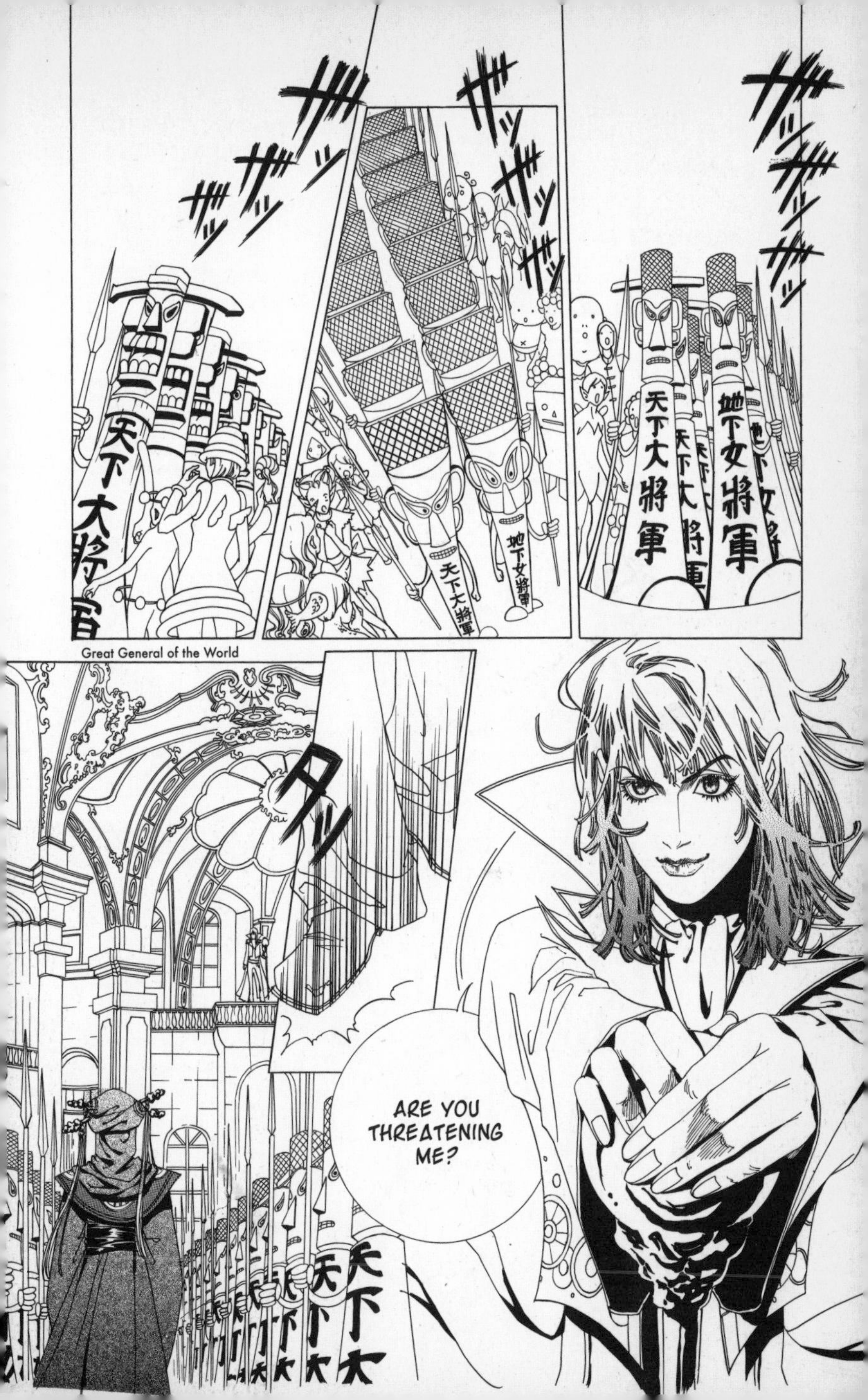

天下大將軍
地下女將軍
Great General of the World
タッ
ARE YOU THREATENING ME?

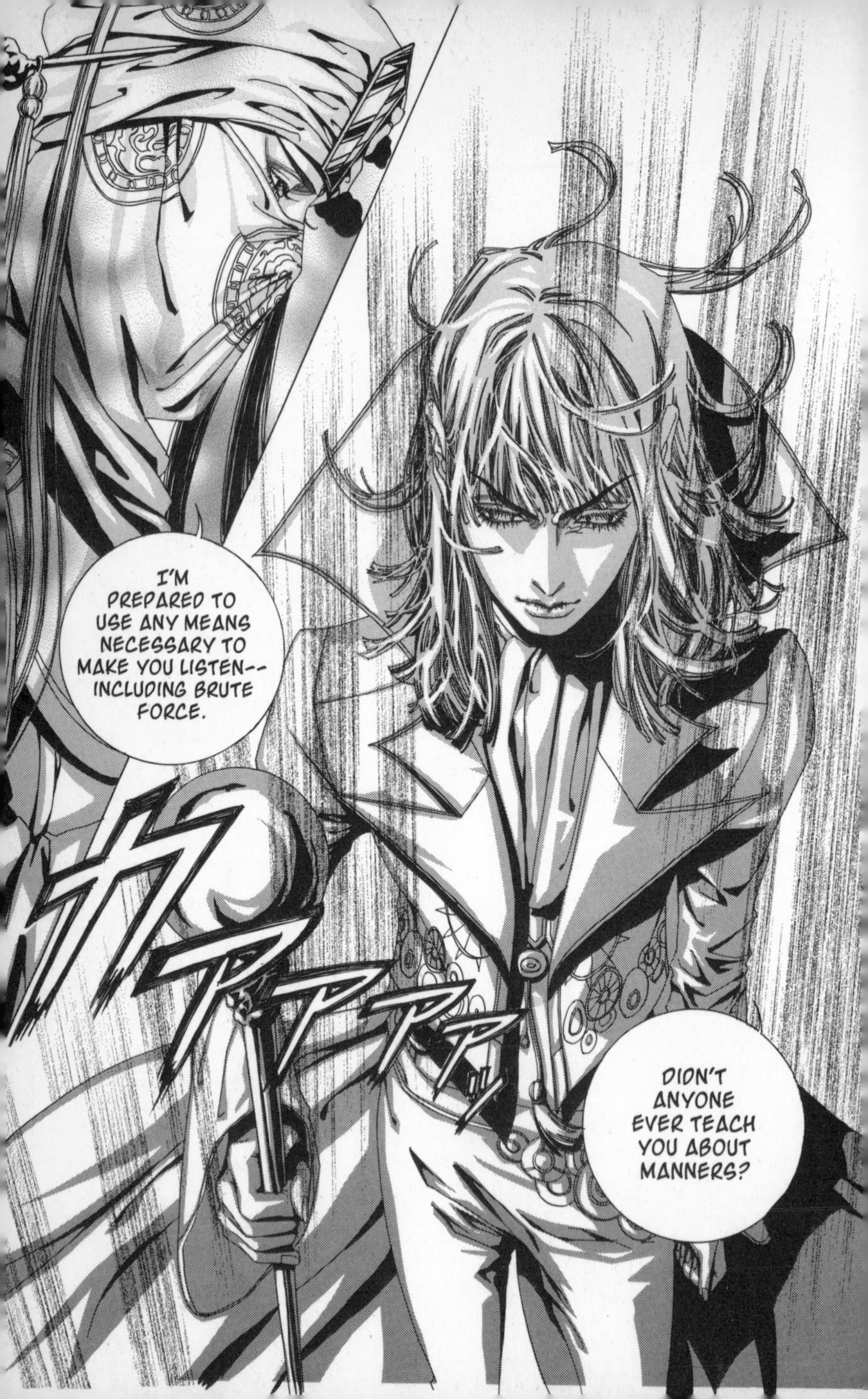
I'M PREPARED TO USE ANY MEANS NECESSARY TO MAKE YOU LISTEN--INCLUDING BRUTE FORCE.
DIDN'T ANYONE EVER TEACH YOU ABOUT MANNERS?

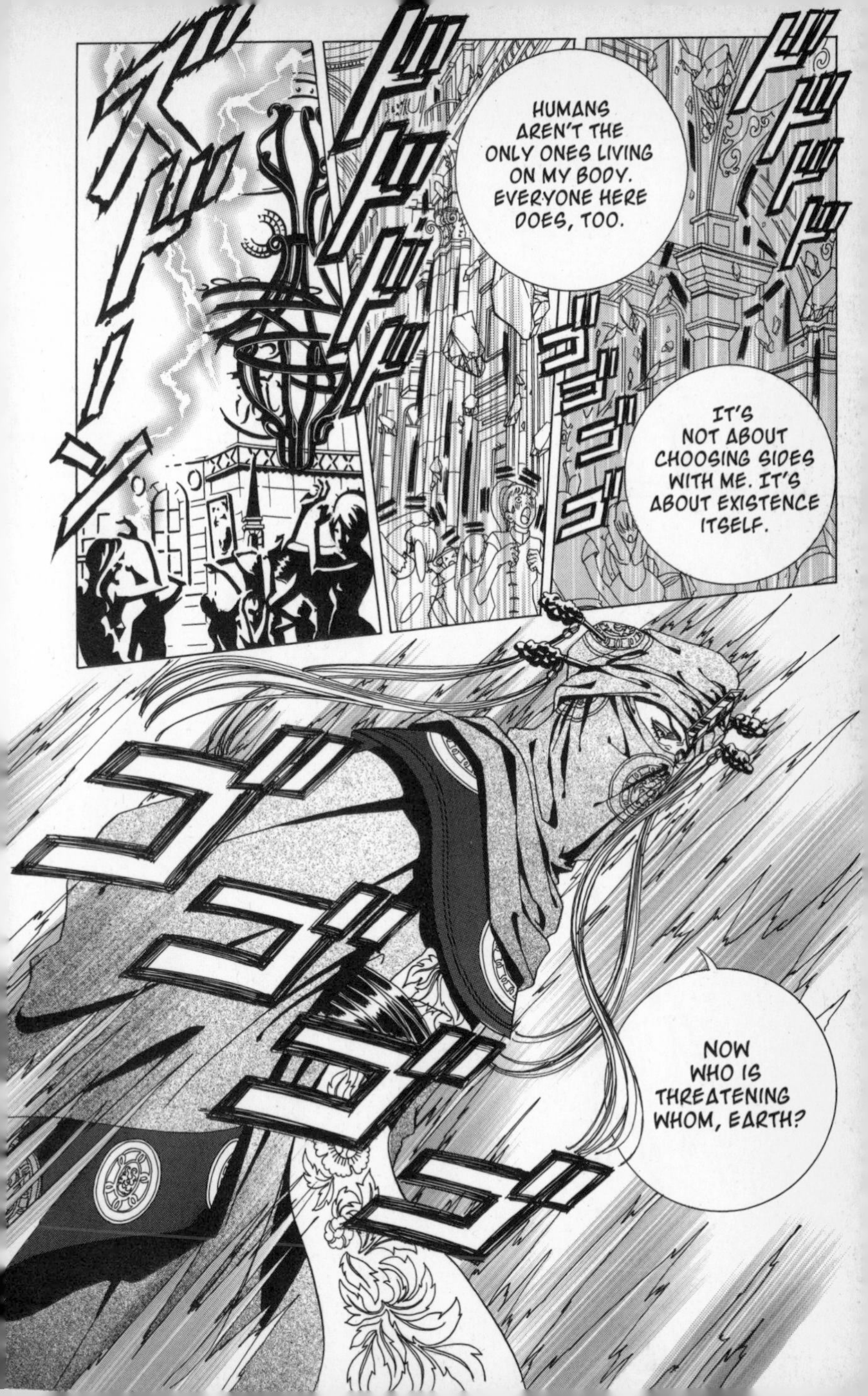
HUMANS AREN'T THE ONLY ONES LIVING ON MY BODY. EVERYONE HERE DOES, TOO.
IT'S NOT ABOUT CHOOSING SIDES WITH ME. IT'S ABOUT EXISTENCE ITSELF.
NOW WHO IS THREATENING WHOM, EARTH?

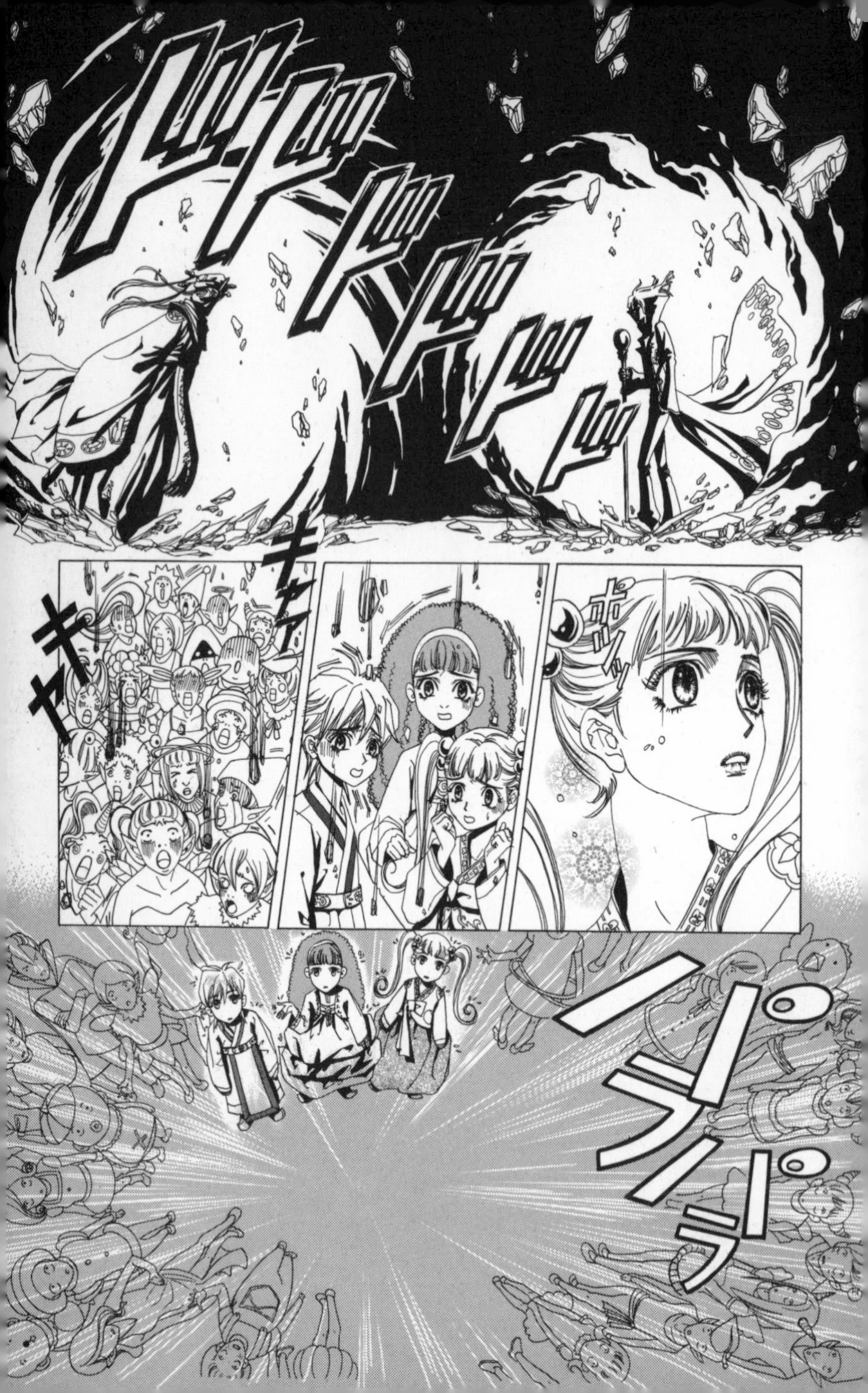
ドドドドドドド
キャア
キャ
パラパラ

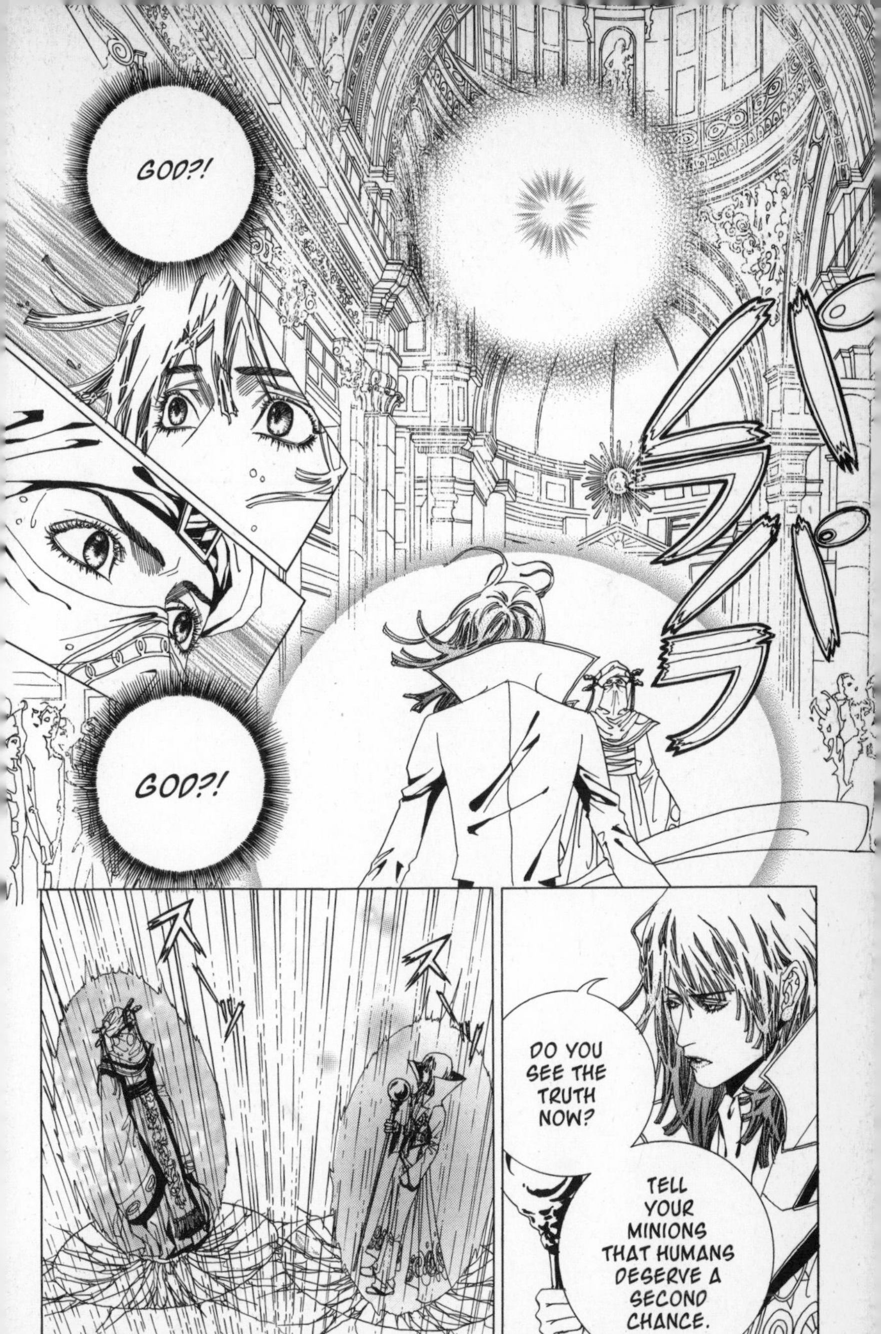
GOD?!
GOD?!
DO YOU SEE THE TRUTH NOW?
TELL YOUR MINIONS THAT HUMANS DESERVE A SECOND CHANCE.

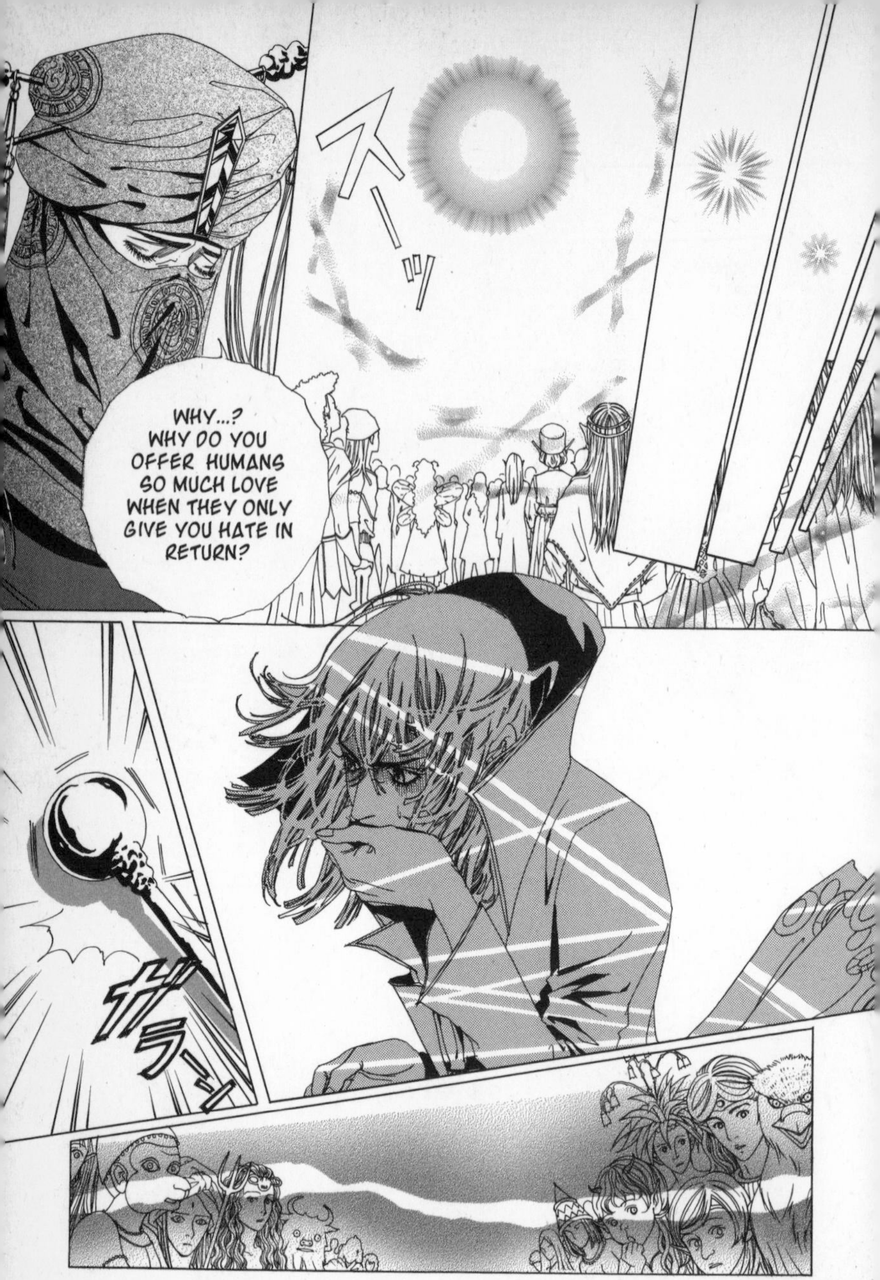
スーッ
WHY...? WHY DO YOU OFFER HUMANS SO MUCH LOVE WHEN THEY ONLY GIVE YOU HATE IN RETURN?
ガラーッ

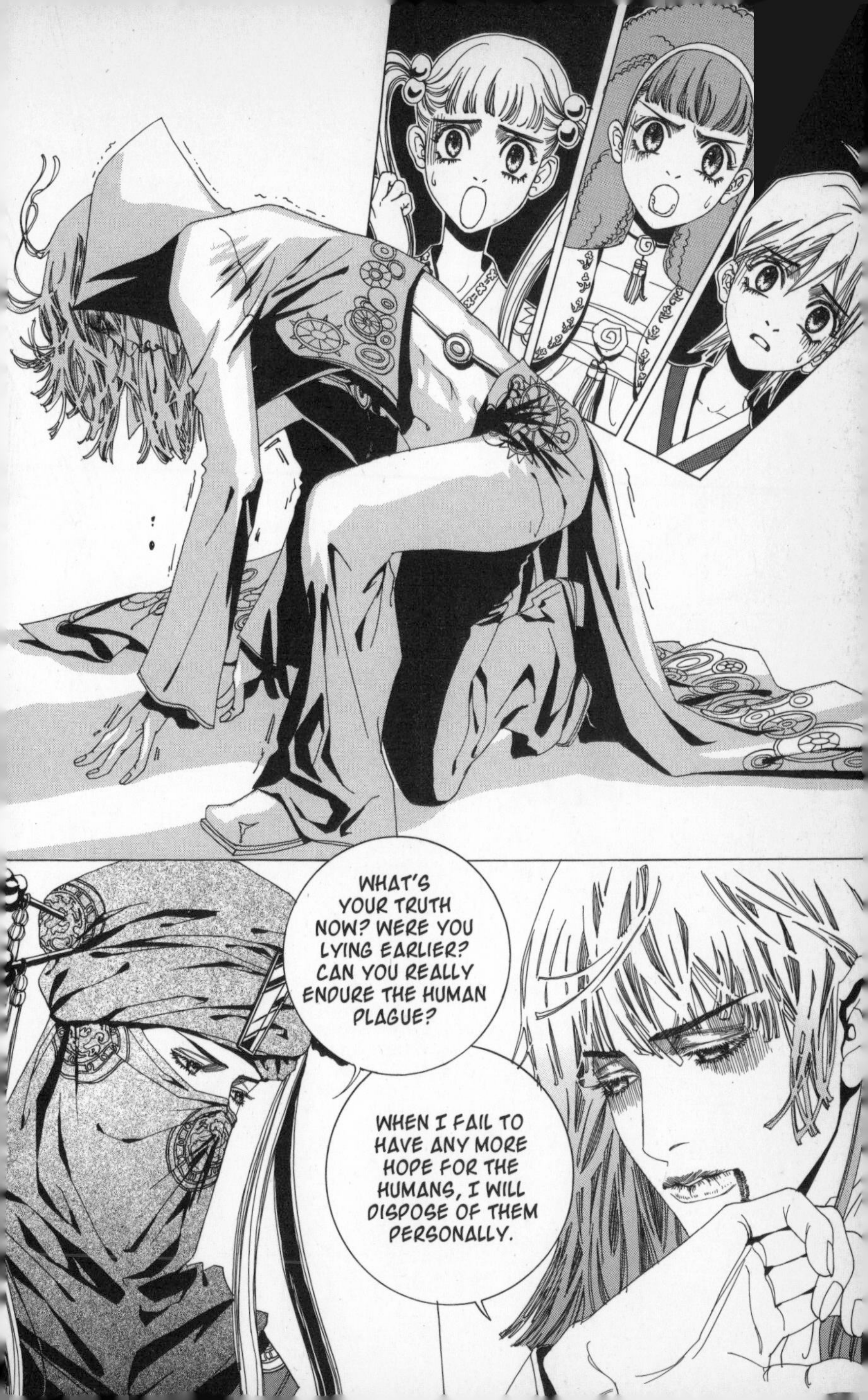
WHAT'S YOUR TRUTH NOW? WERE YOU LYING EARLIER? CAN YOU REALLY ENDURE THE HUMAN PLAGUE?
WHEN I FAIL TO HAVE ANY MORE HOPE FOR THE HUMANS, I WILL DISPOSE OF THEM PERSONALLY.

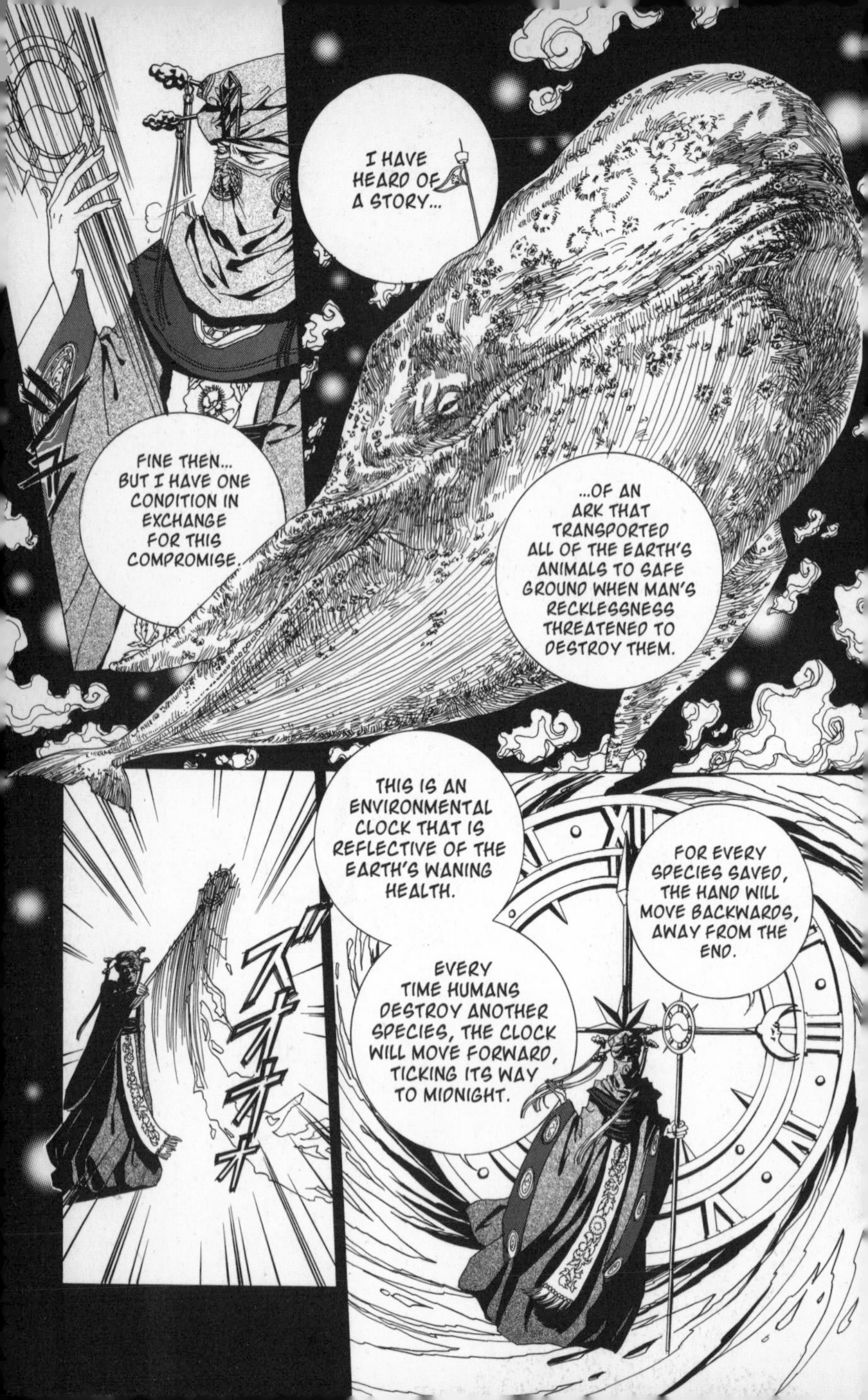
I HAVE HEARD OF A STORY...
...OF AN ARK THAT TRANSPORTED ALL OF THE EARTH'S ANIMALS TO SAFE GROUND WHEN MAN'S RECKLESSNESS THREATENED TO DESTROY THEM.
FINE THEN... BUT I HAVE ONE CONDITION IN EXCHANGE FOR THIS COMPROMISE.
THIS IS AN ENVIRONMENTAL CLOCK THAT IS REFLECTIVE OF THE EARTH'S WANING HEALTH.
EVERY TIME HUMANS DESTROY ANOTHER SPECIES, THE CLOCK WILL MOVE FORWARD, TICKING ITS WAY TO MIDNIGHT.
FOR EVERY SPECIES SAVED, THE HAND WILL MOVE BACKWARDS, AWAY FROM THE END.

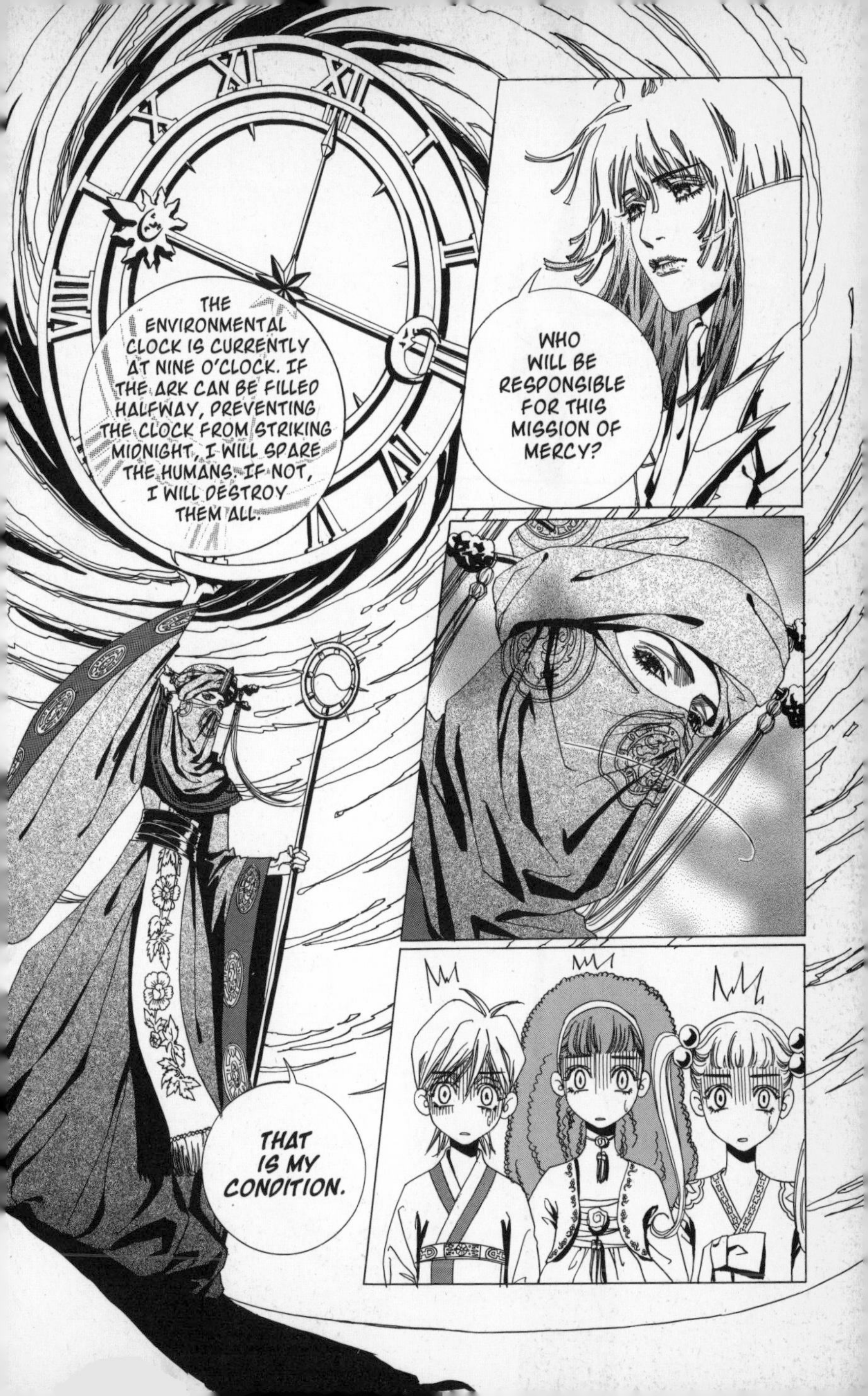
WHO WILL BE RESPONSIBLE FOR THIS MISSION OF MERCY?
THE ENVIRONMENTAL CLOCK IS CURRENTLY AT NINE O'CLOCK. IF THE ARK CAN BE FILLED HALFWAY, PREVENTING THE CLOCK FROM STRIKING MIDNIGHT, I WILL SPARE THE HUMANS. IF NOT, I WILL DESTROY THEM ALL.
THAT IS MY CONDITION.

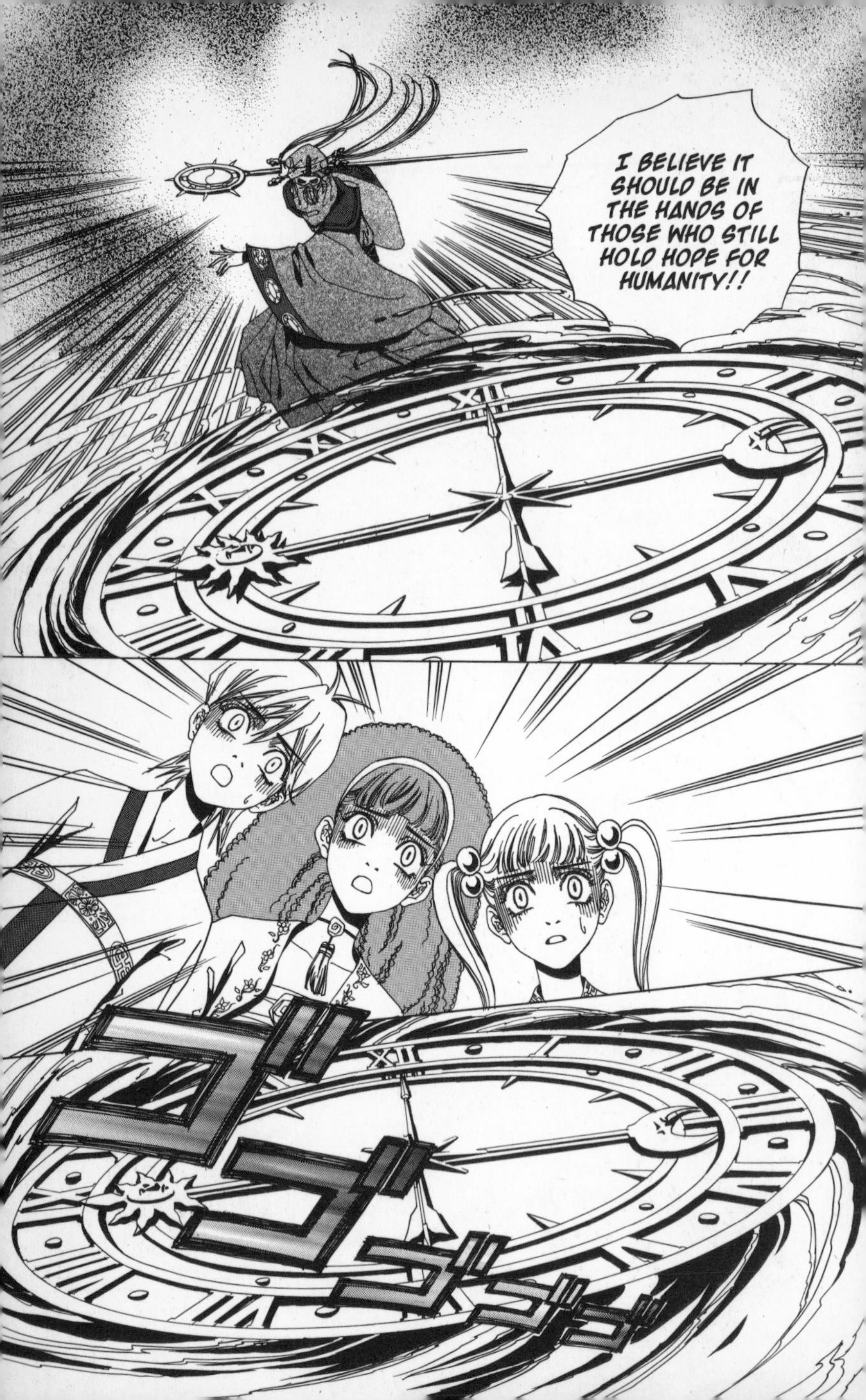
I BELIEVE IT SHOULD BE IN THE HANDS OF THOSE WHO STILL HOLD HOPE FOR HUMANITY!!
ゴゴゴゴ

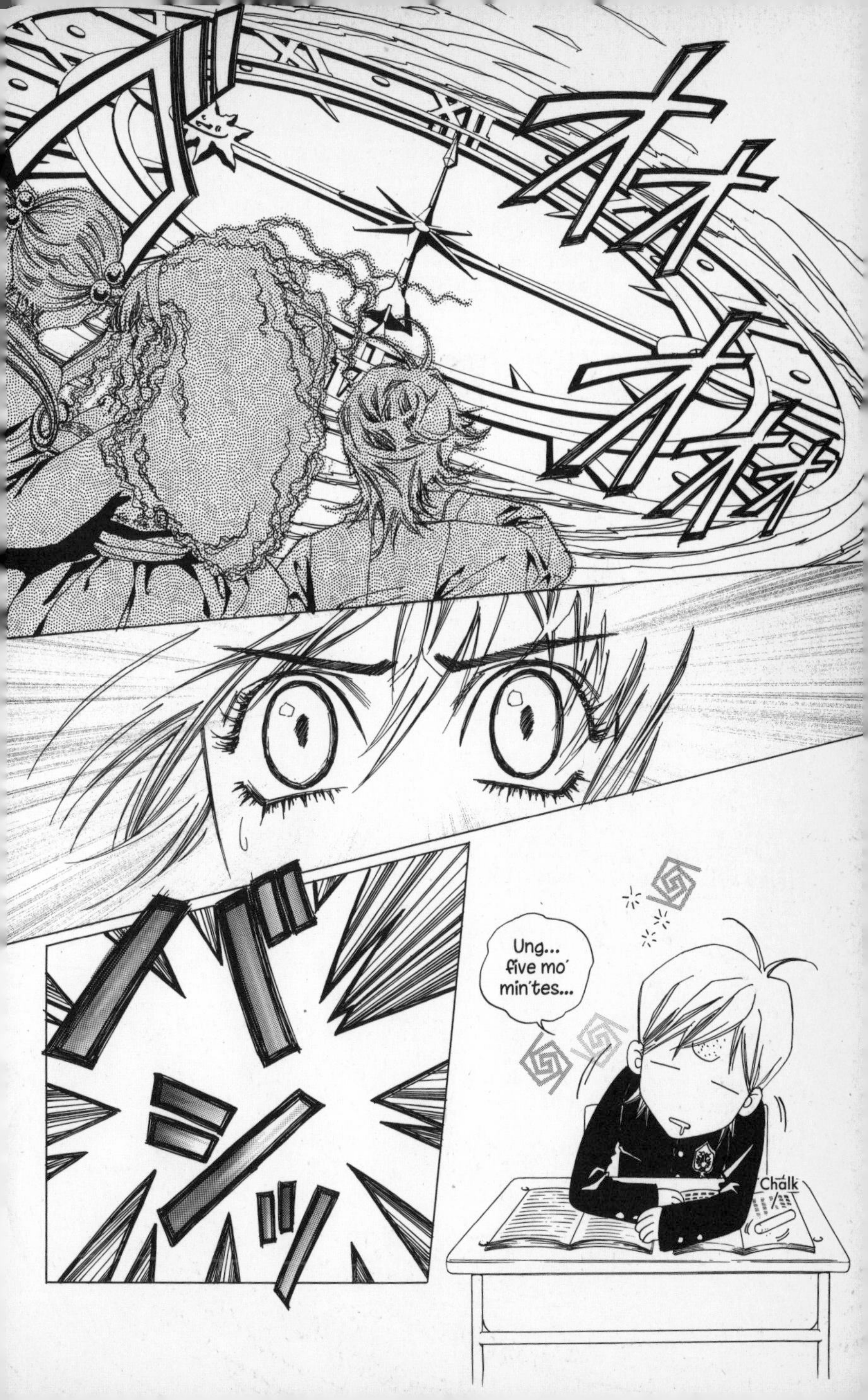
オオオオ
Ung... five mo' min'tes...
Chalk

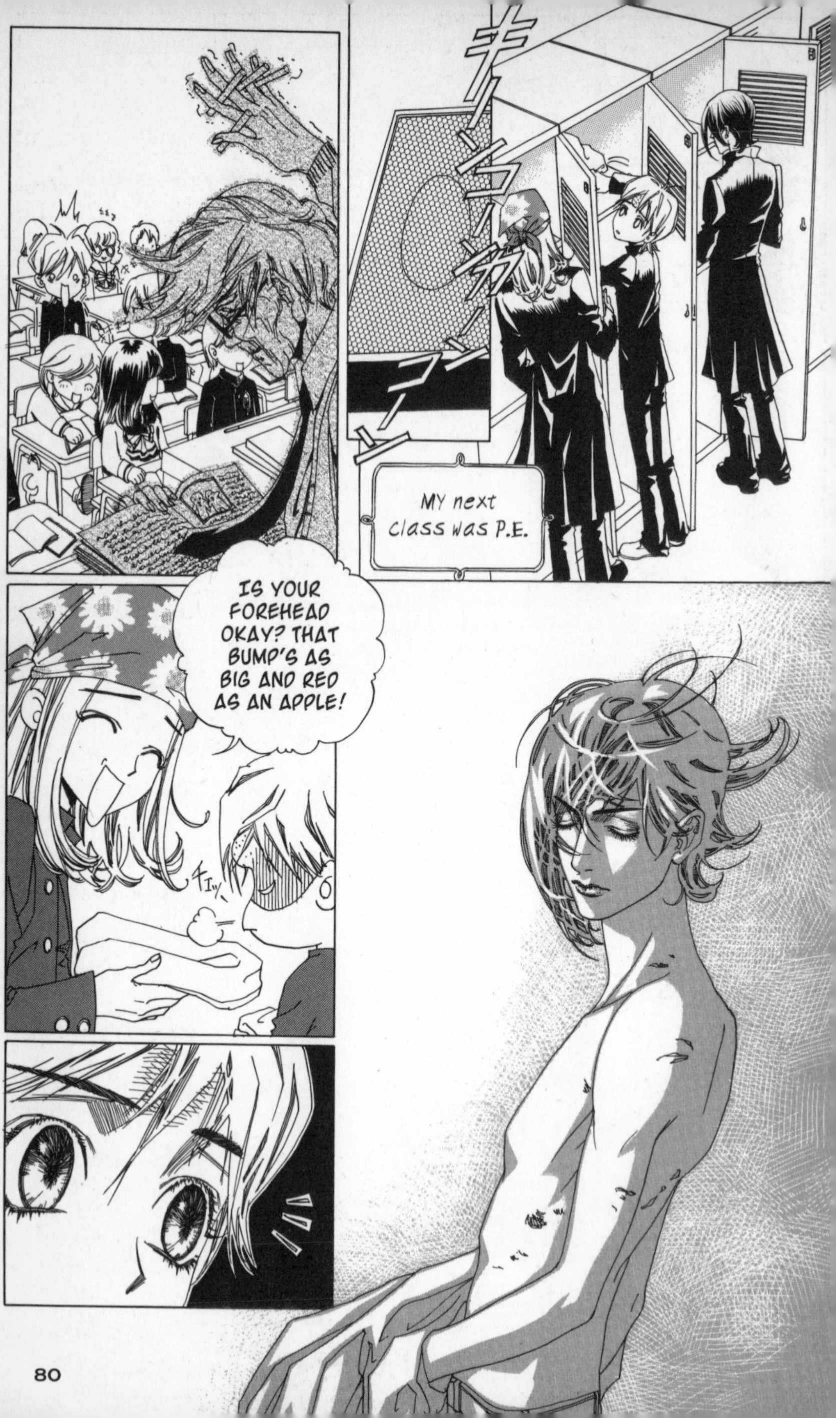
MY next class was P.E.
IS YOUR FOREHEAD OKAY? THAT BUMP'S AS BIG AND RED AS AN APPLE!

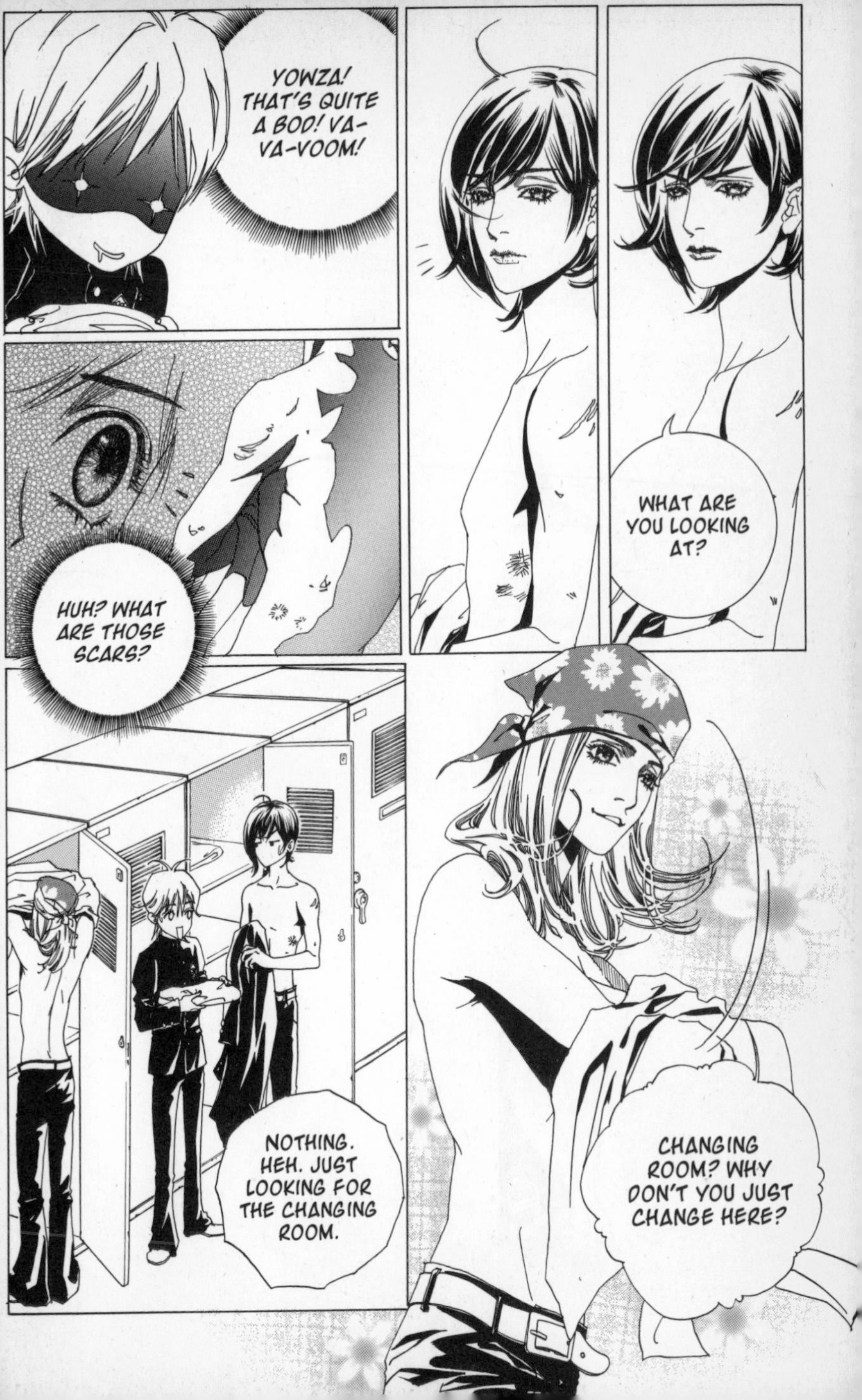
YOWZA! THAT'S QUITE A BOD! VA-VA-VOOM!
HUH? WHAT ARE THOSE SCARS?
WHAT ARE YOU LOOKING AT?
NOTHING. HEH. JUST LOOKING FOR THE CHANGING ROOM.
CHANGING ROOM? WHY DON'T YOU JUST CHANGE HERE?

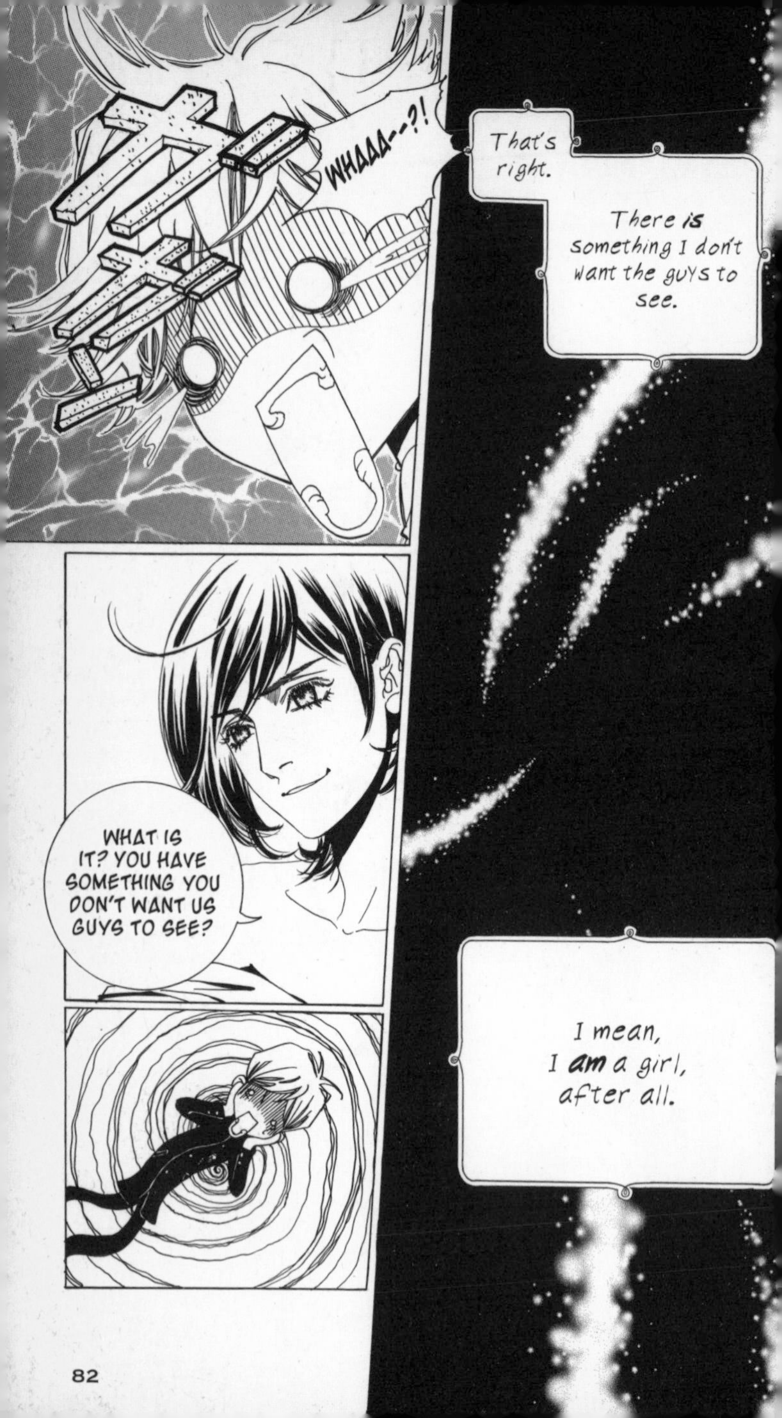
WHAAA--?!
WHAT IS IT? YOU HAVE SOMETHING YOU DON'T WANT US GUYS TO SEE?
That's right.
There *is* something I don't want the guys to see.
I mean, I *am* a girl, after all.

{Chapter 3}

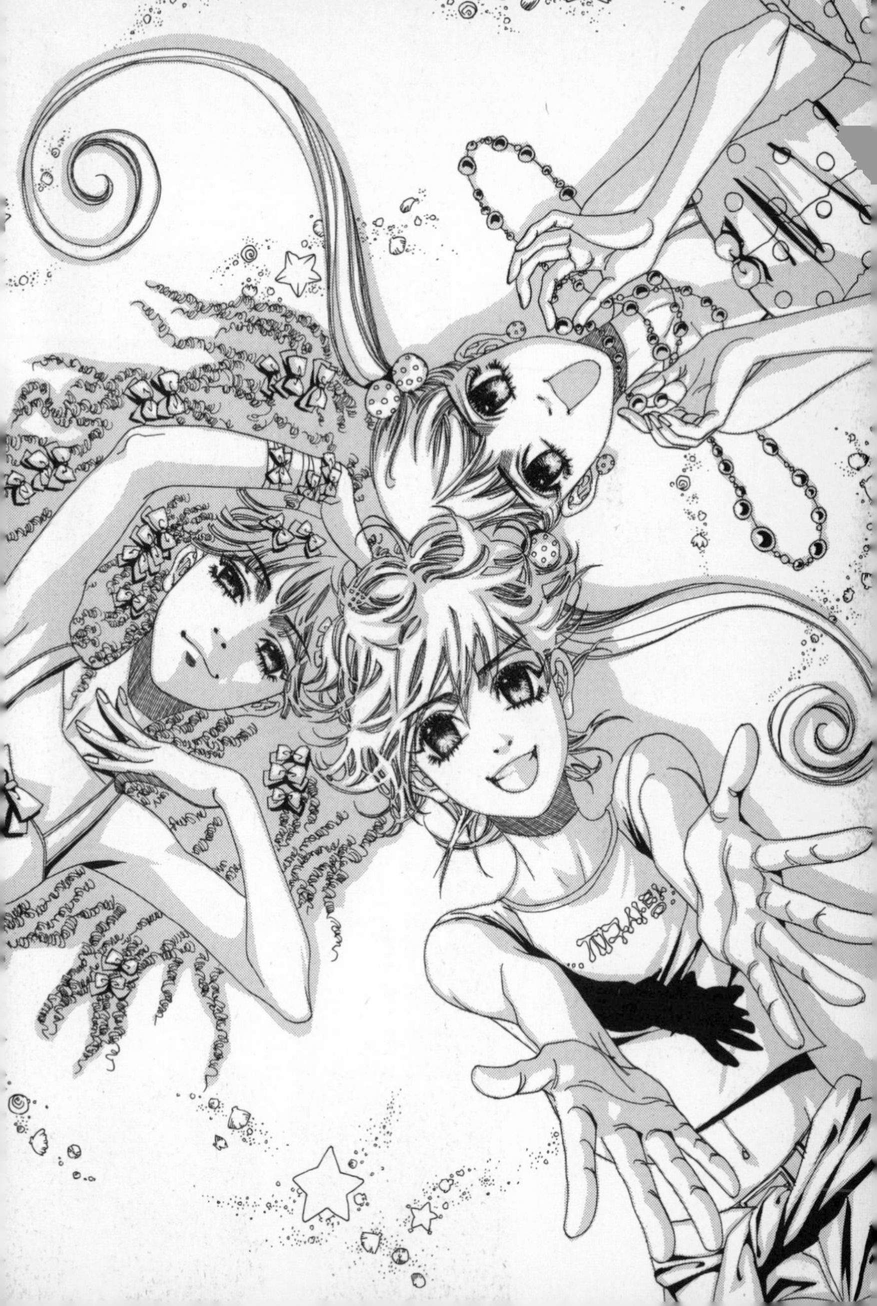

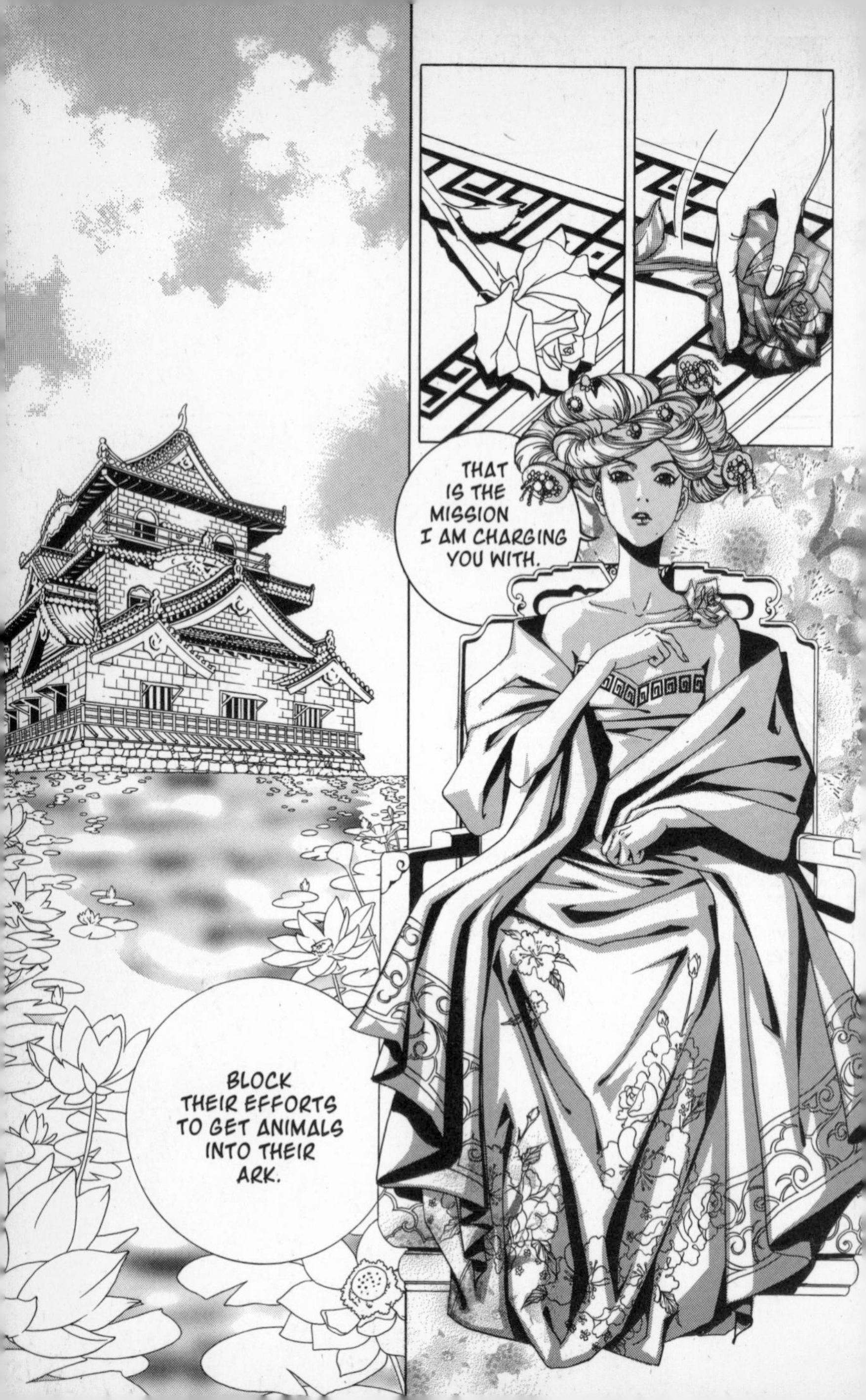
BLOCK THEIR EFFORTS TO GET ANIMALS INTO THEIR ARK.
THAT IS THE MISSION I AM CHARGING YOU WITH.

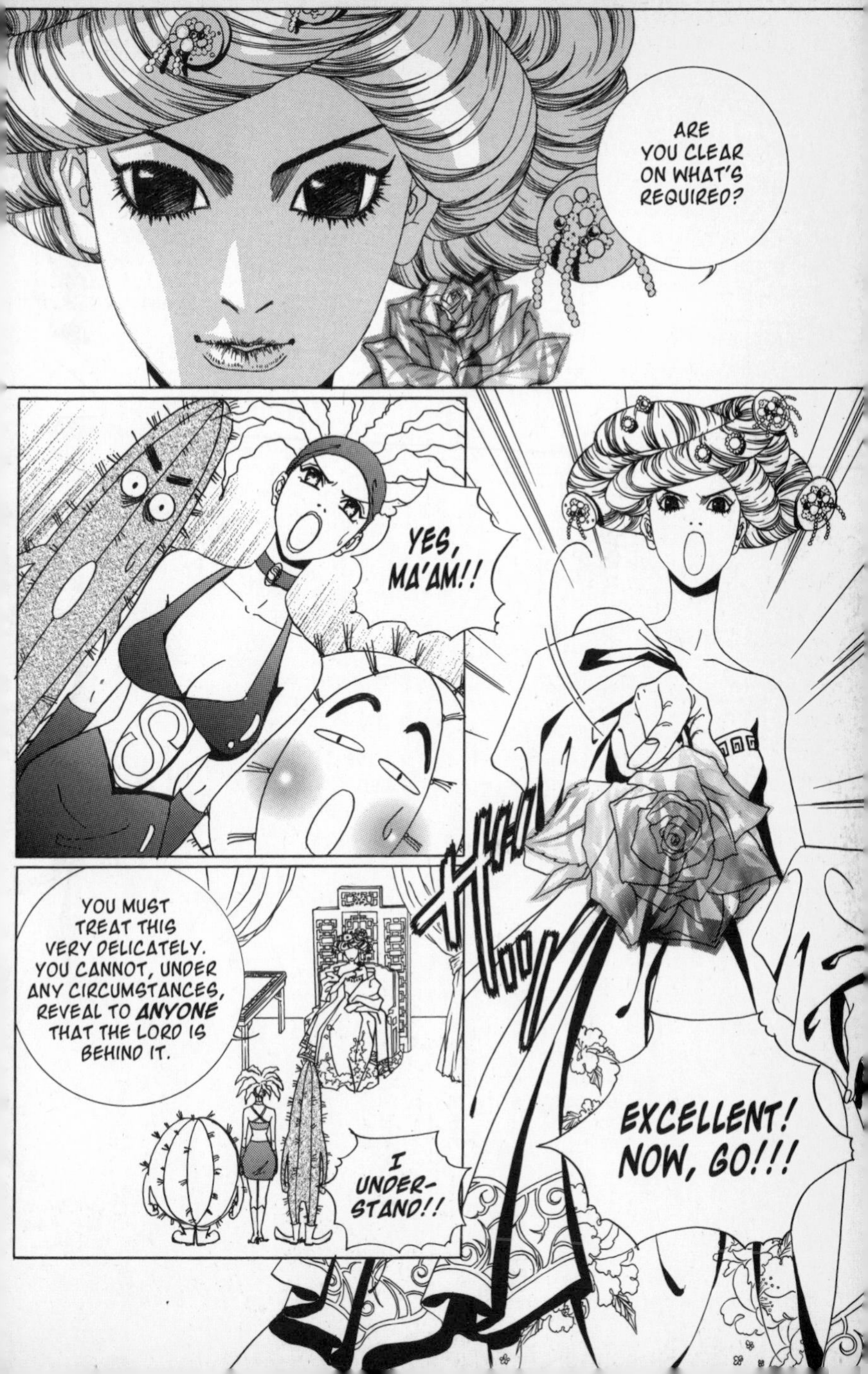
ARE YOU CLEAR ON WHAT'S REQUIRED?
YES, MA'AM!!
YOU MUST TREAT THIS VERY DELICATELY. YOU CANNOT, UNDER ANY CIRCUMSTANCES, REVEAL TO ANYONE THAT THE LORD IS BEHIND IT.
I UNDER-STAND!!
EXCELLENT! NOW, GO!!!

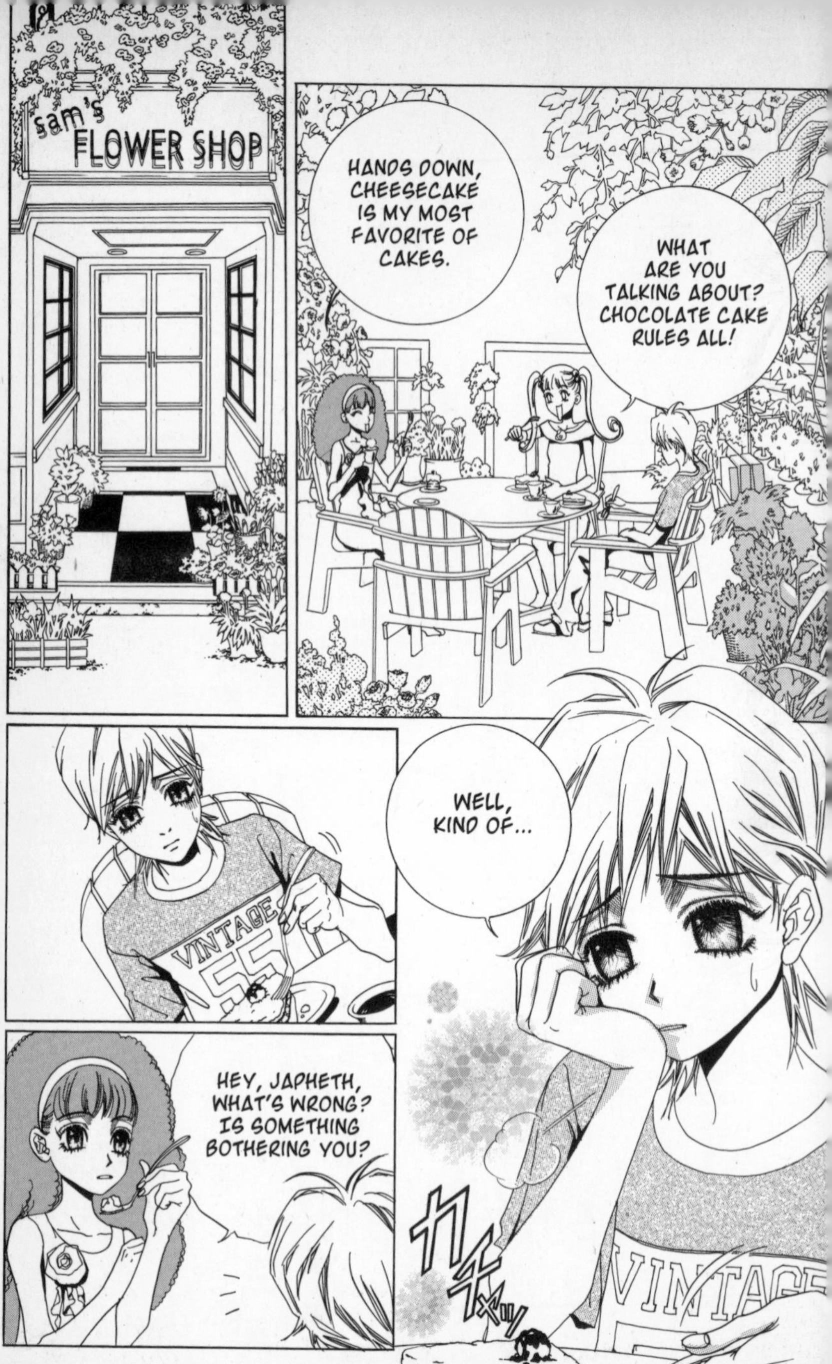
SAM'S
FLOWER SHOP
HANDS DOWN, CHEESECAKE IS MY MOST FAVORITE OF CAKES.
WHAT ARE YOU TALKING ABOUT? CHOCOLATE CAKE RULES ALL!
VINTAGE 55
HEY, JAPHETH, WHAT'S WRONG? IS SOMETHING BOTHERING YOU?
WELL, KIND OF...
VINTAGE

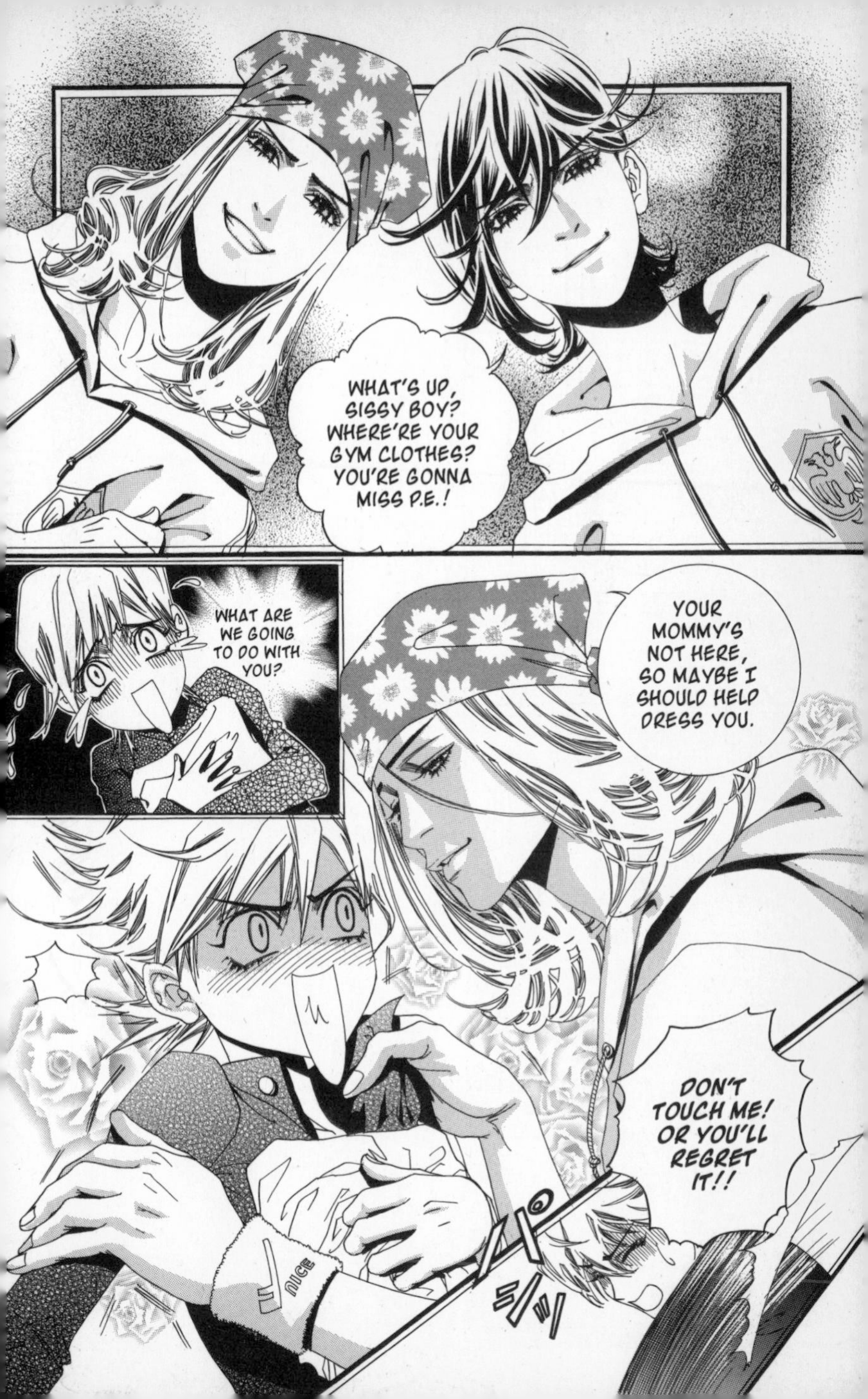
WHAT'S UP, SISSY BOY? WHERE'RE YOUR GYM CLOTHES? YOU'RE GONNA MISS P.E.!
YOUR MOMMY'S NOT HERE, SO MAYBE I SHOULD HELP DRESS YOU.
WHAT ARE WE GOING TO DO WITH YOU?
DON'T TOUCH ME! OR YOU'LL REGRET IT!!
NICE

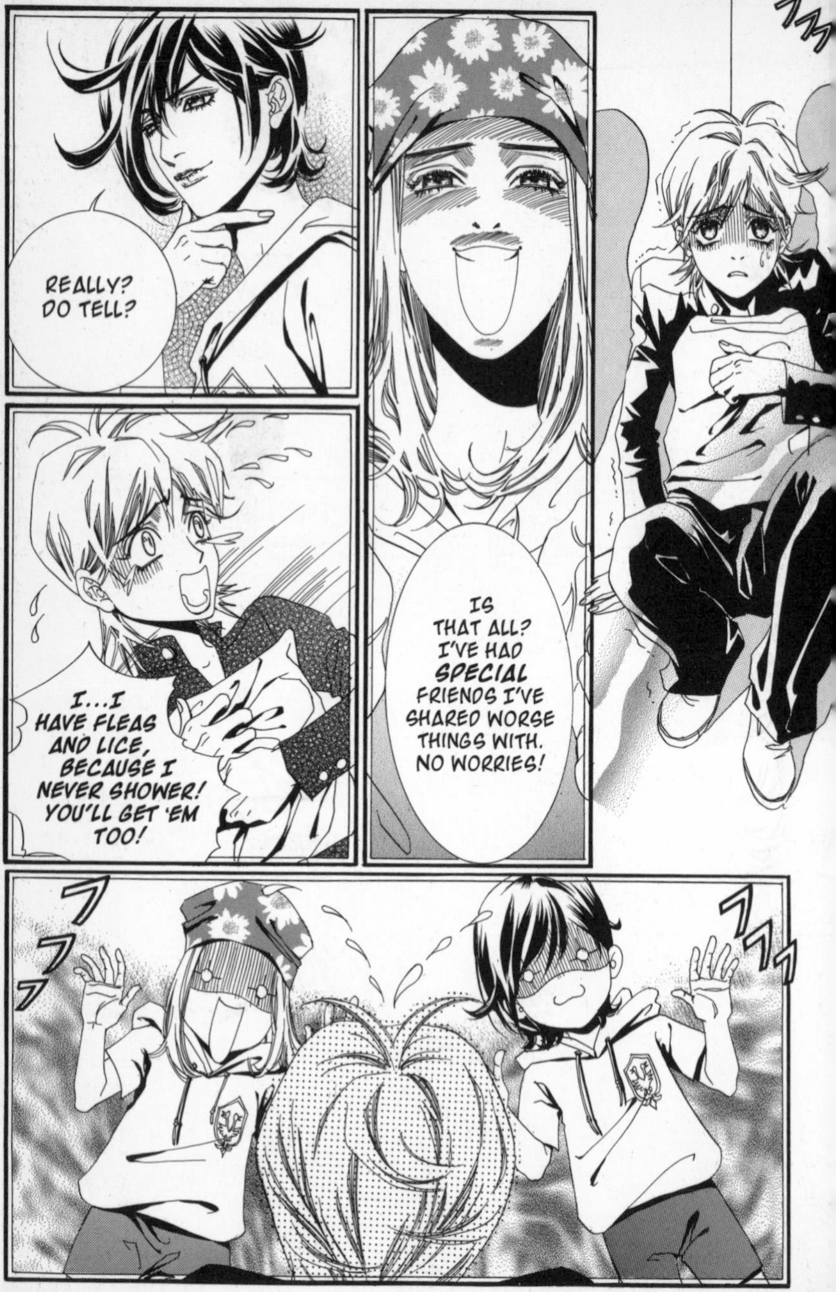
REALLY? DO TELL?
I...I HAVE FLEAS AND LICE, BECAUSE I NEVER SHOWER! YOU'LL GET 'EM TOO!
IS THAT ALL? I'VE HAD SPECIAL FRIENDS I'VE SHARED WORSE THINGS WITH. NO WORRIES!

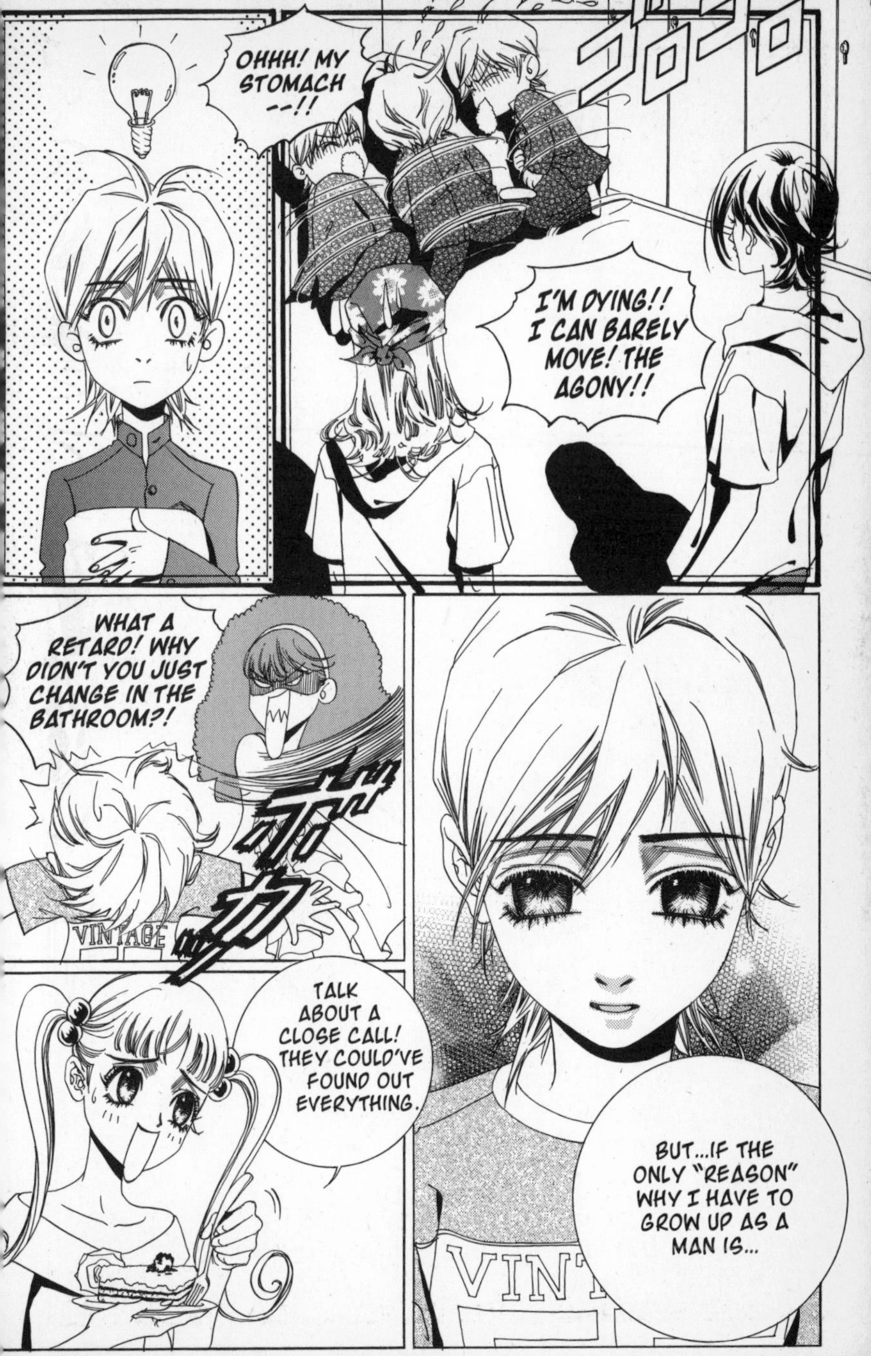
ゴロゴロ
OHHH! MY STOMACH --!!
I'M DYING!! I CAN BARELY MOVE! THE AGONY!!
WHAT A RETARD! WHY DIDN'T YOU JUST CHANGE IN THE BATHROOM?!
VINTAGE
TALK ABOUT A CLOSE CALL! THEY COULD'VE FOUND OUT EVERYTHING.
BUT...IF THE ONLY "REASON" WHY I HAVE TO GROW UP AS A MAN IS...
VINT

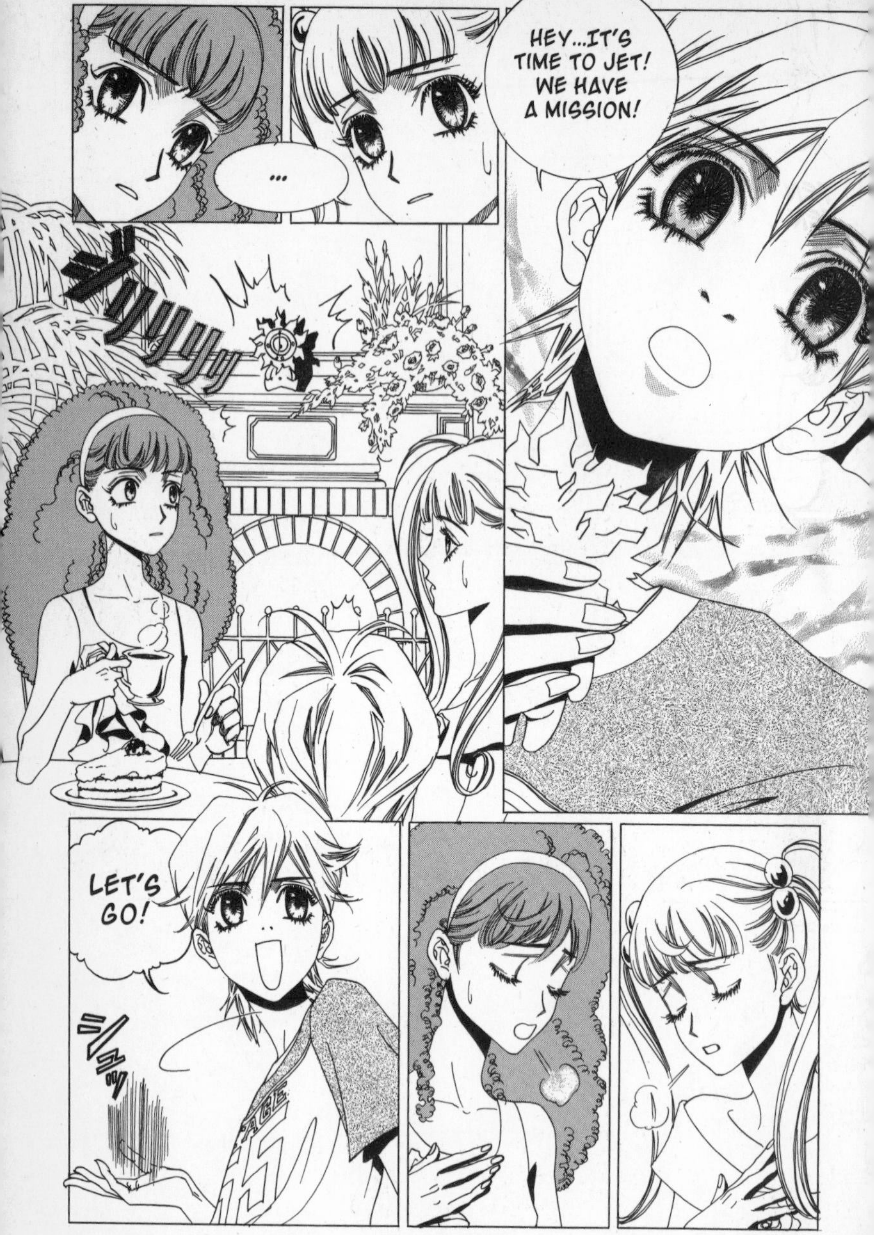
HEY...IT'S TIME TO JET! WE HAVE A MISSION!
...
LET'S GO!

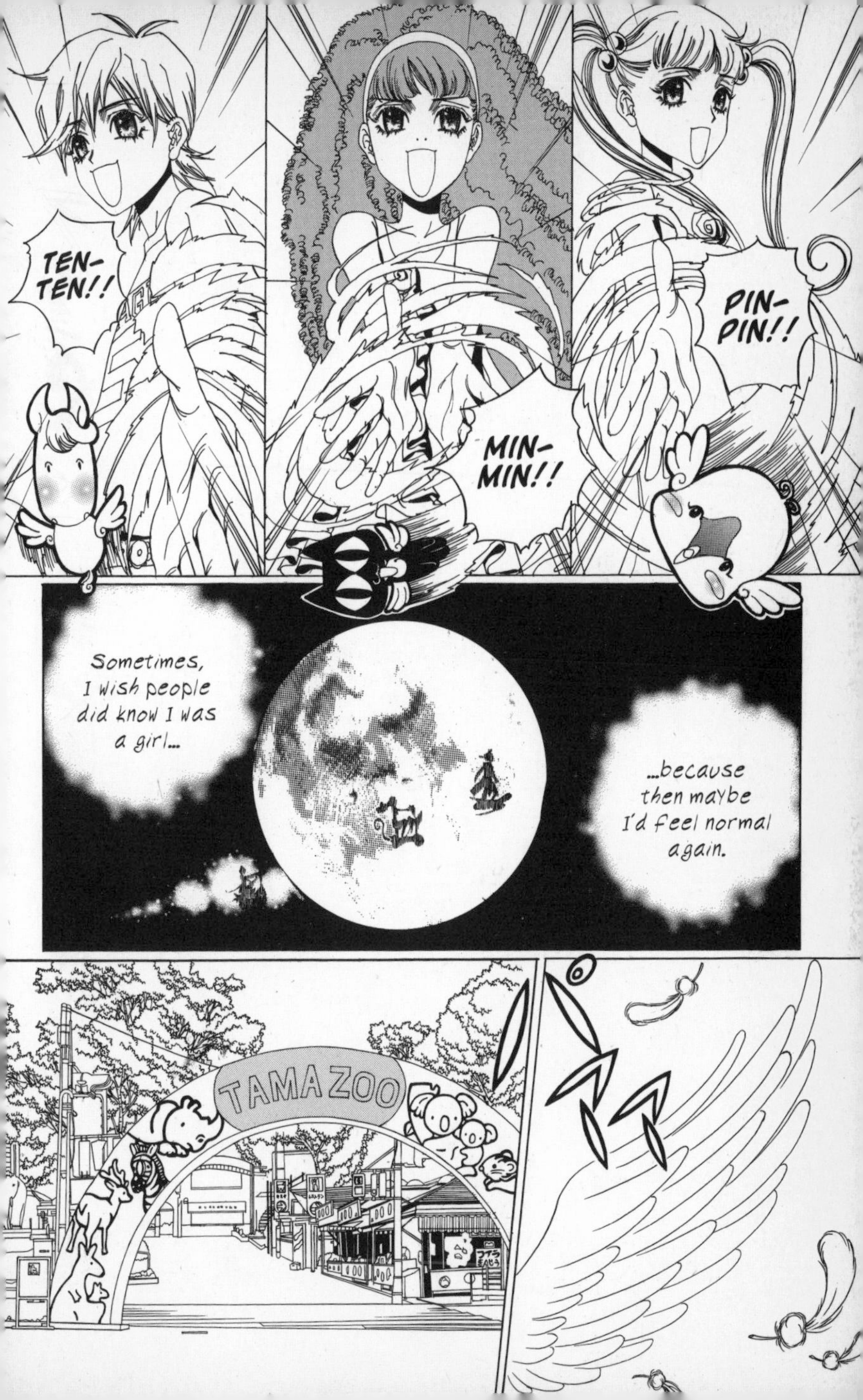
PIN-PIN!!
MIN-MIN!!
TEN-TEN!!
Sometimes, I wish people did know I was a girl...
...because then maybe I'd feel normal again.
TAMA ZOO

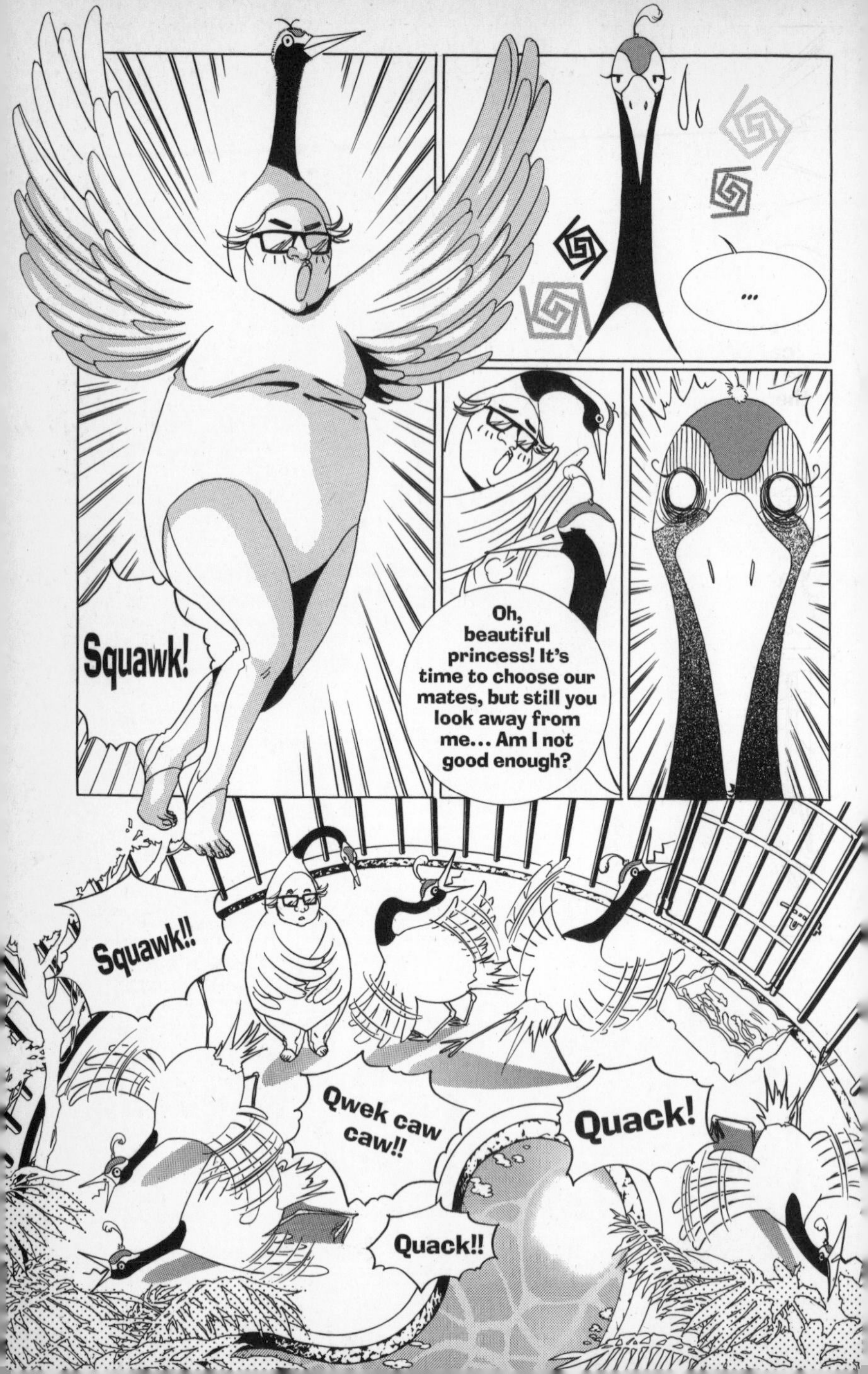
...
Oh, beautiful princess! It's time to choose our mates, but still you look away from me... Am I not good enough?
Squawk!
Squawk!!
Quack!
Qwek caw caw!!
Quack!!

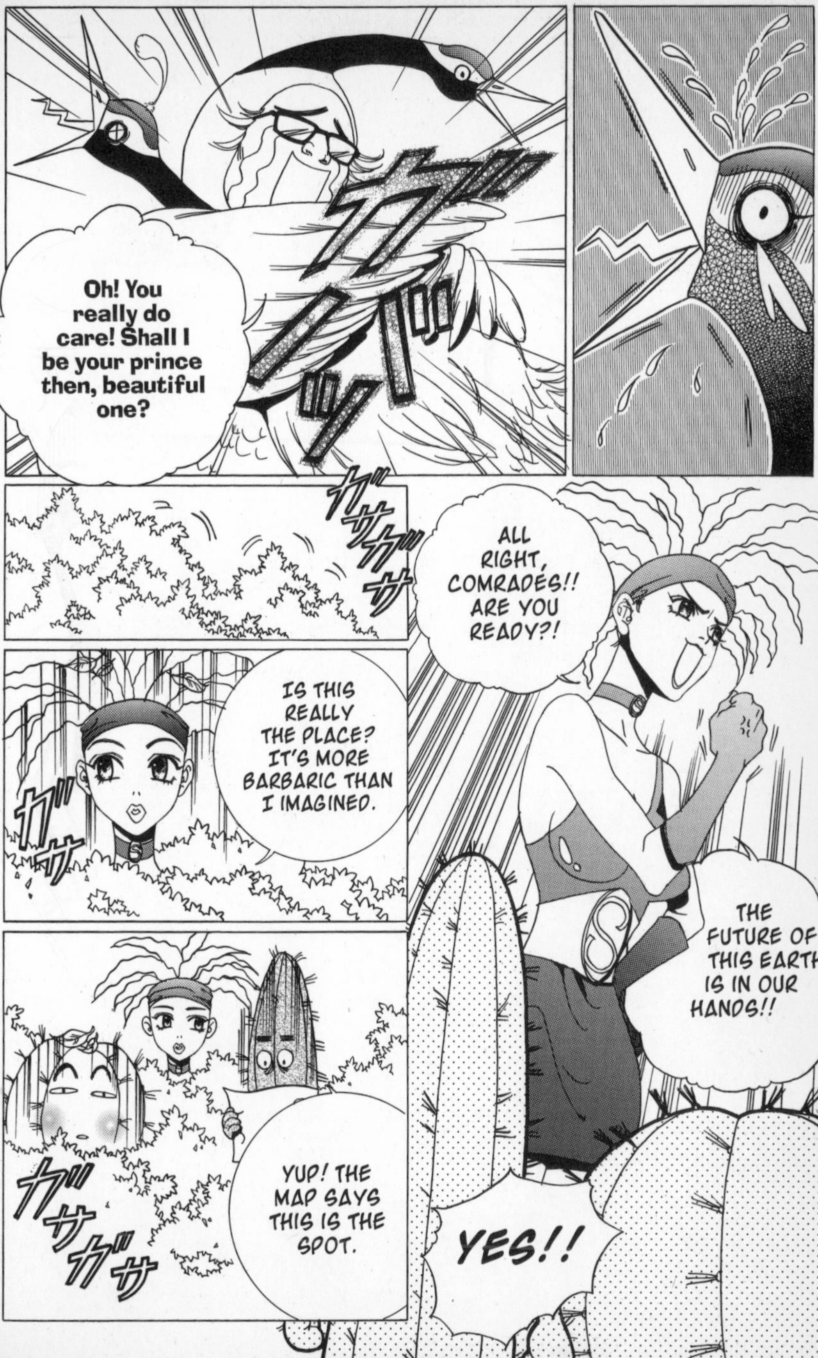
Oh! You really do care! Shall I be your prince then, beautiful one?
ガサガサ
ALL RIGHT, COMRADES!! ARE YOU READY?!
THE FUTURE OF THIS EARTH IS IN OUR HANDS!!
YES!!
ガサ
IS THIS REALLY THE PLACE? IT'S MORE BARBARIC THAN I IMAGINED.
ガサガサ
YUP! THE MAP SAYS THIS IS THE SPOT.

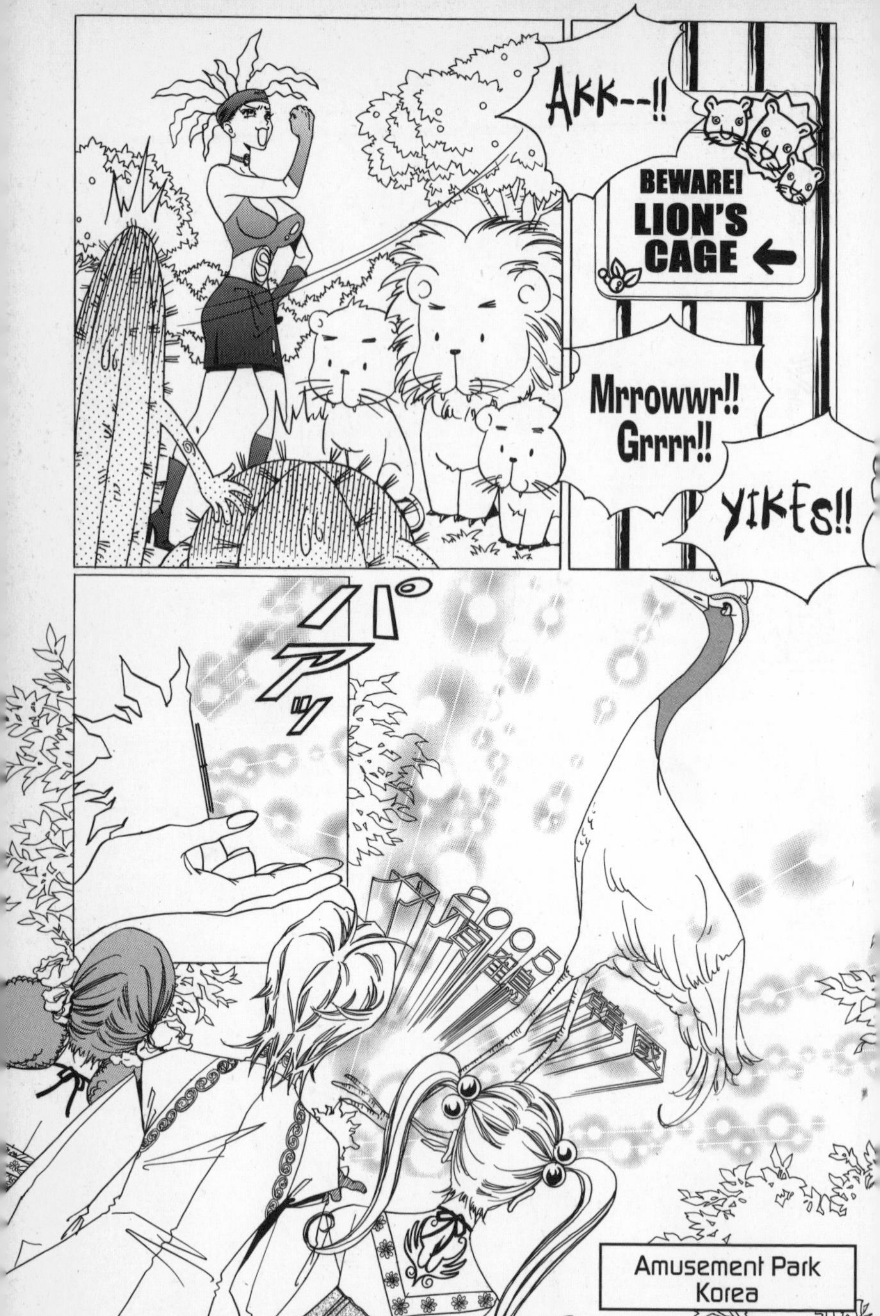
AKK--!!
BEWARE! LION'S CAGE
Mrrowwr!! Grrrr!!
YIKES!!
パアッ
Amusement Park
Korea

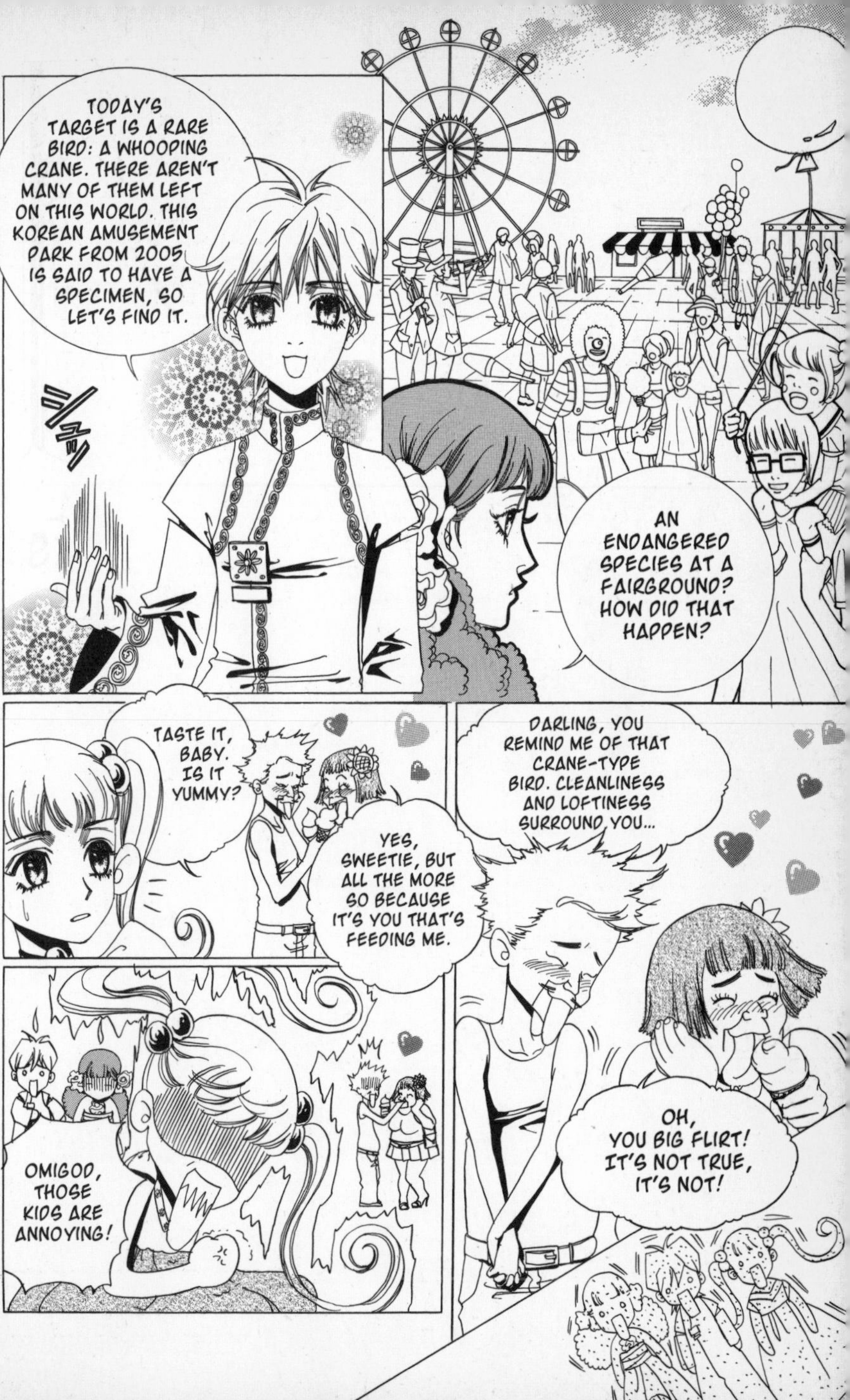
TODAY'S TARGET IS A RARE BIRD: A WHOOPING CRANE. THERE AREN'T MANY OF THEM LEFT ON THIS WORLD. THIS KOREAN AMUSEMENT PARK FROM 2005 IS SAID TO HAVE A SPECIMEN, SO LET'S FIND IT.
AN ENDANGERED SPECIES AT A FAIRGROUND? HOW DID THAT HAPPEN?
TASTE IT, BABY. IS IT YUMMY?
YES, SWEETIE, BUT ALL THE MORE SO BECAUSE IT'S YOU THAT'S FEEDING ME.
DARLING, YOU REMIND ME OF THAT CRANE-TYPE BIRD. CLEANLINESS AND LOFTINESS SURROUND YOU...
OH, YOU BIG FLIRT! IT'S NOT TRUE, IT'S NOT!
OMIGOD, THOSE KIDS ARE ANNOYING!

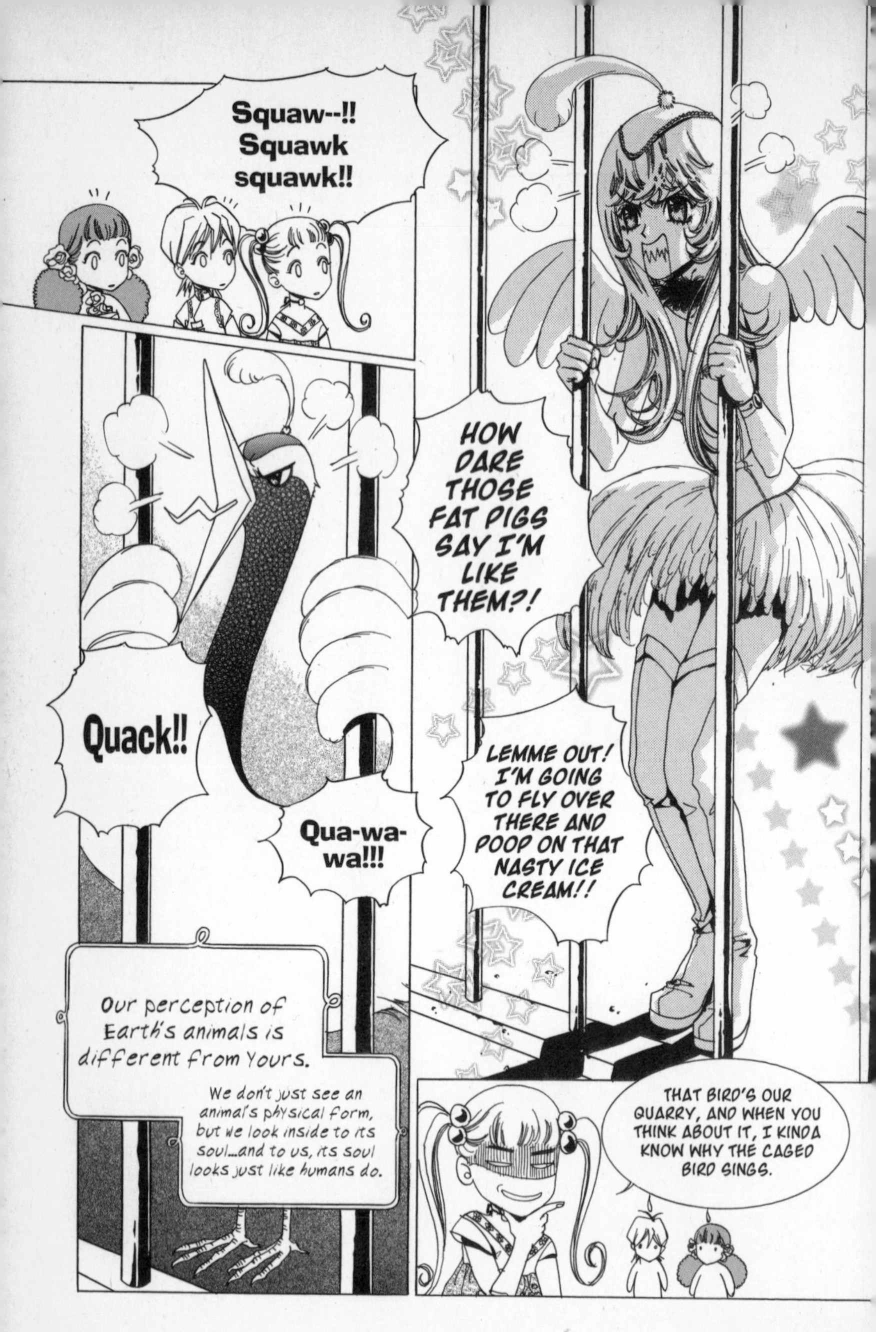
Squaw--!! Squawk squawk!!
Quack!!
Qua-wa-wa!!!
Our perception of Earth's animals is different from yours.
We don't just see an animal's physical form, but we look inside to its soul...and to us, its soul looks just like humans do.
HOW DARE THOSE FAT PIGS SAY I'M LIKE THEM?!
LEMME OUT! I'M GOING TO FLY OVER THERE AND POOP ON THAT NASTY ICE CREAM!!
THAT BIRD'S OUR QUARRY, AND WHEN YOU THINK ABOUT IT, I KINDA KNOW WHY THE CAGED BIRD SINGS.

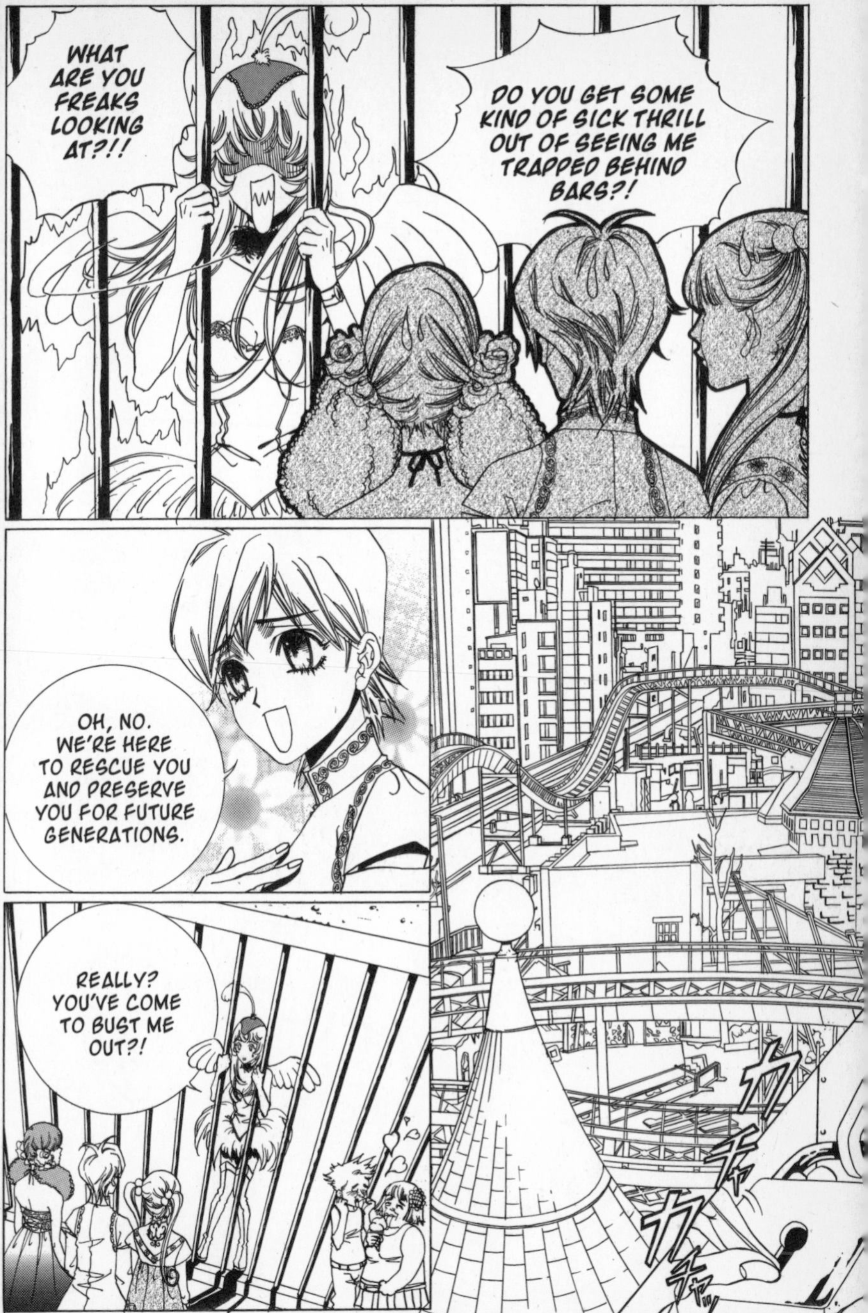
WHAT ARE YOU FREAKS LOOKING AT?!!
DO YOU GET SOME KIND OF SICK THRILL OUT OF SEEING ME TRAPPED BEHIND BARS?!
OH, NO. WE'RE HERE TO RESCUE YOU AND PRESERVE YOU FOR FUTURE GENERATIONS.
REALLY? YOU'VE COME TO BUST ME OUT?!
カチャ
カチャッ

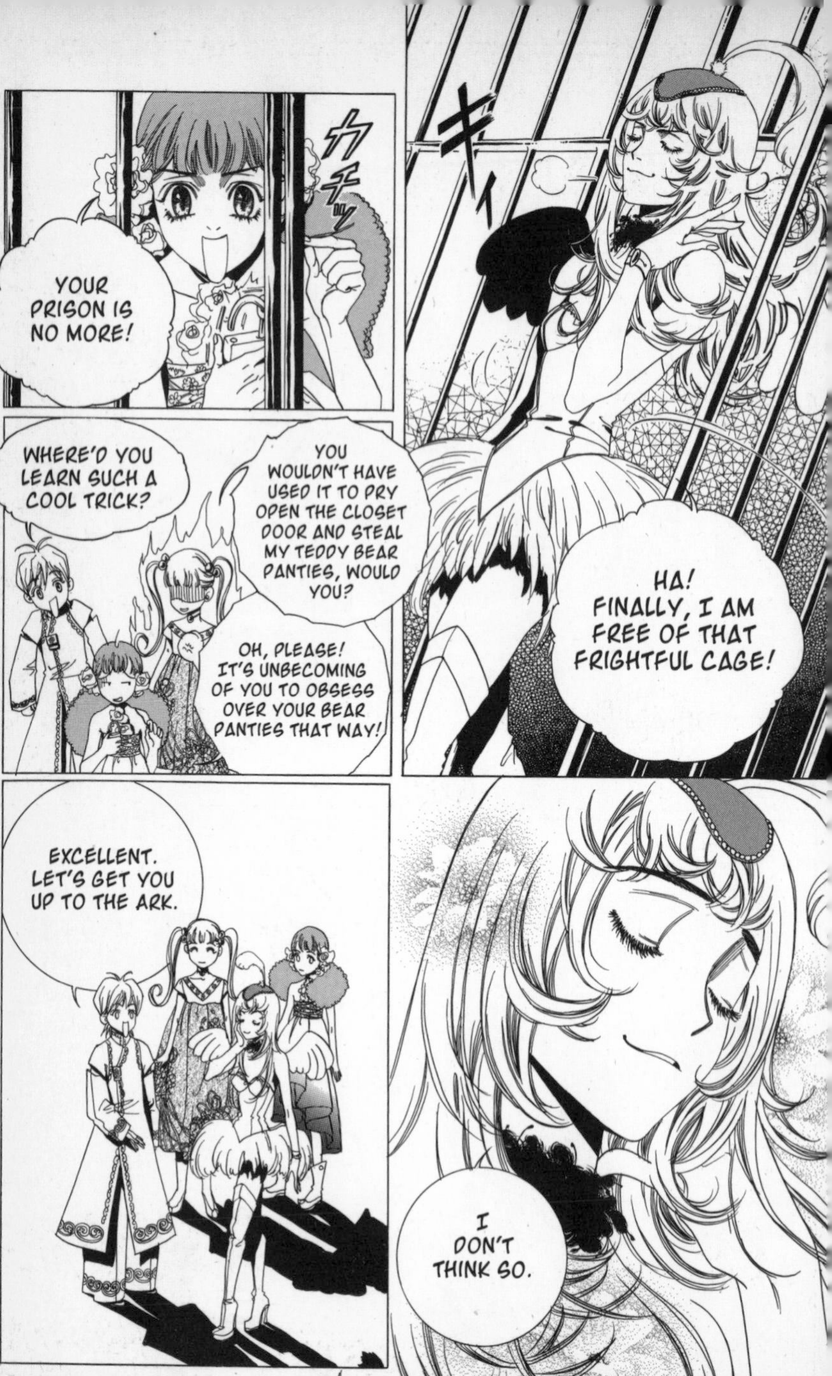
カチッ
YOUR PRISON IS NO MORE!
WHERE'D YOU LEARN SUCH A COOL TRICK?
YOU WOULDN'T HAVE USED IT TO PRY OPEN THE CLOSET DOOR AND STEAL MY TEDDY BEAR PANTIES, WOULD YOU?
OH, PLEASE! IT'S UNBECOMING OF YOU TO OBSESS OVER YOUR BEAR PANTIES THAT WAY!
キィ
HA! FINALLY, I AM FREE OF THAT FRIGHTFUL CAGE!
EXCELLENT. LET'S GET YOU UP TO THE ARK.
I DON'T THINK SO.

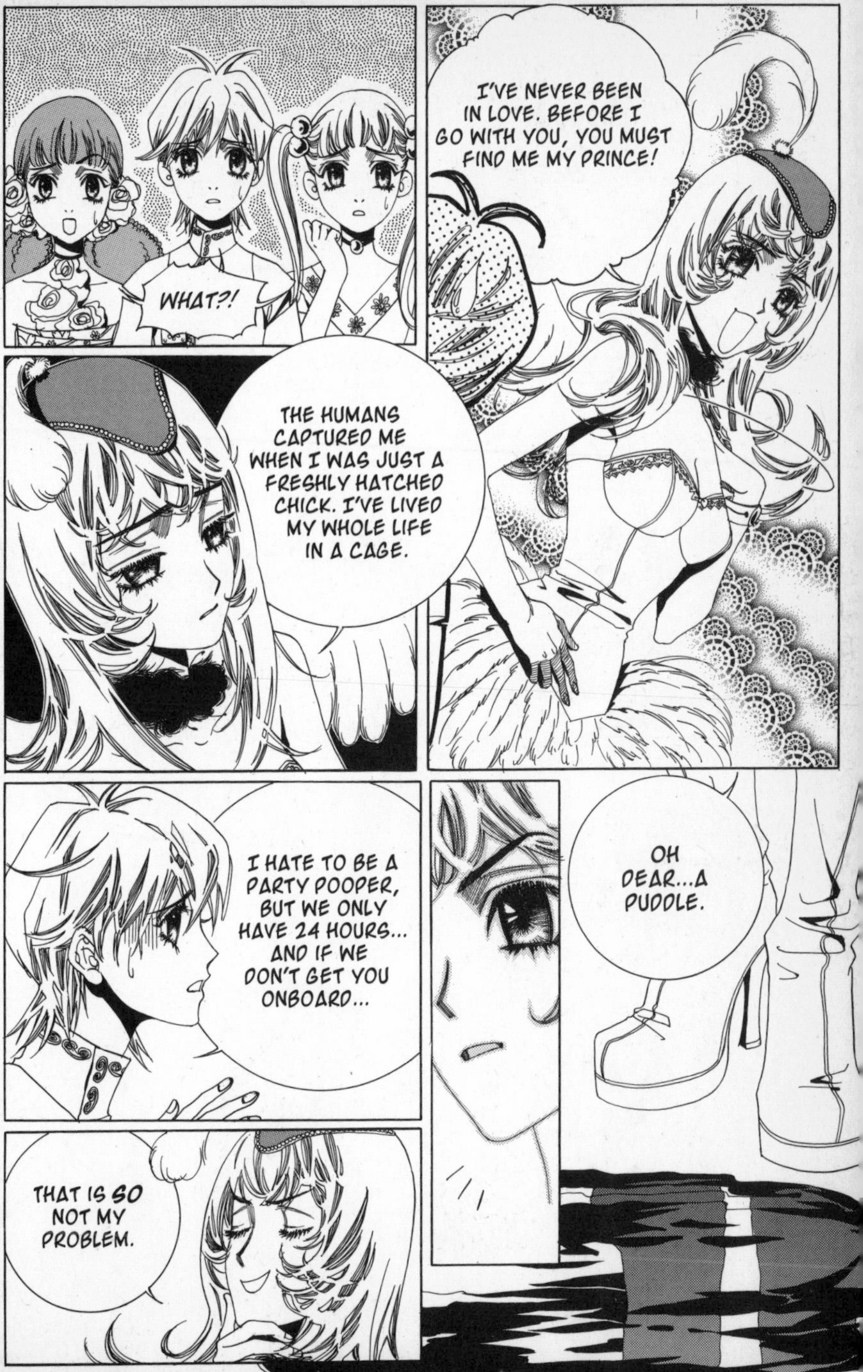
I'VE NEVER BEEN IN LOVE. BEFORE I GO WITH YOU, YOU MUST FIND ME MY PRINCE!
WHAT?!
THE HUMANS CAPTURED ME WHEN I WAS JUST A FRESHLY HATCHED CHICK. I'VE LIVED MY WHOLE LIFE IN A CAGE.
OH DEAR...A PUDDLE.
I HATE TO BE A PARTY POOPER, BUT WE ONLY HAVE 24 HOURS... AND IF WE DON'T GET YOU ONBOARD...
THAT IS SO NOT MY PROBLEM.

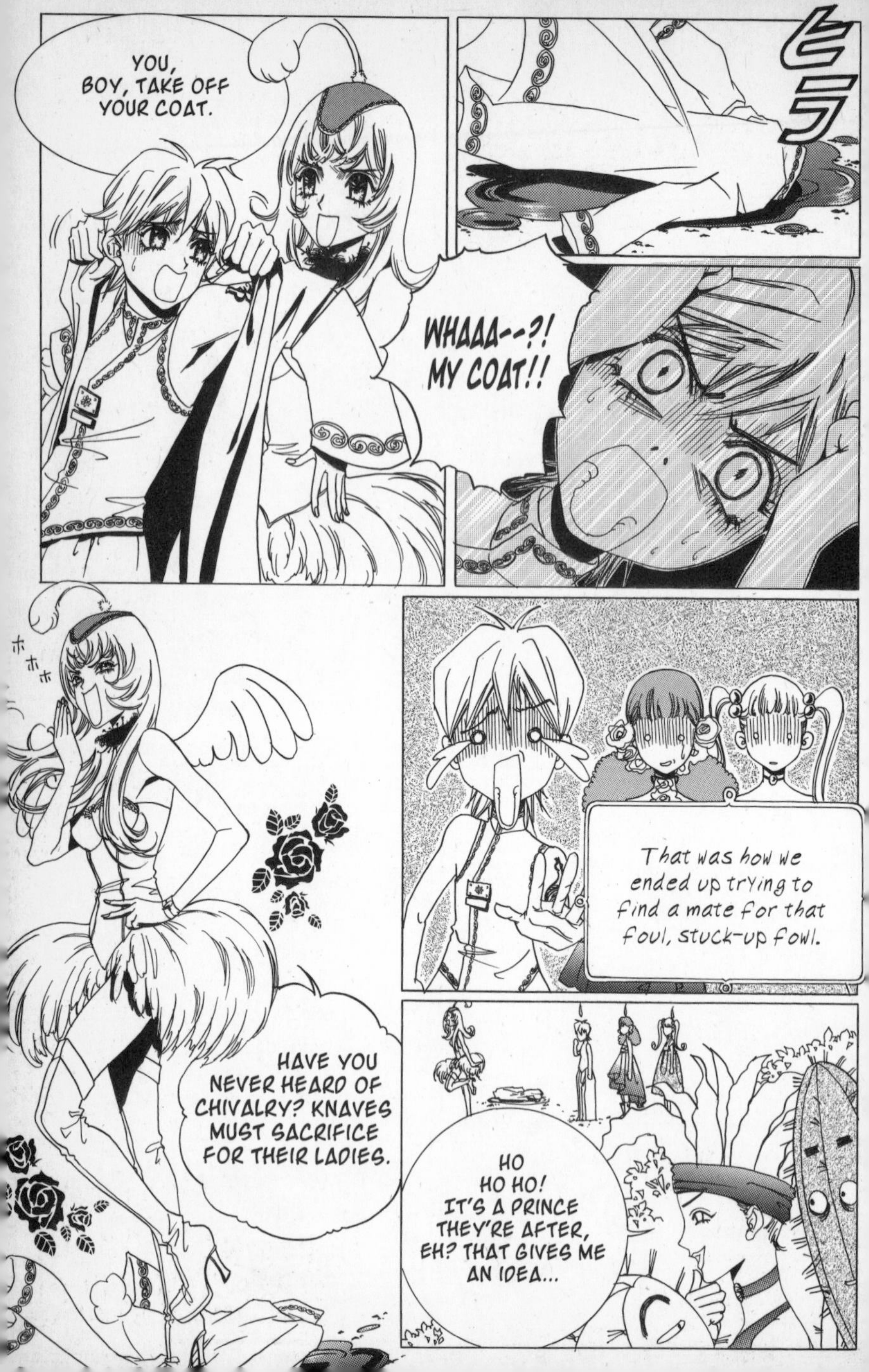
ヒラ
WHAAA--?! MY COAT!!
YOU, BOY, TAKE OFF YOUR COAT.
That was how we ended up trying to find a mate for that foul, stuck-up fowl.
HO HO HO! IT'S A PRINCE THEY'RE AFTER, EH? THAT GIVES ME AN IDEA...
ホホホ
HAVE YOU NEVER HEARD OF CHIVALRY? KNAVES MUST SACRIFICE FOR THEIR LADIES.

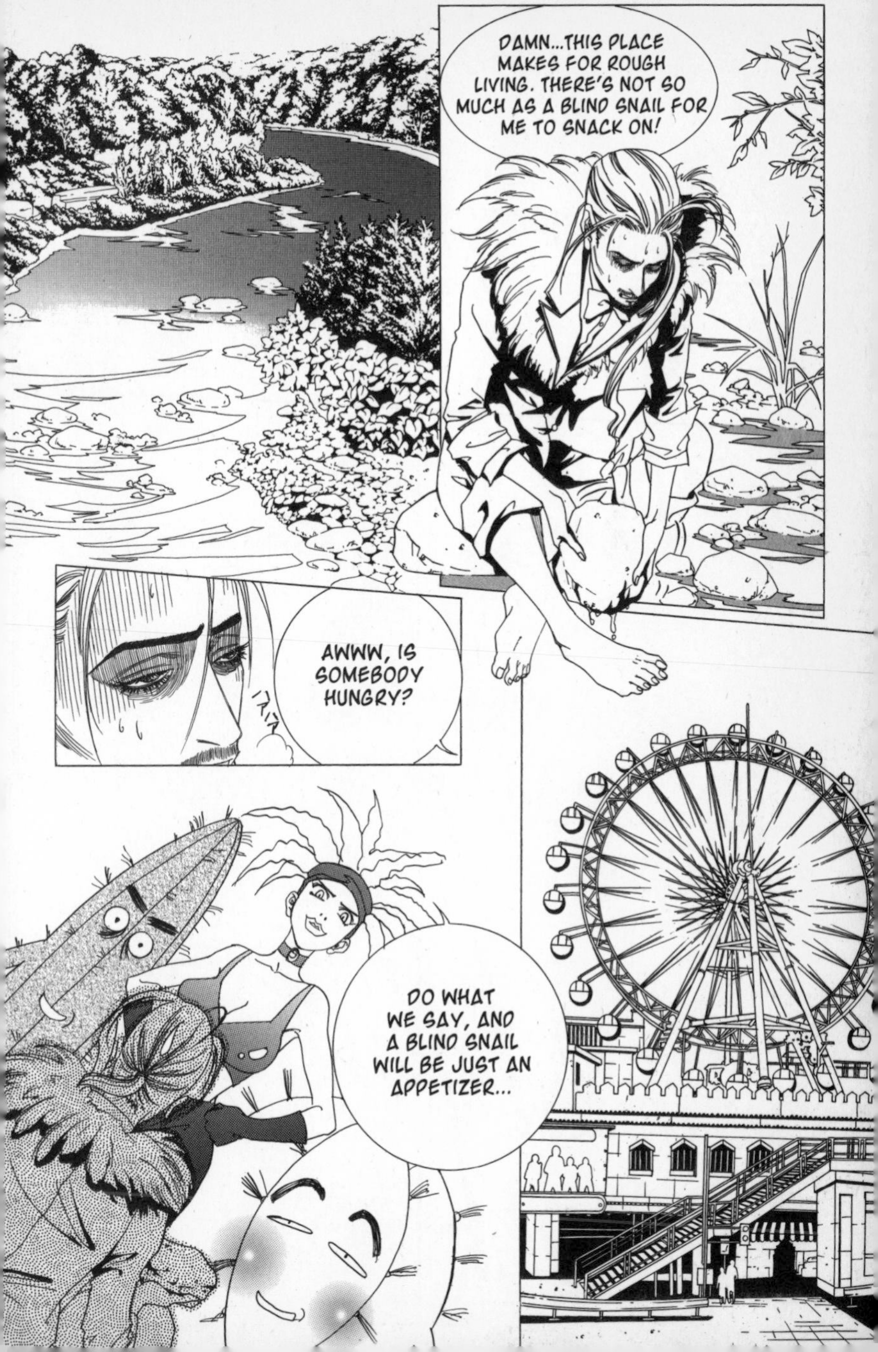
DAMN...THIS PLACE MAKES FOR ROUGH LIVING. THERE'S NOT SO MUCH AS A BLIND SNAIL FOR ME TO SNACK ON!
AWWW, IS SOMEBODY HUNGRY?
DO WHAT WE SAY, AND A BLIND SNAIL WILL BE JUST AN APPETIZER...

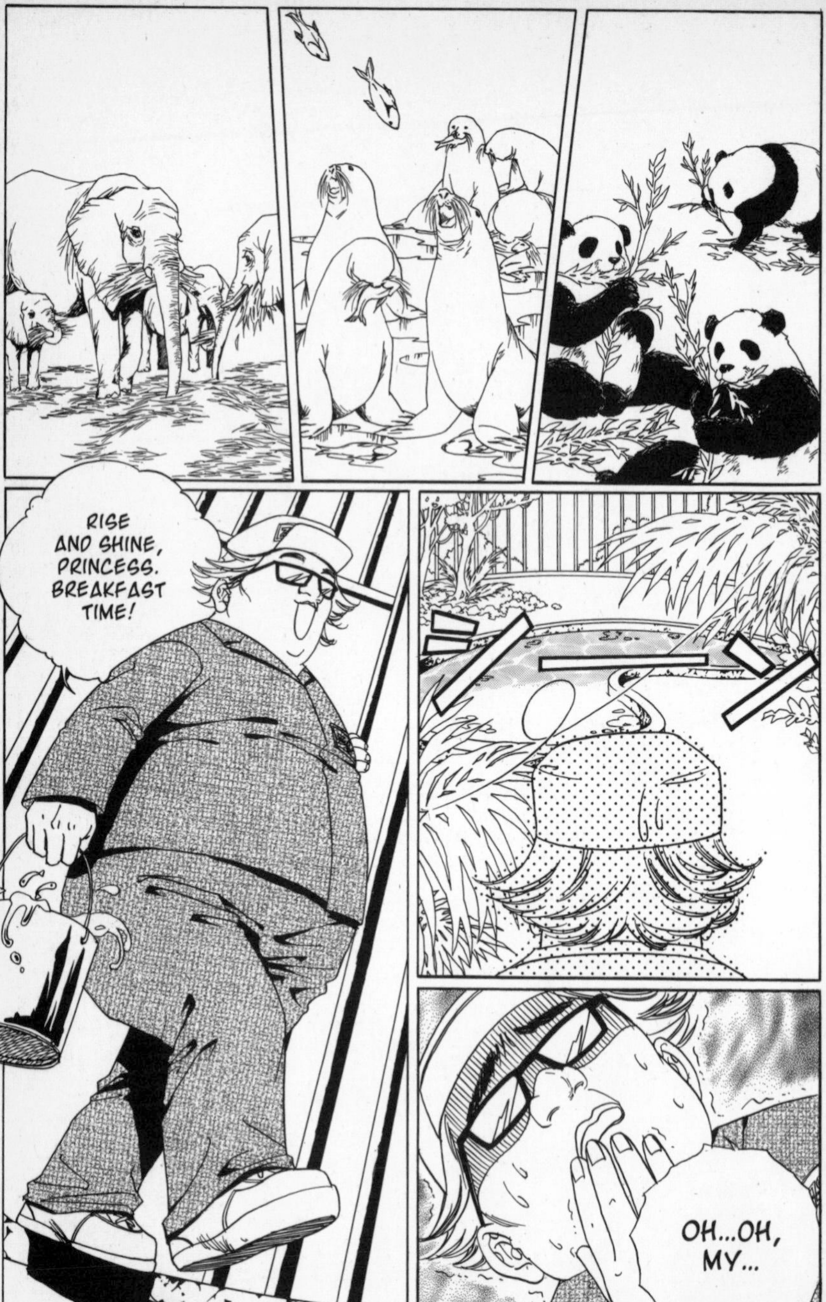
RISE AND SHINE, PRINCESS. BREAKFAST TIME!
OH...OH, MY...

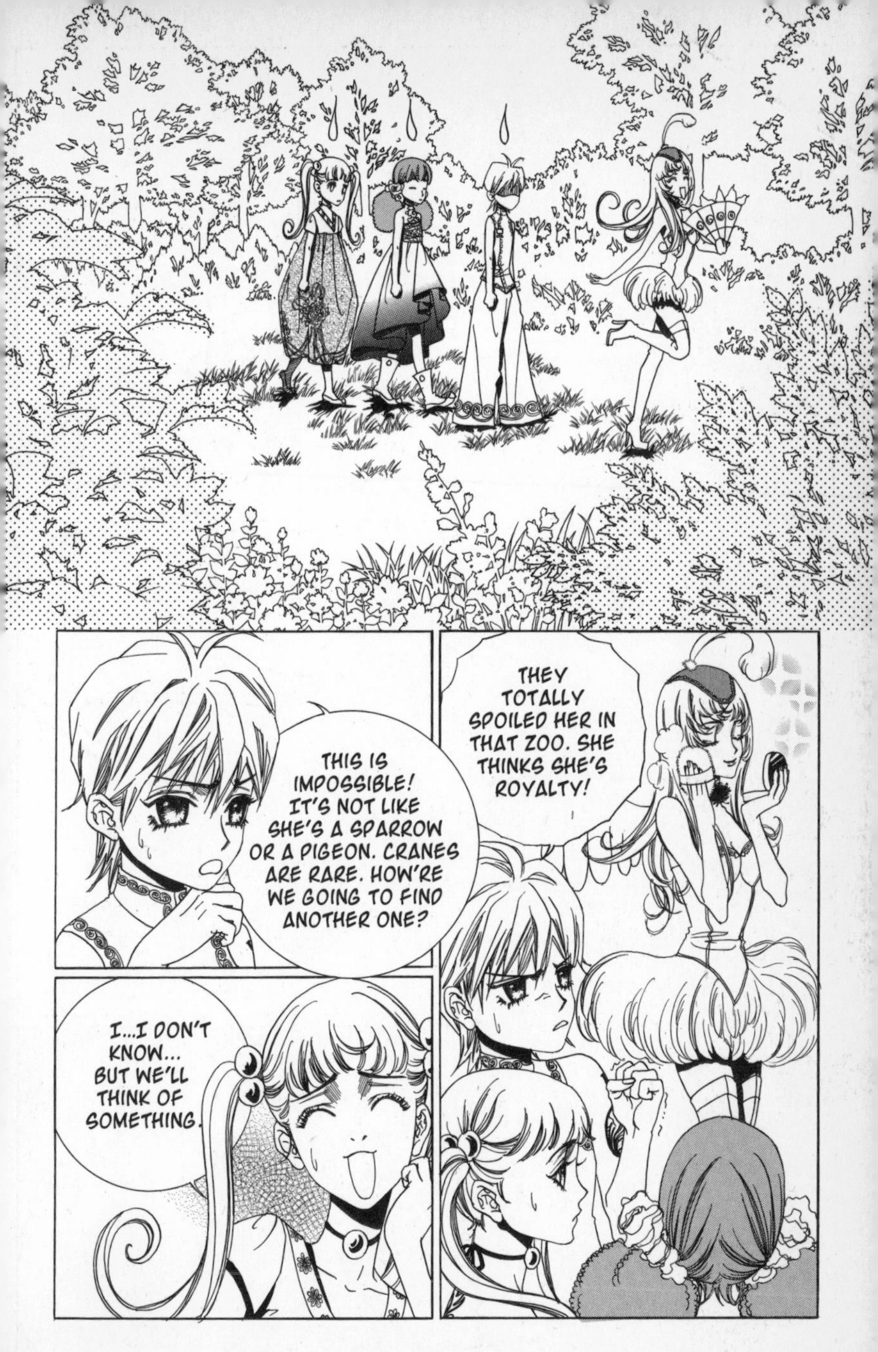
THIS IS IMPOSSIBLE! IT'S NOT LIKE SHE'S A SPARROW OR A PIGEON. CRANES ARE RARE. HOW'RE WE GOING TO FIND ANOTHER ONE?
I...I DON'T KNOW... BUT WE'LL THINK OF SOMETHING.
THEY TOTALLY SPOILED HER IN THAT ZOO. SHE THINKS SHE'S ROYALTY!

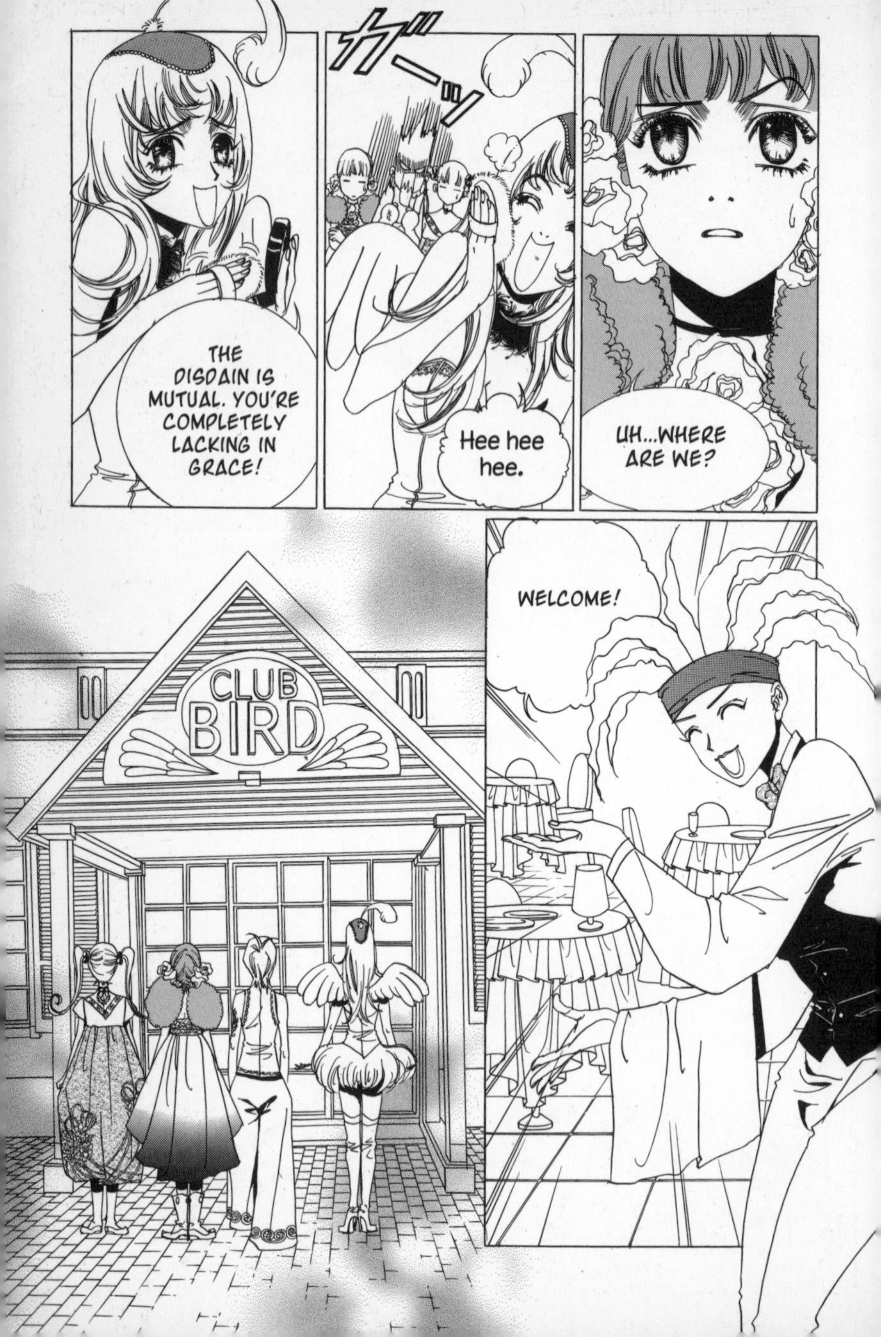
UH...WHERE ARE WE?
ガーッ
Hee hee hee.
THE DISDAIN IS MUTUAL. YOU'RE COMPLETELY LACKING IN GRACE!
WELCOME!
CLUB BIRD

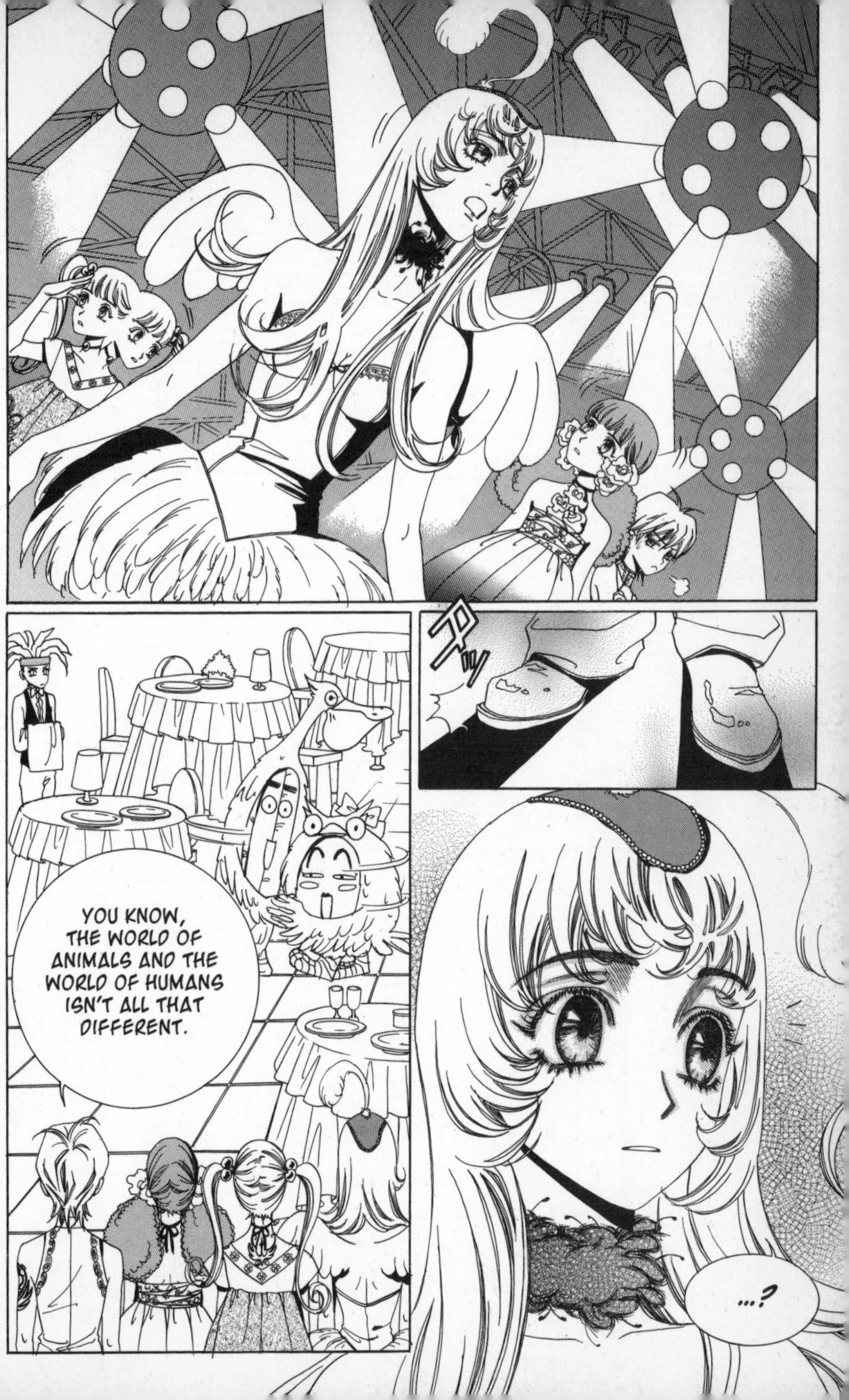
YOU KNOW, THE WORLD OF ANIMALS AND THE WORLD OF HUMANS ISN'T ALL THAT DIFFERENT.
...?

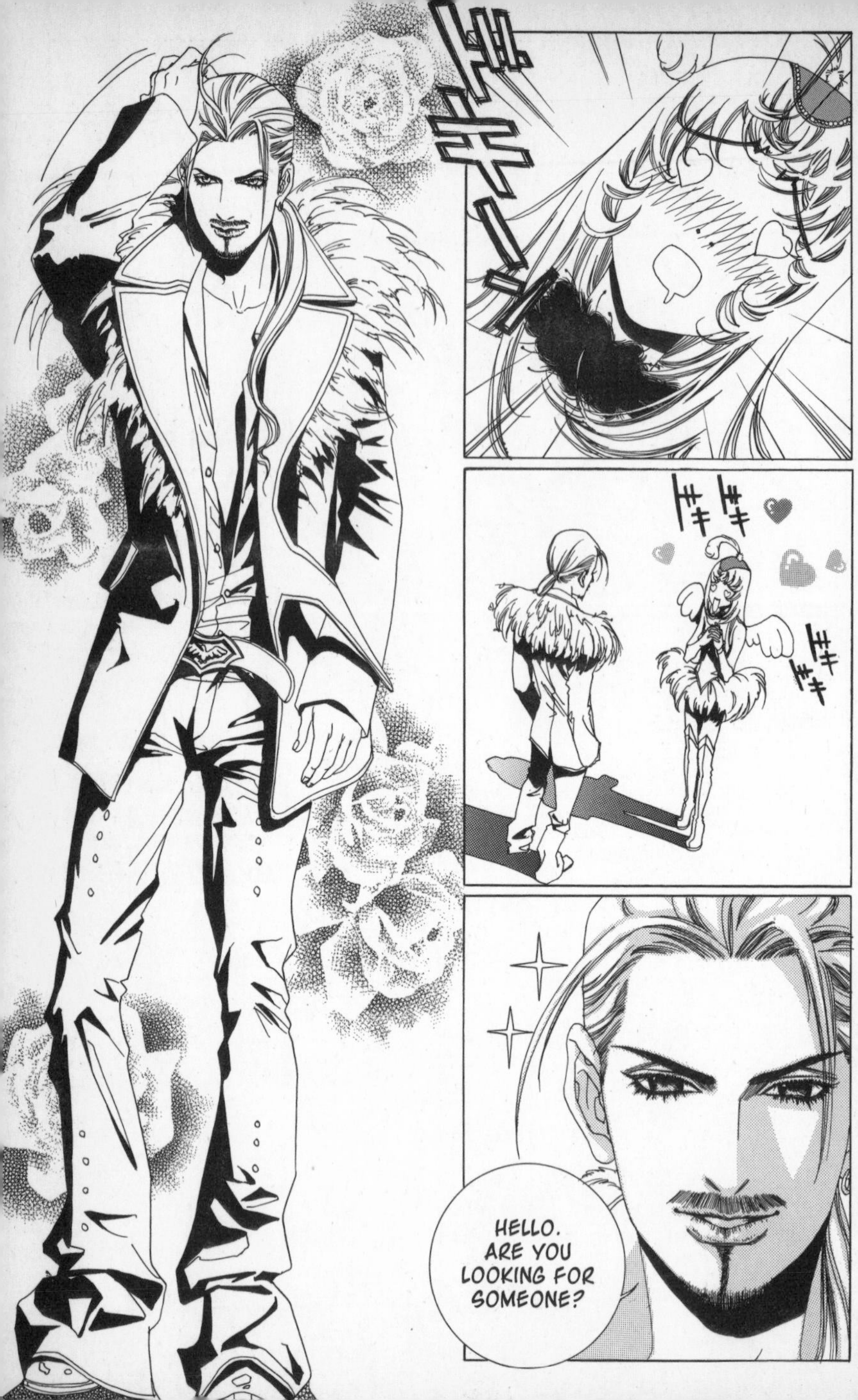
HELLO. ARE YOU LOOKING FOR SOMEONE?

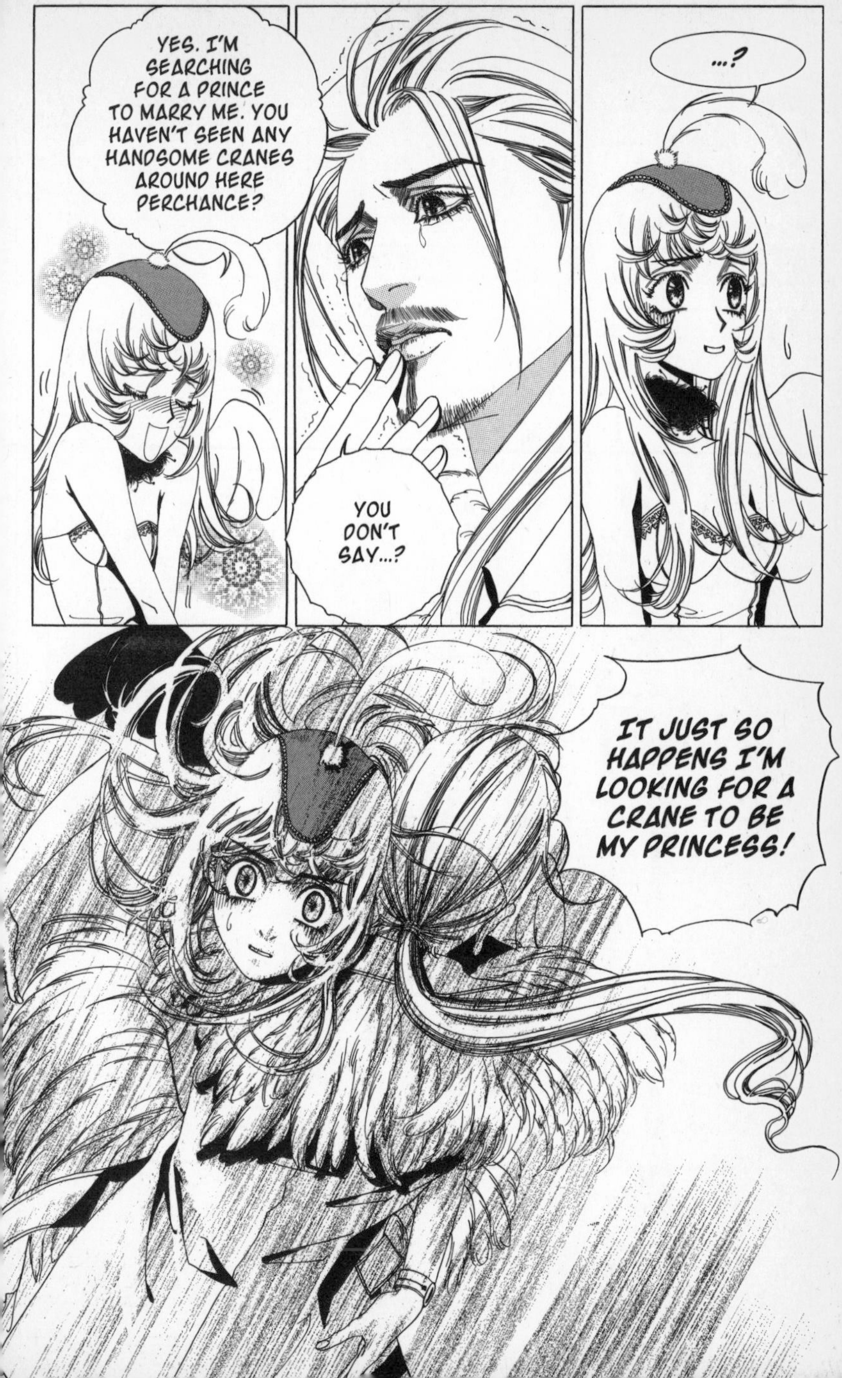
YES. I'M SEARCHING FOR A PRINCE TO MARRY ME. YOU HAVEN'T SEEN ANY HANDSOME CRANES AROUND HERE PERCHANCE?
YOU DON'T SAY...?
...?
IT JUST SO HAPPENS I'M LOOKING FOR A CRANE TO BE MY PRINCESS!

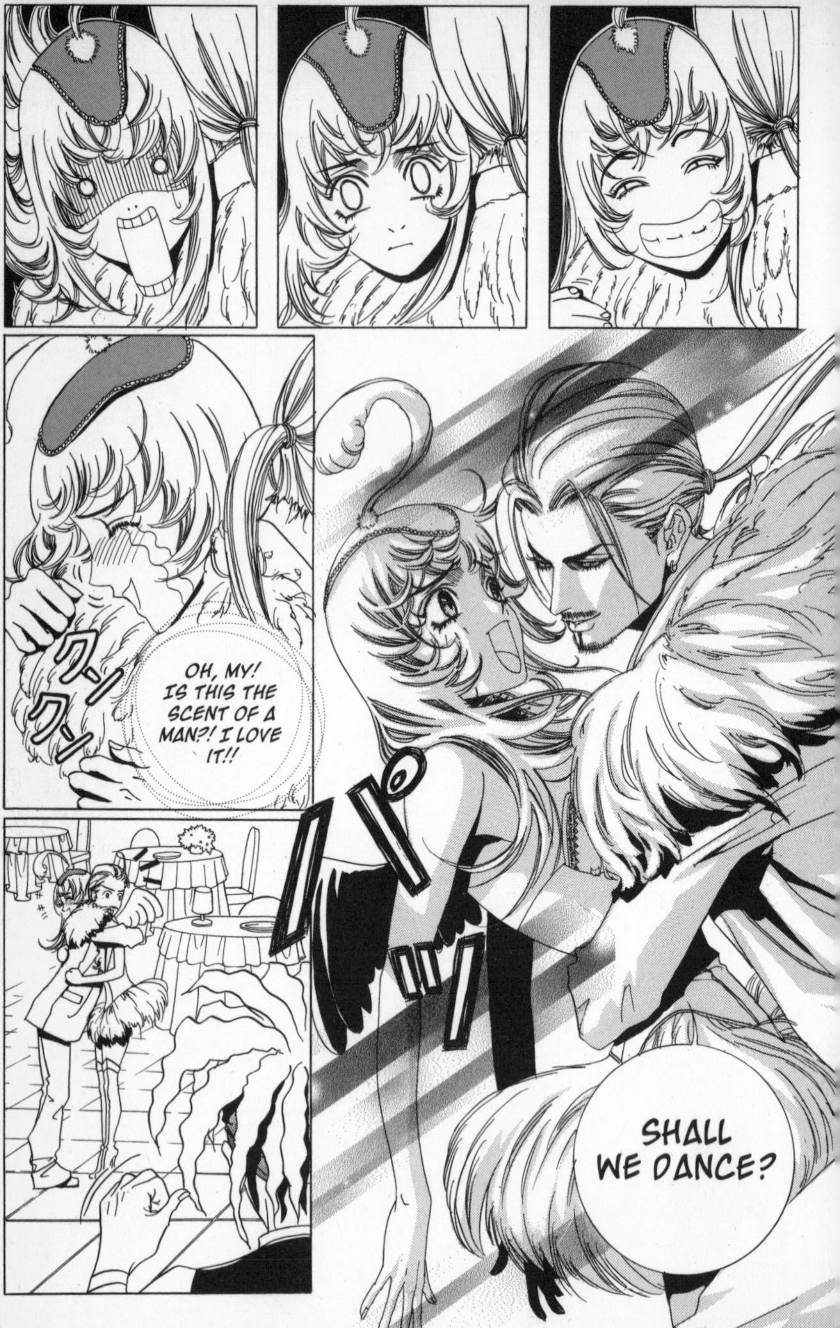
クンクン
OH, MY! IS THIS THE SCENT OF A MAN?! I LOVE IT!!
パッ
SHALL WE DANCE?

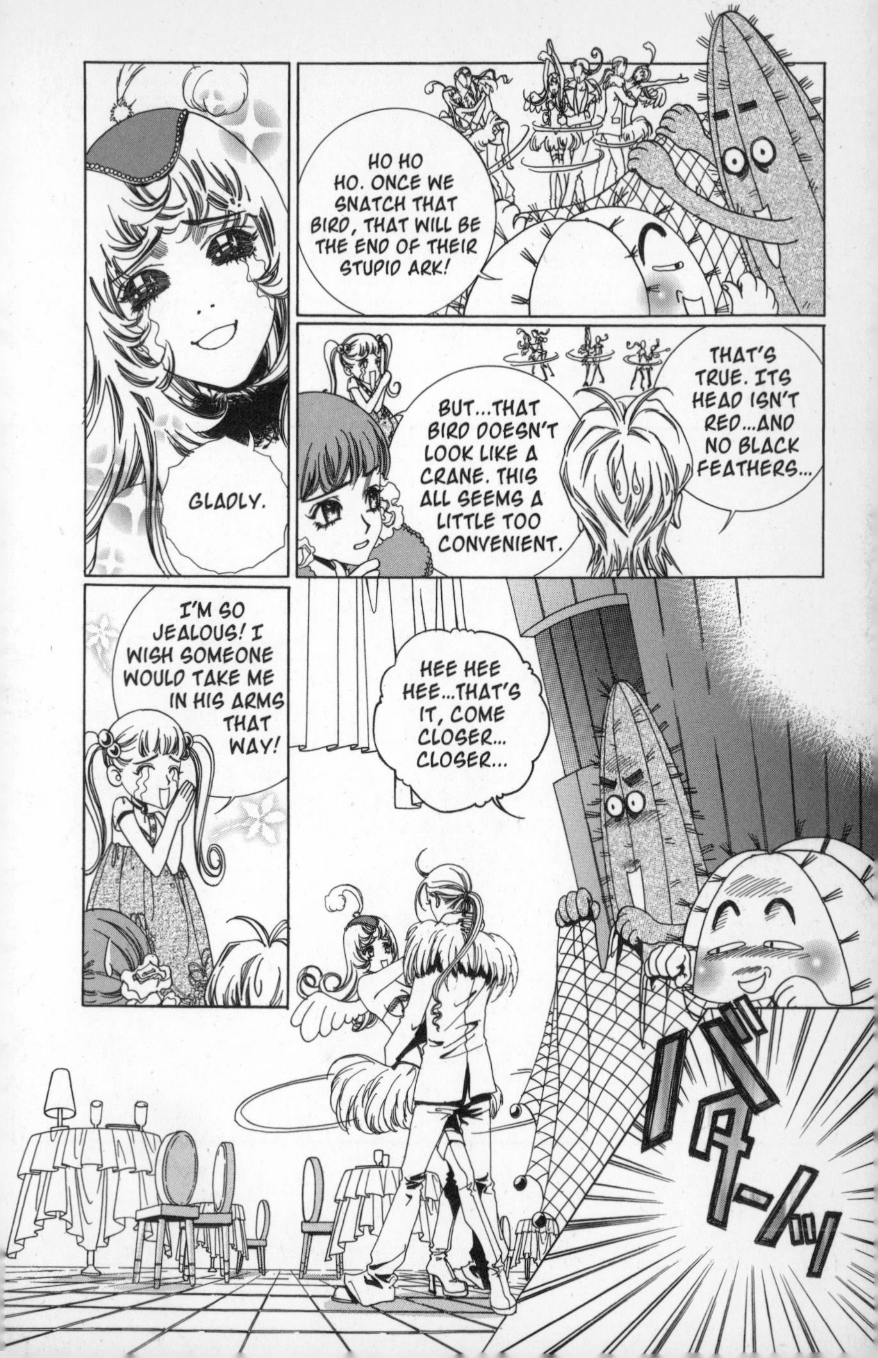
HO HO HO. ONCE WE SNATCH THAT BIRD, THAT WILL BE THE END OF THEIR STUPID ARK!
BUT...THAT BIRD DOESN'T LOOK LIKE A CRANE. THIS ALL SEEMS A LITTLE TOO CONVENIENT.
THAT'S TRUE. ITS HEAD ISN'T RED...AND NO BLACK FEATHERS...
GLADLY.
I'M SO JEALOUS! I WISH SOMEONE WOULD TAKE ME IN HIS ARMS THAT WAY!
HEE HEE HEE...THAT'S IT, COME CLOSER... CLOSER...

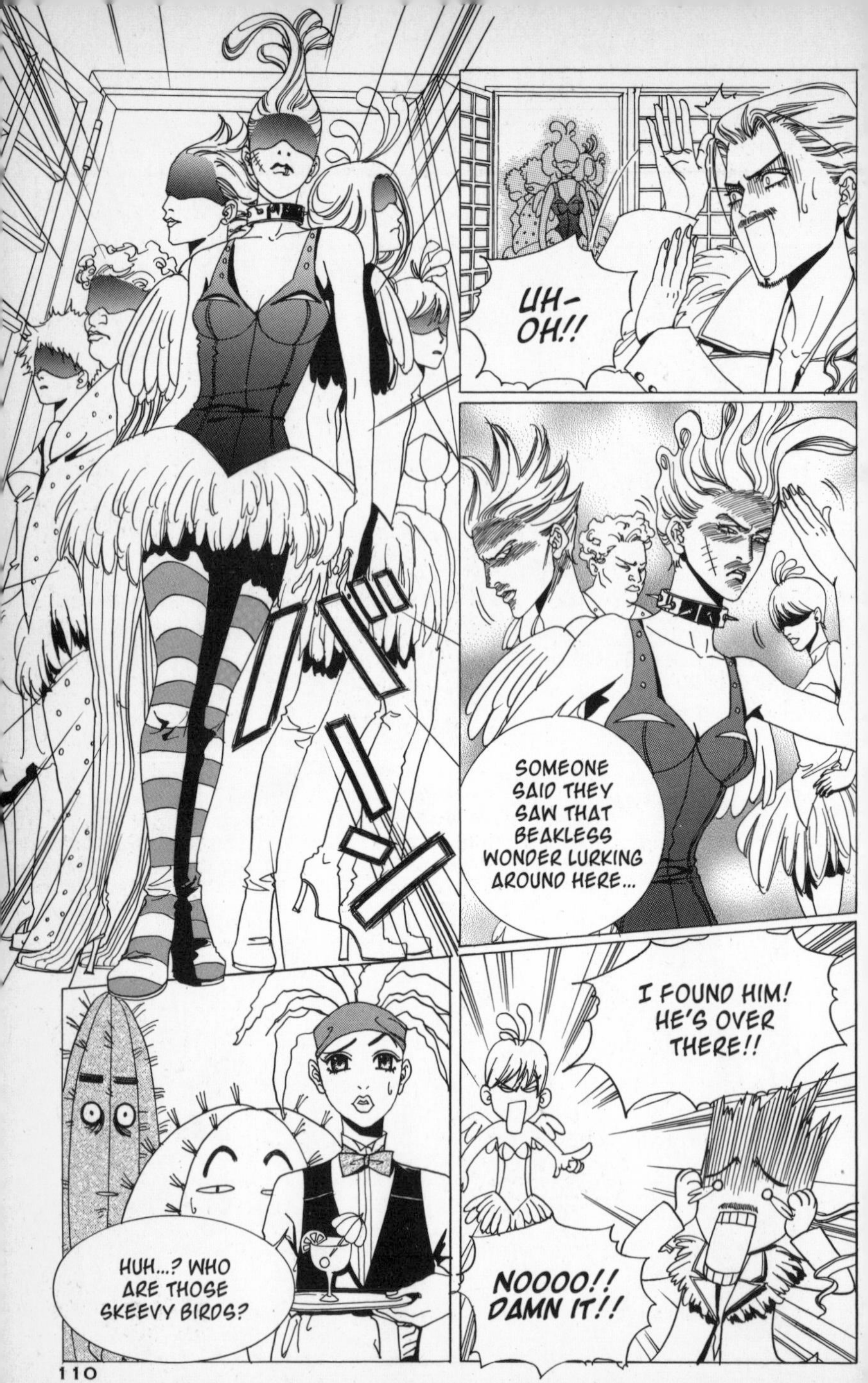
UH-OH!!
SOMEONE SAID THEY SAW THAT BEAKLESS WONDER LURKING AROUND HERE...
I FOUND HIM! HE'S OVER THERE!!
NOOOO!! DAMN IT!!
HUH...? WHO ARE THOSE SKEEVY BIRDS?

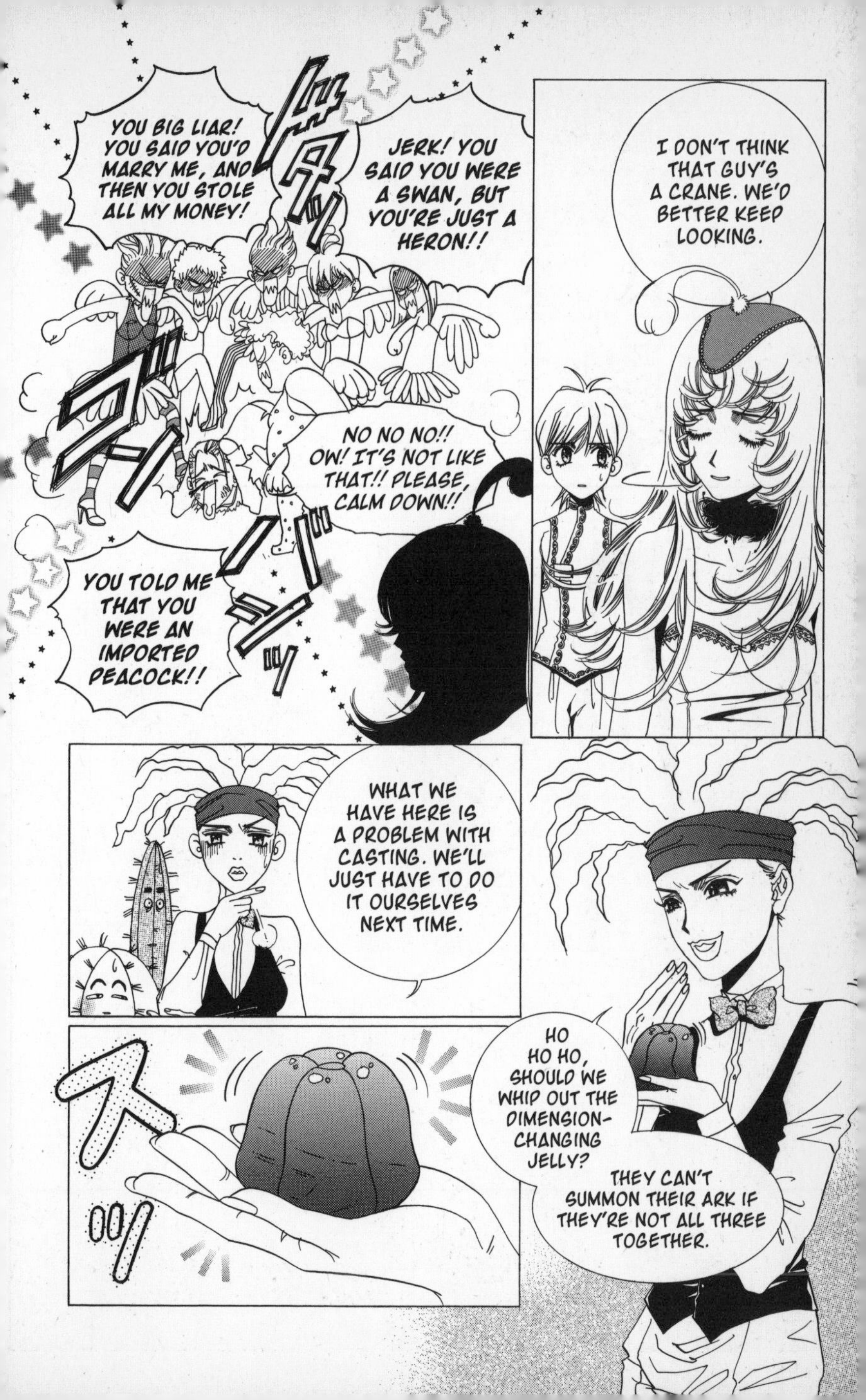
I DON'T THINK THAT GUY'S A CRANE. WE'D BETTER KEEP LOOKING.
JERK! YOU SAID YOU WERE A SWAN, BUT YOU'RE JUST A HERON!!
YOU BIG LIAR! YOU SAID YOU'D MARRY ME, AND THEN YOU STOLE ALL MY MONEY!
NO NO NO!! OW! IT'S NOT LIKE THAT!! PLEASE, CALM DOWN!!
YOU TOLD ME THAT YOU WERE AN IMPORTED PEACOCK!!
HO HO HO, SHOULD WE WHIP OUT THE DIMENSION-CHANGING JELLY?
THEY CAN'T SUMMON THEIR ARK IF THEY'RE NOT ALL THREE TOGETHER.
WHAT WE HAVE HERE IS A PROBLEM WITH CASTING. WE'LL JUST HAVE TO DO IT OURSELVES NEXT TIME.

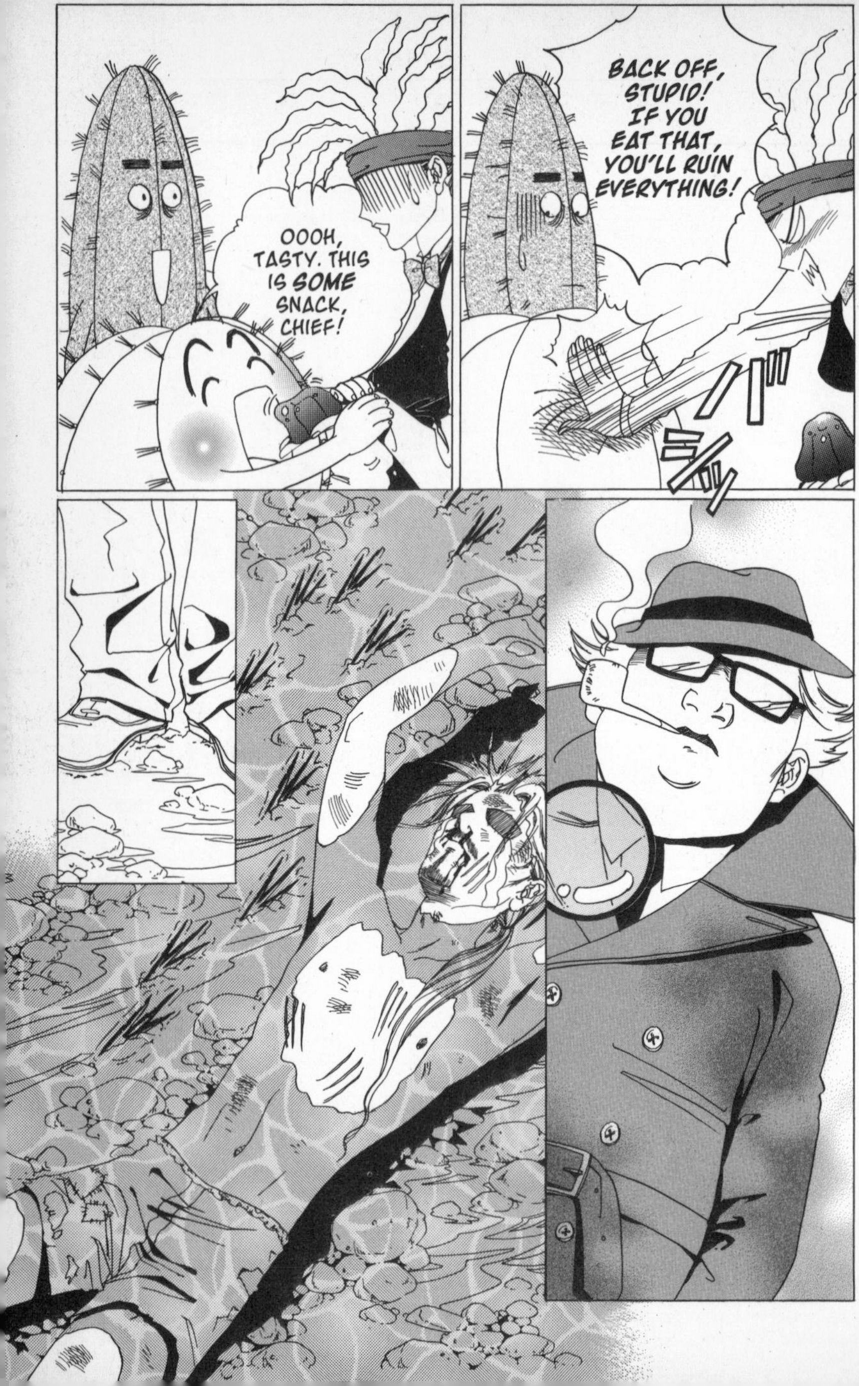
OOOH, TASTY. THIS IS SOME SNACK, CHIEF!
BACK OFF, STUPID! IF YOU EAT THAT, YOU'LL RUIN EVERYTHING!

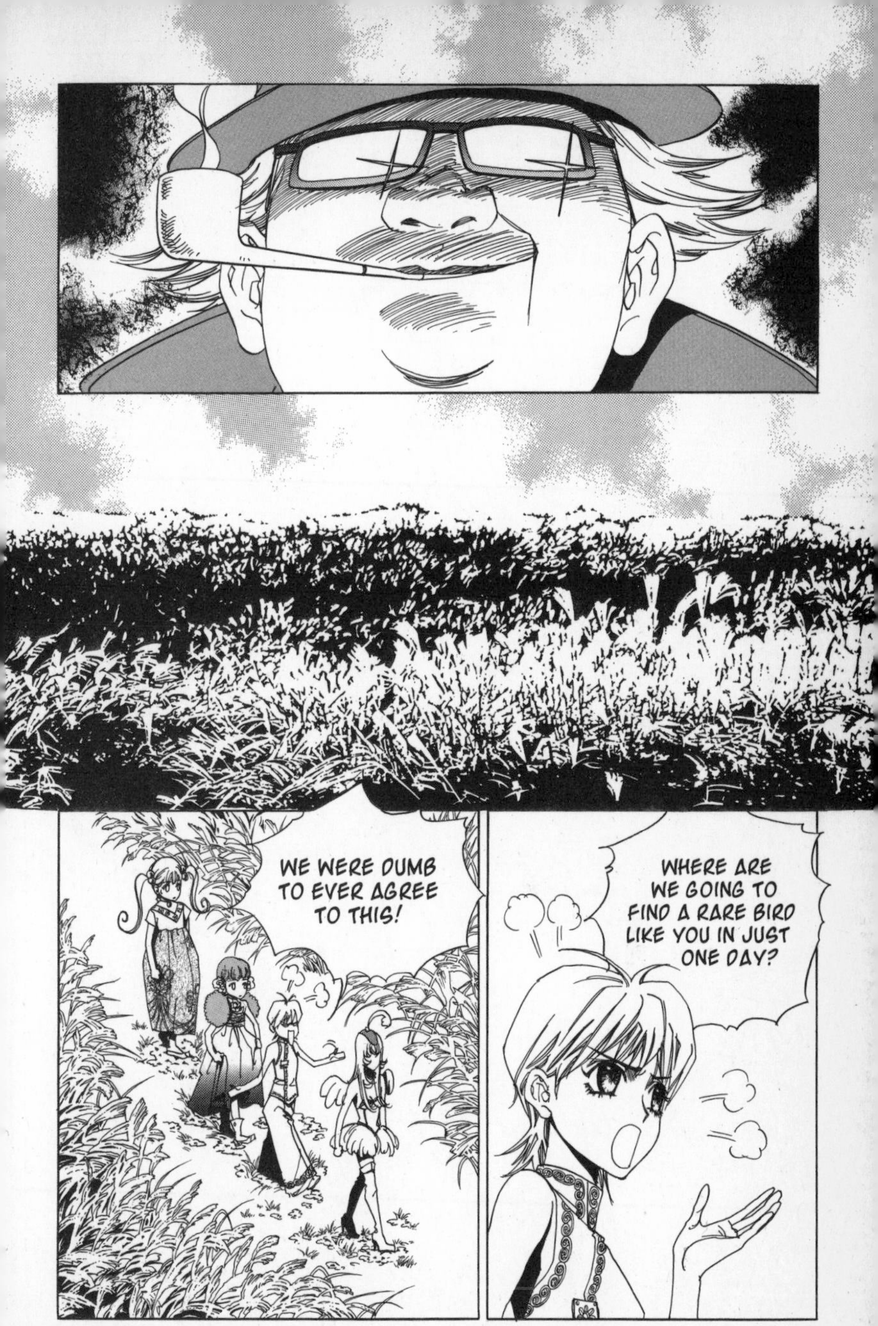
WHERE ARE WE GOING TO FIND A RARE BIRD LIKE YOU IN JUST ONE DAY?
WE WERE DUMB TO EVER AGREE TO THIS!

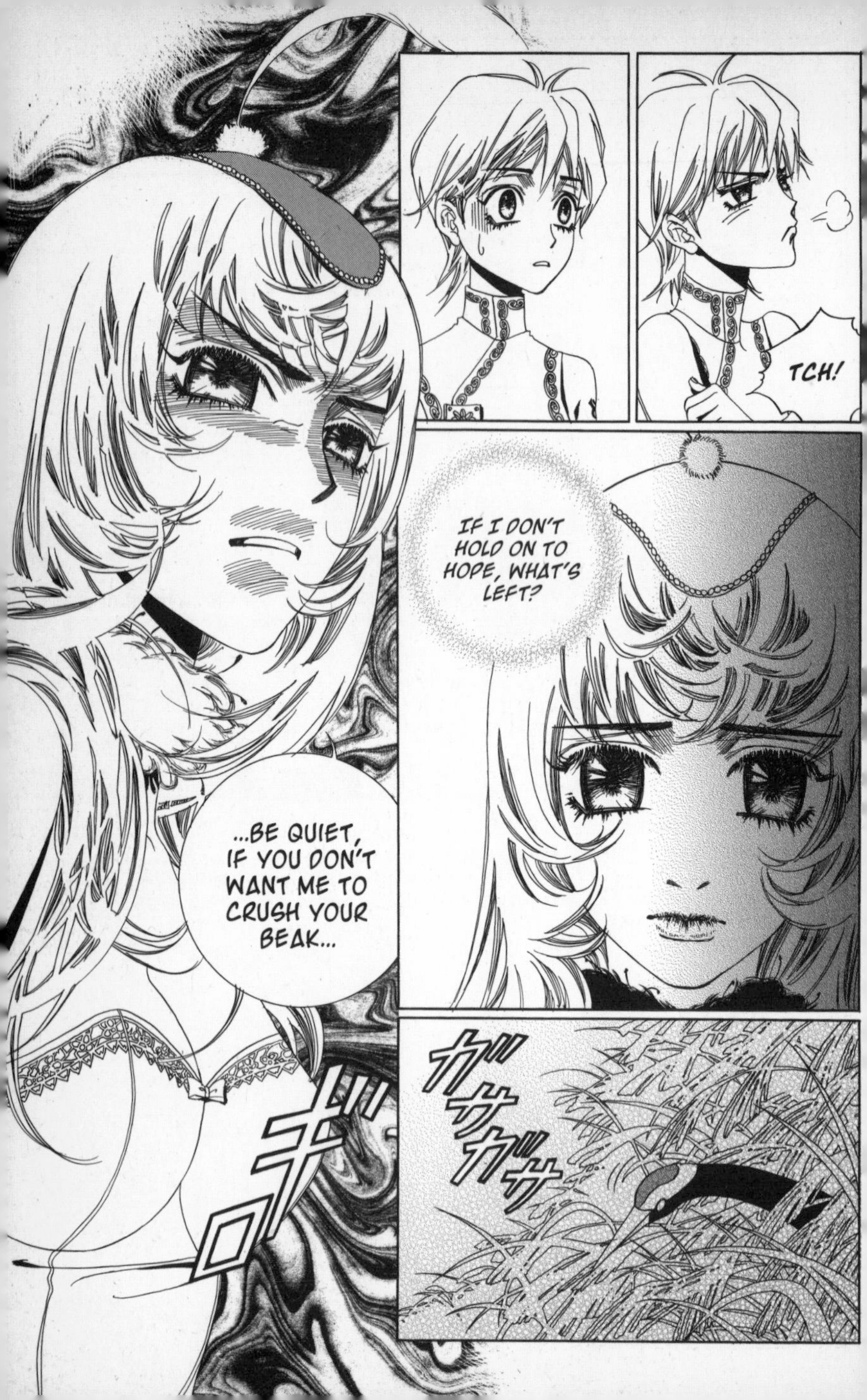
TCH!
IF I DON'T HOLD ON TO HOPE, WHAT'S LEFT?
ガサガサ
...BE QUIET, IF YOU DON'T WANT ME TO CRUSH YOUR BEAK...

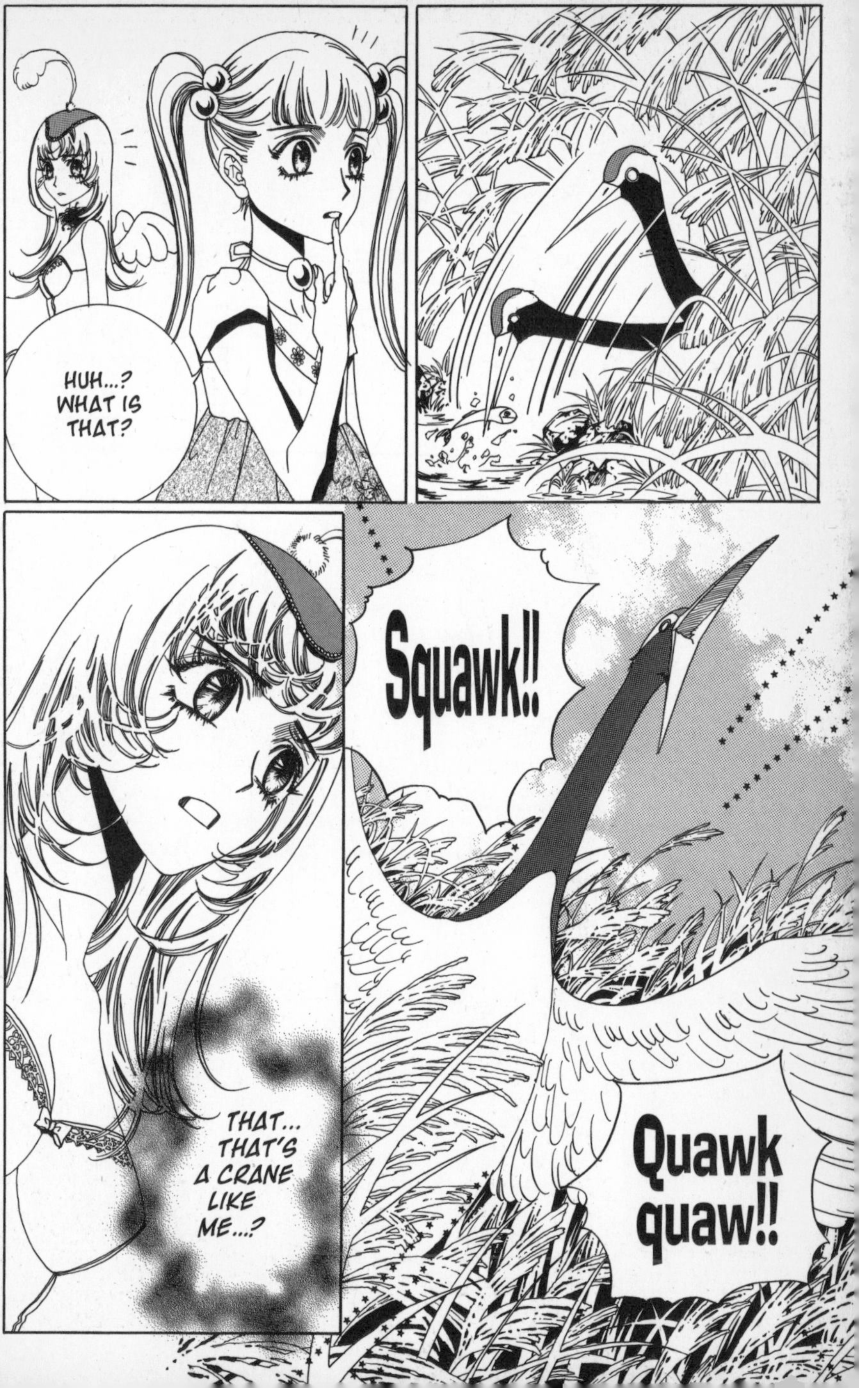
HUH...? WHAT IS THAT?
Squawk!!
Quawk quaw!!
THAT... THAT'S A CRANE LIKE ME...?

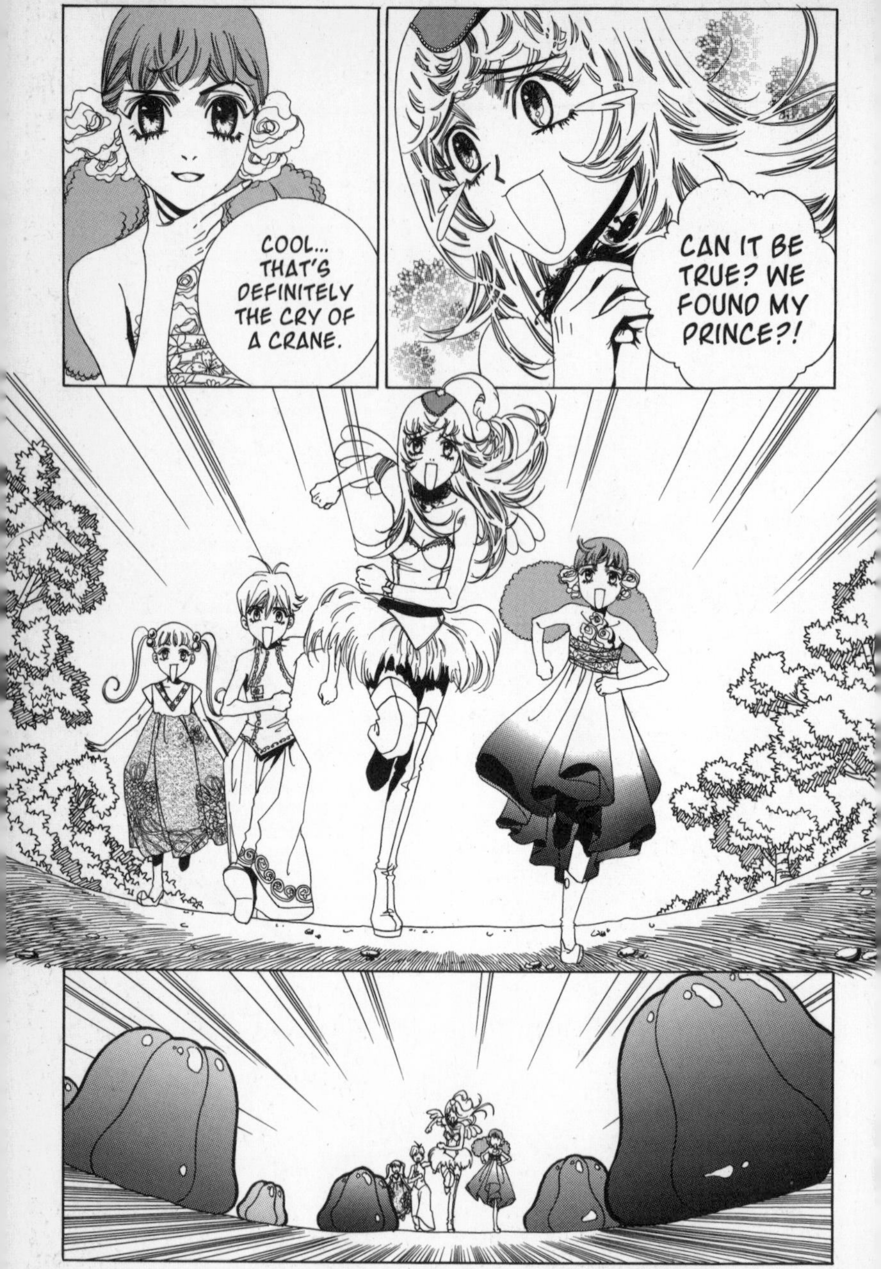
COOL... THAT'S DEFINITELY THE CRY OF A CRANE.
CAN IT BE TRUE? WE FOUND MY PRINCE?!

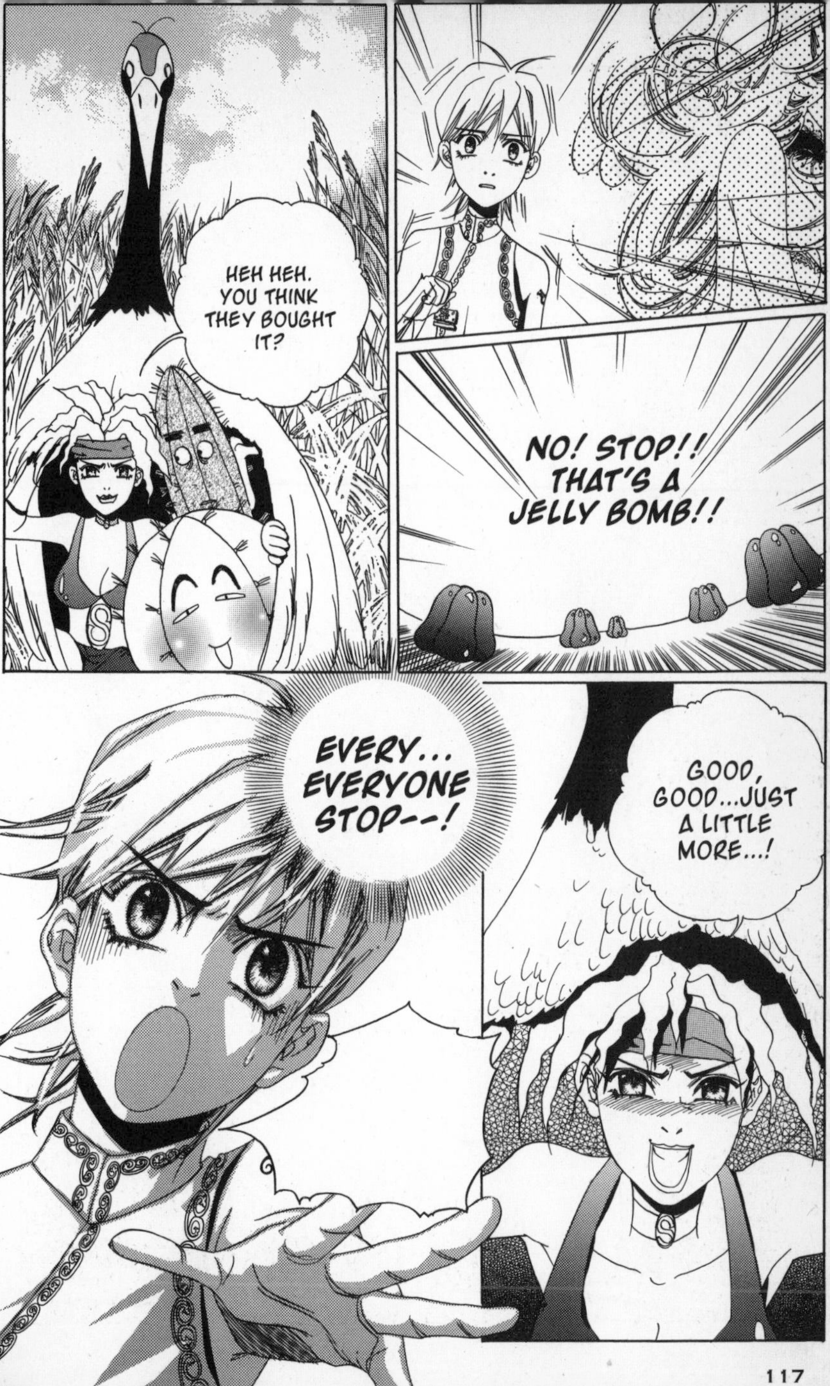
HEH HEH. YOU THINK THEY BOUGHT IT?
NO! STOP!! THAT'S A JELLY BOMB!!
EVERY... EVERYONE STOP--!
GOOD, GOOD...JUST A LITTLE MORE...!

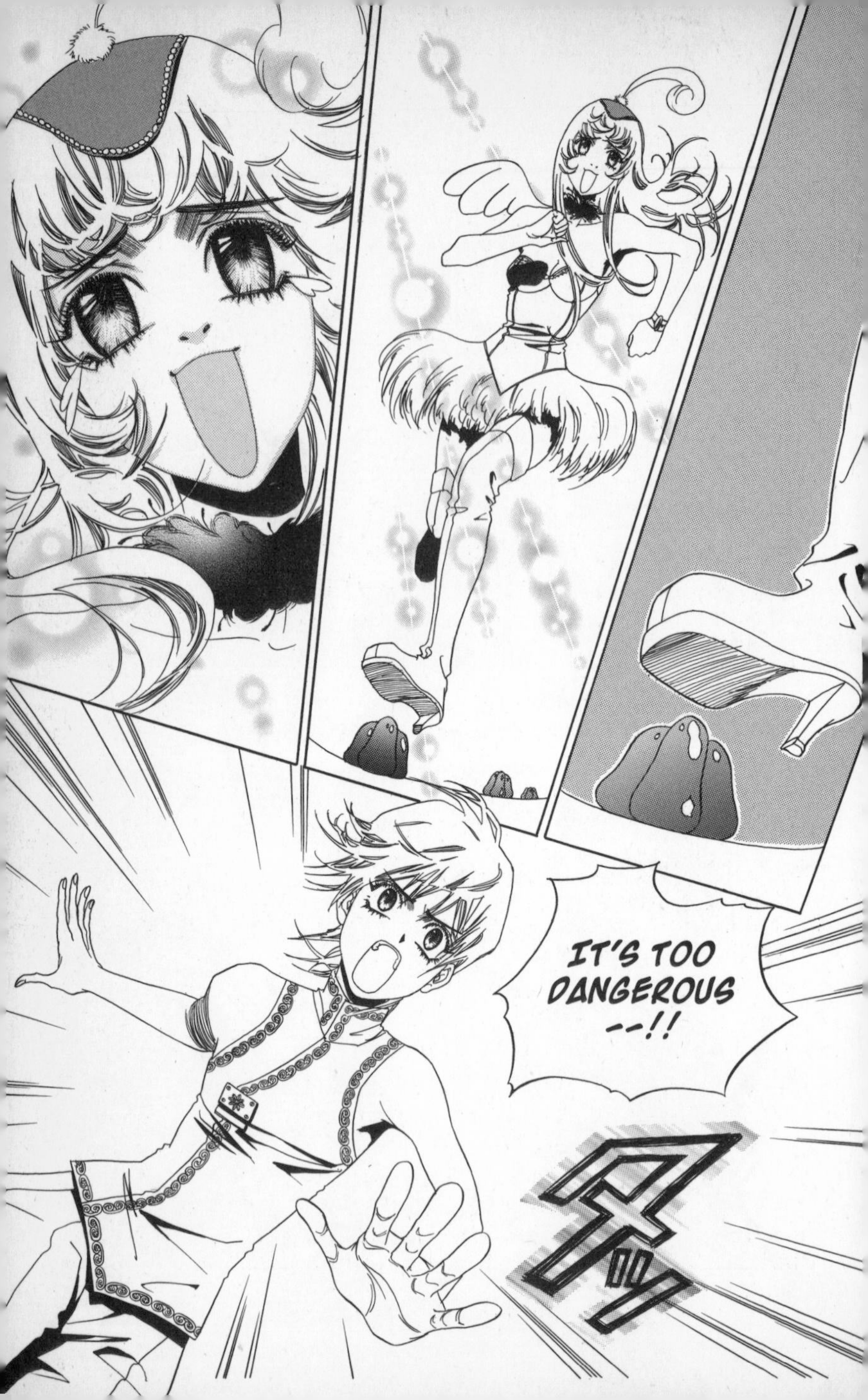
IT'S TOO DANGEROUS --!!

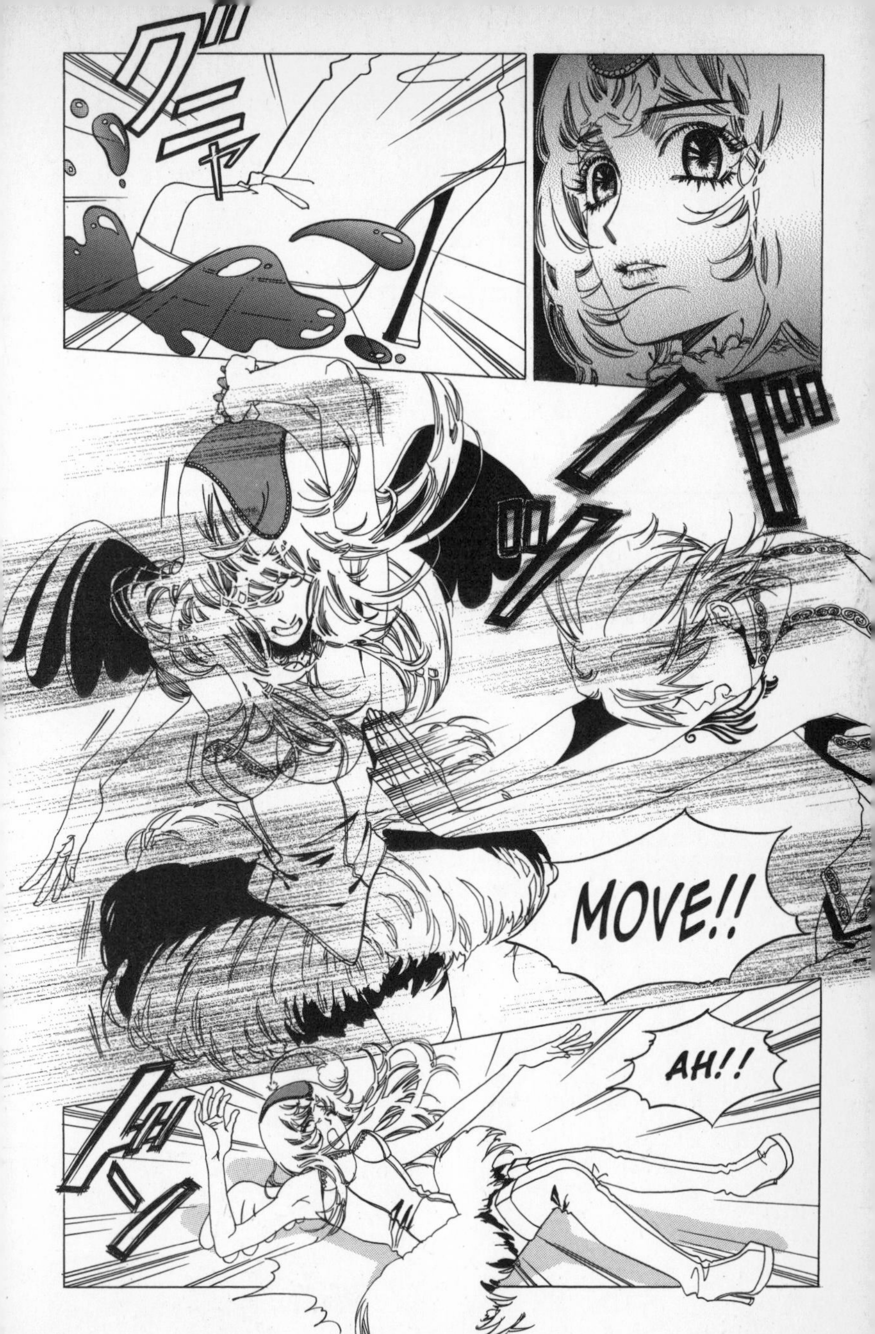
MOVE!!
AH!!

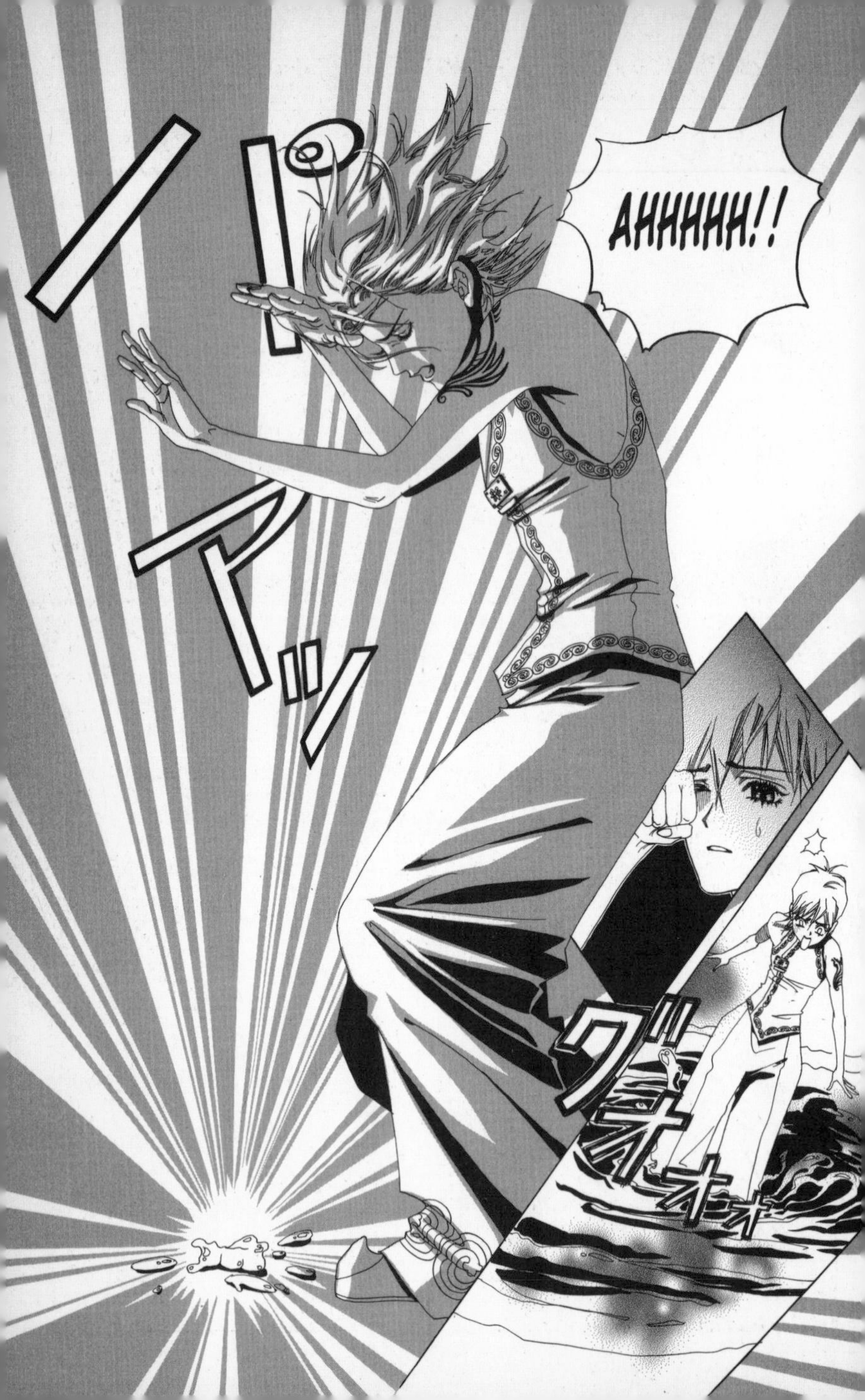
AHHHHH!!

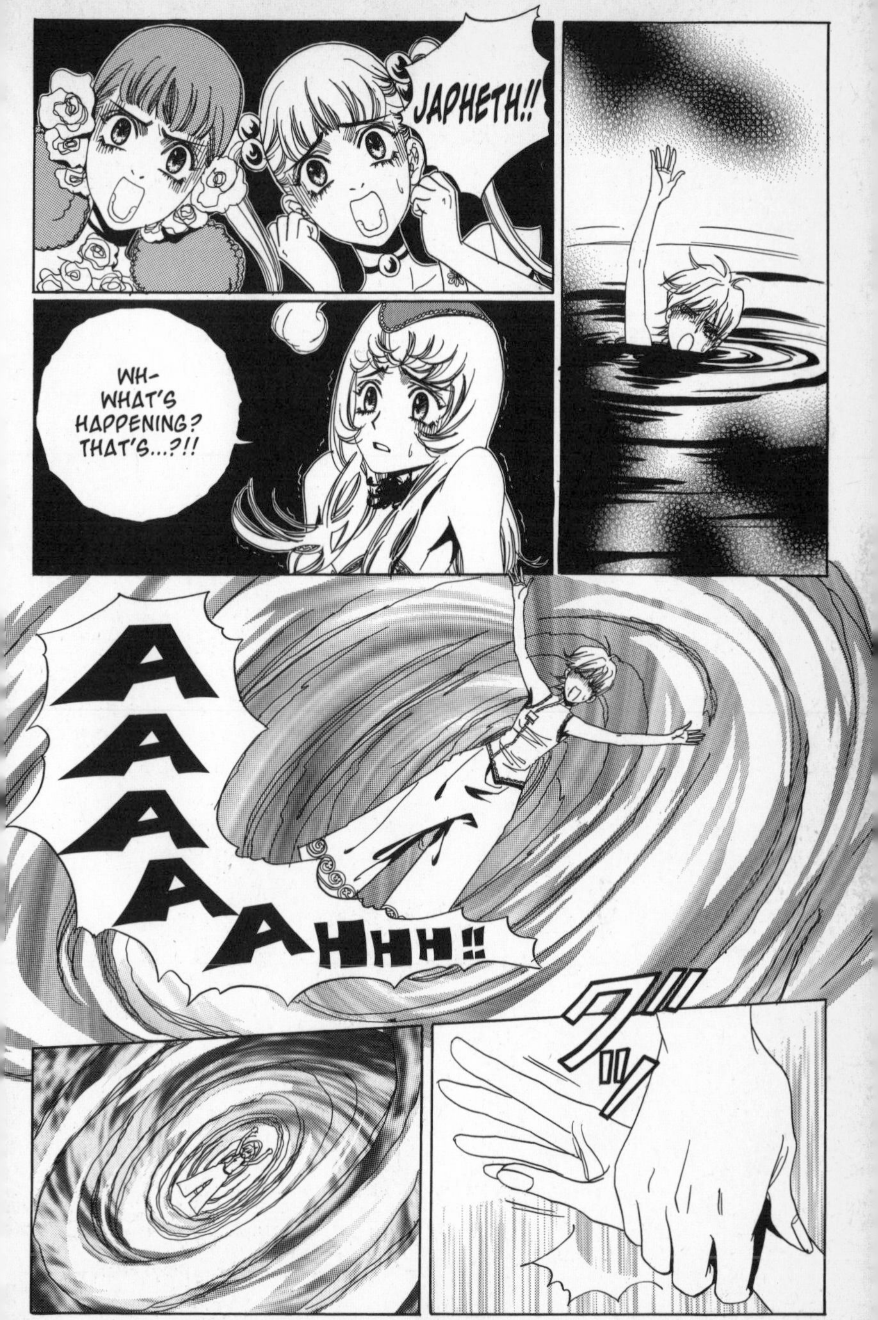
JAPHETH!!
WH- WHAT'S HAPPENING? THAT'S...?!!
AAAAAAHHH!!
ツ゛ッ

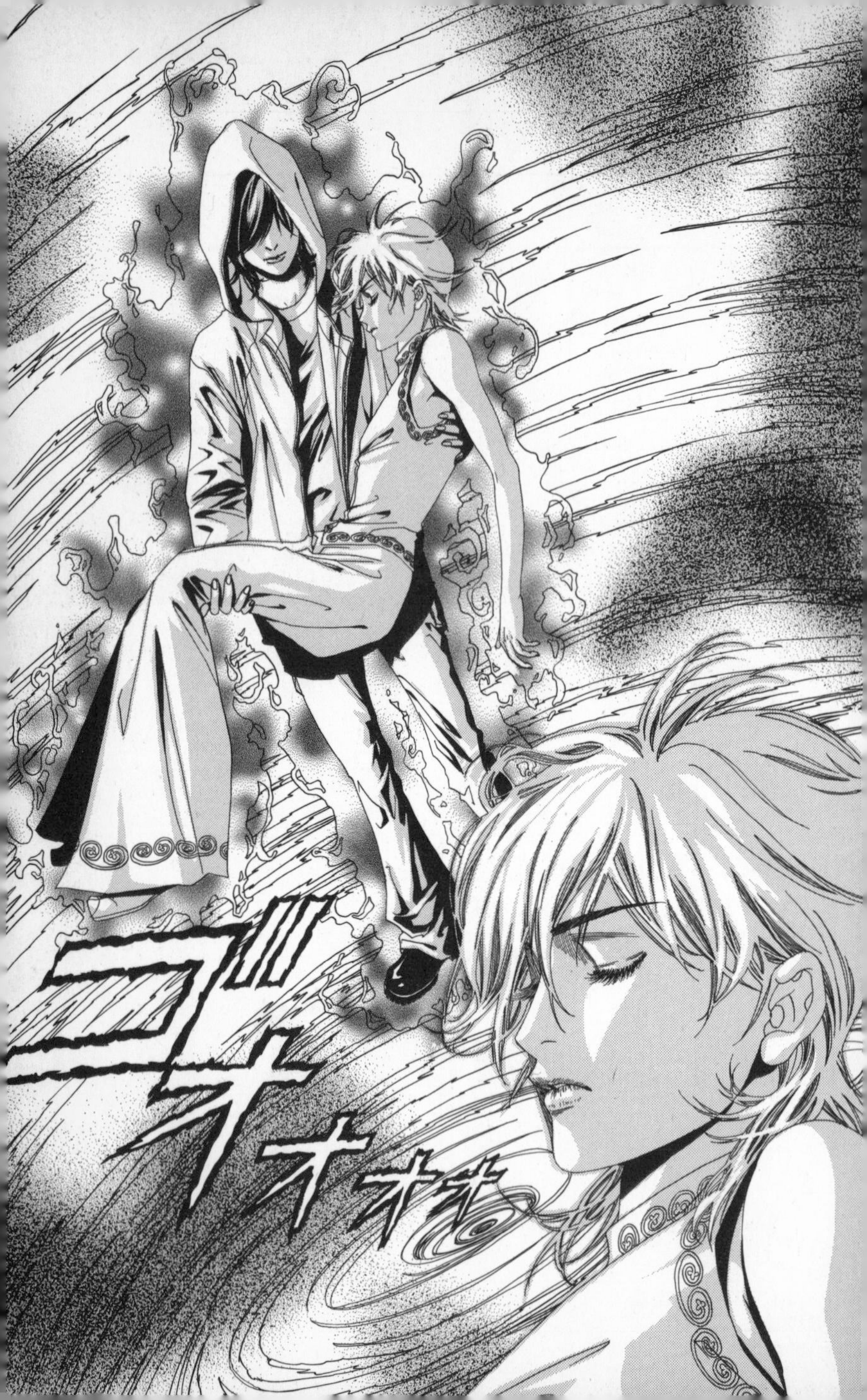
ゴオオォ

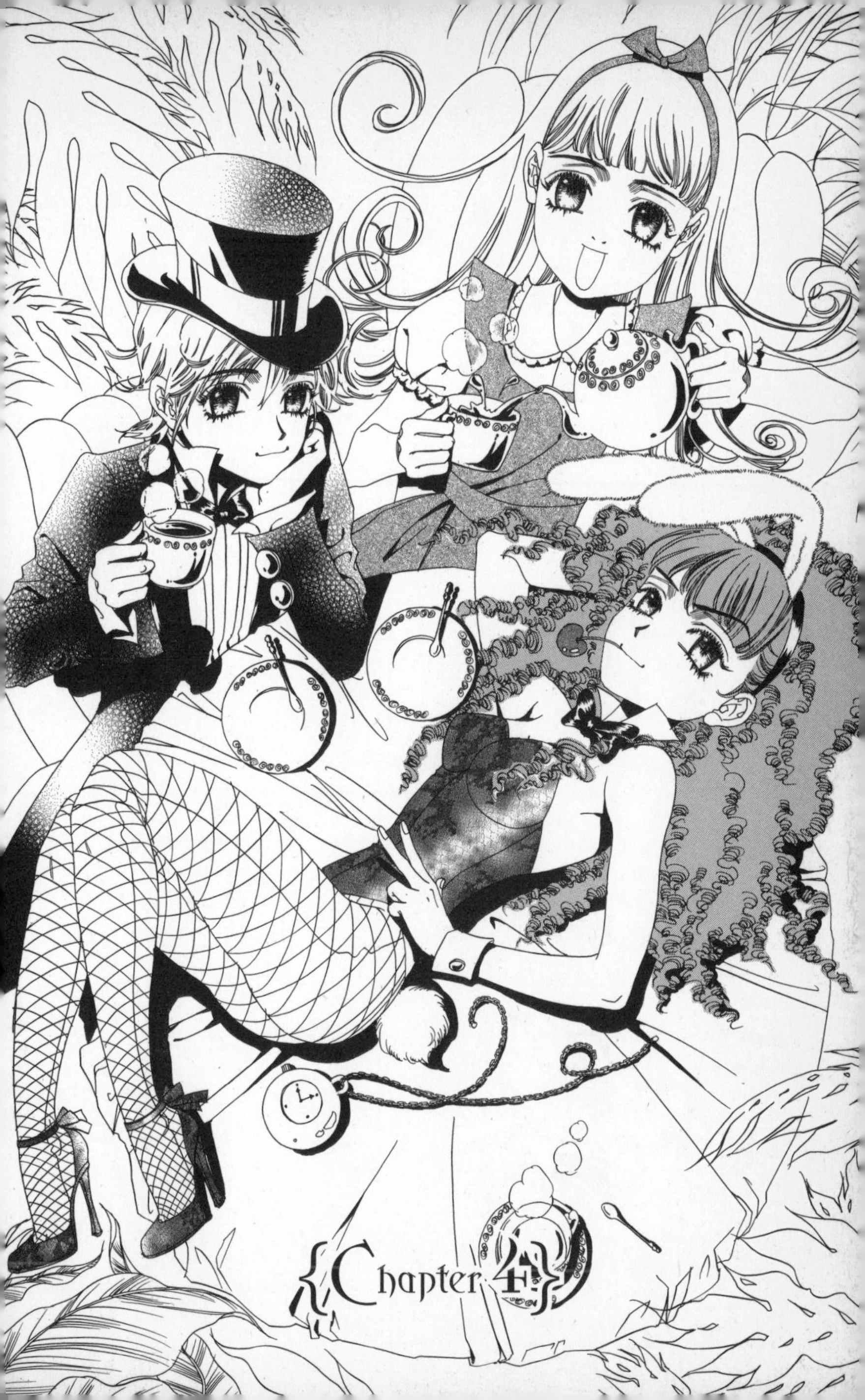
Chapter 4

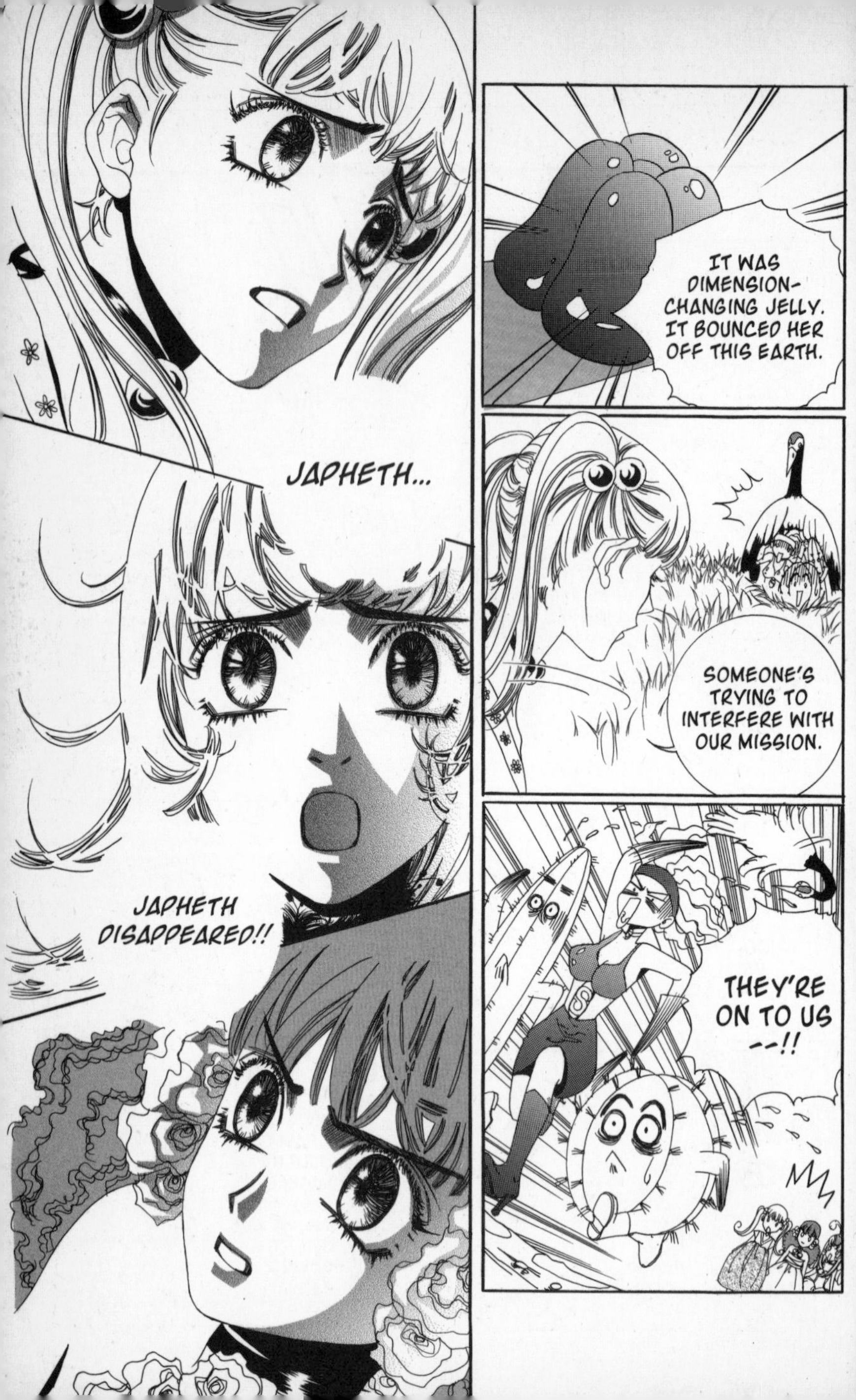
IT WAS DIMENSION-CHANGING JELLY. IT BOUNCED HER OFF THIS EARTH.
SOMEONE'S TRYING TO INTERFERE WITH OUR MISSION.
THEY'RE ON TO US --!!
JAPHETH...
JAPHETH DISAPPEARED!!

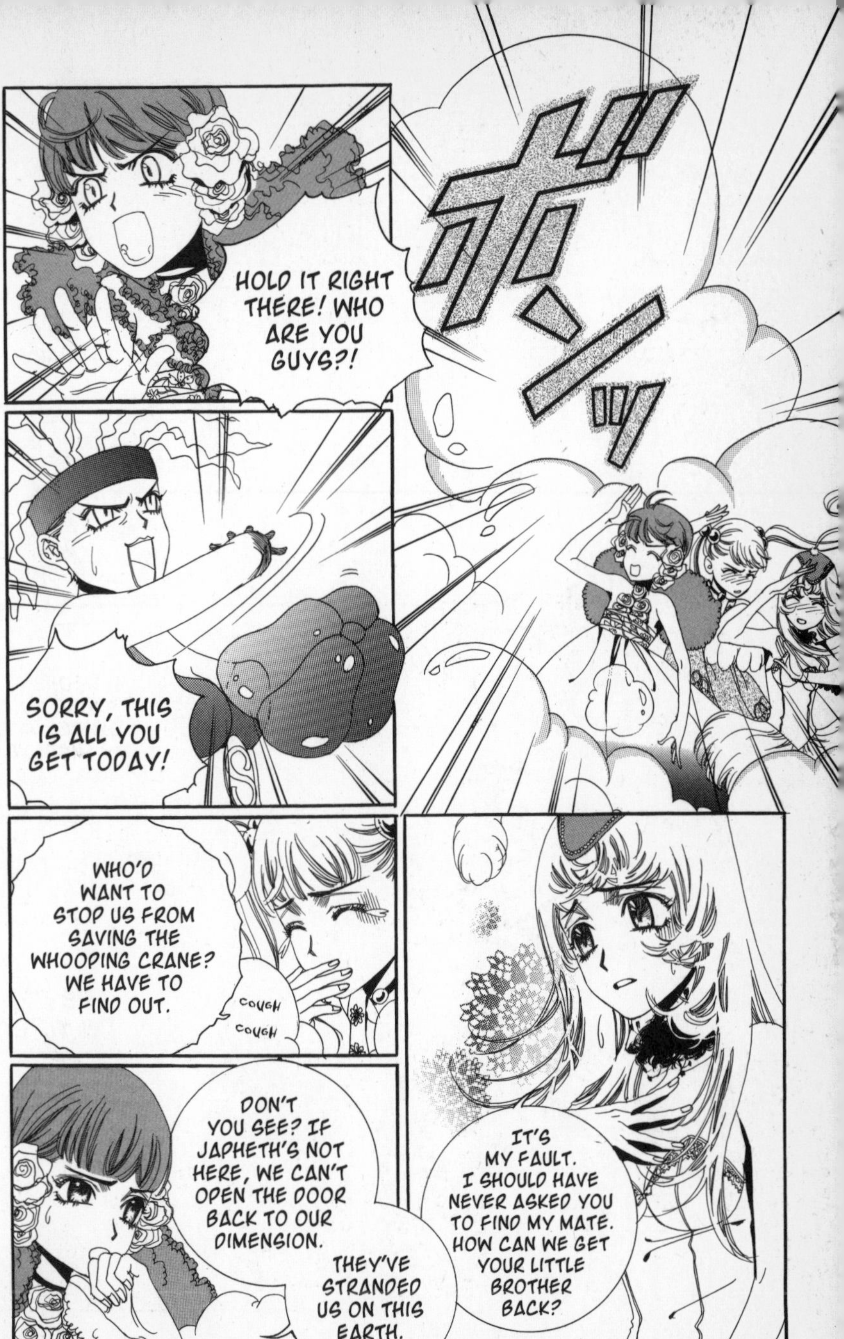
HOLD IT RIGHT THERE! WHO ARE YOU GUYS?!
SORRY, THIS IS ALL YOU GET TODAY!
ボンッ
WHO'D WANT TO STOP US FROM SAVING THE WHOOPING CRANE? WE HAVE TO FIND OUT.
COUGH
COUGH
DON'T YOU SEE? IF JAPHETH'S NOT HERE, WE CAN'T OPEN THE DOOR BACK TO OUR DIMENSION.
THEY'VE STRANDED US ON THIS EARTH.
IT'S MY FAULT. I SHOULD HAVE NEVER ASKED YOU TO FIND MY MATE. HOW CAN WE GET YOUR LITTLE BROTHER BACK?

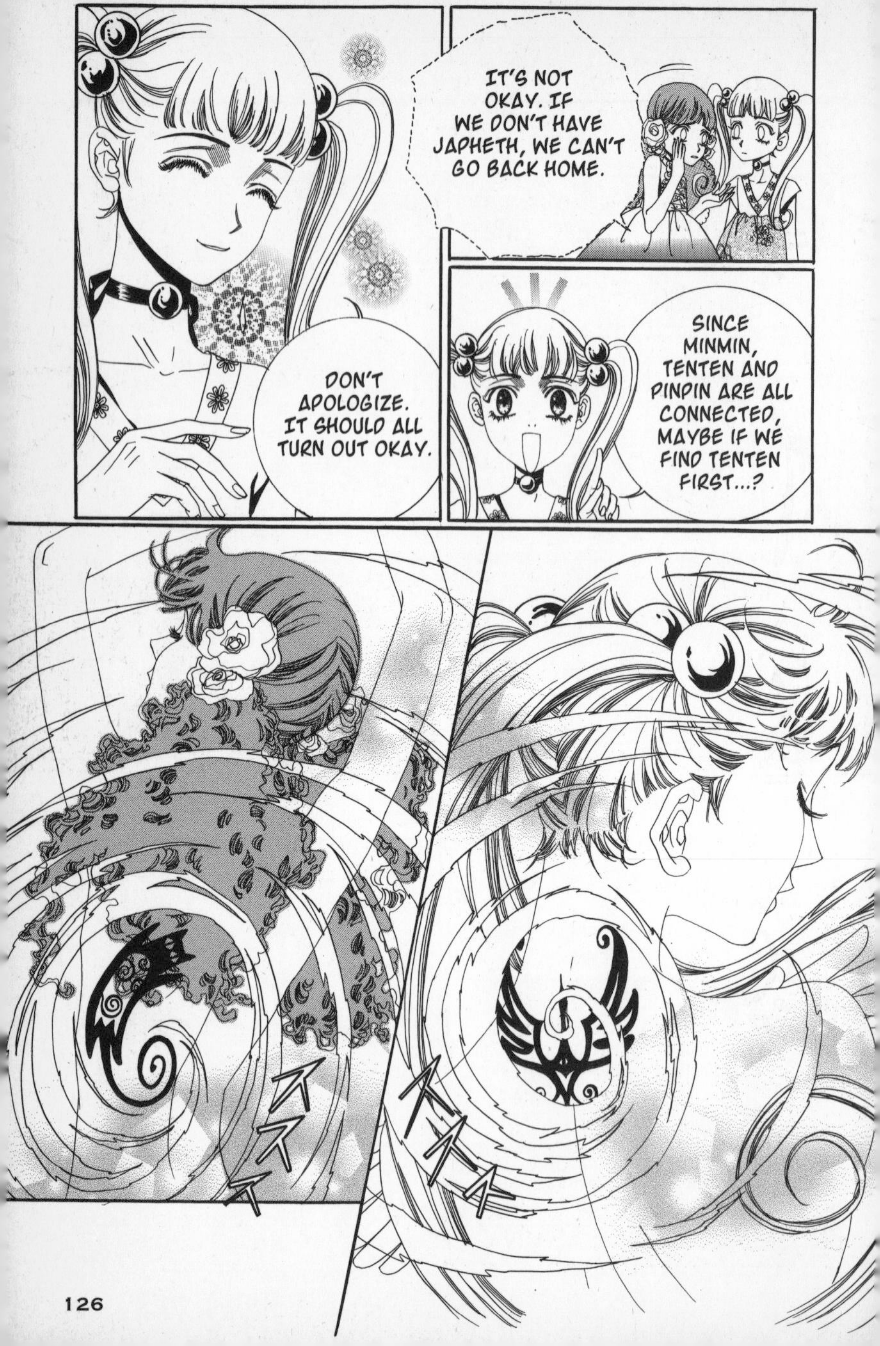
DON'T APOLOGIZE. IT SHOULD ALL TURN OUT OKAY.
IT'S NOT OKAY. IF WE DON'T HAVE JAPHETH, WE CAN'T GO BACK HOME.
SINCE MINMIN, TENTEN AND PINPIN ARE ALL CONNECTED, MAYBE IF WE FIND TENTEN FIRST...?

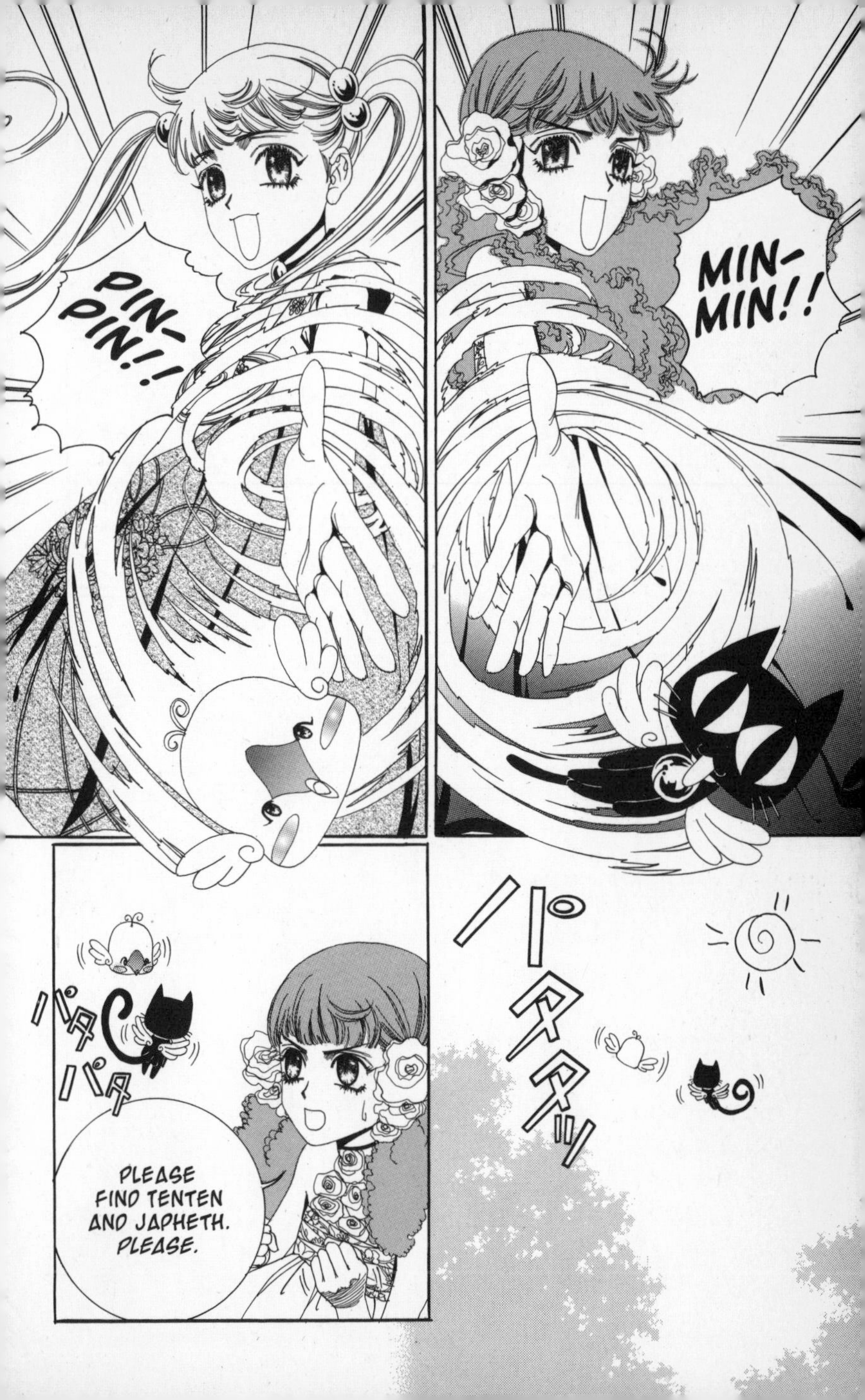
MIN-MIN!!
PIN-PIN!!
パタタッ
パタパタ
PLEASE FIND TENTEN AND JAPHETH. PLEASE.

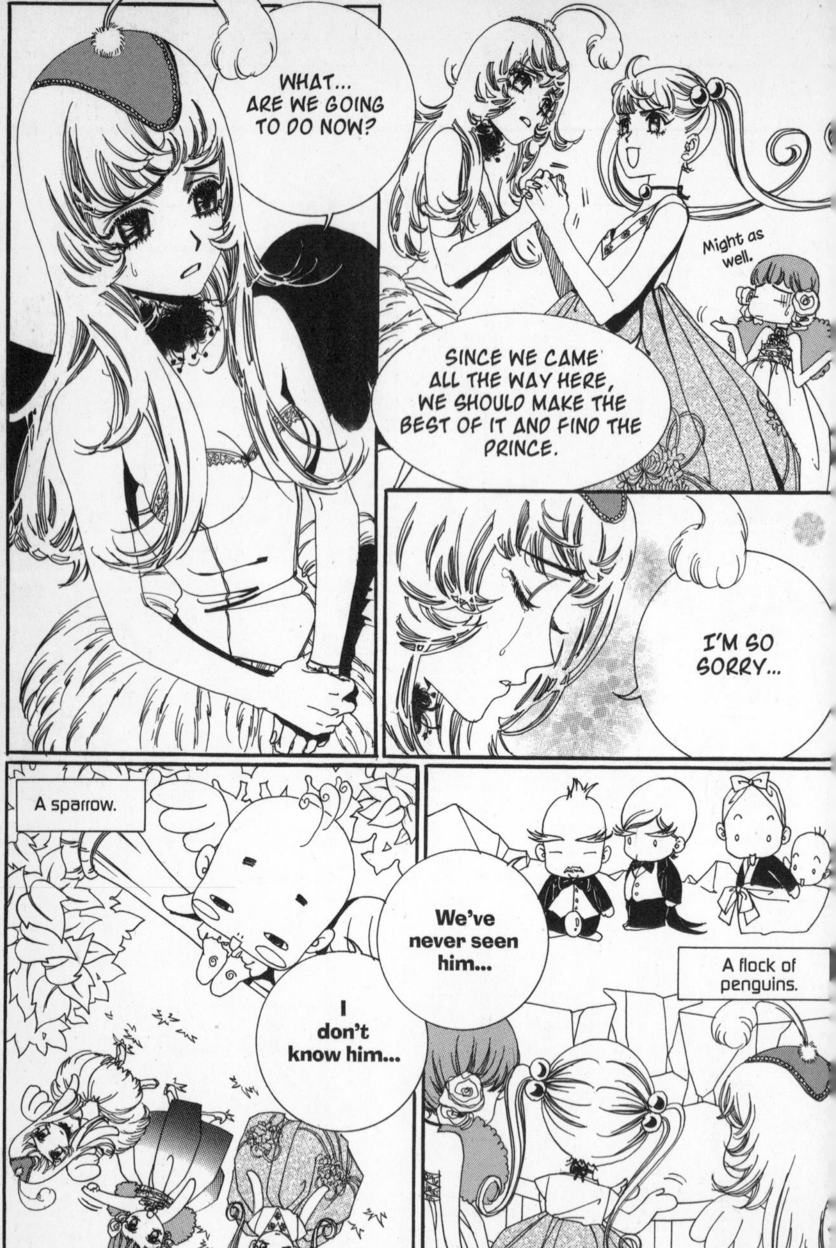
WHAT... ARE WE GOING TO DO NOW?
SINCE WE CAME ALL THE WAY HERE, WE SHOULD MAKE THE BEST OF IT AND FIND THE PRINCE.
Might as well.
I'M SO SORRY...
A sparrow.
I don't know him...
We've never seen him...
A flock of penguins.

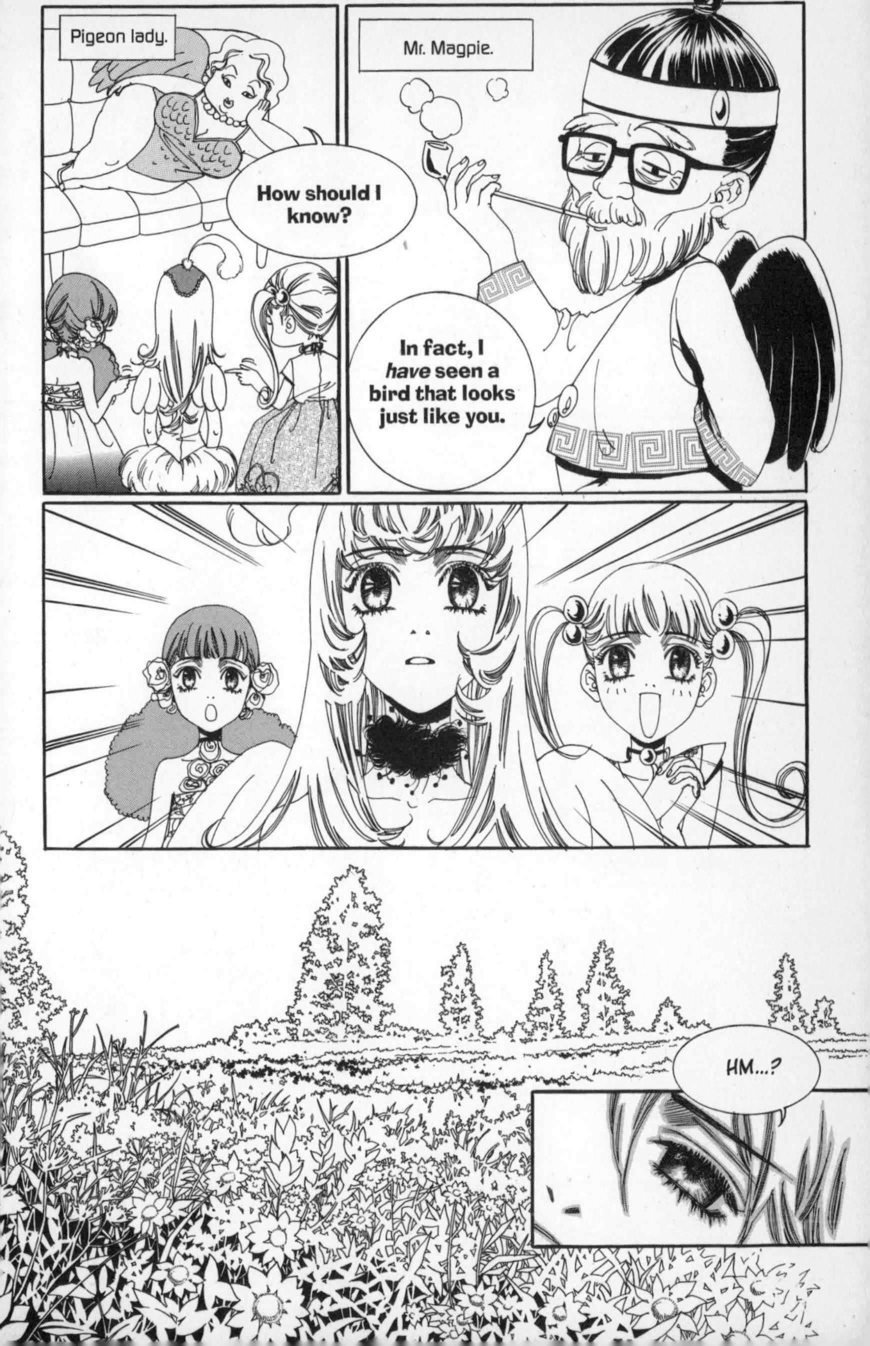
Pigeon lady.
How should I know?
Mr. Magpie.
In fact, I *have* seen a bird that looks just like you.
HM...?

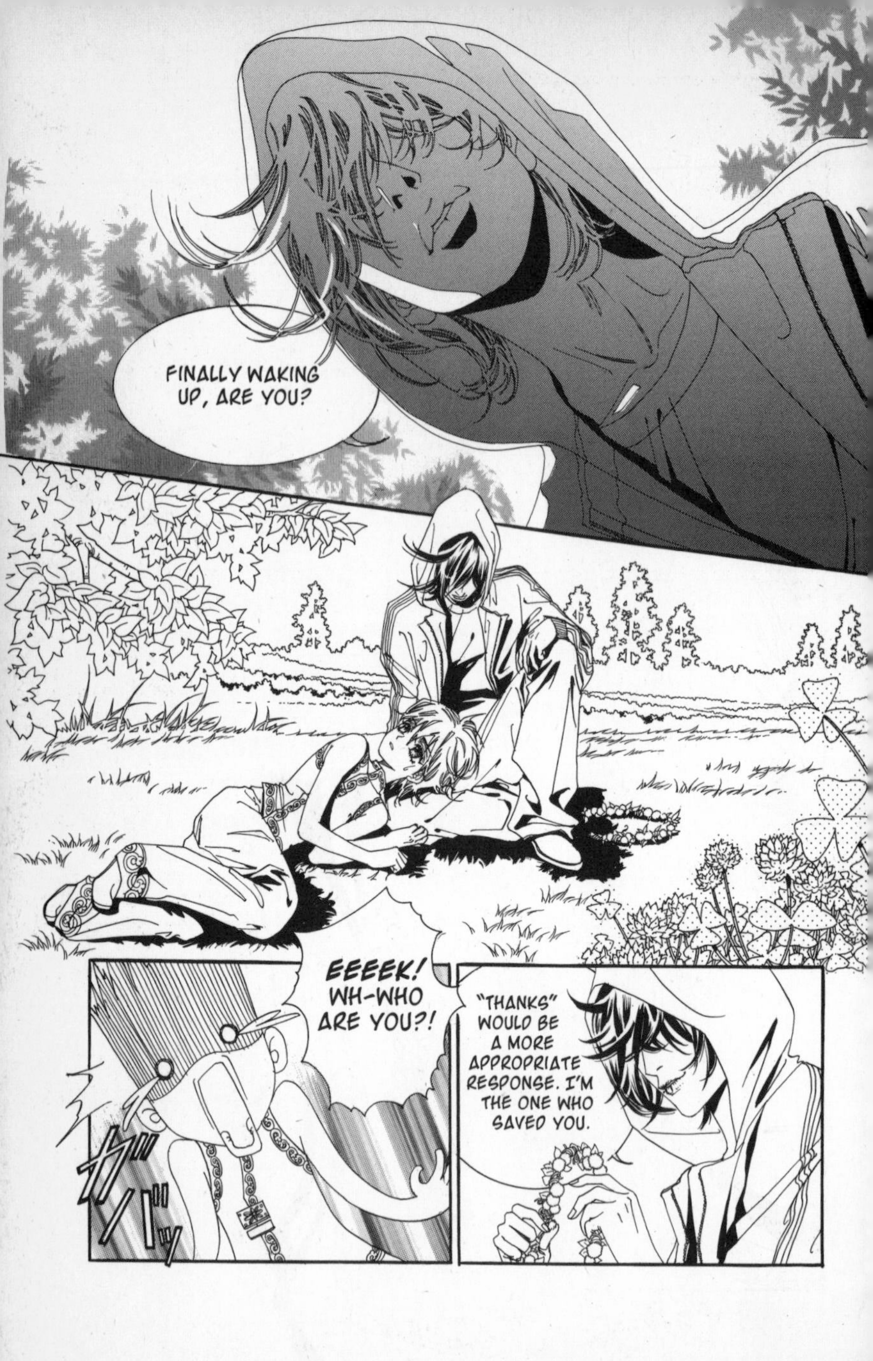
FINALLY WAKING UP, ARE YOU?
EEEEK! WH-WHO ARE YOU?!
ガバッ
"THANKS" WOULD BE A MORE APPROPRIATE RESPONSE. I'M THE ONE WHO SAVED YOU.

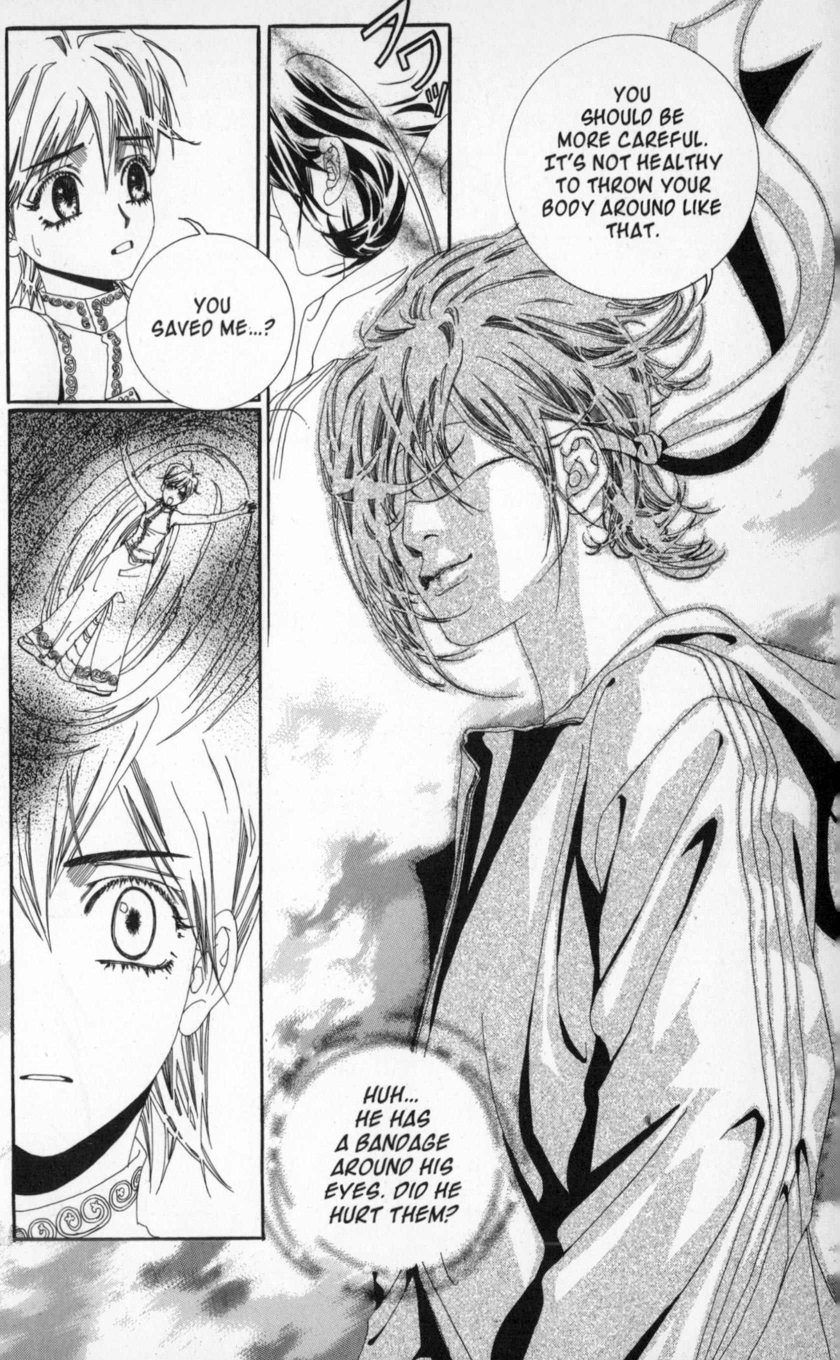
YOU SHOULD BE MORE CAREFUL. IT'S NOT HEALTHY TO THROW YOUR BODY AROUND LIKE THAT.
YOU SAVED ME...?
HUH... HE HAS A BANDAGE AROUND HIS EYES. DID HE HURT THEM?

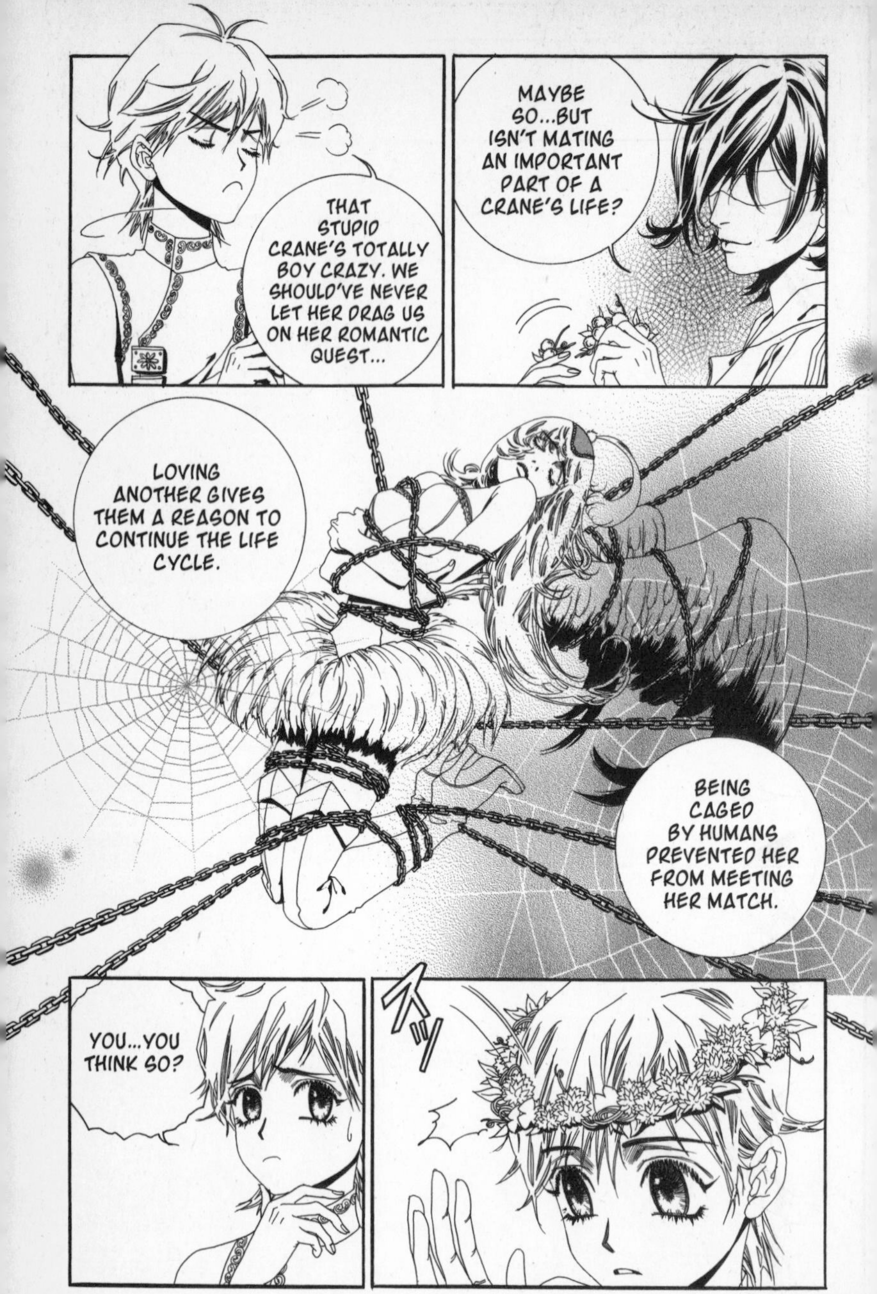
THAT STUPID CRANE'S TOTALLY BOY CRAZY. WE SHOULD'VE NEVER LET HER DRAG US ON HER ROMANTIC QUEST...
MAYBE SO...BUT ISN'T MATING AN IMPORTANT PART OF A CRANE'S LIFE?
LOVING ANOTHER GIVES THEM A REASON TO CONTINUE THE LIFE CYCLE.
BEING CAGED BY HUMANS PREVENTED HER FROM MEETING HER MATCH.
YOU...YOU THINK SO?

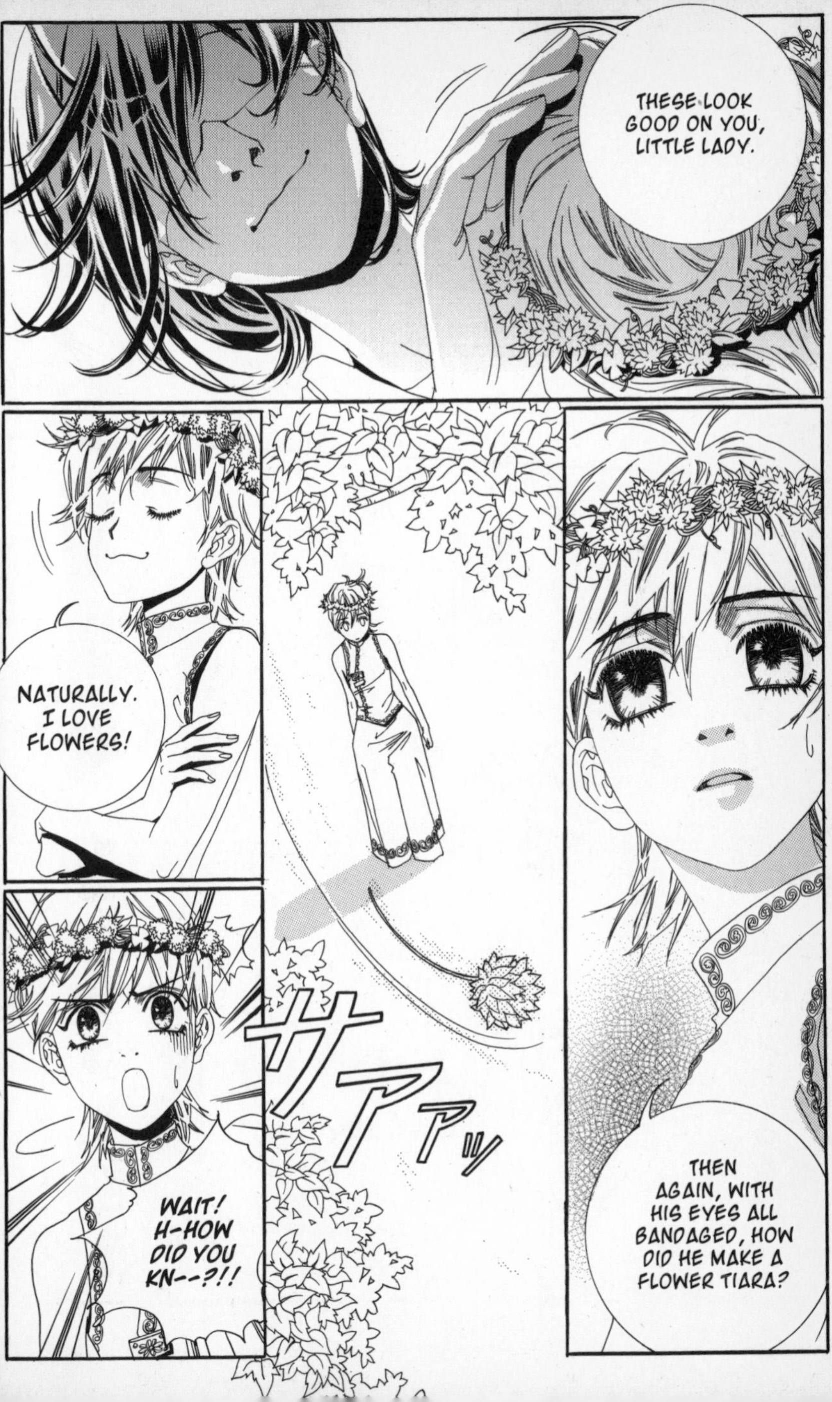
THESE LOOK GOOD ON YOU, LITTLE LADY.
NATURALLY. I LOVE FLOWERS!
WAIT! H-HOW DID YOU KN--?!!
サアァッ
THEN AGAIN, WITH HIS EYES ALL BANDAGED, HOW DID HE MAKE A FLOWER TIARA?

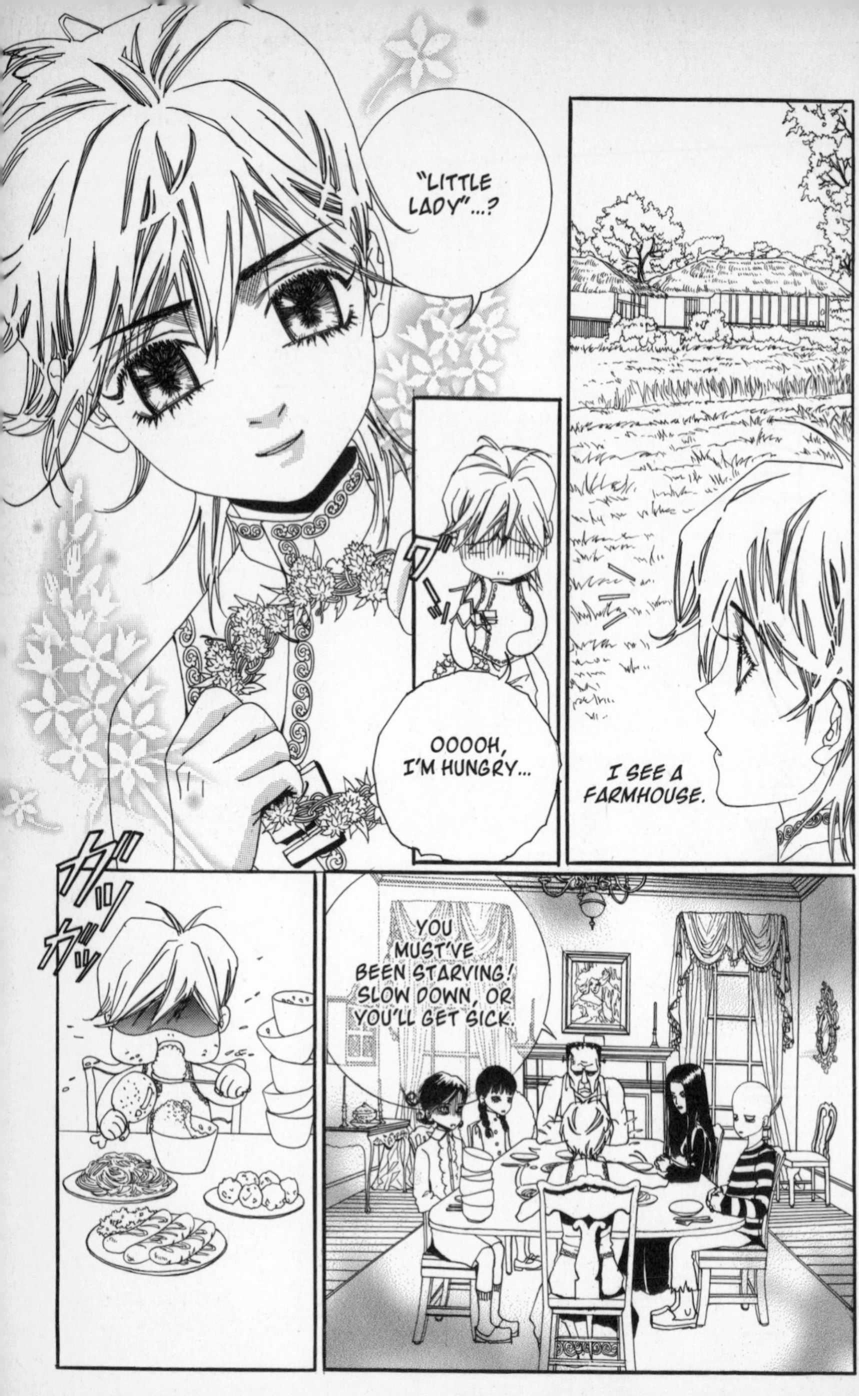
"LITTLE LADY"...?
I SEE A FARMHOUSE.
OOOOH, I'M HUNGRY...
YOU MUST'VE BEEN STARVING! SLOW DOWN, OR YOU'LL GET SICK.

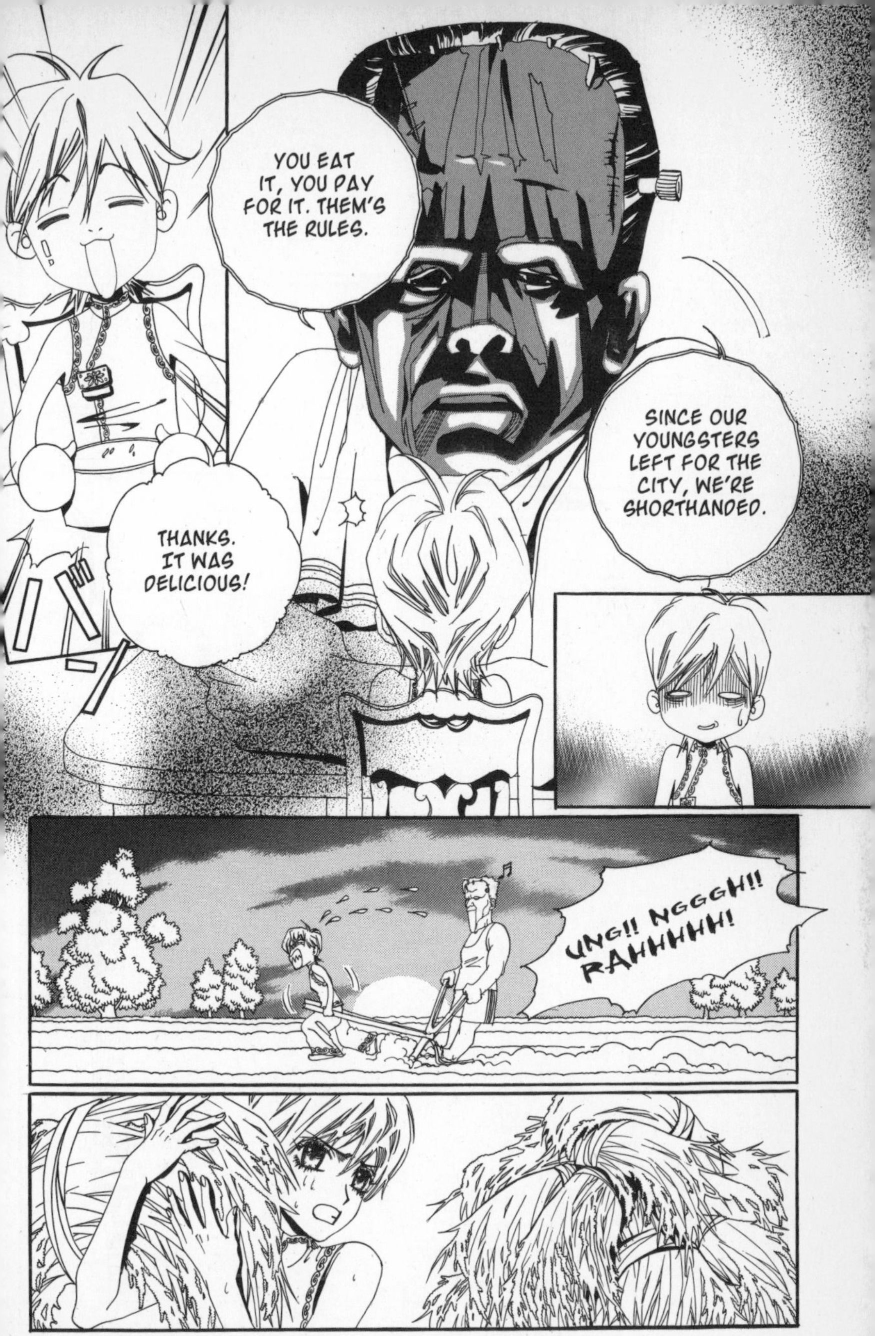
YOU EAT IT, YOU PAY FOR IT. THEM'S THE RULES.
THANKS. IT WAS DELICIOUS!
SINCE OUR YOUNGSTERS LEFT FOR THE CITY, WE'RE SHORTHANDED.
UNG!! NGGGH!! RAHHHHHH!

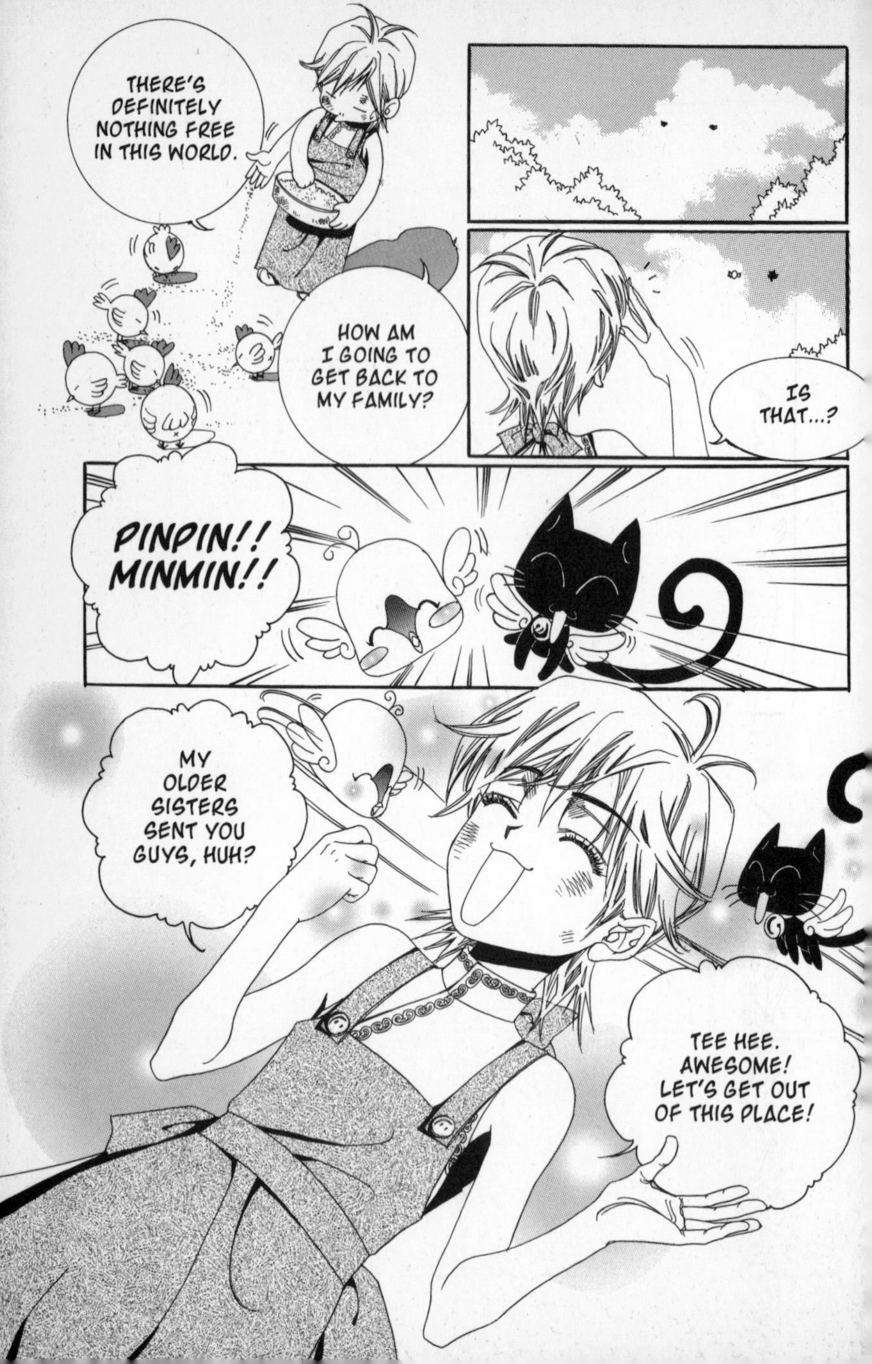
THERE'S DEFINITELY NOTHING FREE IN THIS WORLD.
HOW AM I GOING TO GET BACK TO MY FAMILY?
IS THAT...?
PINPIN!! MINMIN!!
MY OLDER SISTERS SENT YOU GUYS, HUH?
TEE HEE. AWESOME! LET'S GET OUT OF THIS PLACE!

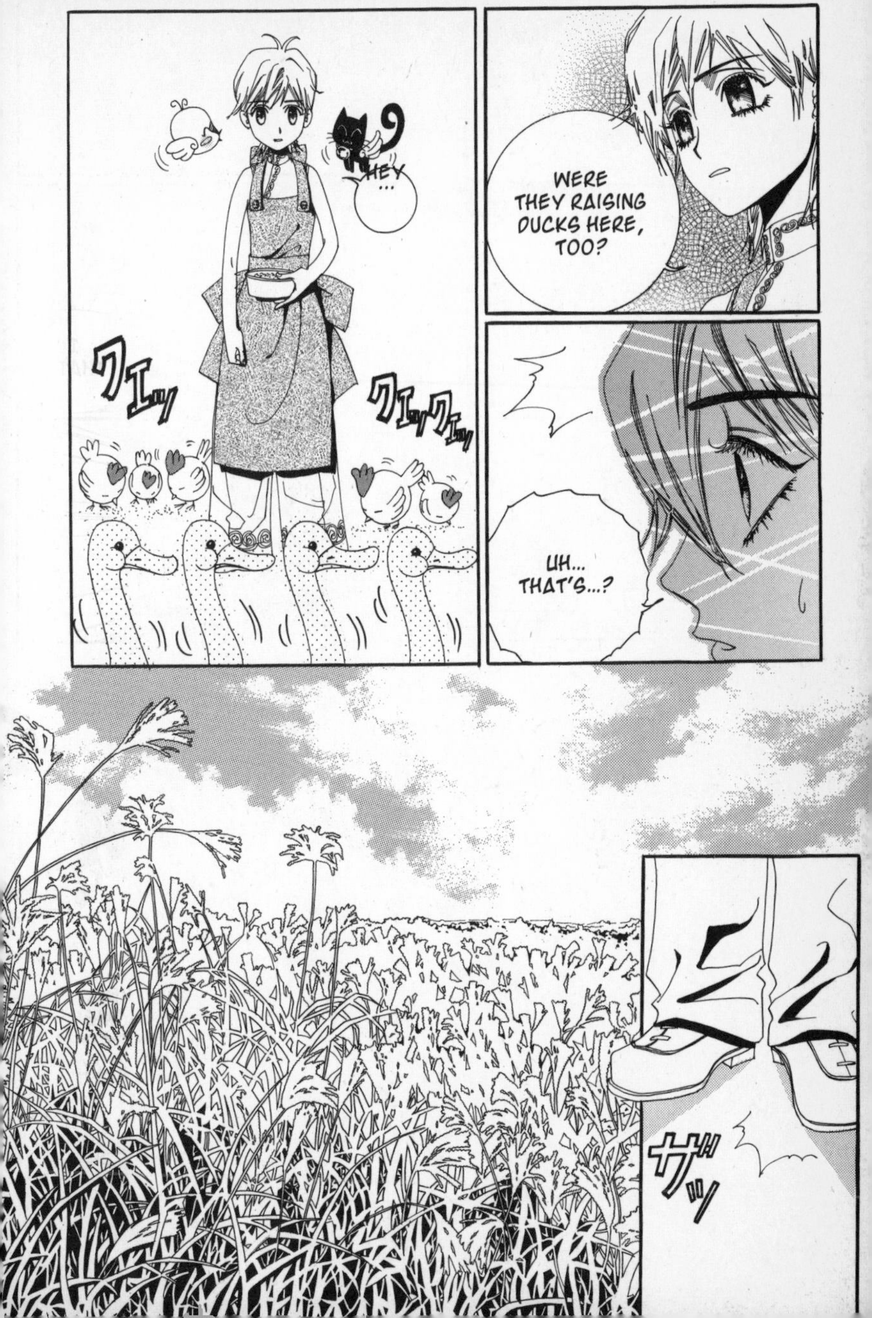
WERE THEY RAISING DUCKS HERE, TOO?
UH... THAT'S...?
HEY ...
クエッ
クエックエッ
ザッ

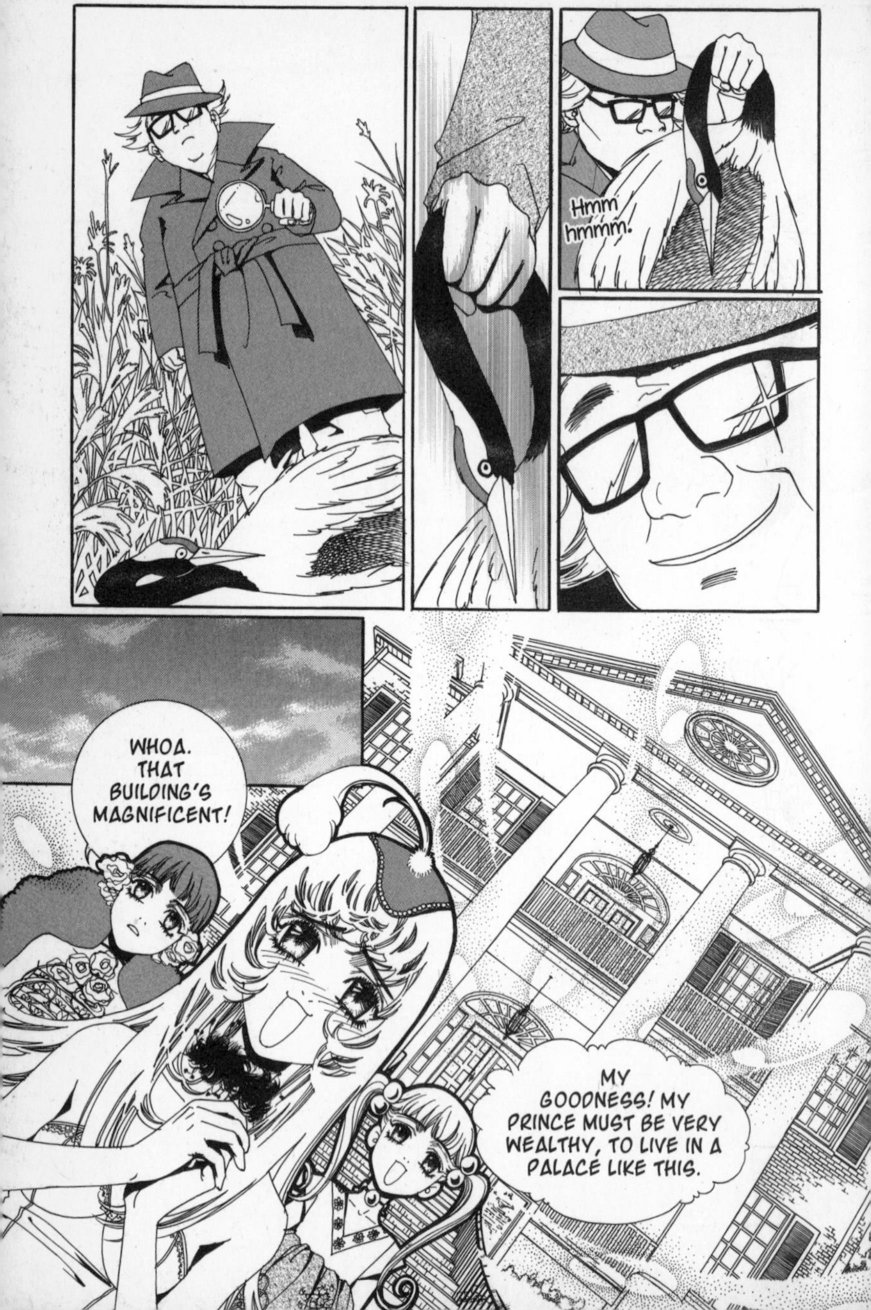
Hmm hmmm.
WHOA. THAT BUILDING'S MAGNIFICENT!
MY GOODNESS! MY PRINCE MUST BE VERY WEALTHY, TO LIVE IN A PALACE LIKE THIS.

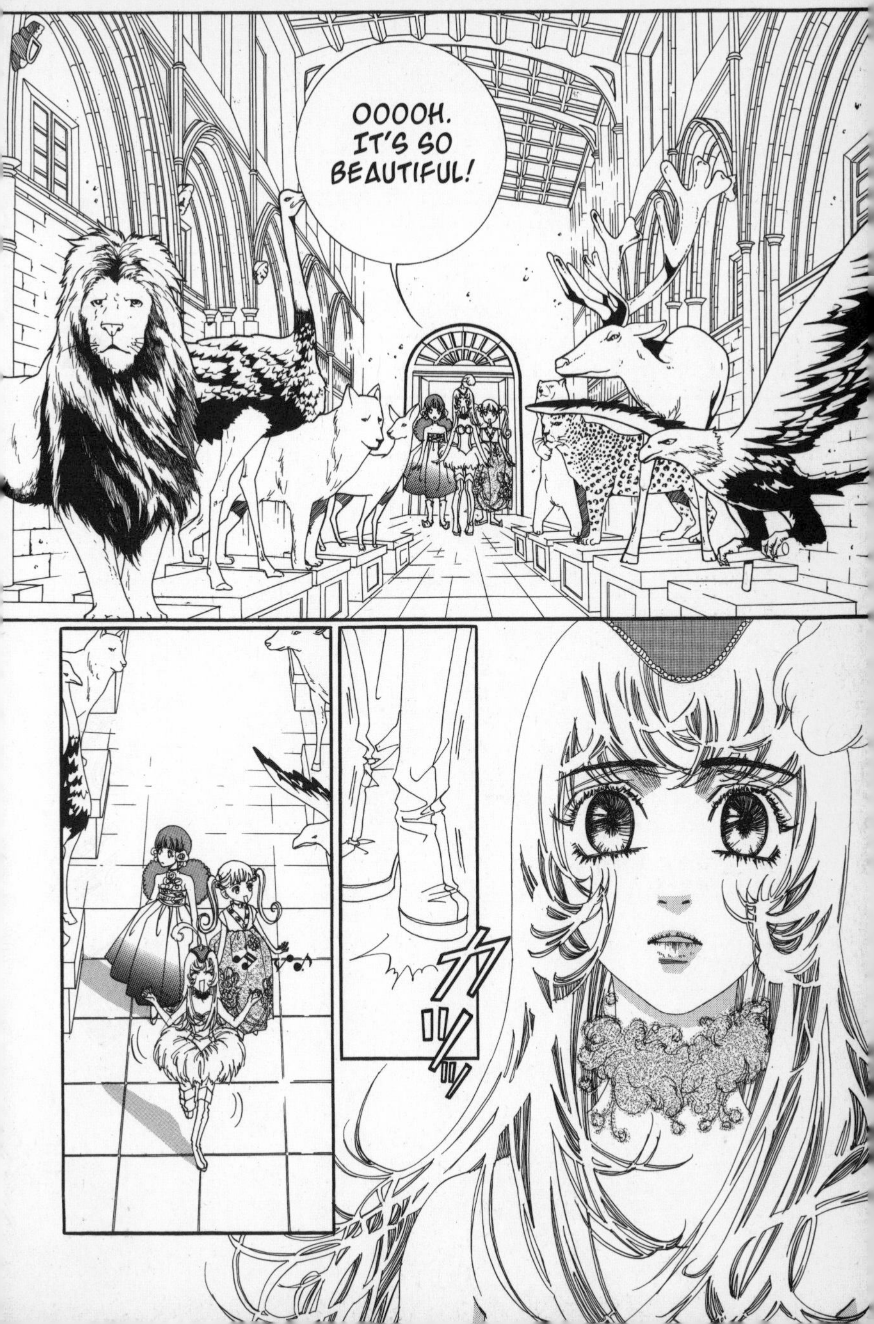
OOOOH. IT'S SO BEAUTIFUL!

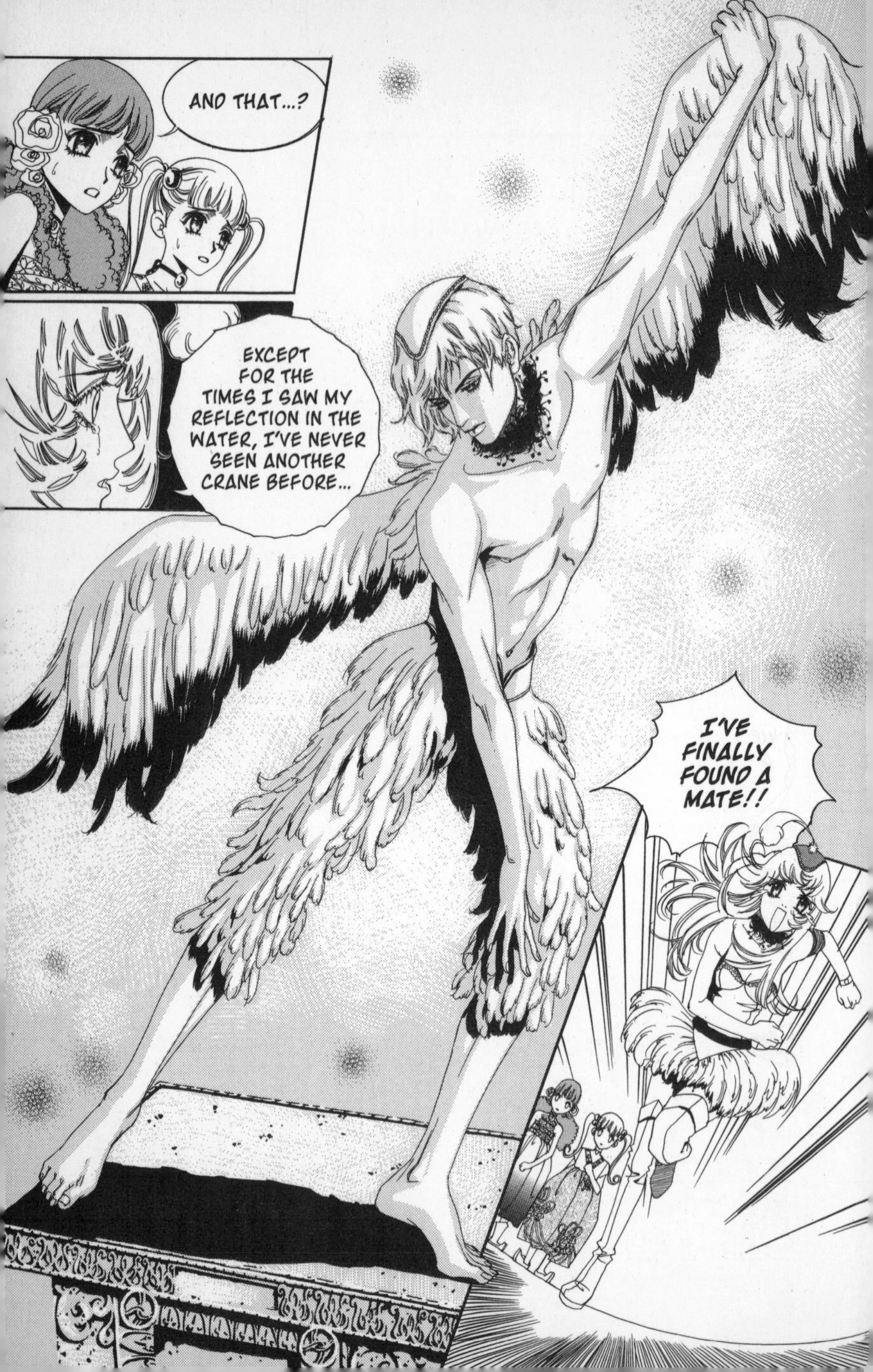
AND THAT...?
EXCEPT FOR THE TIMES I SAW MY REFLECTION IN THE WATER, I'VE NEVER SEEN ANOTHER CRANE BEFORE...
I'VE FINALLY FOUND A MATE!!

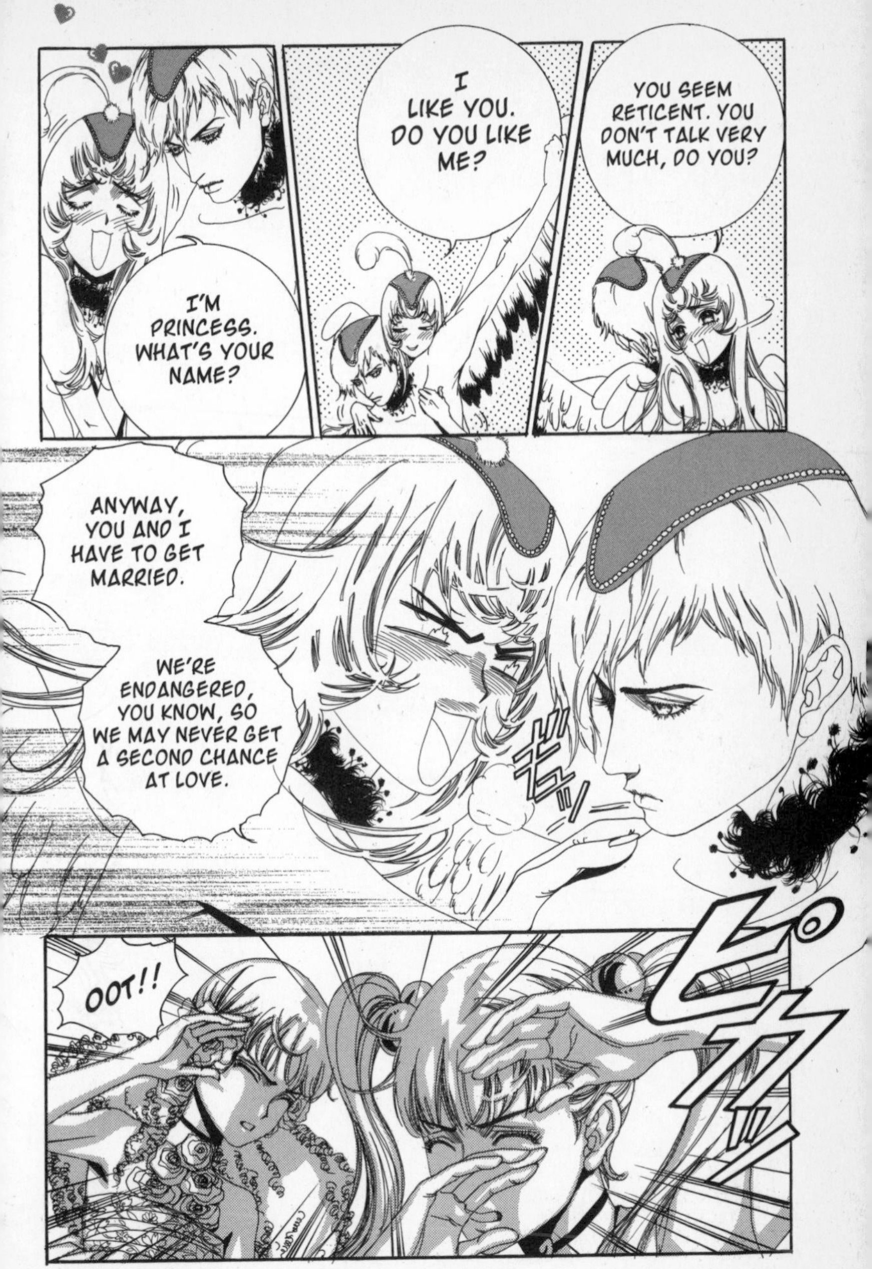
I'M PRINCESS. WHAT'S YOUR NAME?
I LIKE YOU. DO YOU LIKE ME?
YOU SEEM RETICENT. YOU DON'T TALK VERY MUCH, DO YOU?
ANYWAY, YOU AND I HAVE TO GET MARRIED.
WE'RE ENDANGERED, YOU KNOW, SO WE MAY NEVER GET A SECOND CHANCE AT LOVE.
ぎゅッ
ピタッ
OOT!!

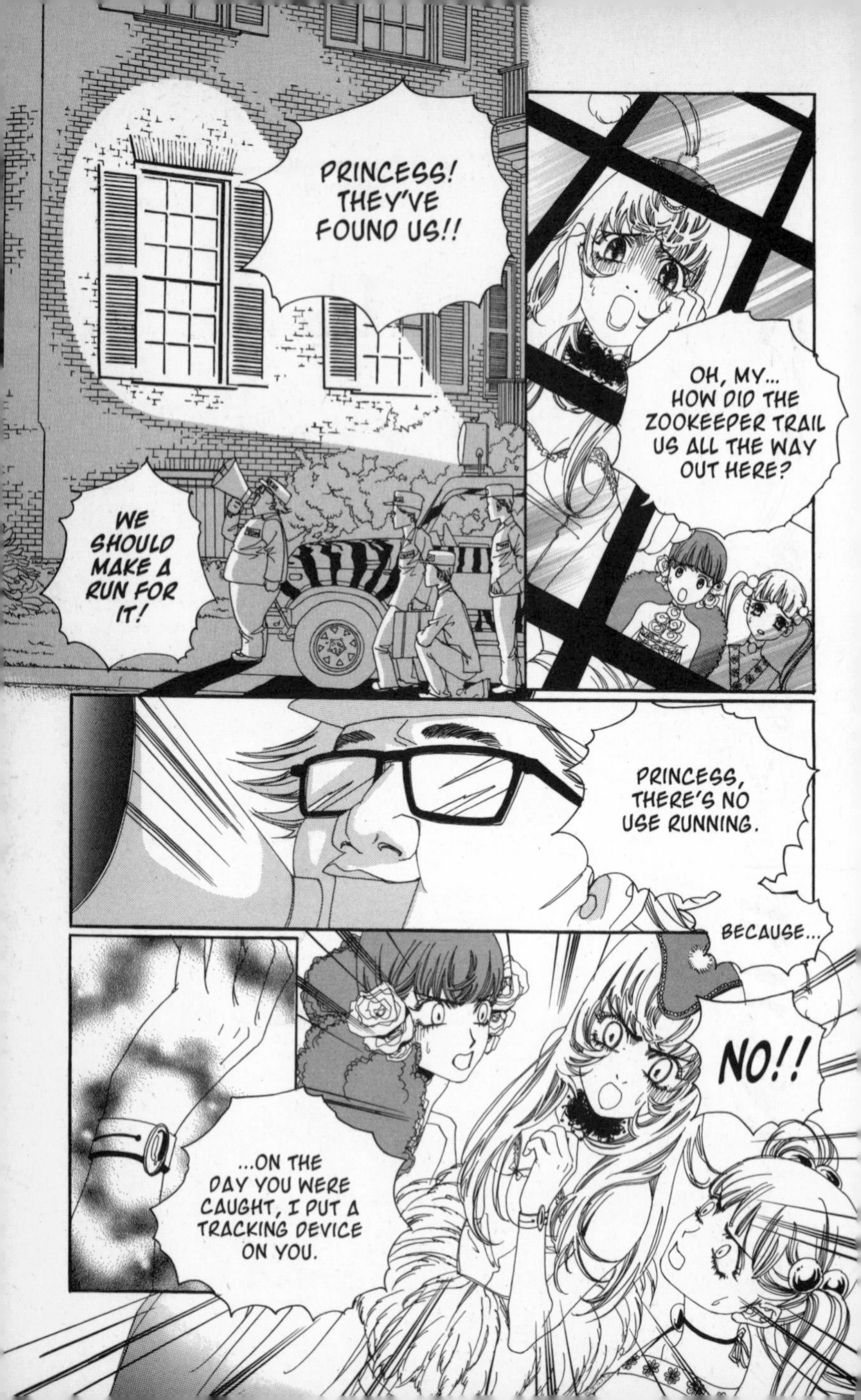
PRINCESS! THEY'VE FOUND US!!
OH, MY... HOW DID THE ZOOKEEPER TRAIL US ALL THE WAY OUT HERE?
WE SHOULD MAKE A RUN FOR IT!
PRINCESS, THERE'S NO USE RUNNING.
BECAUSE...
...ON THE DAY YOU WERE CAUGHT, I PUT A TRACKING DEVICE ON YOU.
NO!!

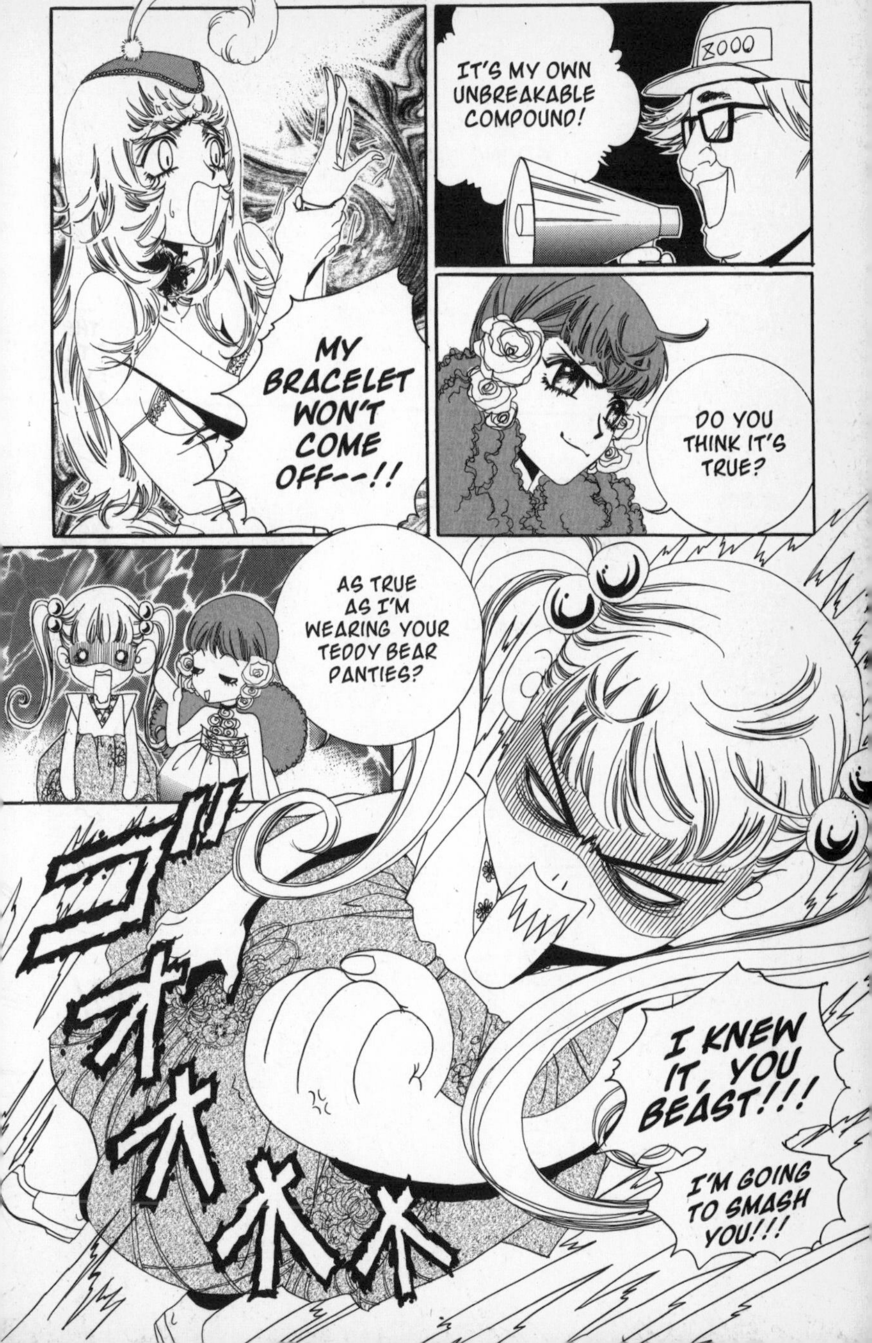
IT'S MY OWN UNBREAKABLE COMPOUND!
DO YOU THINK IT'S TRUE?
MY BRACELET WON'T COME OFF--!!
AS TRUE AS I'M WEARING YOUR TEDDY BEAR PANTIES?
I KNEW IT, YOU BEAST!!!
I'M GOING TO SMASH YOU!!!
ゴオオオ

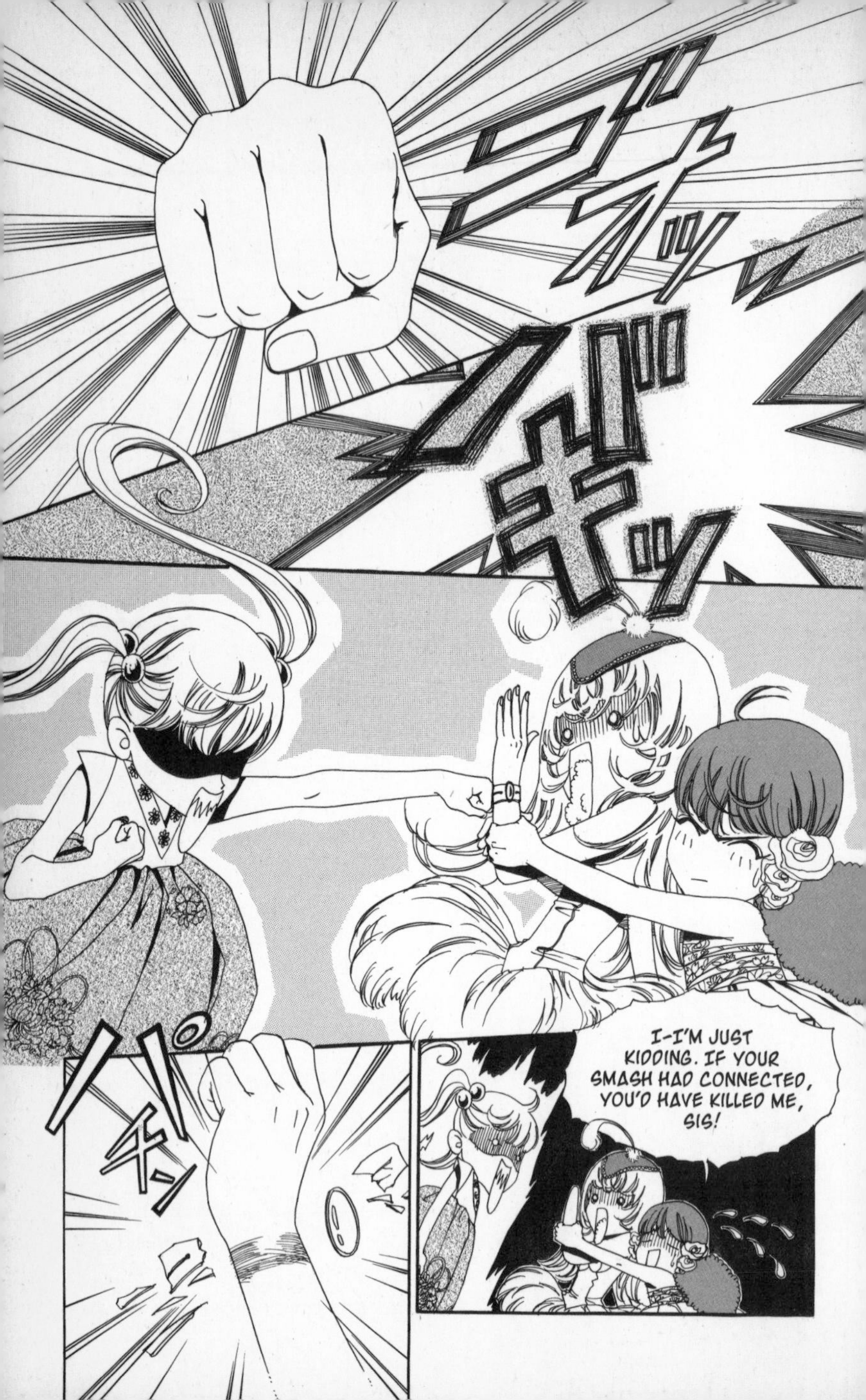
I-I'M JUST KIDDING. IF YOUR SMASH HAD CONNECTED, YOU'D HAVE KILLED ME, SIS!

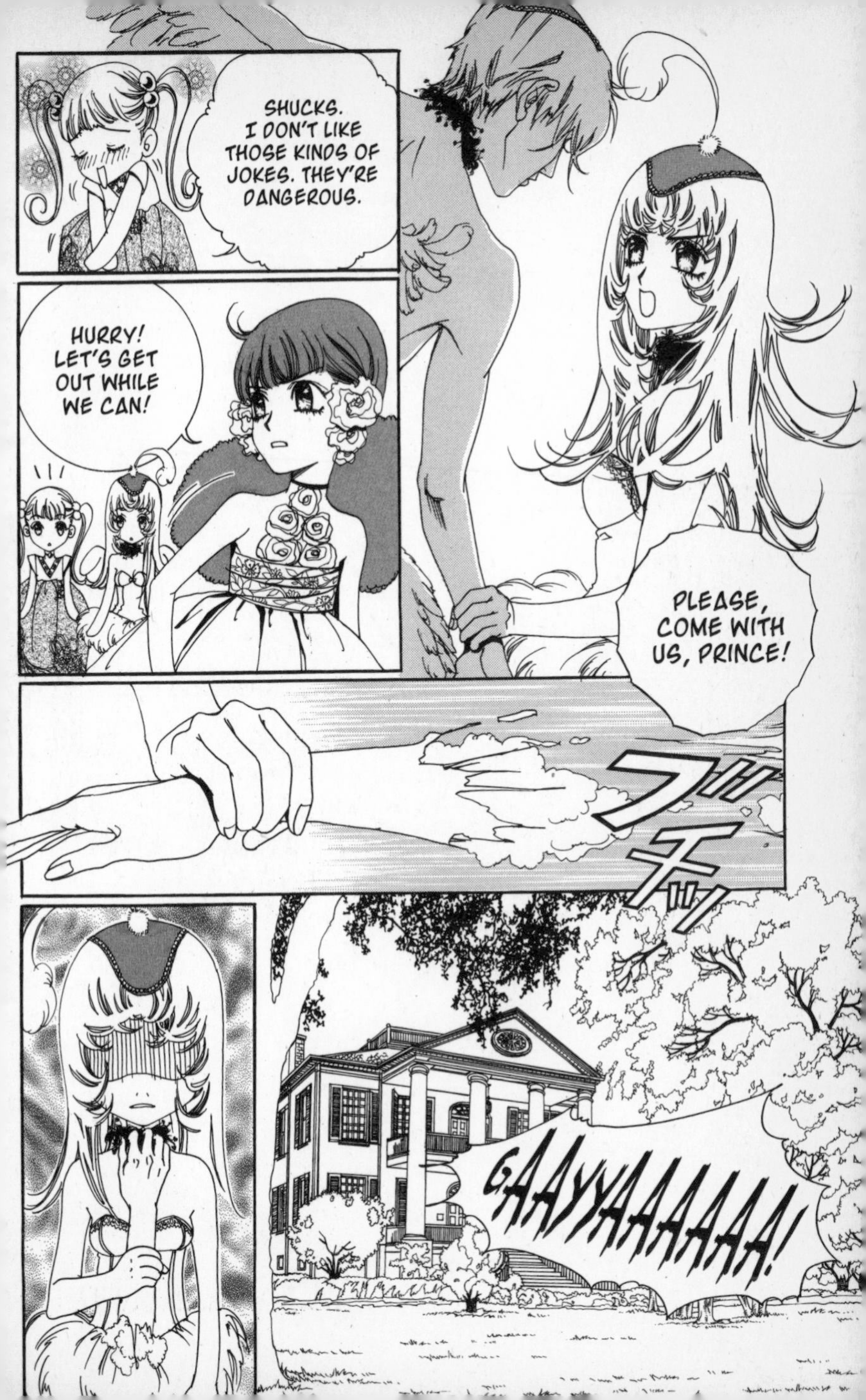
SHUCKS. I DON'T LIKE THOSE KINDS OF JOKES. THEY'RE DANGEROUS.
HURRY! LET'S GET OUT WHILE WE CAN!
PLEASE, COME WITH US, PRINCE!
ブチッ
GAAYYAAAAAA!

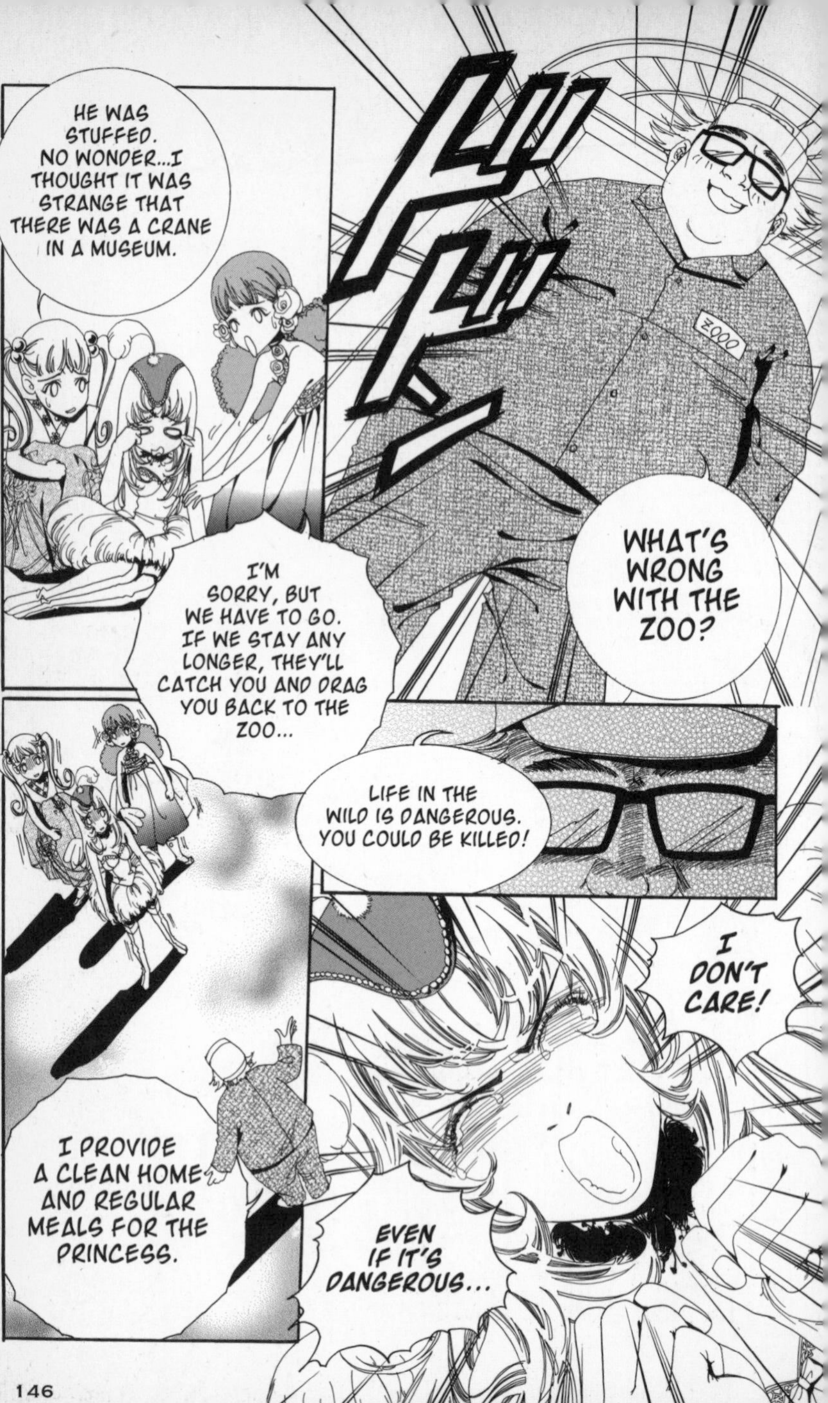
HE WAS STUFFED. NO WONDER...I THOUGHT IT WAS STRANGE THAT THERE WAS A CRANE IN A MUSEUM.
I'M SORRY, BUT WE HAVE TO GO. IF WE STAY ANY LONGER, THEY'LL CATCH YOU AND DRAG YOU BACK TO THE ZOO...
WHAT'S WRONG WITH THE ZOO?
ZOO
LIFE IN THE WILD IS DANGEROUS. YOU COULD BE KILLED!
I PROVIDE A CLEAN HOME AND REGULAR MEALS FOR THE PRINCESS.
I DON'T CARE!
EVEN IF IT'S DANGEROUS...

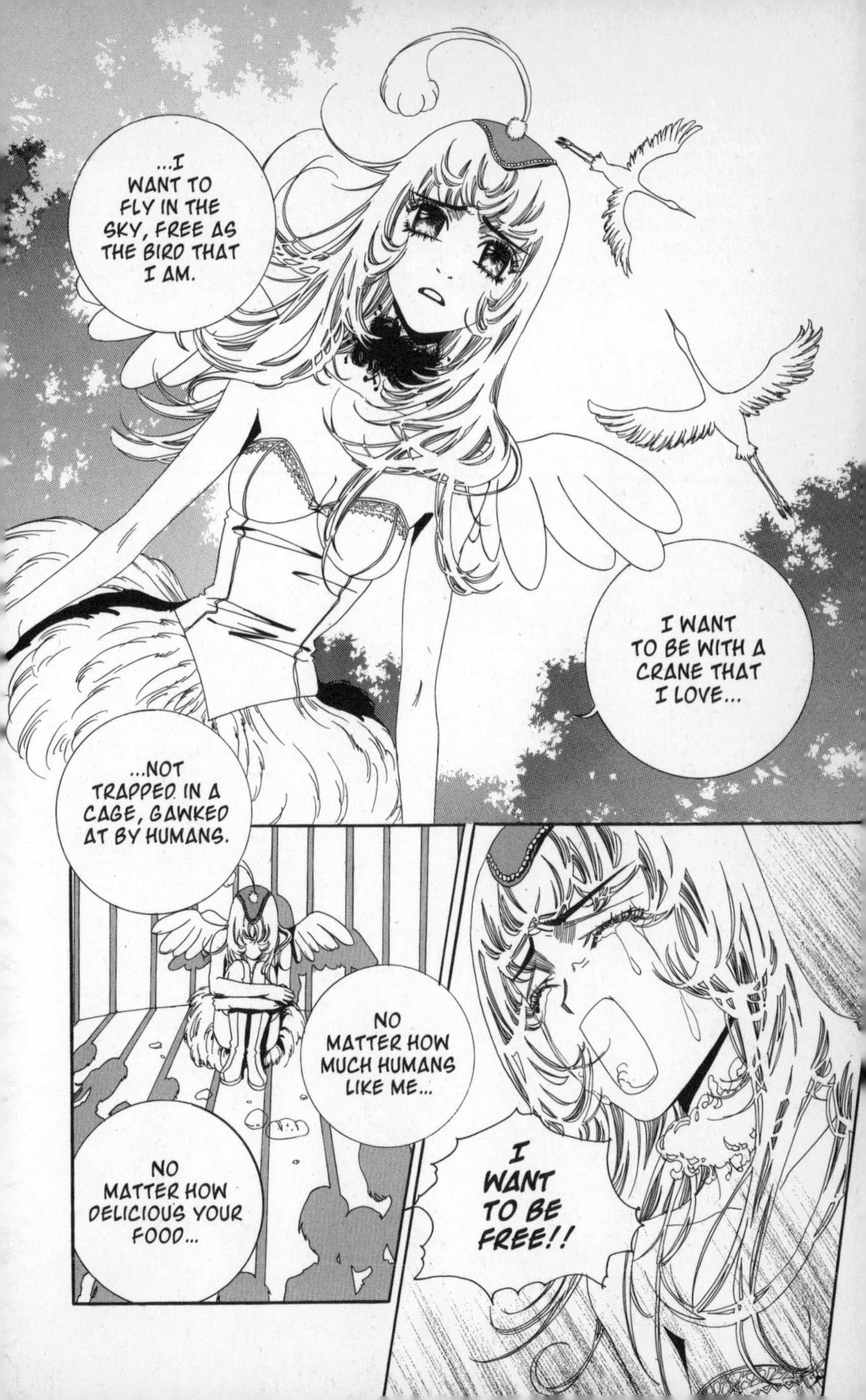
...I WANT TO FLY IN THE SKY, FREE AS THE BIRD THAT I AM.
I WANT TO BE WITH A CRANE THAT I LOVE...
...NOT TRAPPED IN A CAGE, GAWKED AT BY HUMANS.
NO MATTER HOW MUCH HUMANS LIKE ME...
NO MATTER HOW DELICIOUS YOUR FOOD...
I WANT TO BE FREE!!

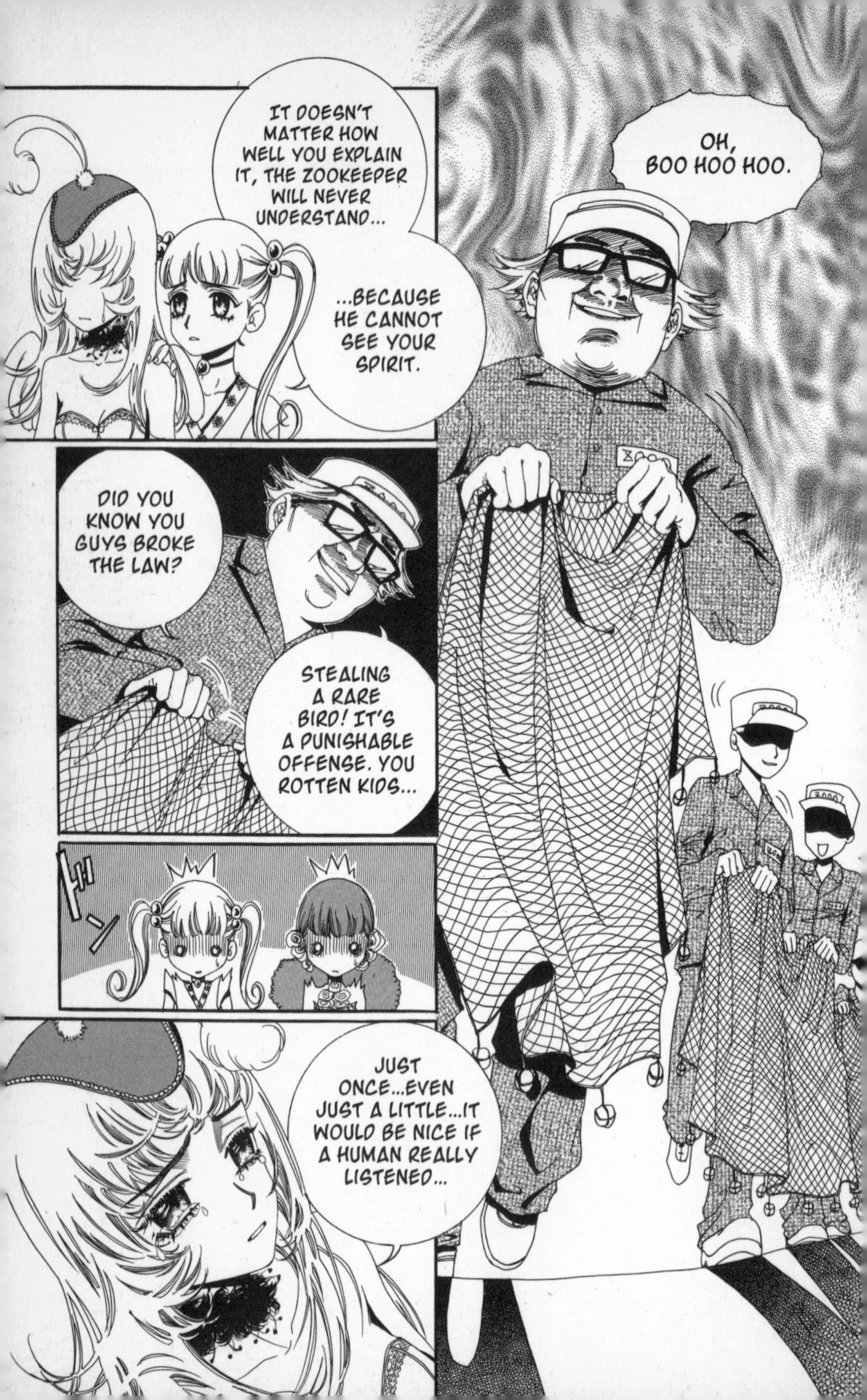
OH, BOO HOO HOO.
IT DOESN'T MATTER HOW WELL YOU EXPLAIN IT, THE ZOOKEEPER WILL NEVER UNDERSTAND...
...BECAUSE HE CANNOT SEE YOUR SPIRIT.
DID YOU KNOW YOU GUYS BROKE THE LAW?
STEALING A RARE BIRD! IT'S A PUNISHABLE OFFENSE. YOU ROTTEN KIDS...
JUST ONCE...EVEN JUST A LITTLE...IT WOULD BE NICE IF A HUMAN REALLY LISTENED...

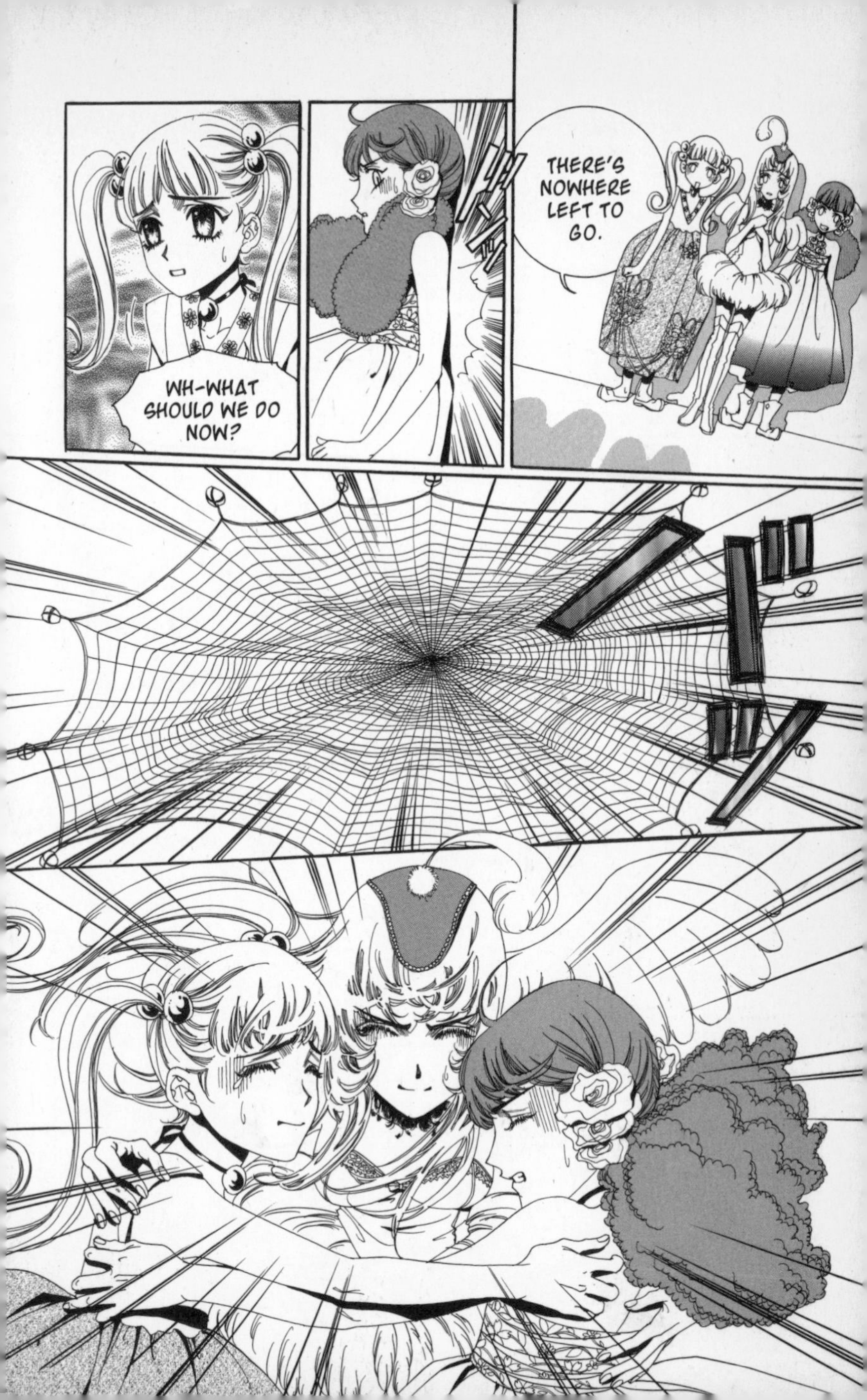
THERE'S NOWHERE LEFT TO GO.
WH-WHAT SHOULD WE DO NOW?

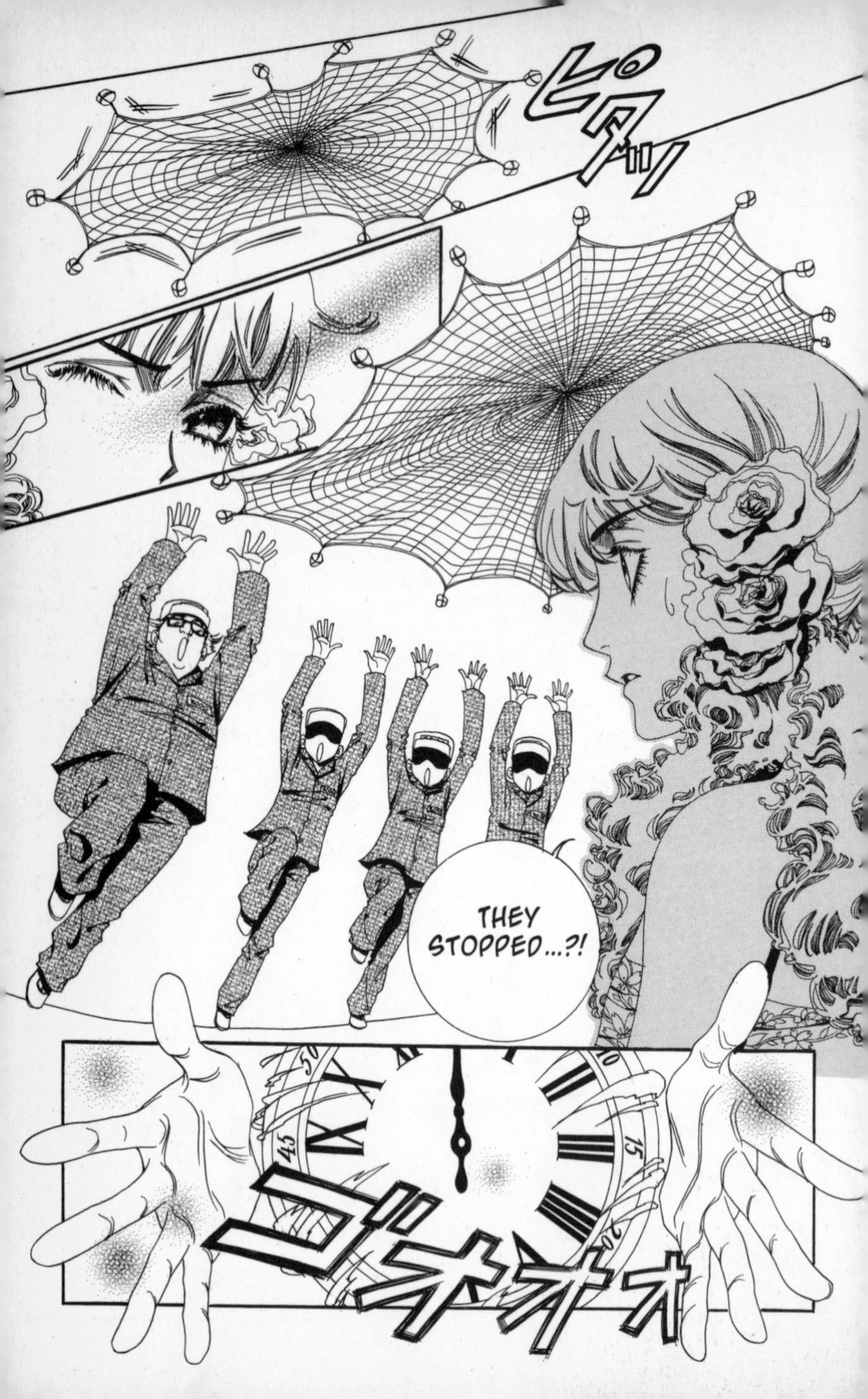
ピタッ
THEY STOPPED...?!
ゴォオオ

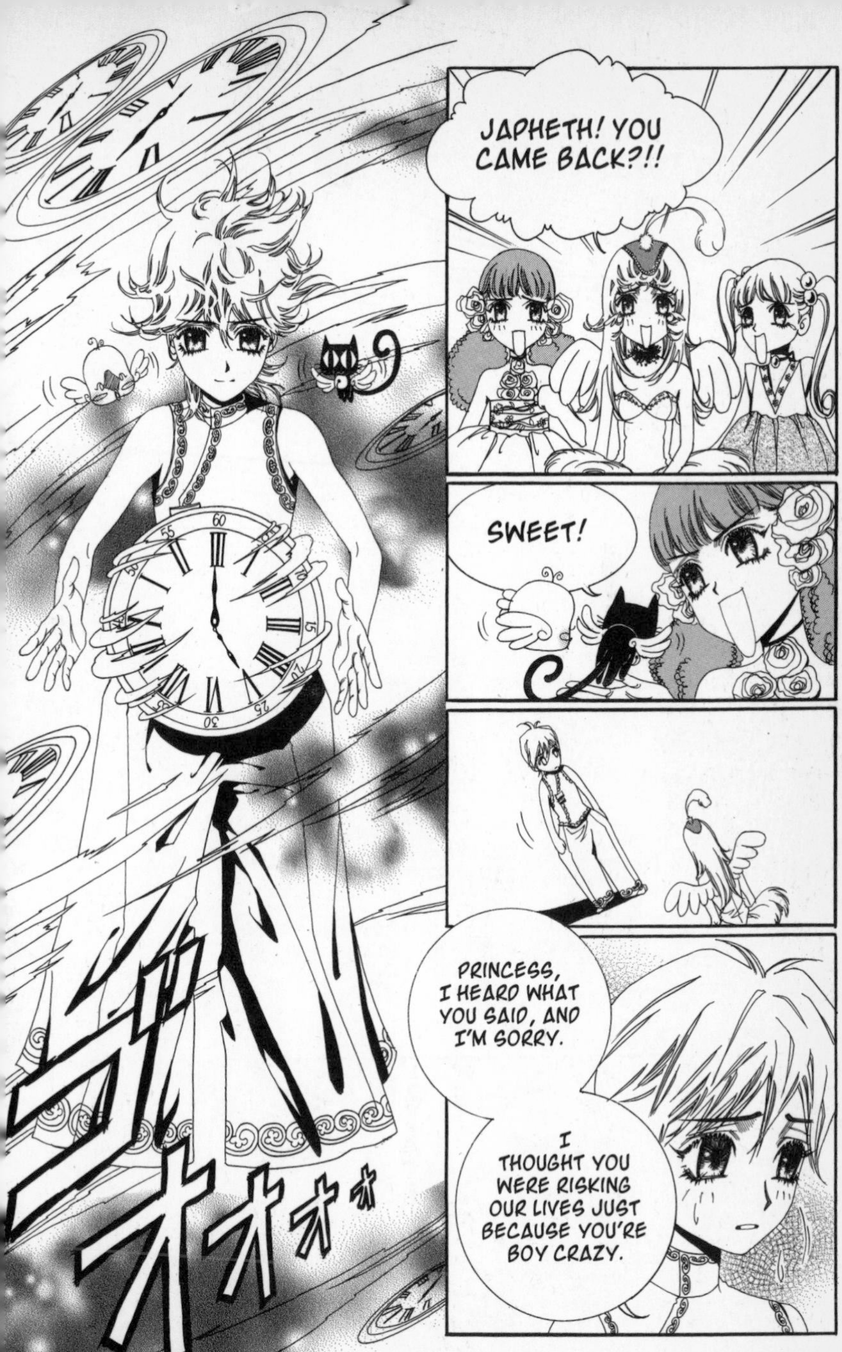
JAPHETH! YOU CAME BACK?!!
SWEET!
PRINCESS, I HEARD WHAT YOU SAID, AND I'M SORRY.
I THOUGHT YOU WERE RISKING OUR LIVES JUST BECAUSE YOU'RE BOY CRAZY.
ゴオオオォ

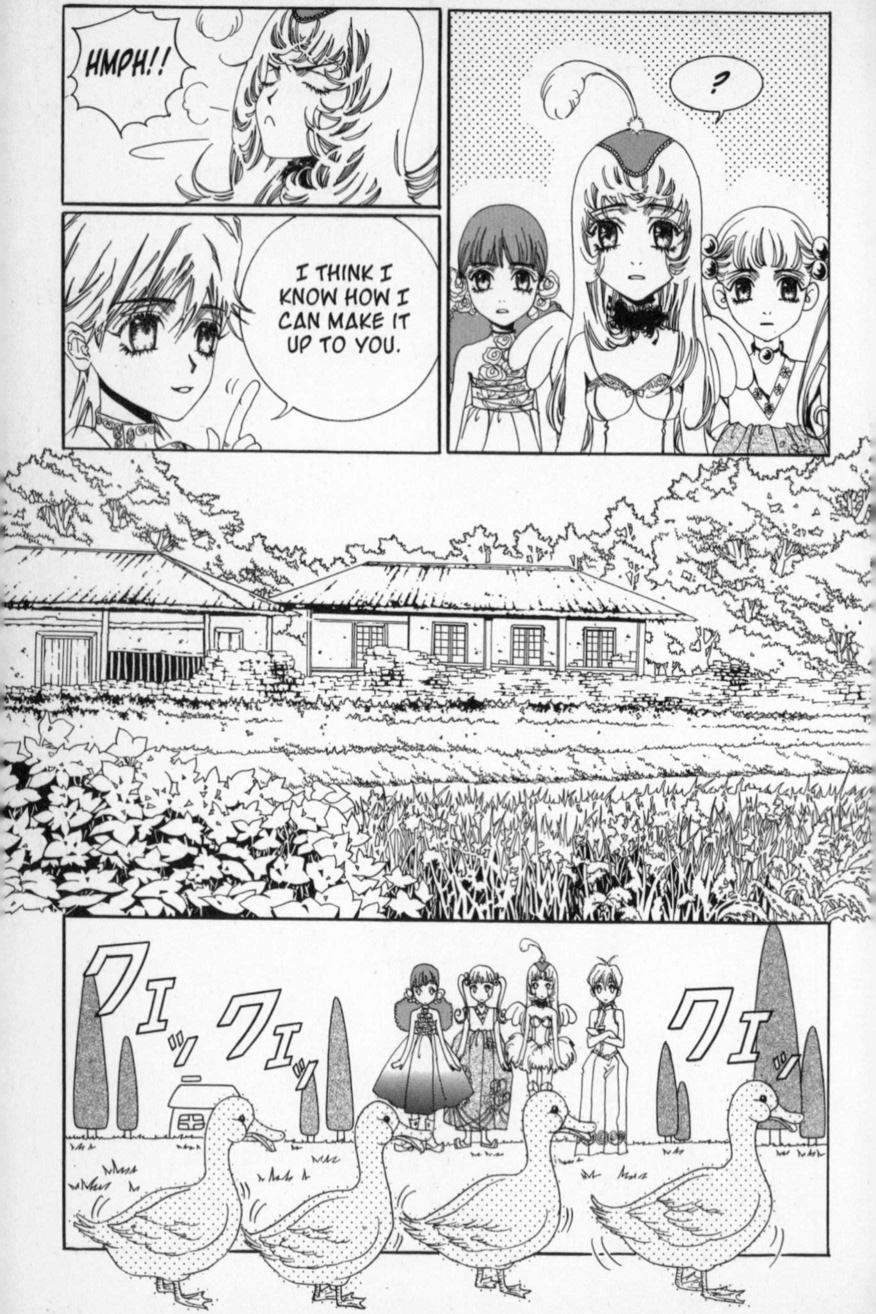
?
HMPH!!
I THINK I KNOW HOW I CAN MAKE IT UP TO YOU.
ワエッ
ワエッ
ワエッ

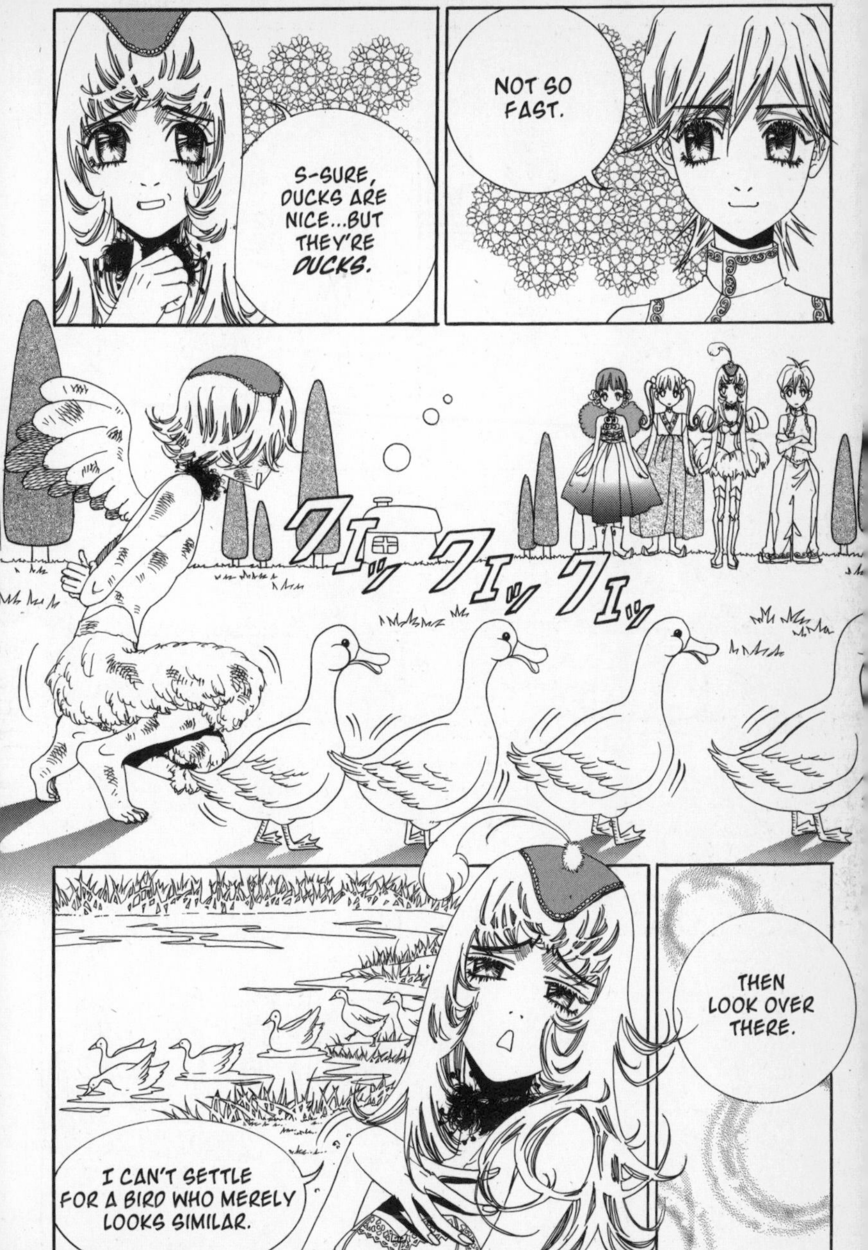
S-SURE, DUCKS ARE NICE...BUT THEY'RE *DUCKS.*
NOT SO FAST.
クエッ クエッ クエッ
I CAN'T SETTLE FOR A BIRD WHO MERELY LOOKS SIMILAR.
THEN LOOK OVER THERE.

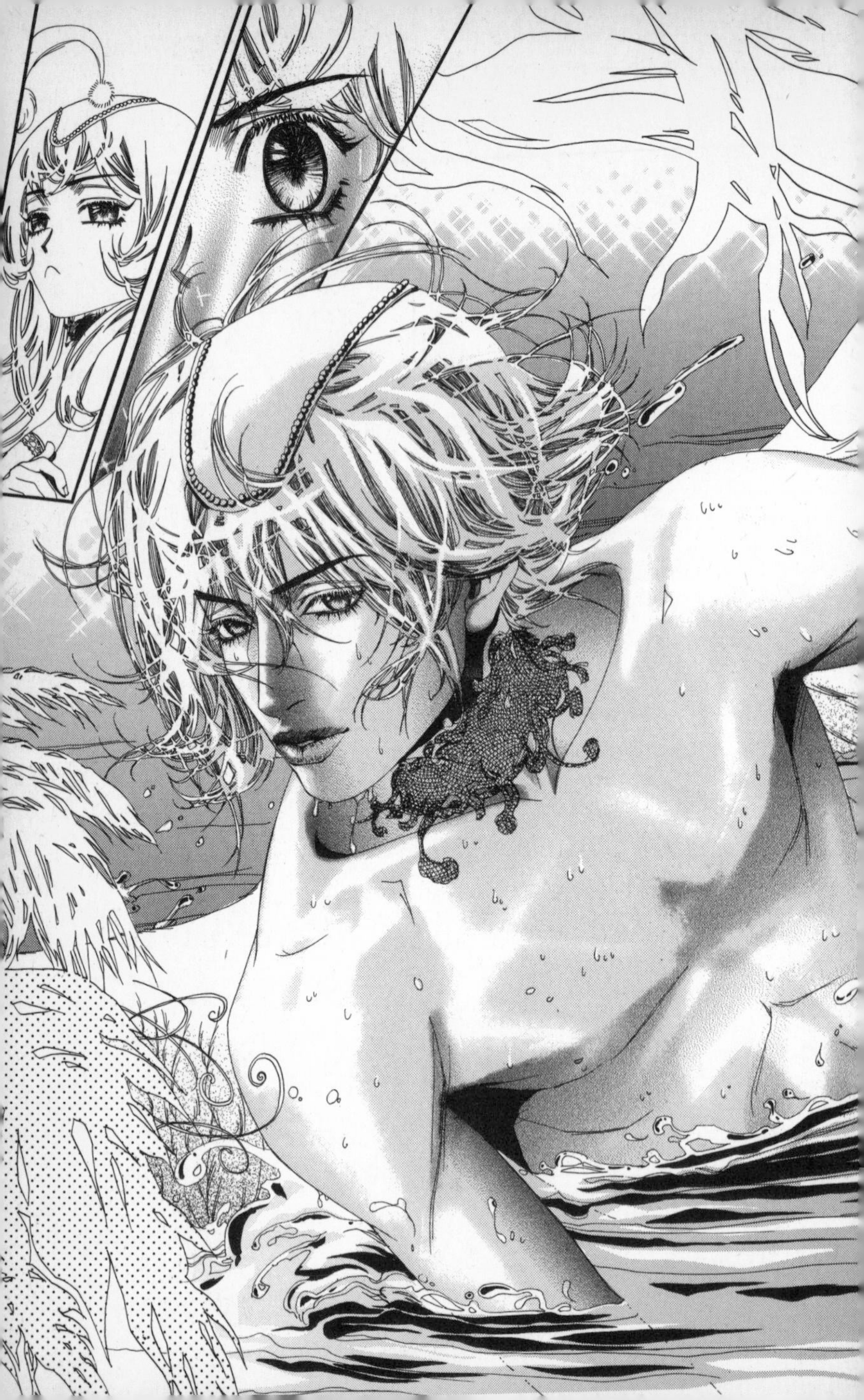

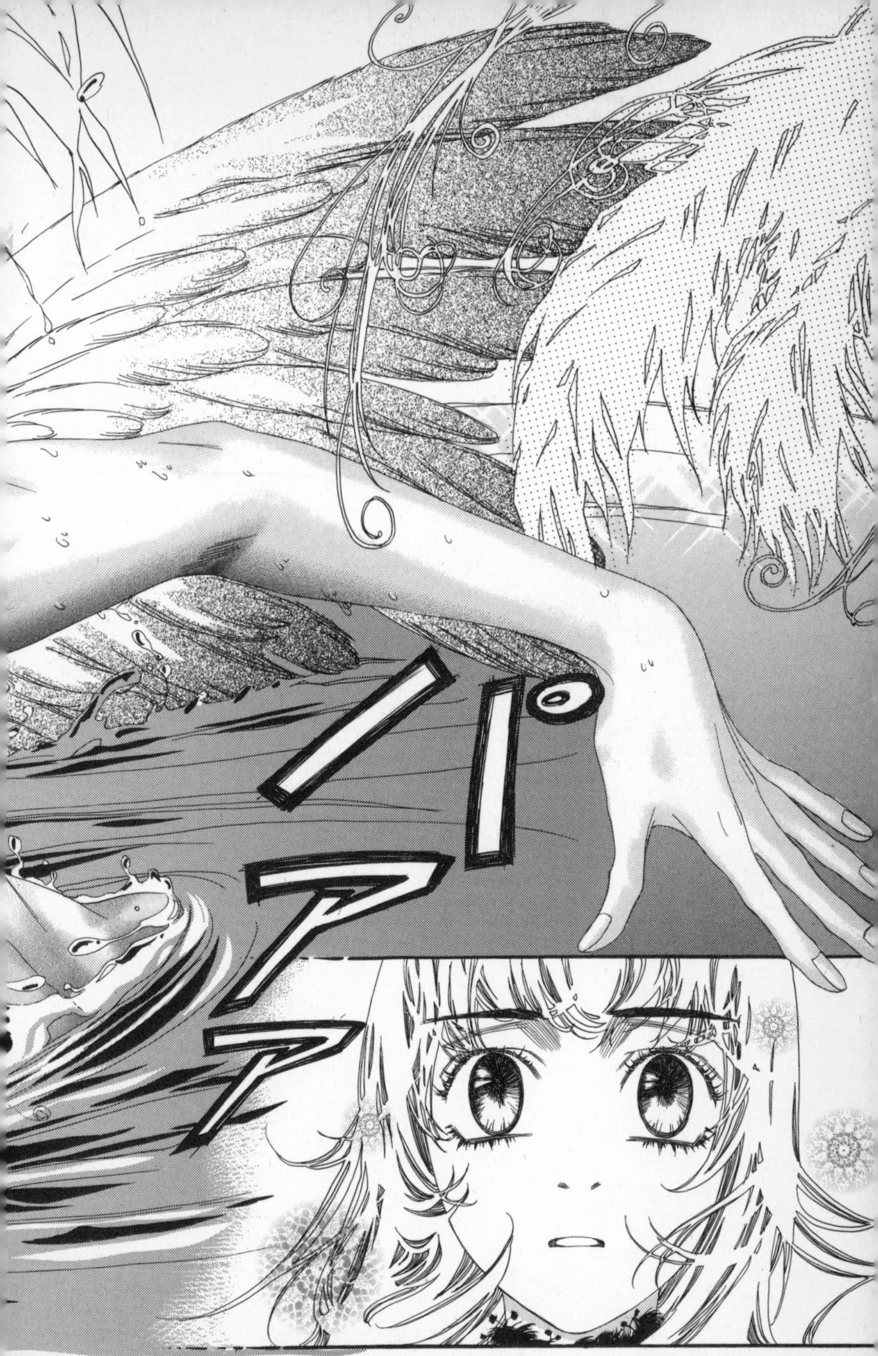
パアア

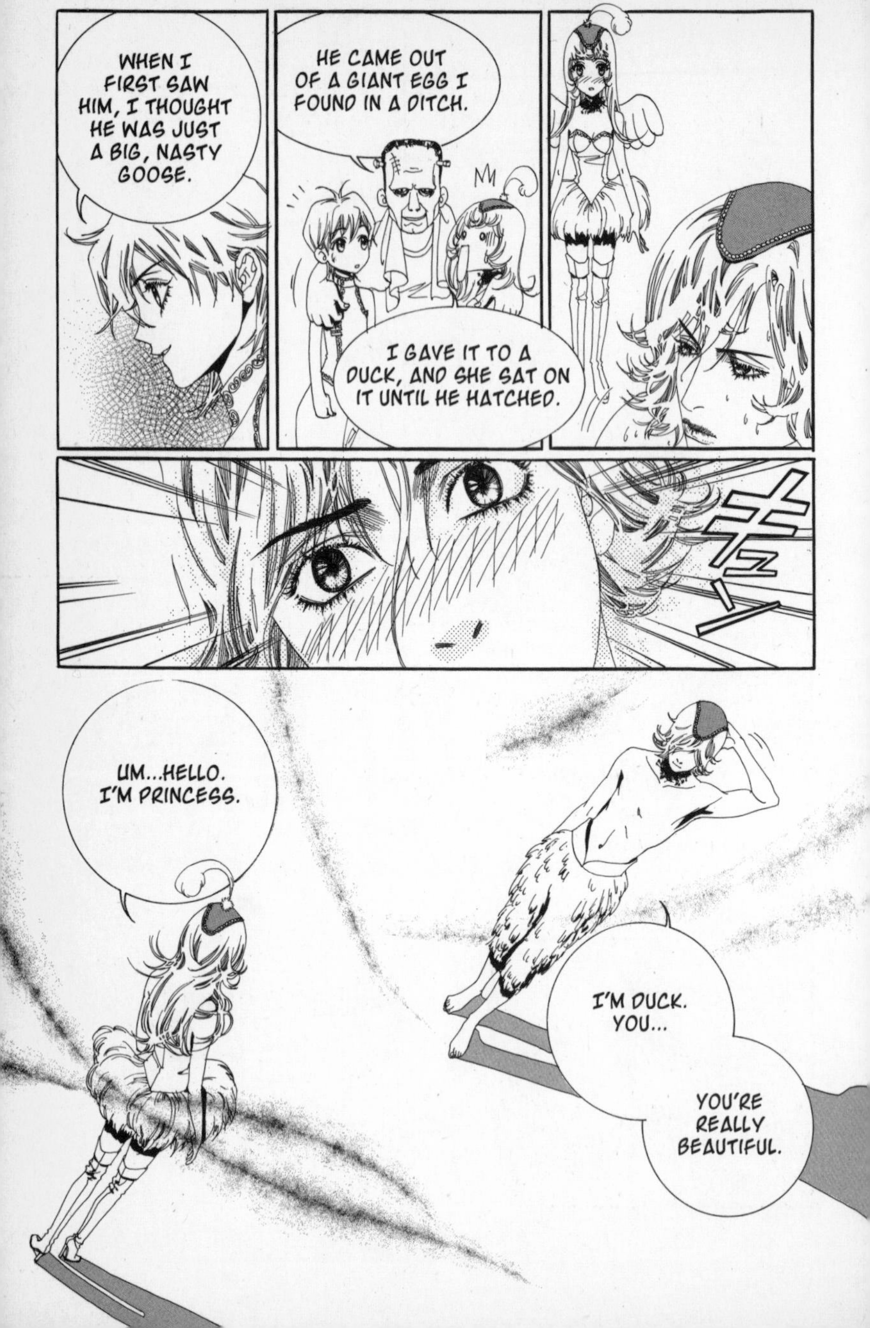
WHEN I FIRST SAW HIM, I THOUGHT HE WAS JUST A BIG, NASTY GOOSE.
HE CAME OUT OF A GIANT EGG I FOUND IN A DITCH.
I GAVE IT TO A DUCK, AND SHE SAT ON IT UNTIL HE HATCHED.
UM...HELLO. I'M PRINCESS.
I'M DUCK. YOU...
YOU'RE REALLY BEAUTIFUL.

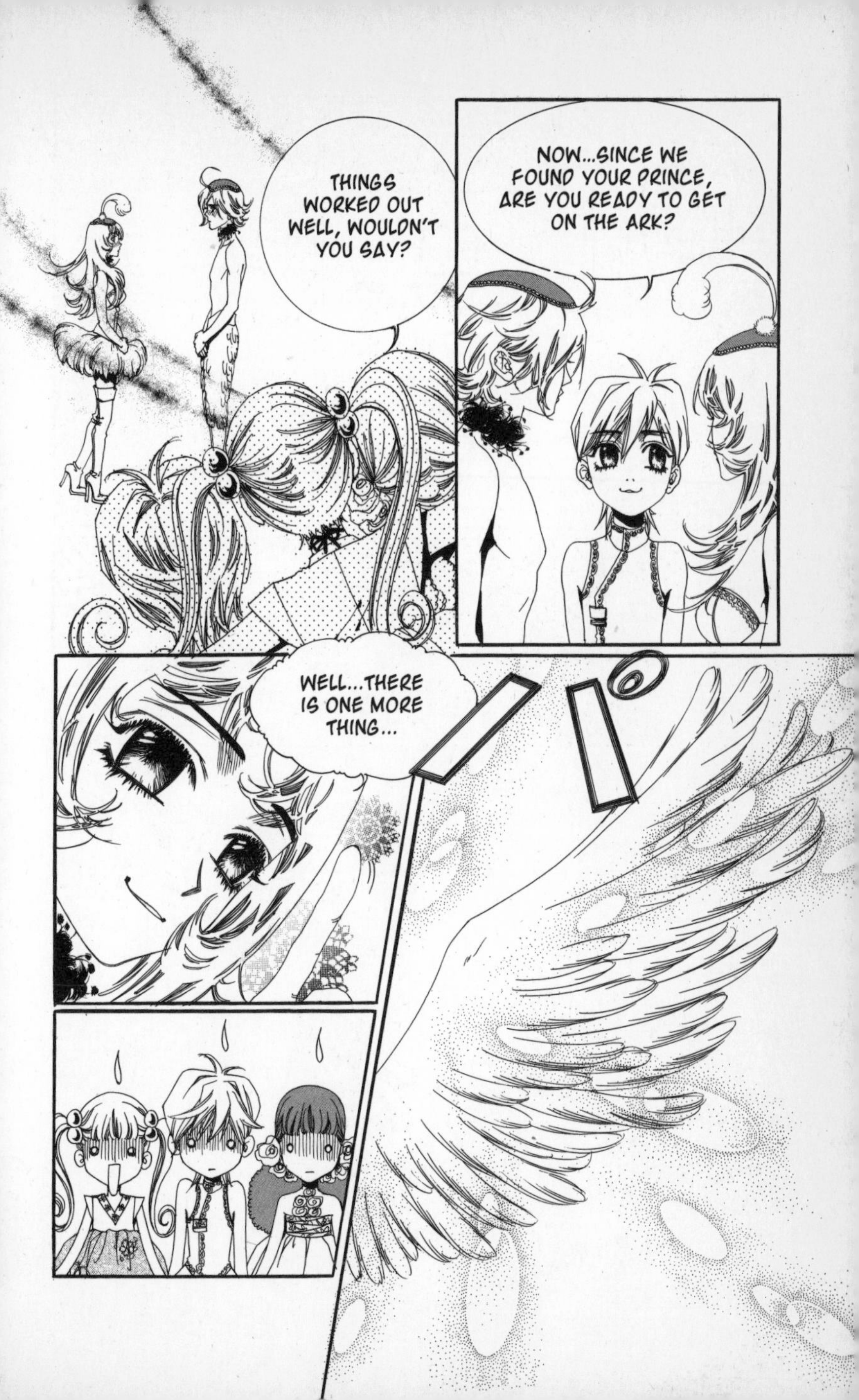
NOW...SINCE WE FOUND YOUR PRINCE, ARE YOU READY TO GET ON THE ARK?
THINGS WORKED OUT WELL, WOULDN'T YOU SAY?
WELL...THERE IS ONE MORE THING...

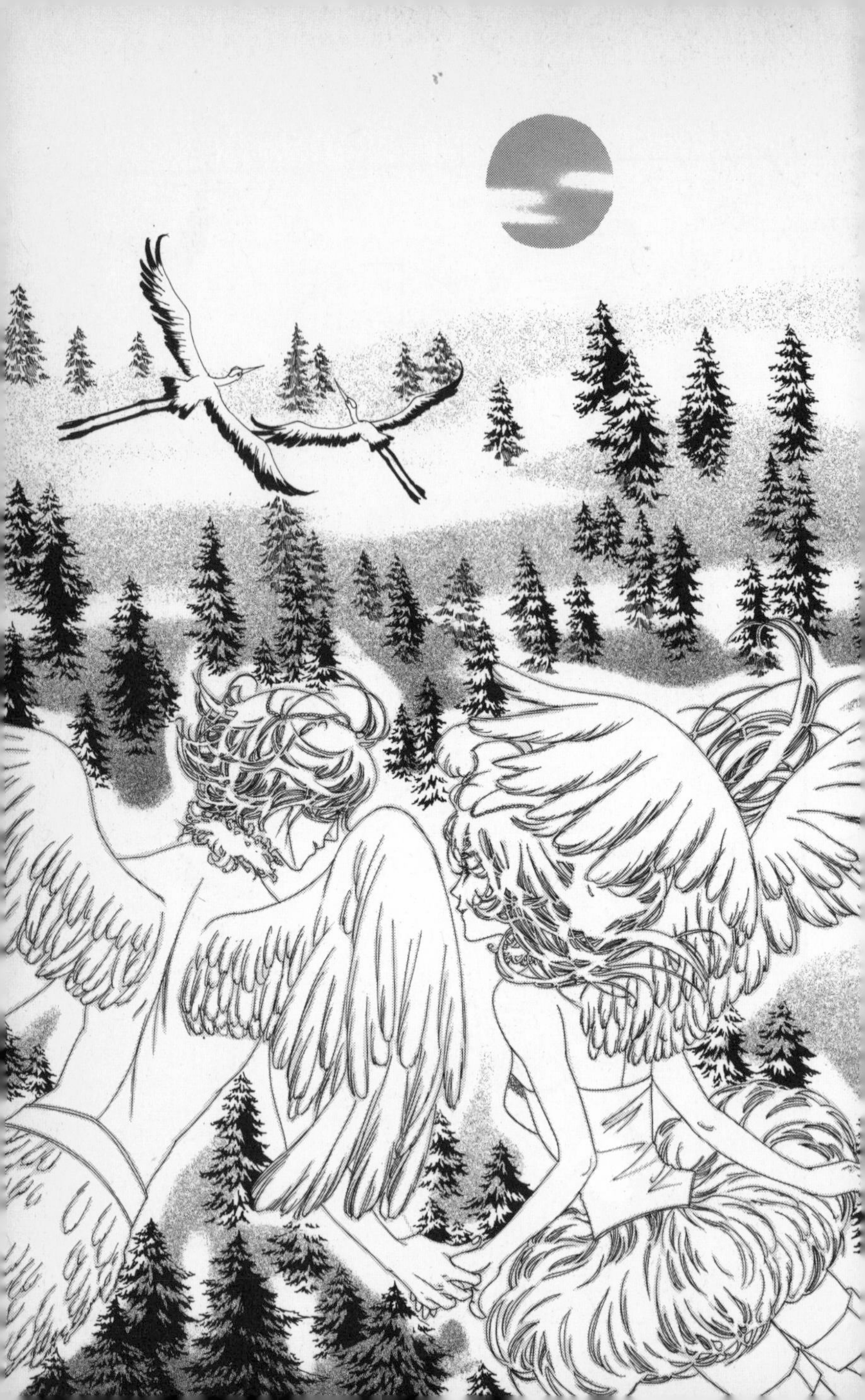

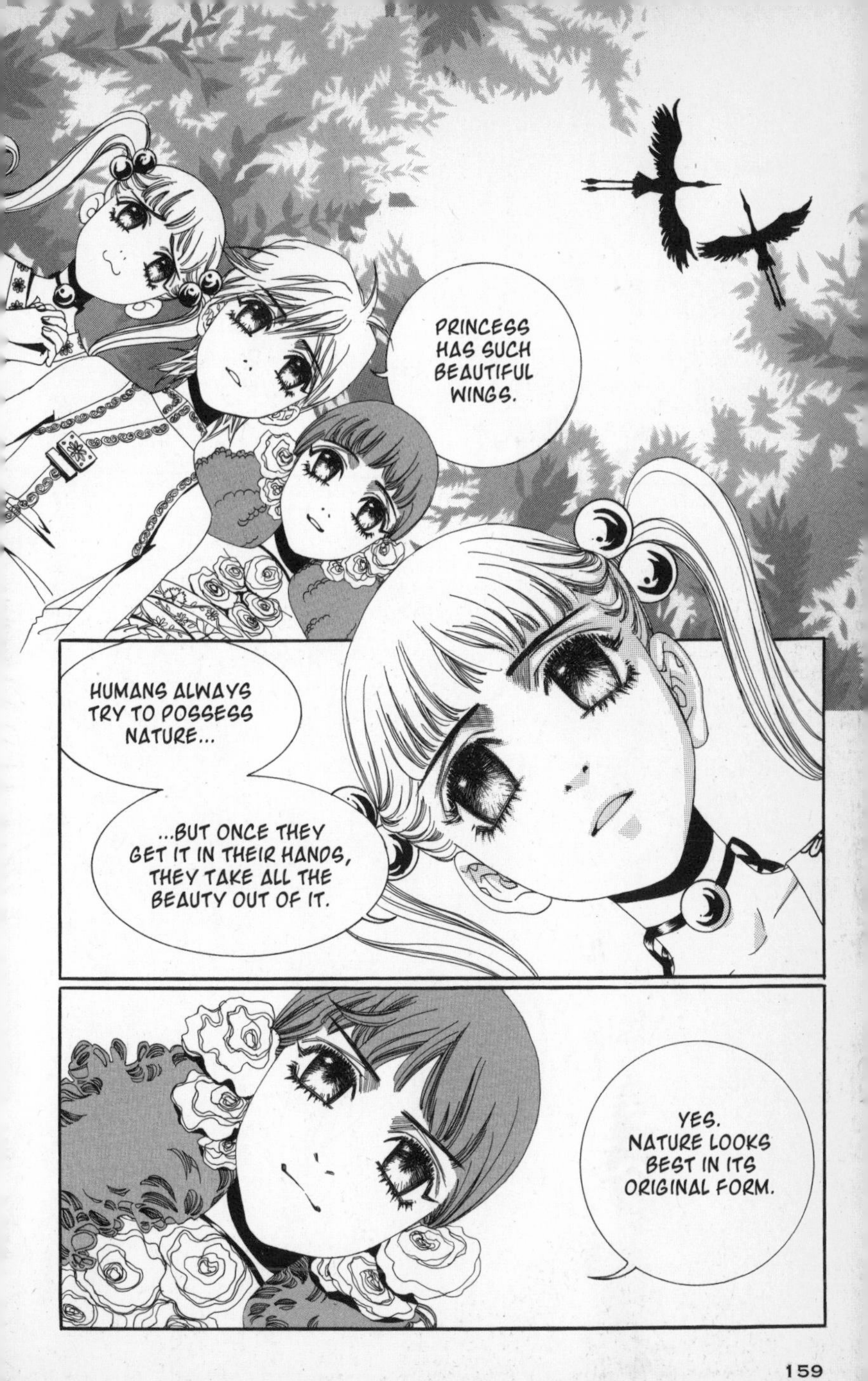
PRINCESS HAS SUCH BEAUTIFUL WINGS.
HUMANS ALWAYS TRY TO POSSESS NATURE...
...BUT ONCE THEY GET IT IN THEIR HANDS, THEY TAKE ALL THE BEAUTY OUT OF IT.
YES. NATURE LOOKS BEST IN ITS ORIGINAL FORM.

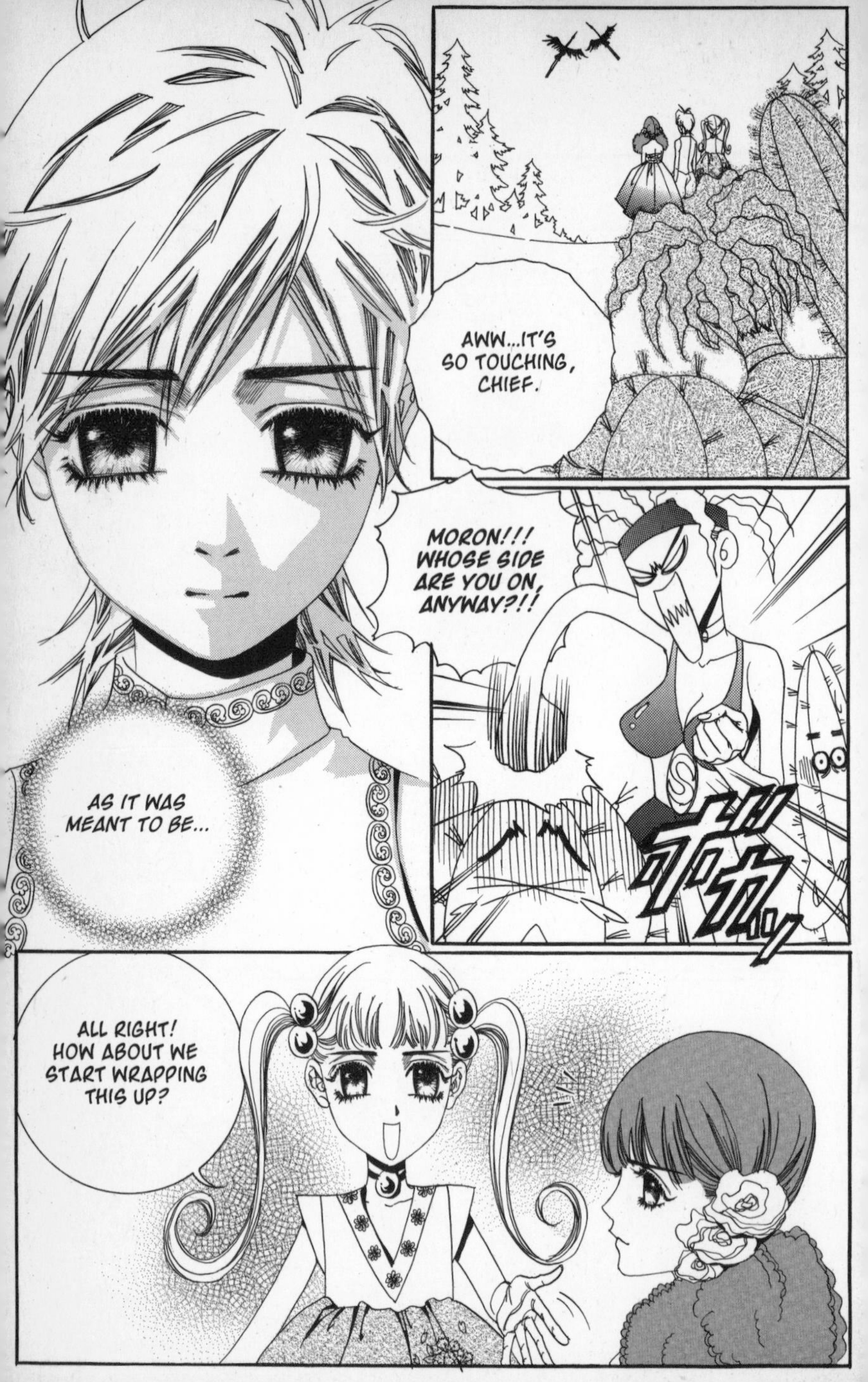
AWW...IT'S SO TOUCHING, CHIEF.
MORON!!! WHOSE SIDE ARE YOU ON, ANYWAY?!!
AS IT WAS MEANT TO BE...
ALL RIGHT! HOW ABOUT WE START WRAPPING THIS UP?

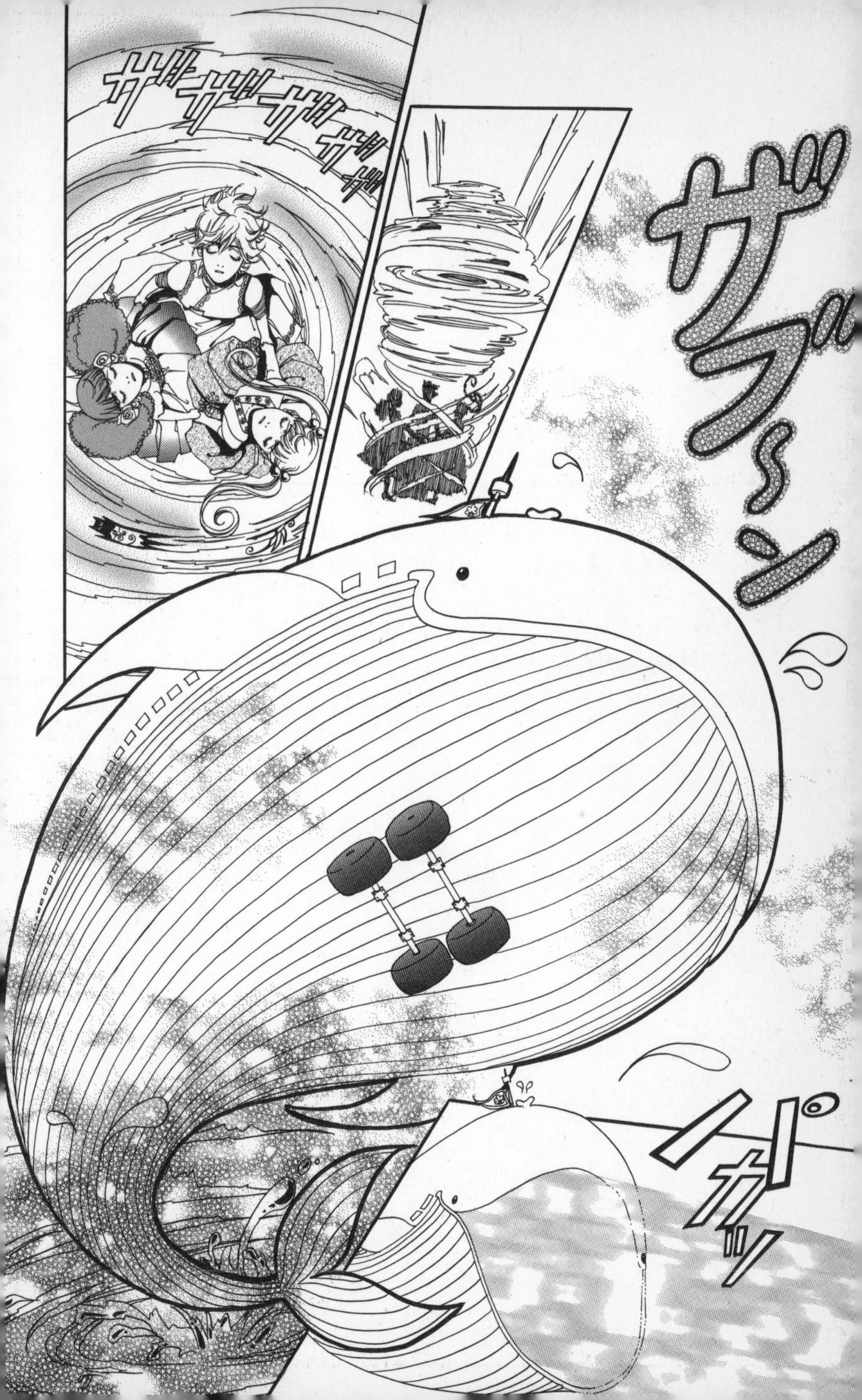
ザザザザザ
ザブ～ン
パカッ

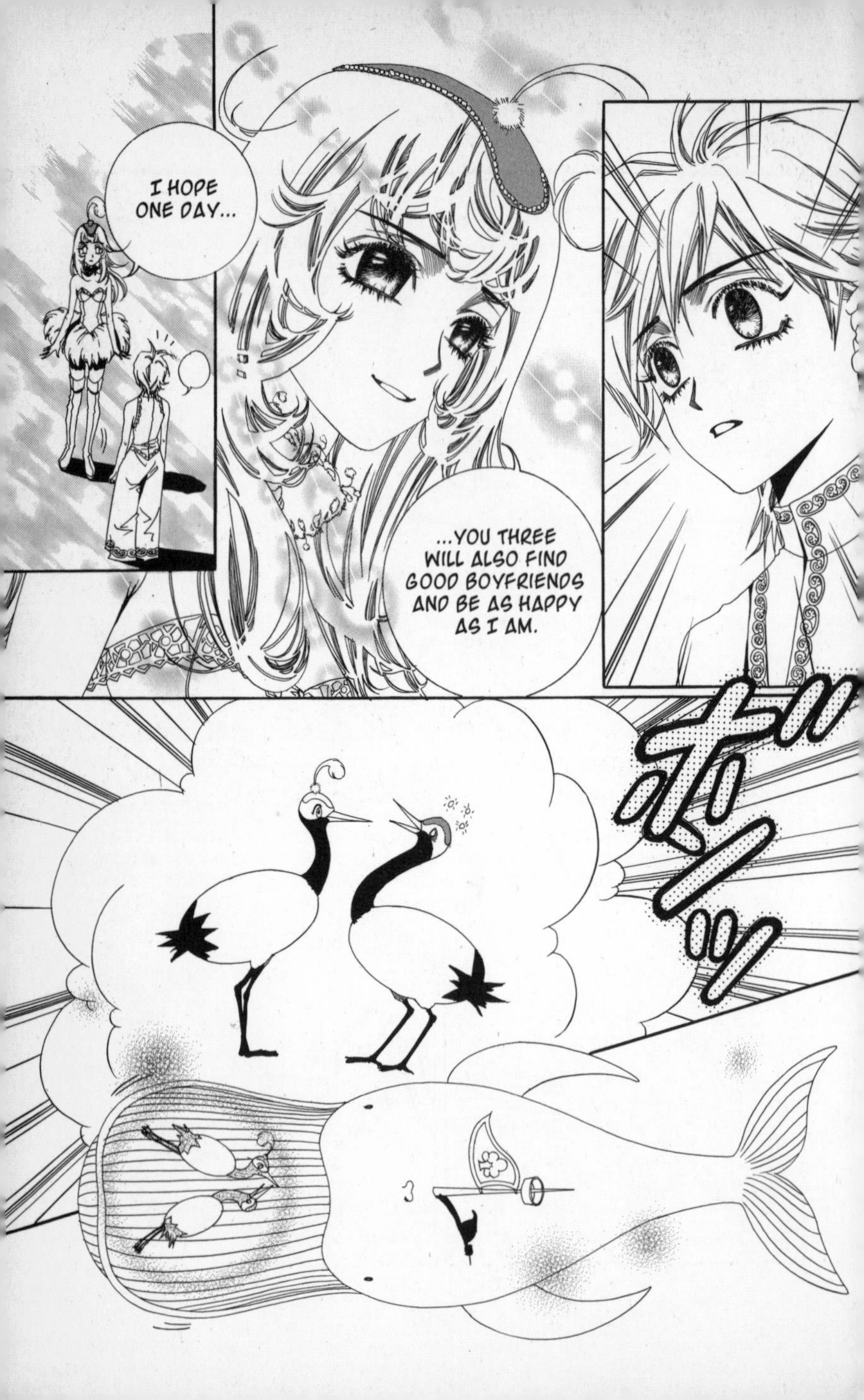
I HOPE ONE DAY...
...YOU THREE WILL ALSO FIND GOOD BOYFRIENDS AND BE AS HAPPY AS I AM.

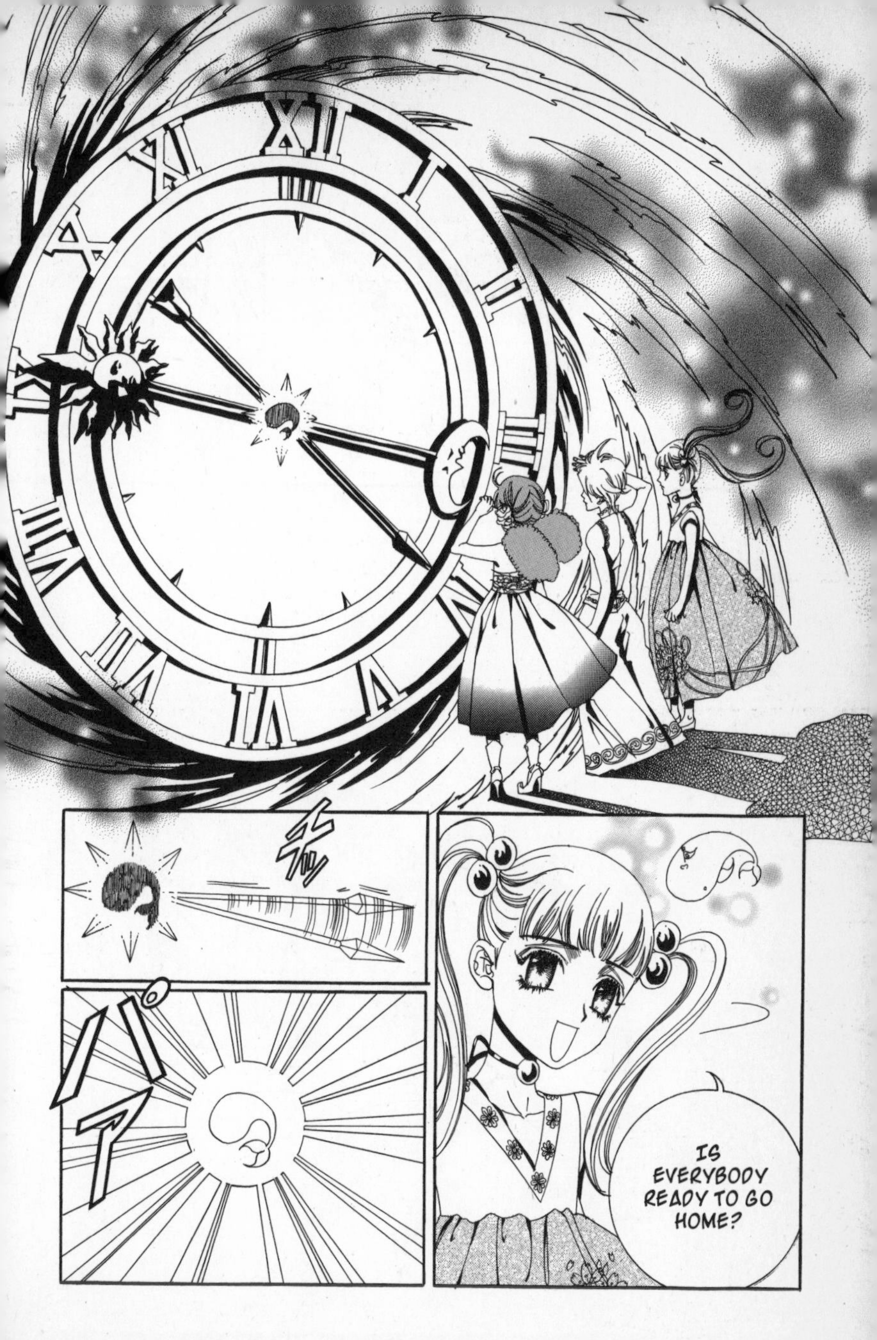
IS EVERYBODY READY TO GO HOME?
チッ
パア

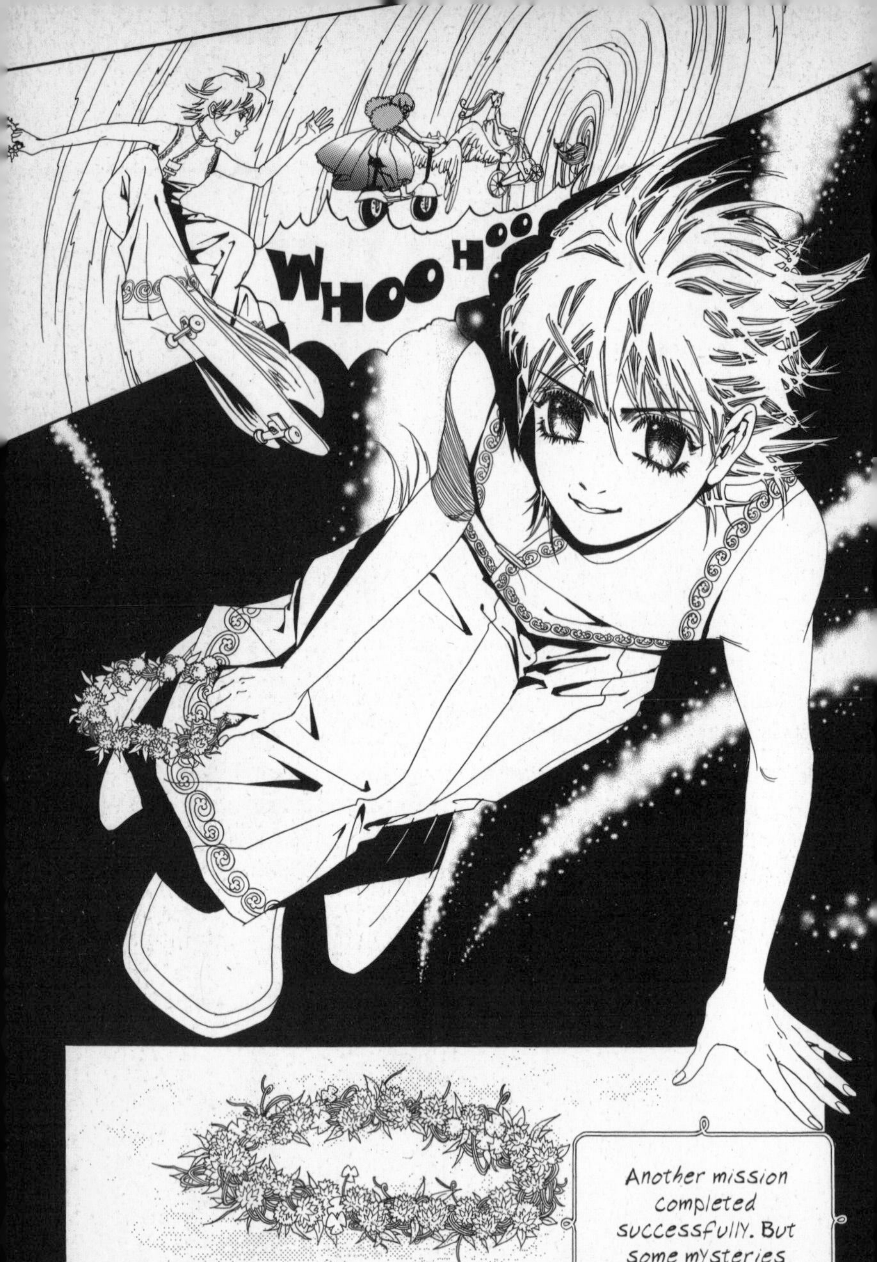
WHOO HOO
Another mission completed successfully. But some mysteries remain...

IN THE NEXT
VOLUME OF

Ark Angels

Next time in Ark Angels...

More adventures of Japheth, Hamu and Shem as the three sisters set out to save a turtle prince, the sole survivor of a race of reptiles that were wiped out by greedy humans who found them to be quite delicious.

Back at school, Japheth's relationship with that pretty boy develops--and secrets are exposed after he collapses from a mysterious disease. Perhaps there is more going on with him than the sisters suspect...

And the identity of the mysterious Cactus Three is revealed.

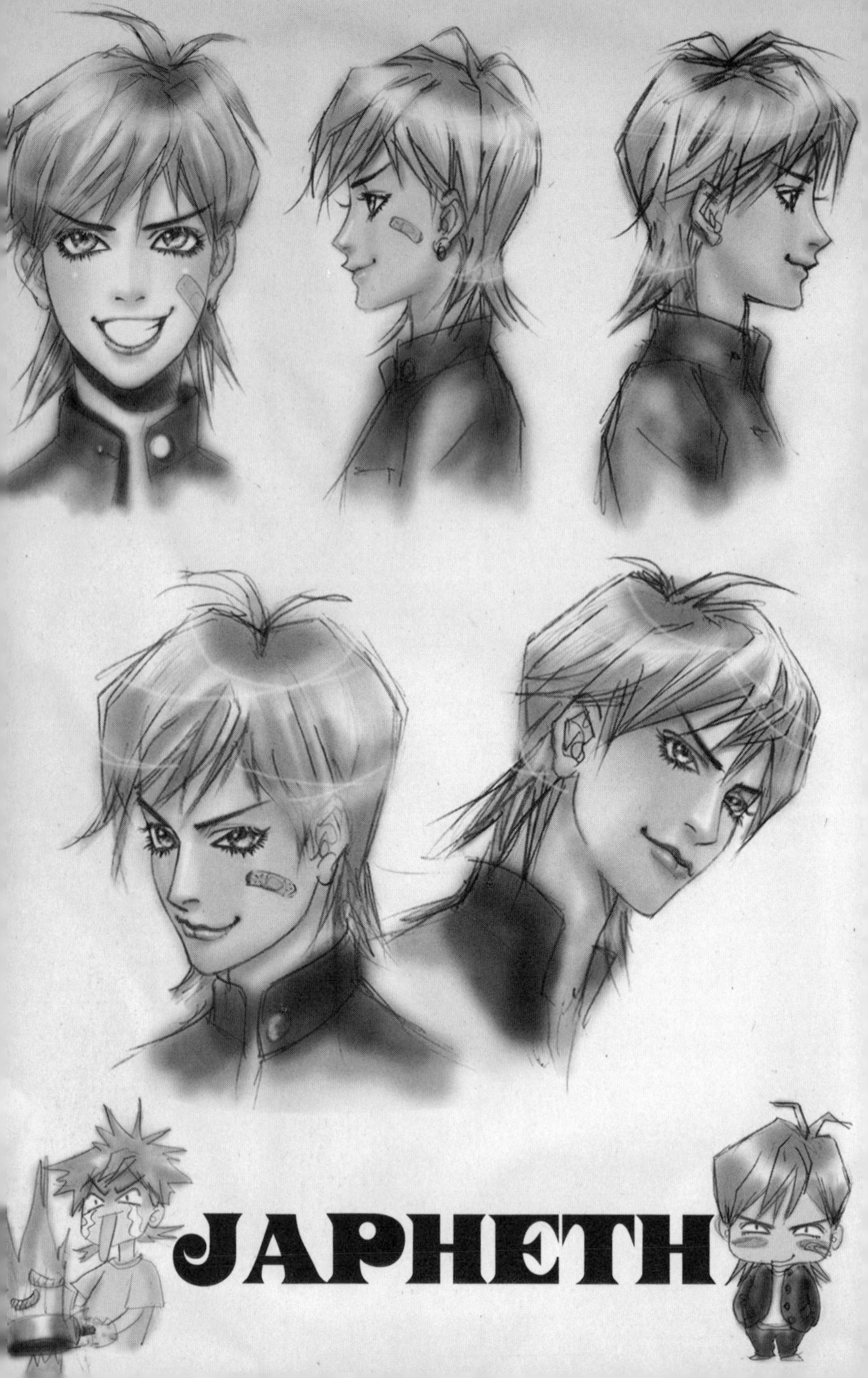
JAPHETH

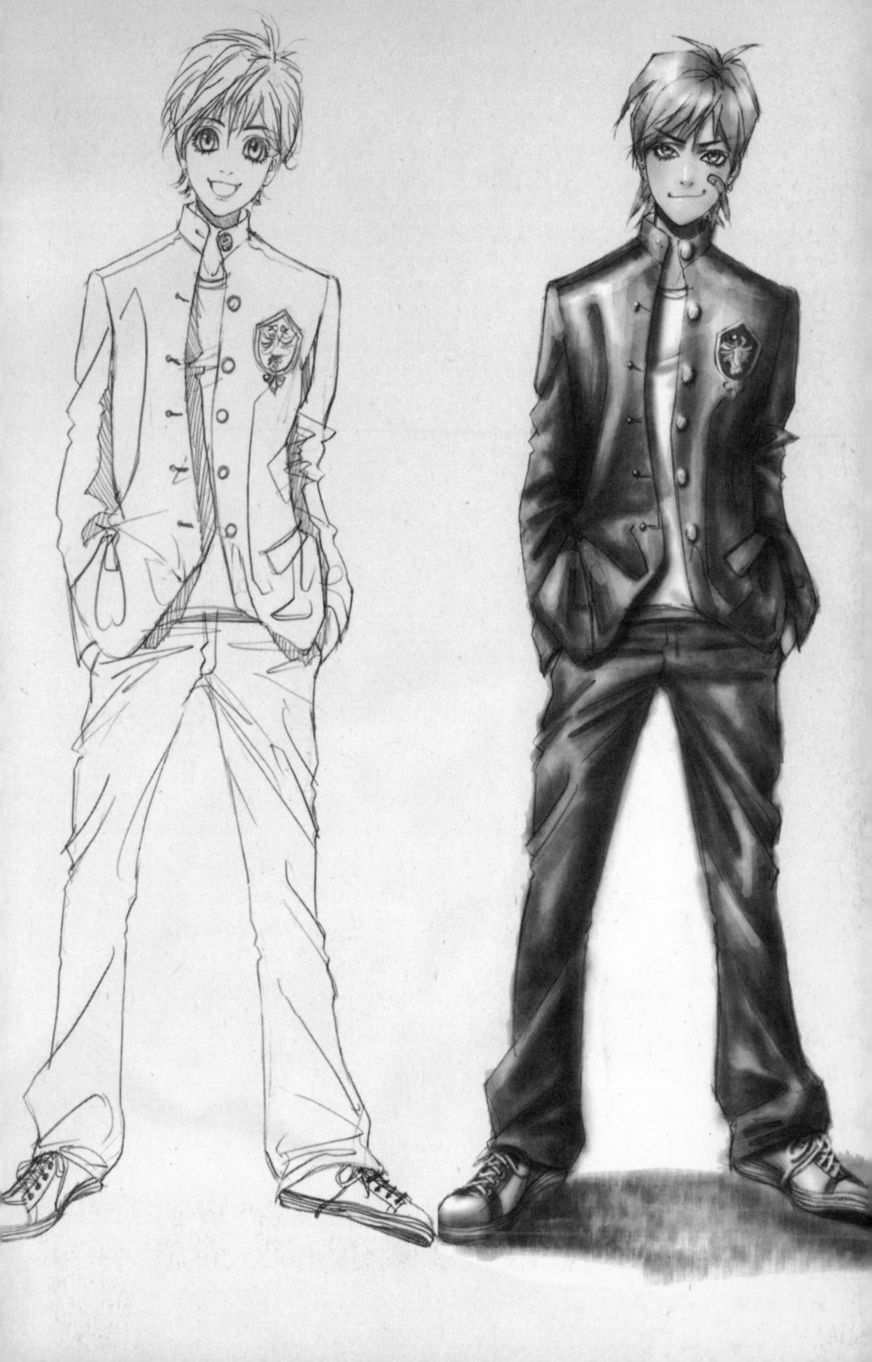

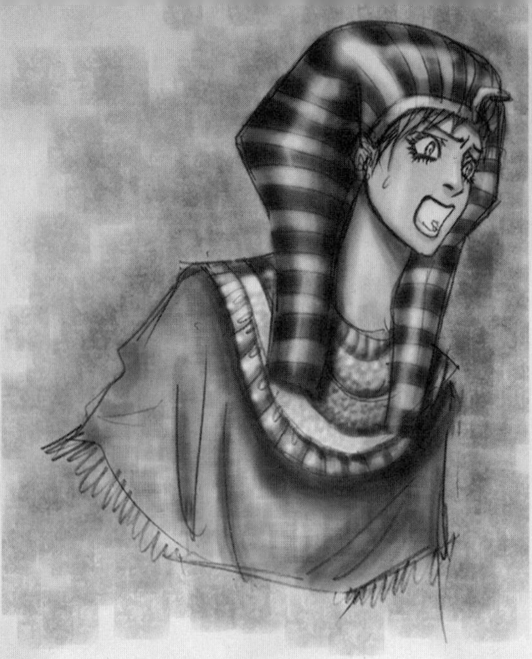

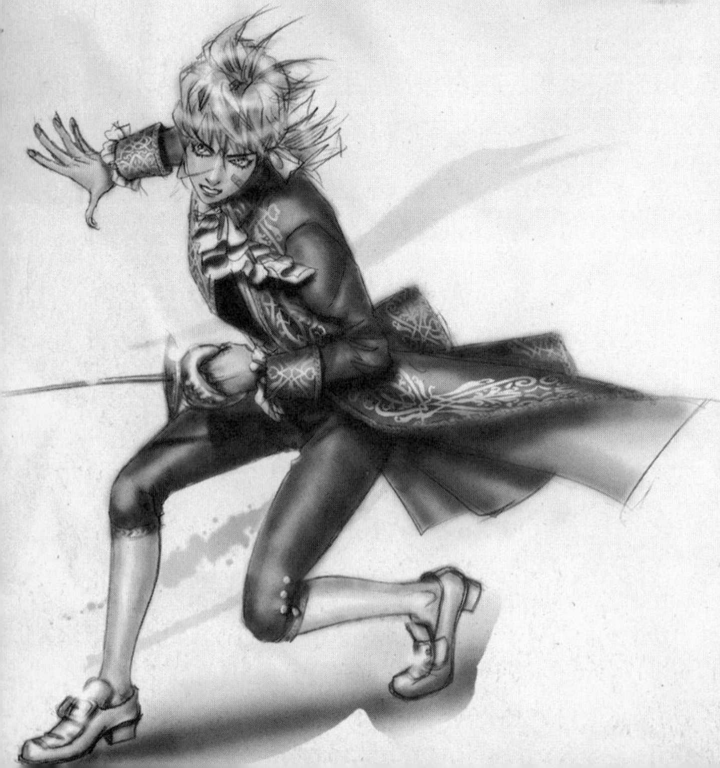

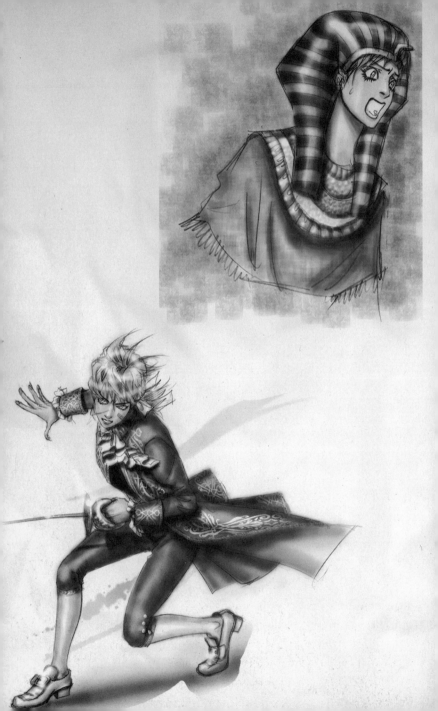

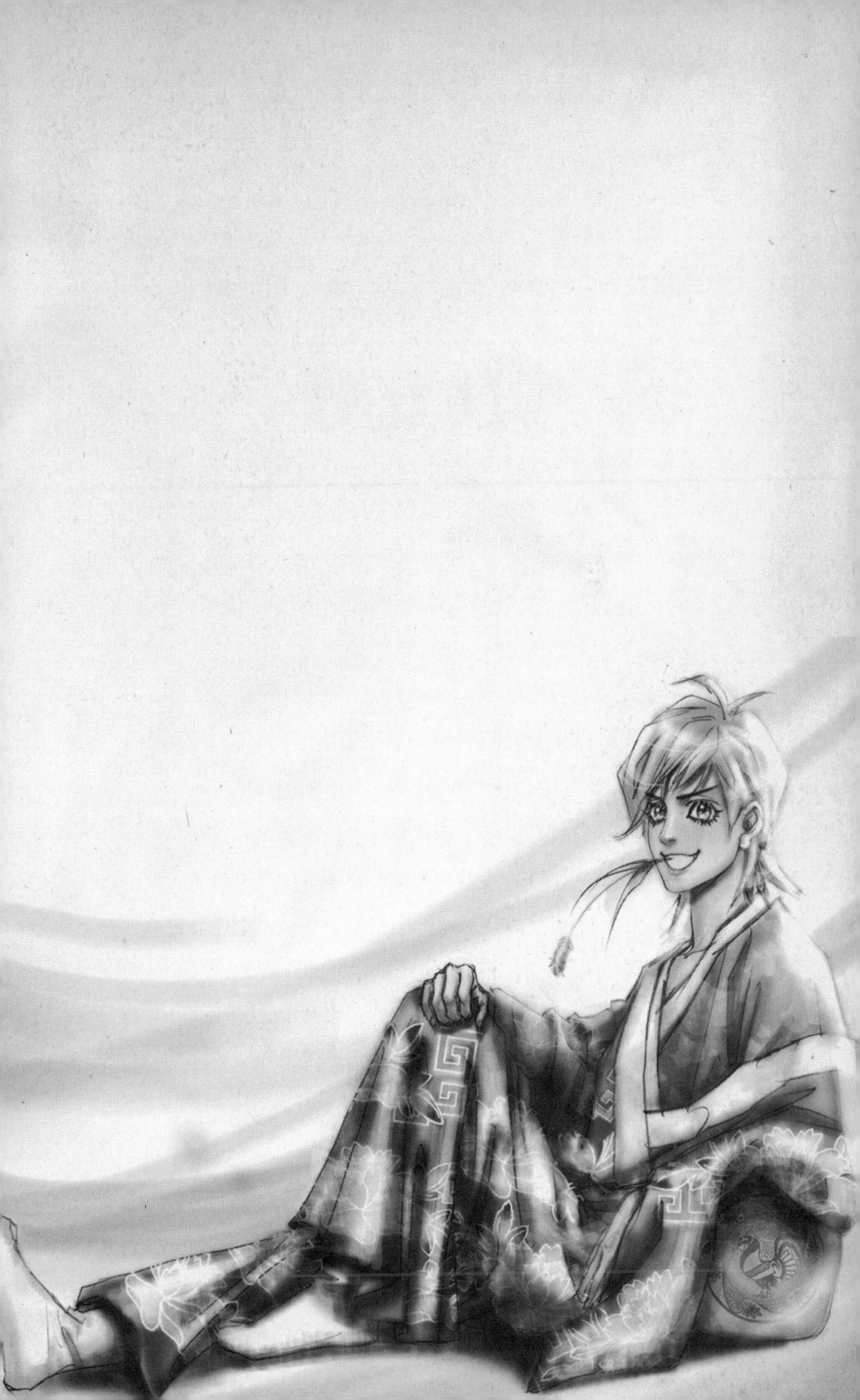

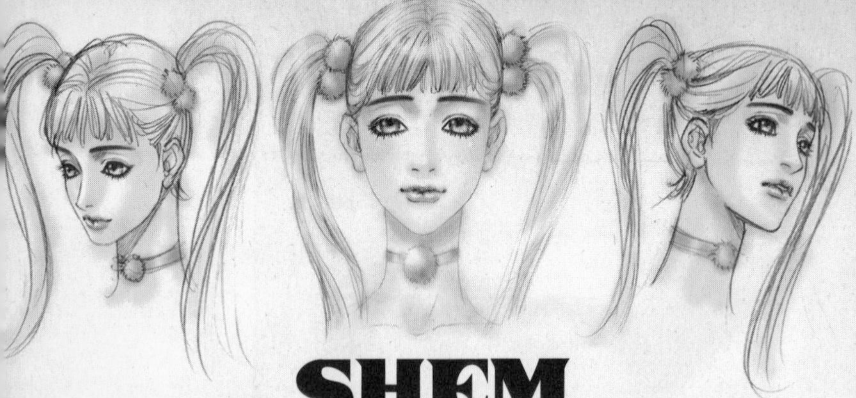

SHEM

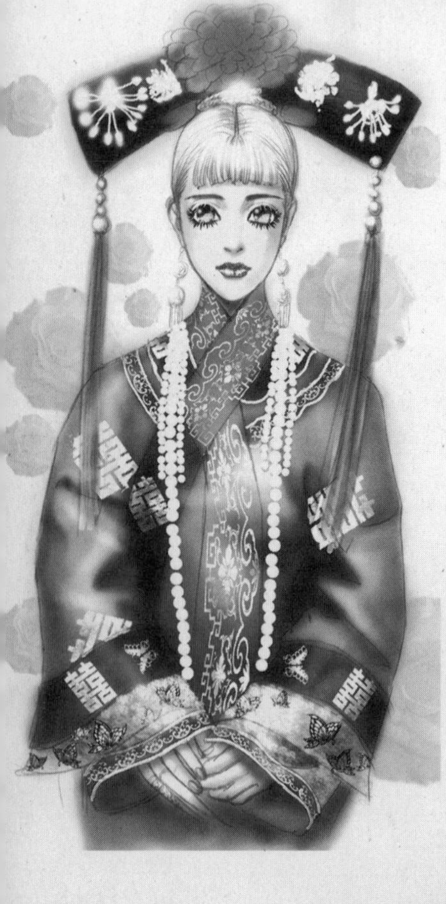

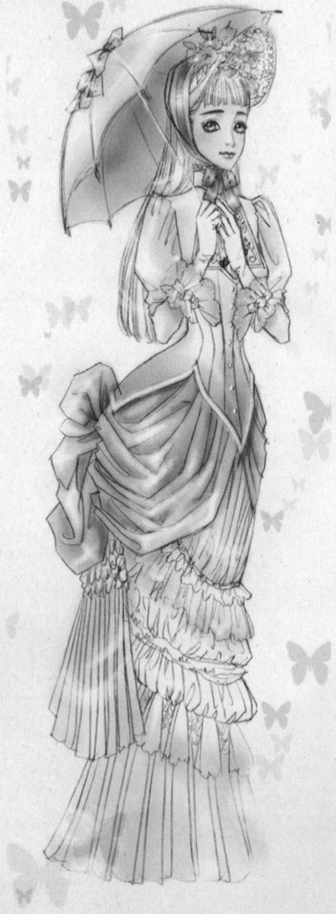

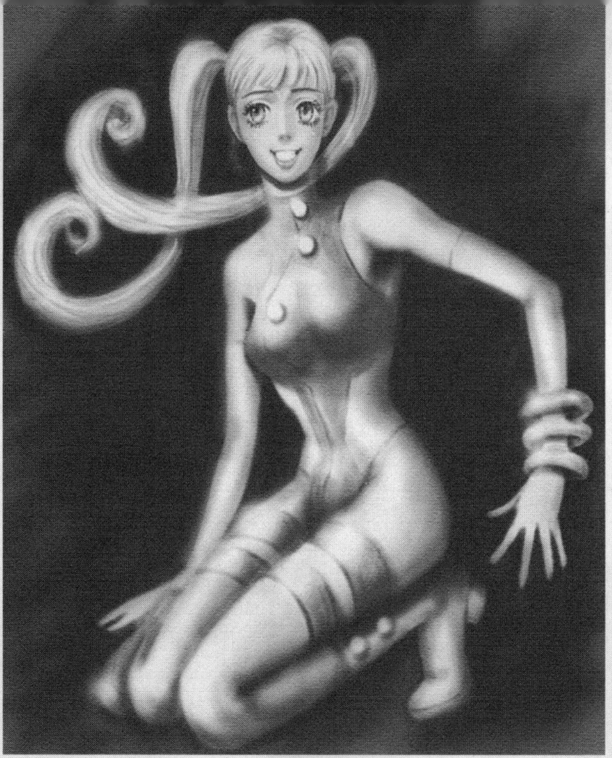

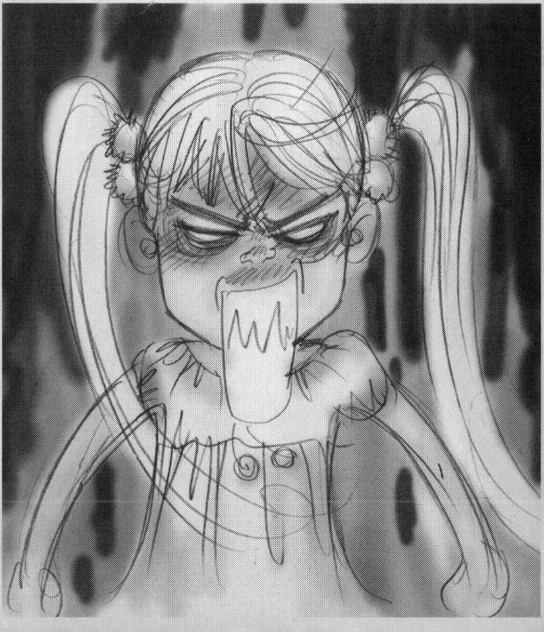

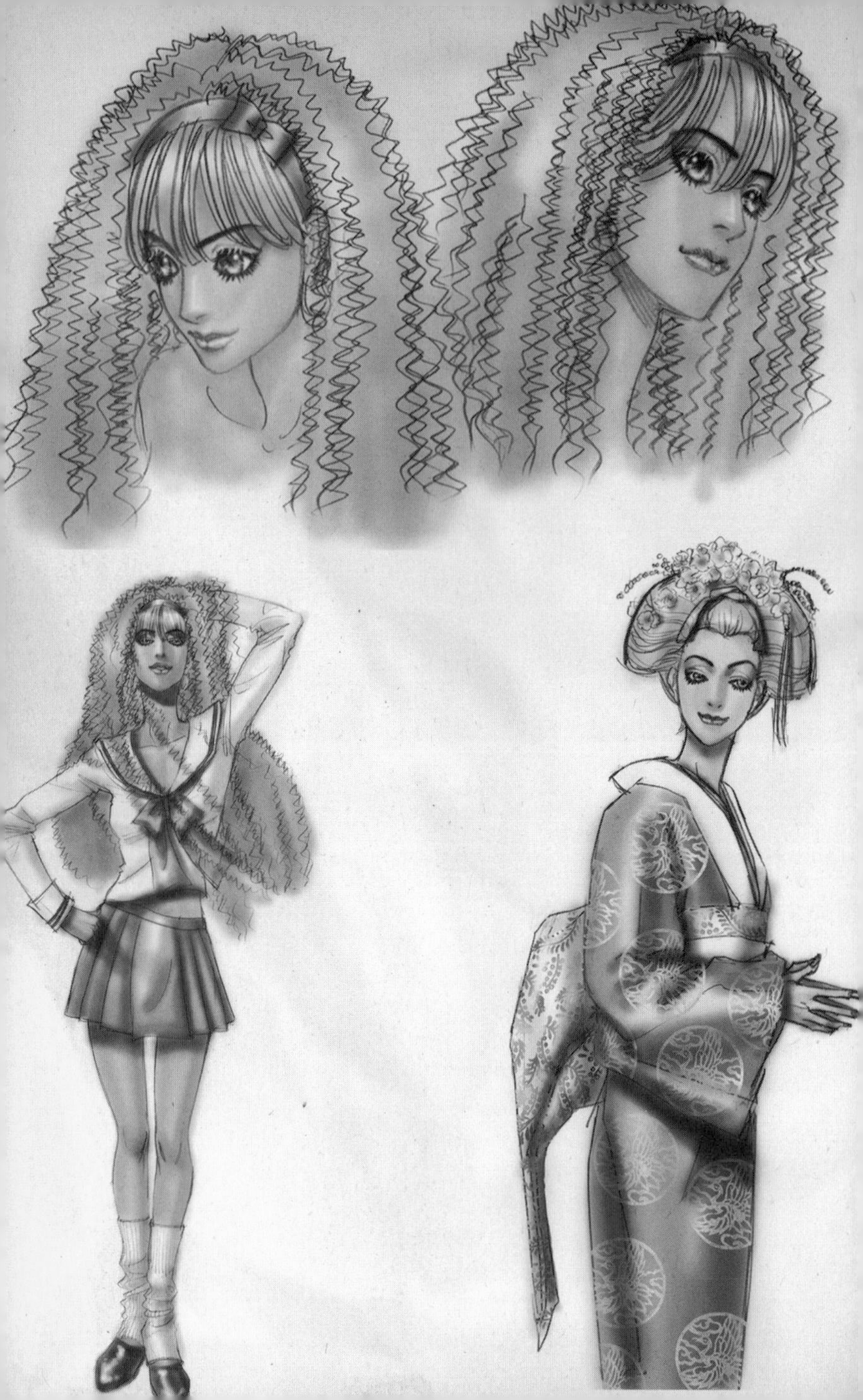

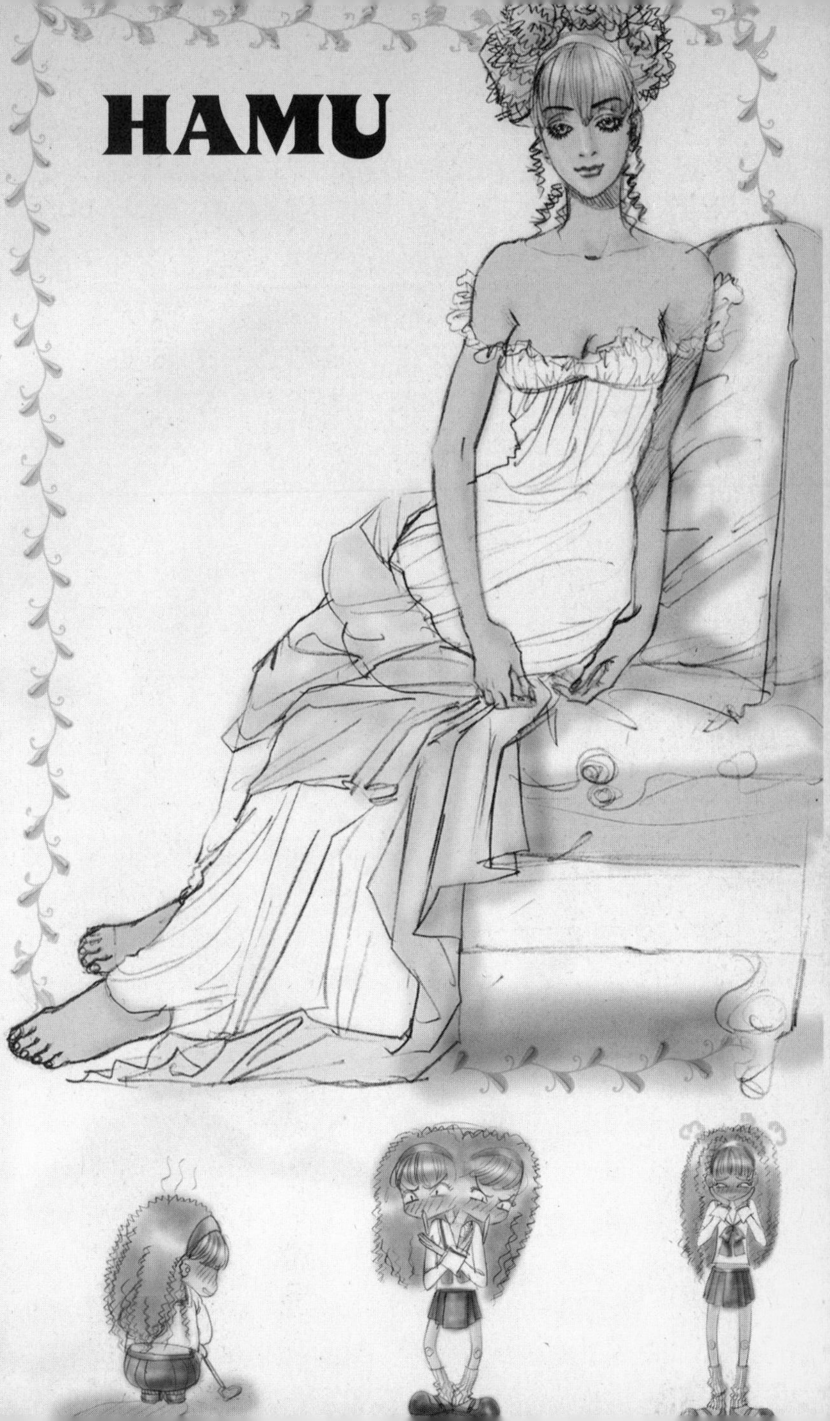
HAMU

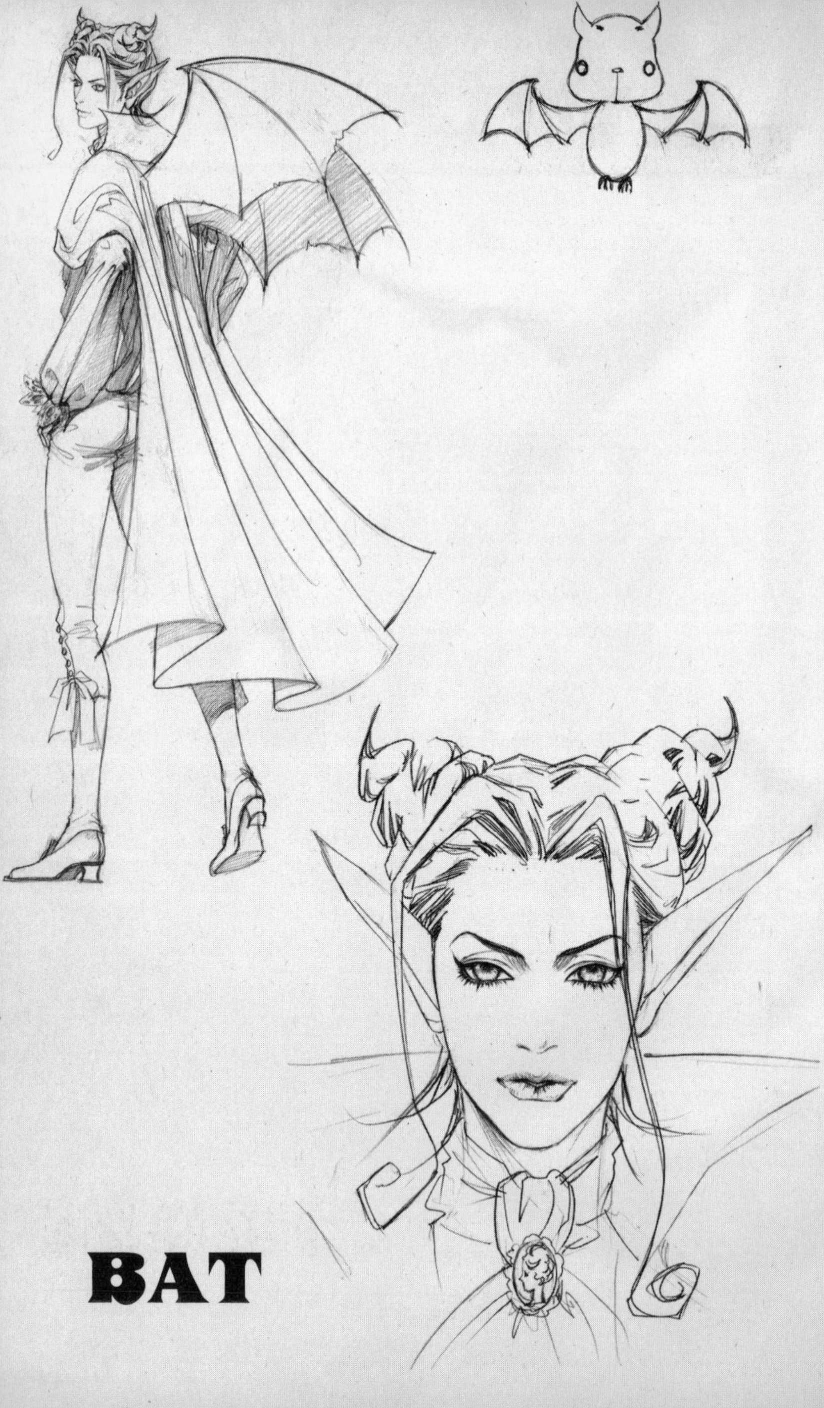

BAT

CRANE

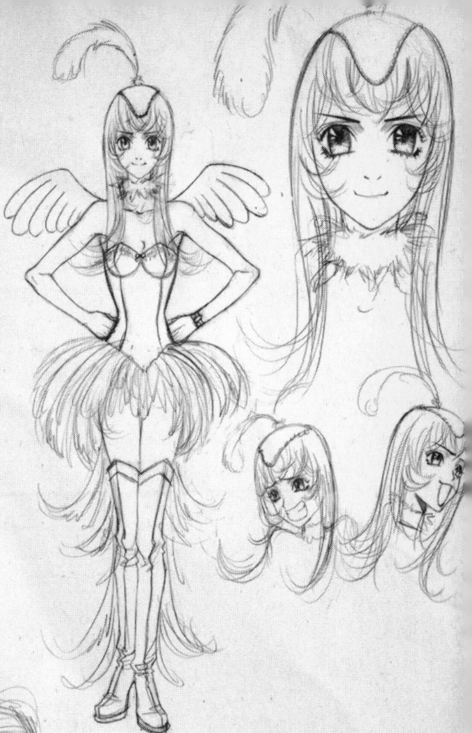

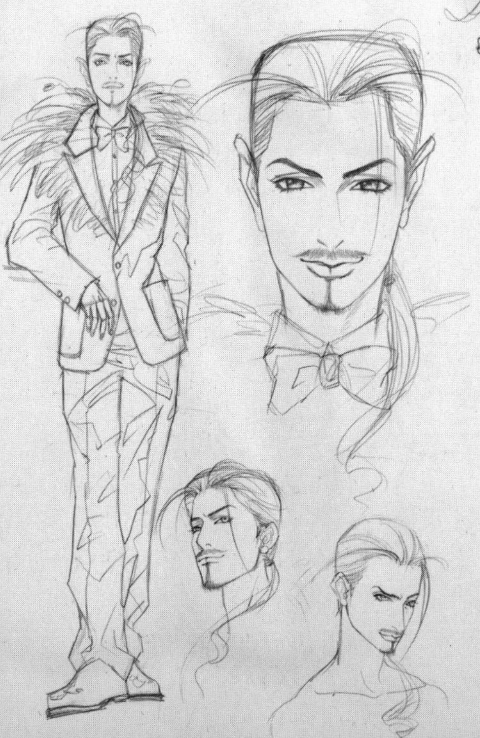

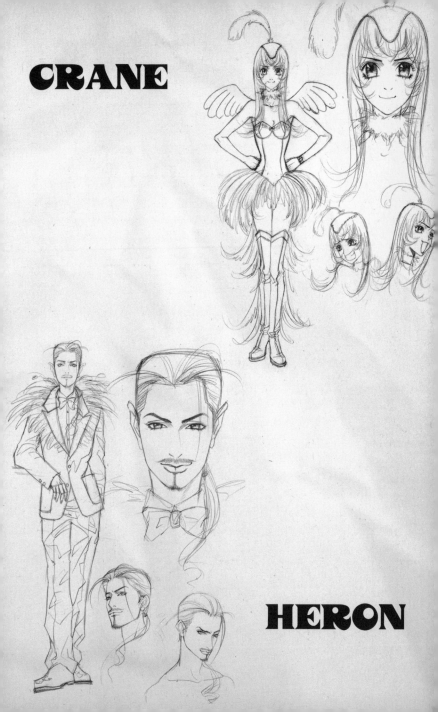

HERON

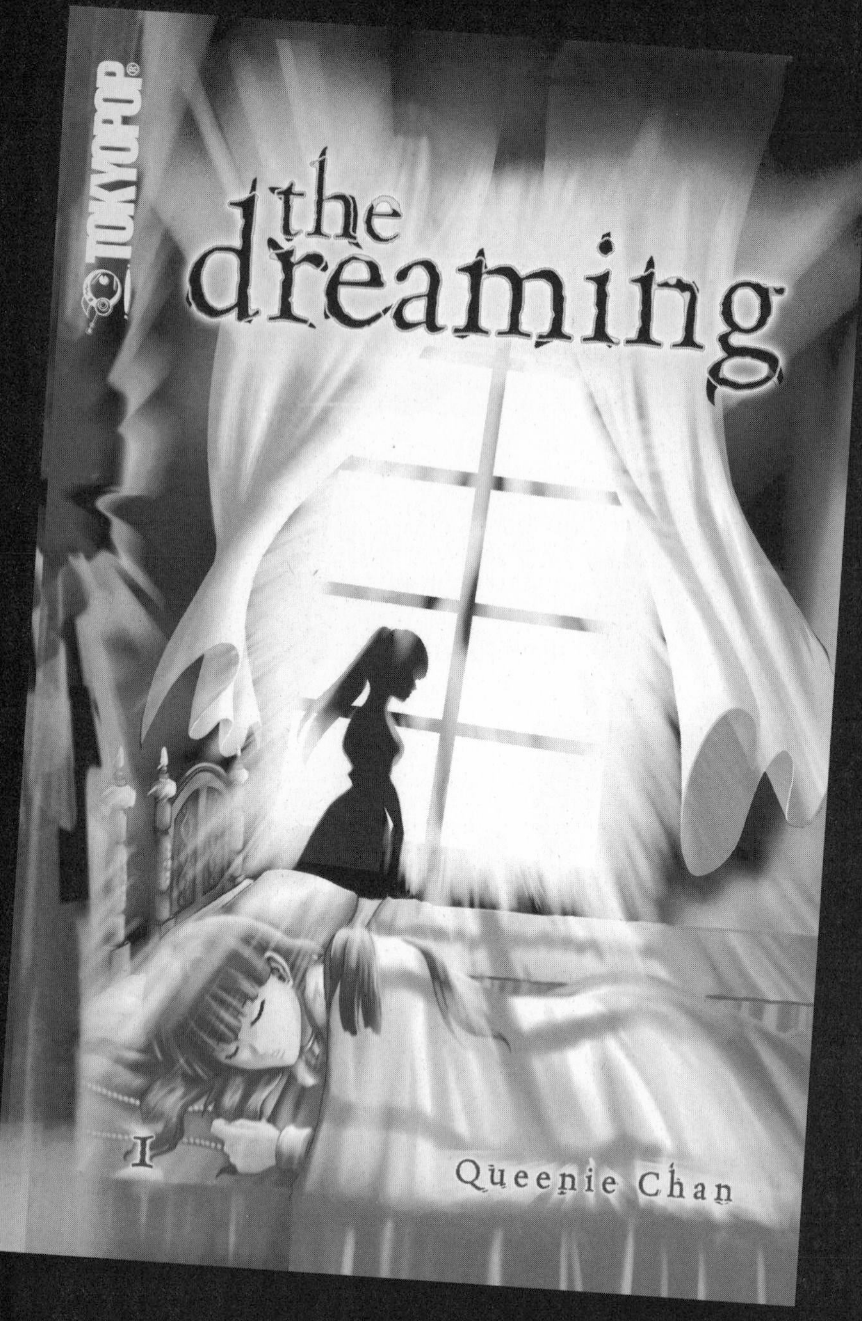
TOKYOPOP
the dreaming
I
Queenie Chan

And now, an exciting first look at a new manga from TOKYOPOP...

When twin sisters Amber and Jeanie are accepted into an exclusive Australian boarding school, their future looks bright. But the school's halls harbor a terrible secret: students have been known to wander into the surrounding bushlands and vanish...without a trace! No one knows where they went--or why. But as Amber and Jeanie are about to learn, the key to the school's dark past may lie in the world of their dreams...

Available Now!

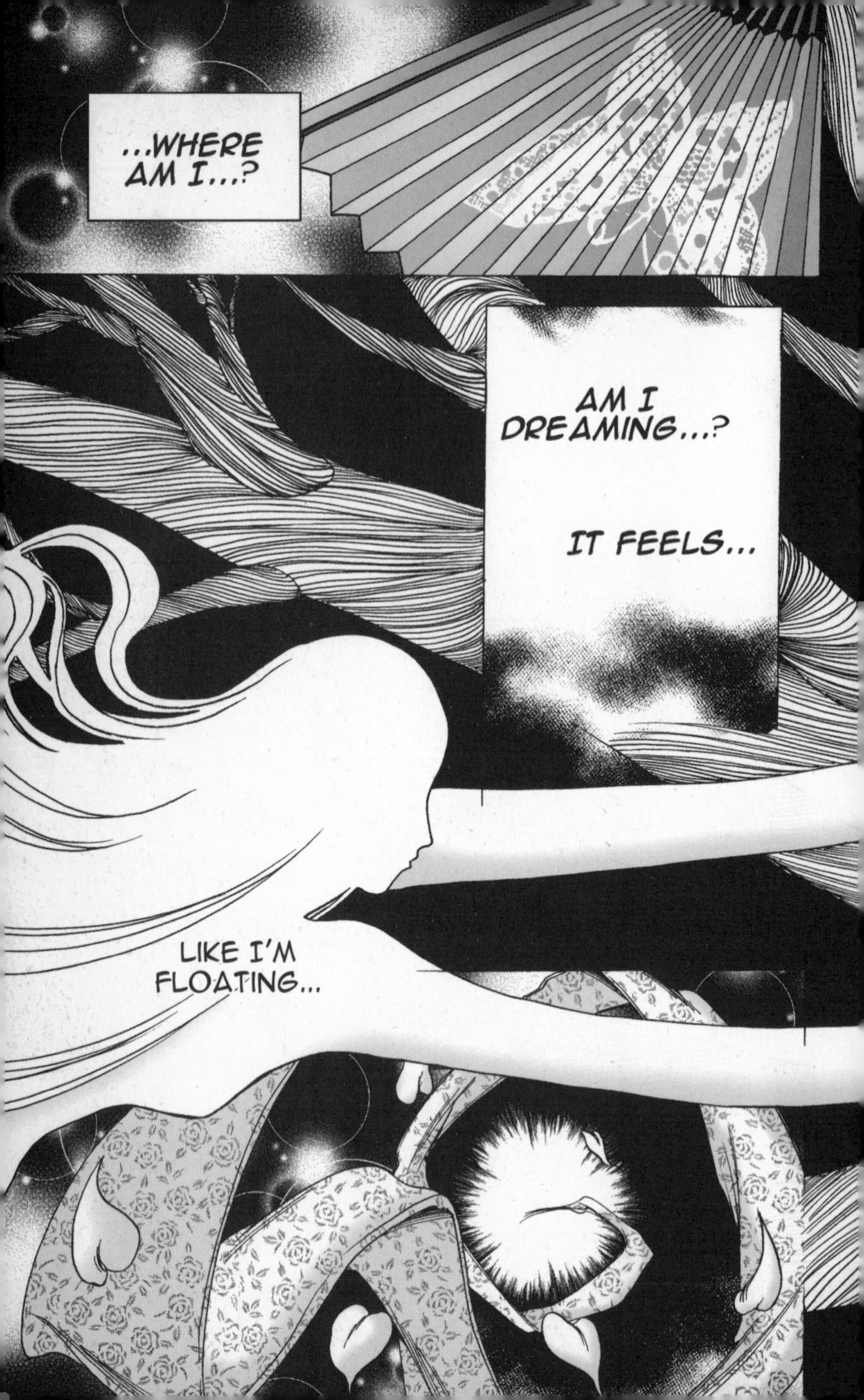
...WHERE AM I...?
AM I DREAMING...?
IT FEELS...
LIKE I'M FLOATING...

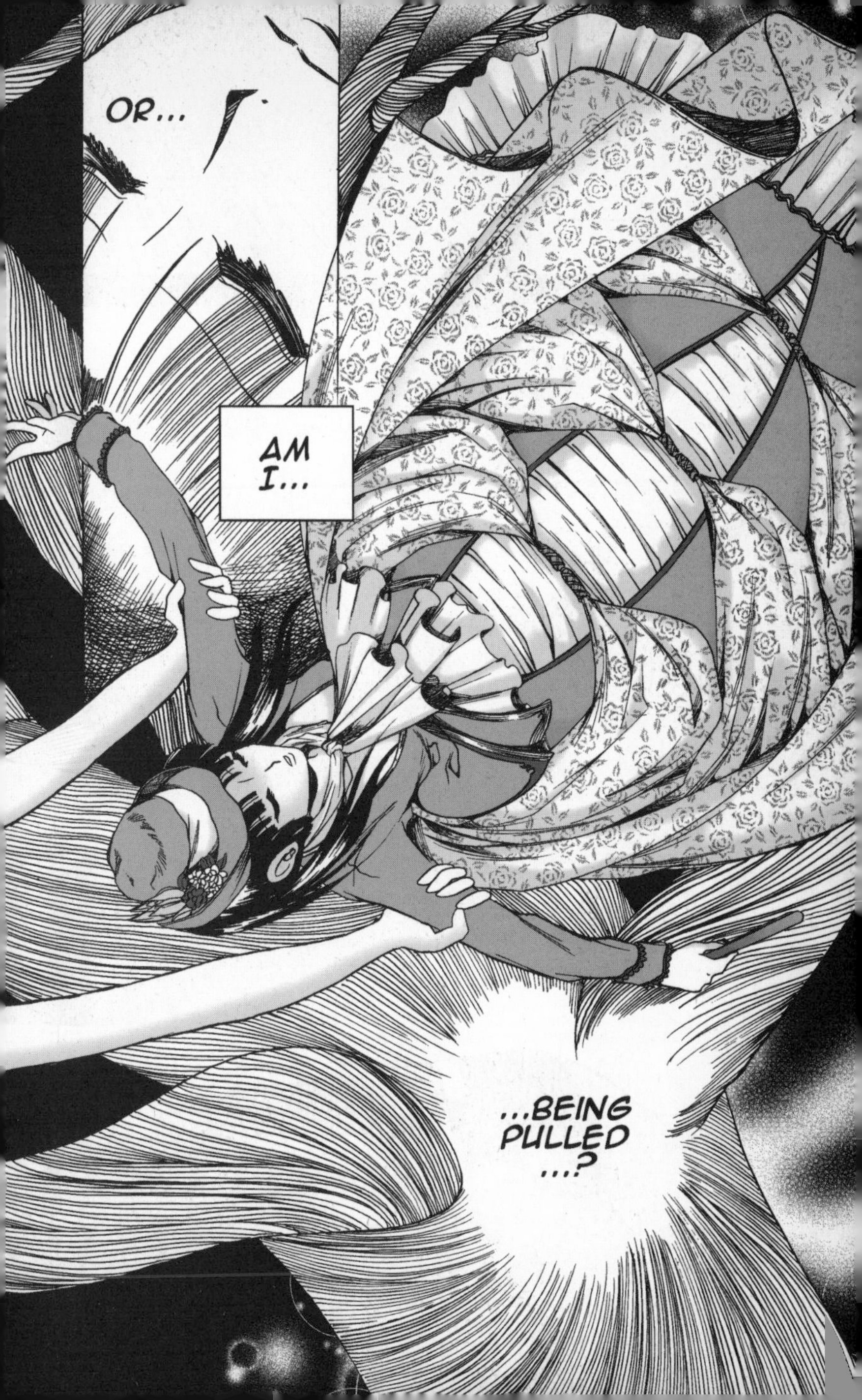
OR...
AM I...
...BEING PULLED ...?

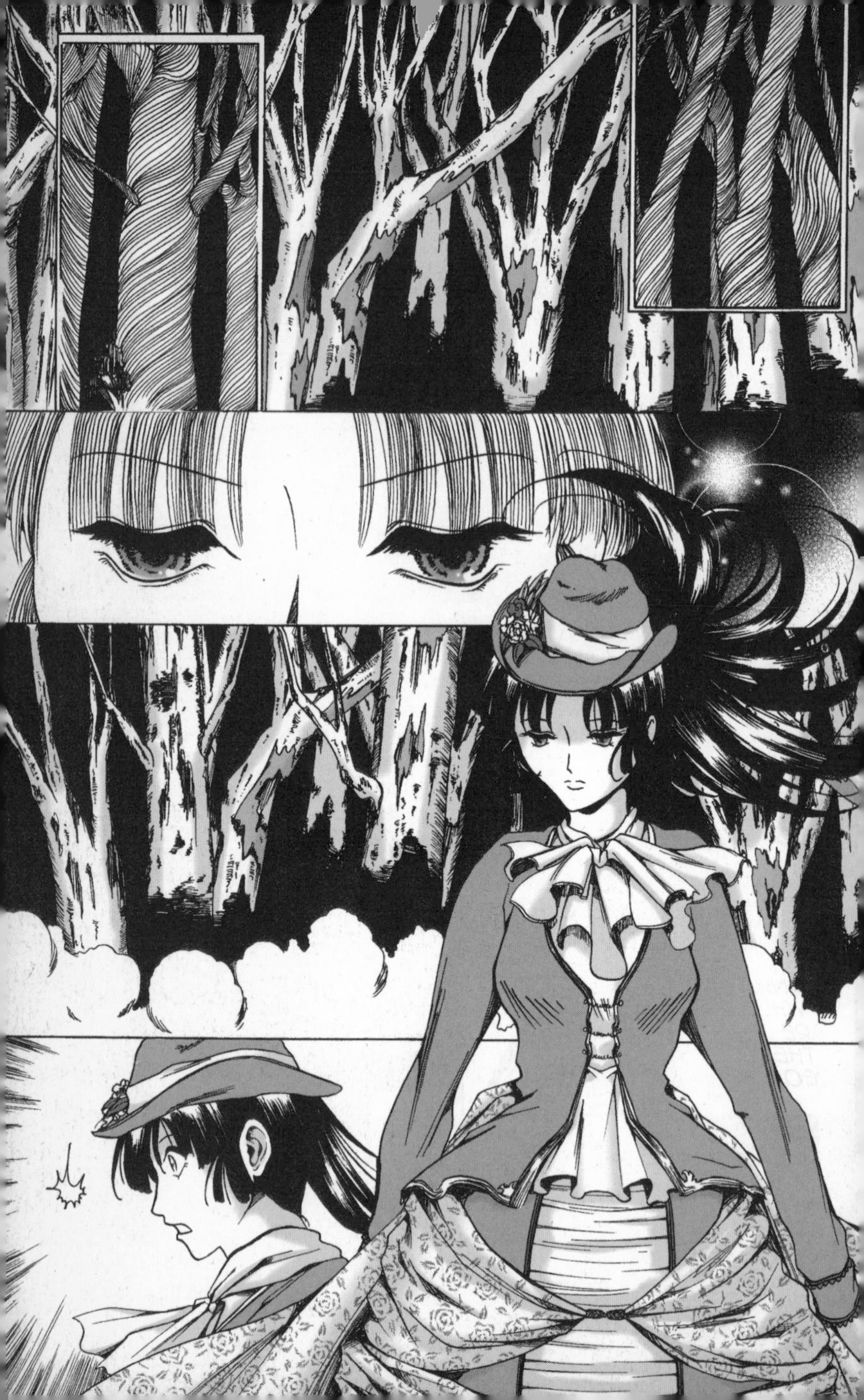

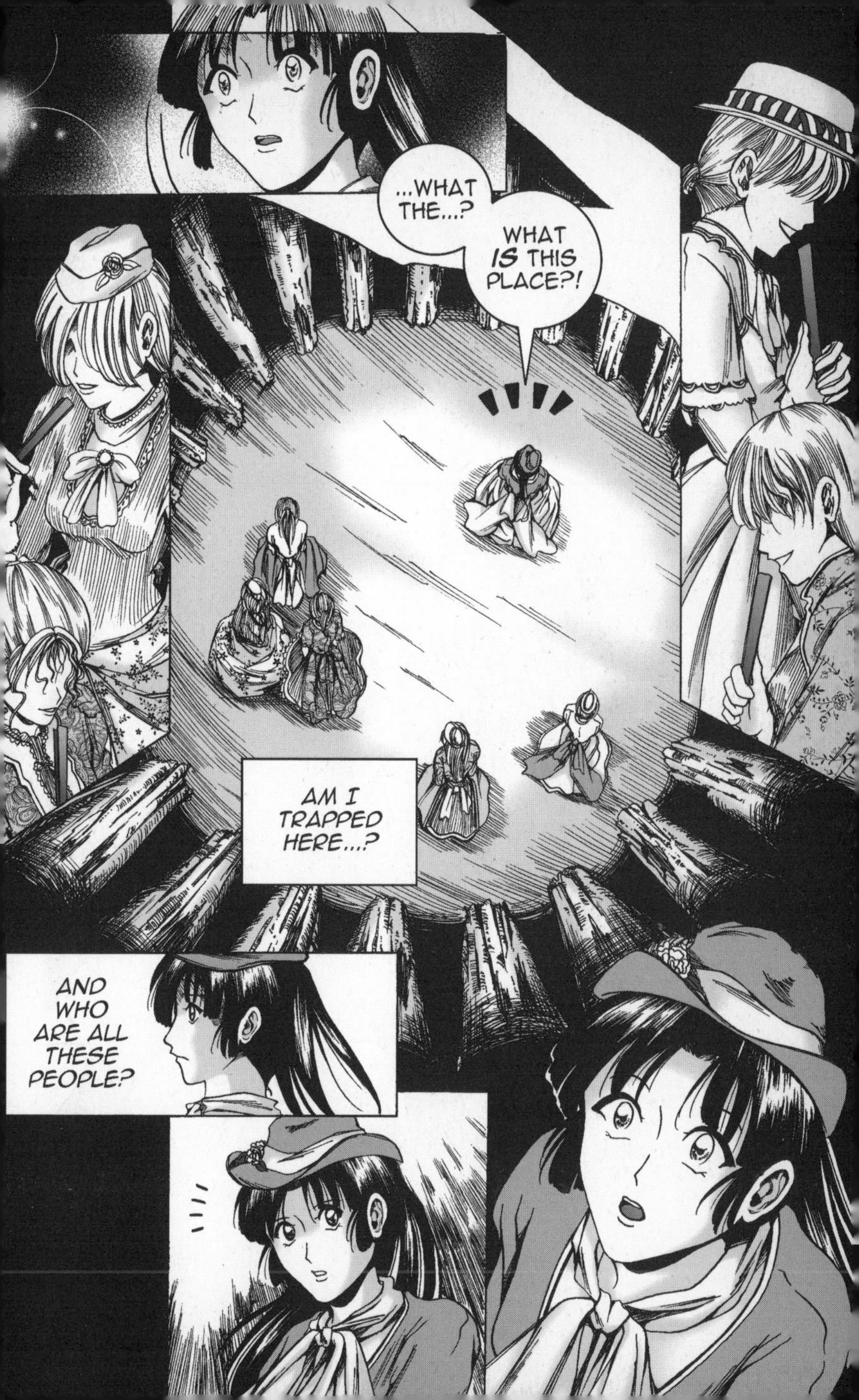
...WHAT THE...?
WHAT *IS* THIS PLACE?!
AM I TRAPPED HERE...?
AND WHO ARE ALL THESE PEOPLE?

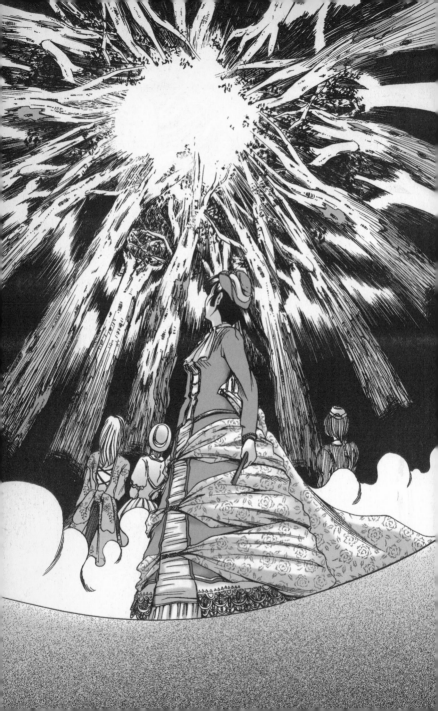

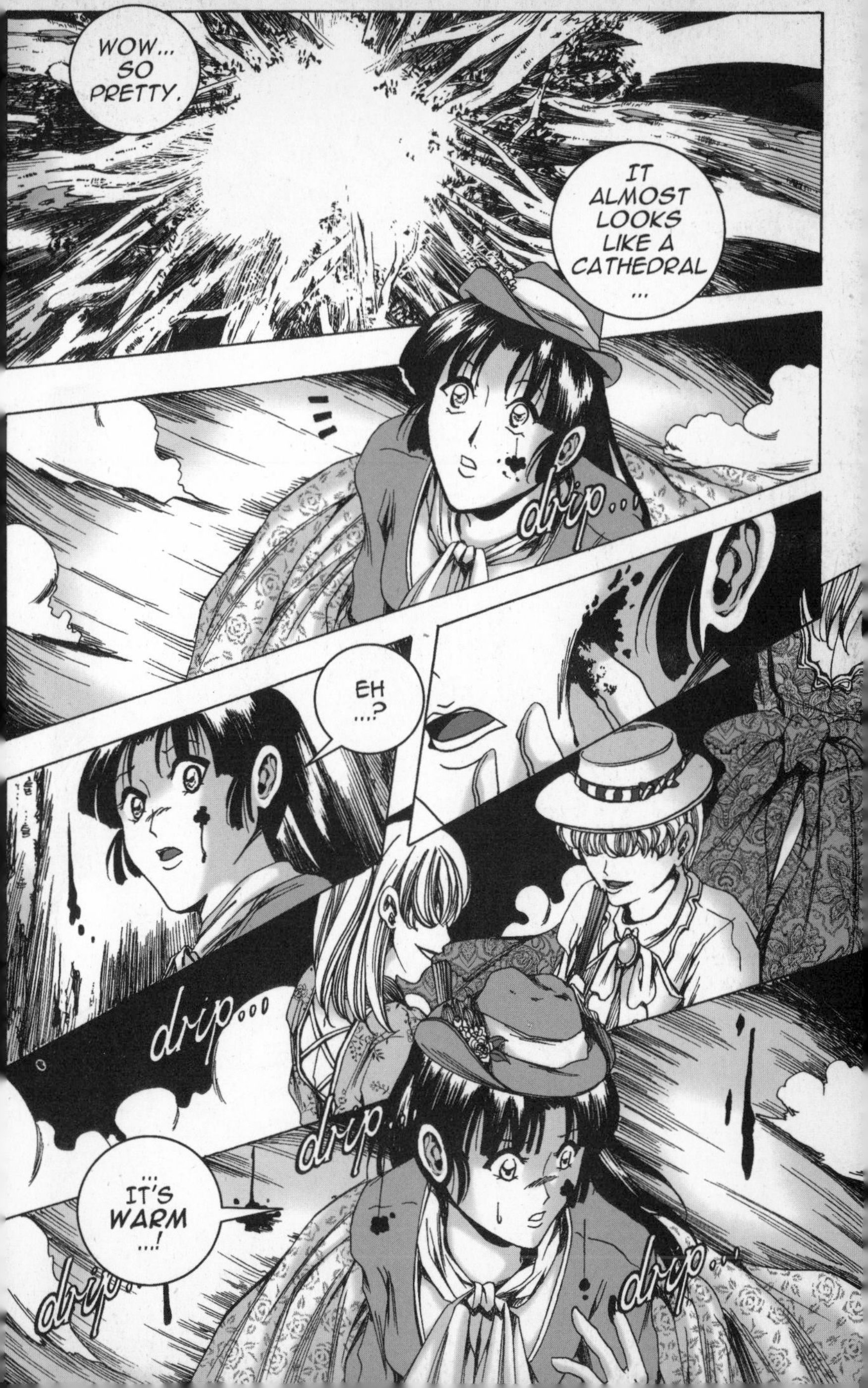
IT ALMOST LOOKS LIKE A CATHEDRAL ...
WOW... SO PRETTY.
drip...
EH ...?
drip...
drip...
... IT'S WARM ...!
drip...
drip...

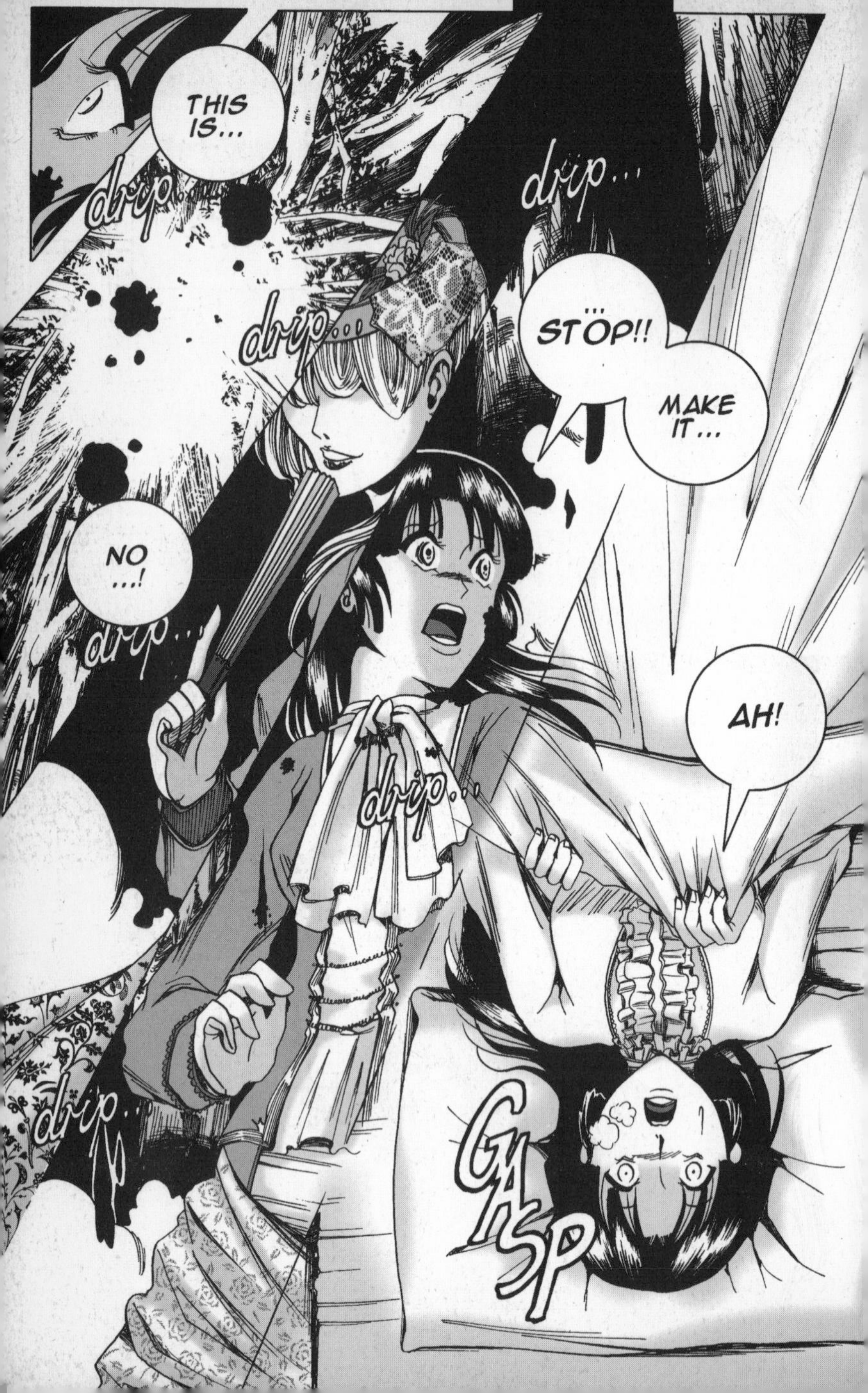
THIS IS...
drip...
drip...
drip...
MAKE IT...
...STOP!!
NO ...!
drip...
AH!
drip...
drip...
GASP

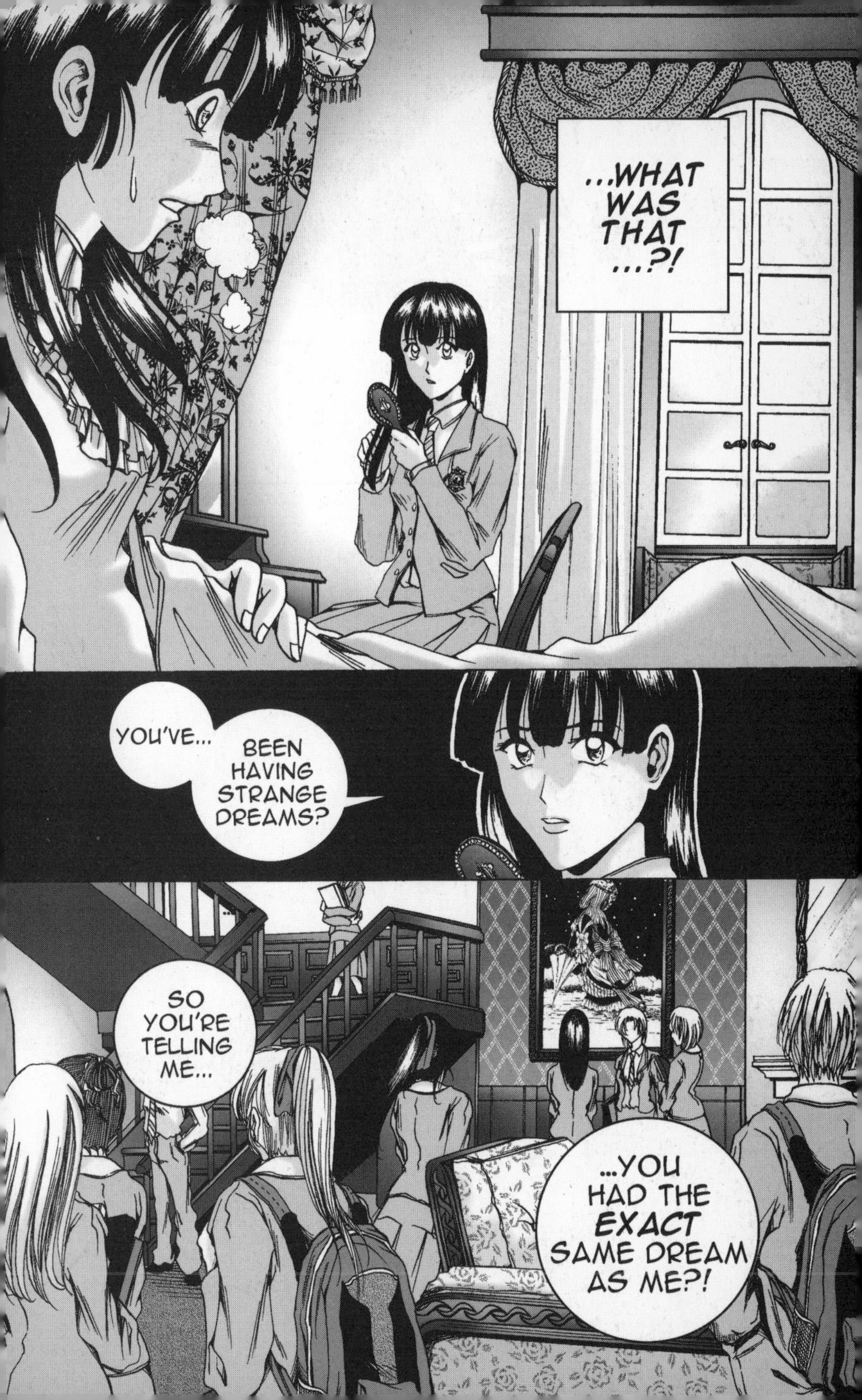
...WHAT WAS THAT ...?!
YOU'VE...
BEEN HAVING STRANGE DREAMS?
SO YOU'RE TELLING ME...
...YOU HAD THE *EXACT* SAME DREAM AS ME?!

TOKYOPOP PRESENTS
MANGA 漫画
THE NEW SIZZLING HOT
MANGA
MAGAZINE
ZELDA AND FRIEND FROM
WAR ON FLESH
©2005 Justin Boring, Greg Hildebrandt and TOKYOPOP
SIGN UP FOR FREE WWW.TOKYOPOP.COM

TOKYOPOP SHOP

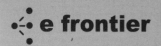

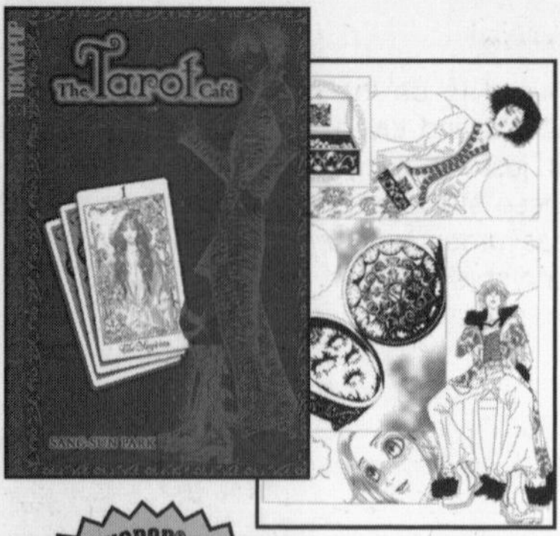
The Tarot Café
SANG-SUN PARK

BY SANG-SUN PARK

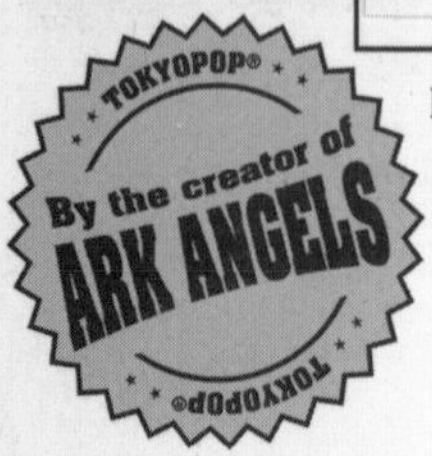
TOKYOPOP®
By the creator of
ARK ANGELS
TOKYOPOP®

THE TAROT CAFÉ

I was always kind of fond of *Petshop of Horrors,* and then along comes *The Tarot Café* and blows me away. It's like *Petshop,* but with a bishonen factor that goes through the roof and into the stratosphere! Sang-Sun Park's art is just unreal. It's beautifully detailed, all the characters are stunning and unique, and while at first the story seems to be yet another Gothy episodic piece of fluff, there is a dark side to Pamela and her powers that I can't wait to read more about. I'm a sucker for teenage werewolves, too.

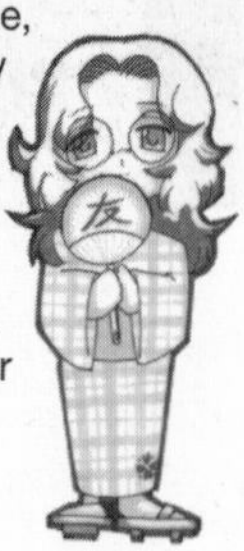

~Lillian Diaz-Pryzbyl, Editor

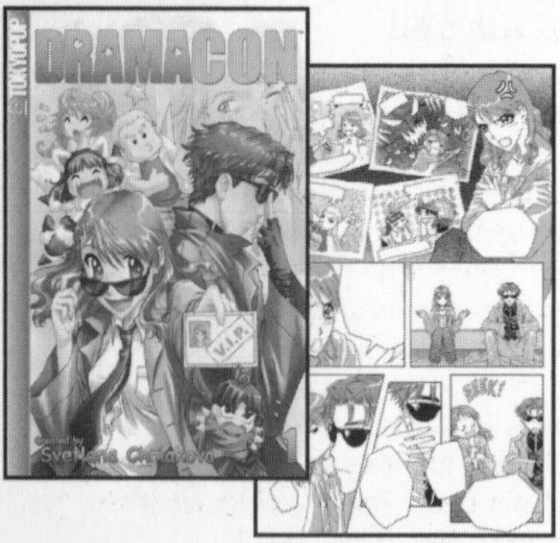
DRAMACON
TOKYOPOP
V.I.P.

BY SVETLANA CHMAKOVA

DRAMACON

I love this manga! First of all, Svetlana is amazing. She's the artist who creates "The Adventures of CosmoGIRL!" manga feature in *CosmoGIRL!* magazine, and she totally rules. *Dramacon* is a juicy romance about a guy and a girl who meet up every year at a crazy anime convention. It grabbed me from the first panel and just wouldn't let go. If you love shojo as much as I do, this book will rock your world.

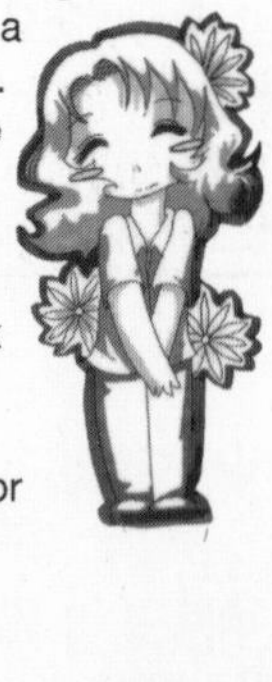

~Julie Taylor, Senior Editor

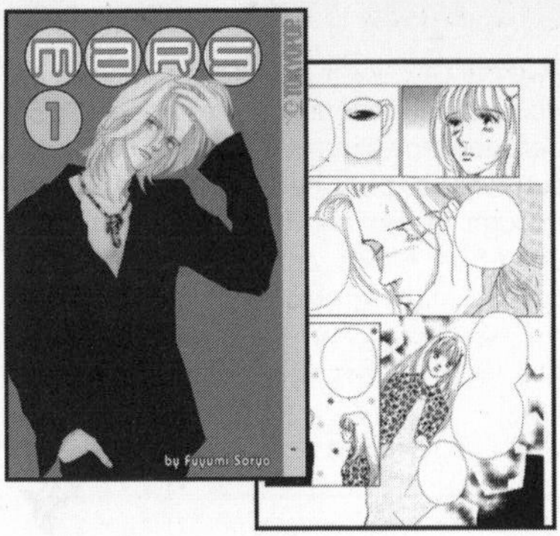
MARS
1
by Fuyumi Soryo

BY FUYUMI SORYO

MARS

I used to do the English adaptation for *MARS* and loved working on it. The art is just amazing—Fuyumi Soryo draws these stunning characters and beautiful backgrounds to boot. I remember this one spread in particular where Rei takes Kira on a ride on his motorcycle past this factory, and it's all lit up like Christmas and the most gorgeous thing you've ever seen—and it's a factory! And the story is a super-juicy soap opera that kept me on the edge of my seat just dying to get the next volume every time I'd finish one.

~Elizabeth Hurchalla, Sr. Editor

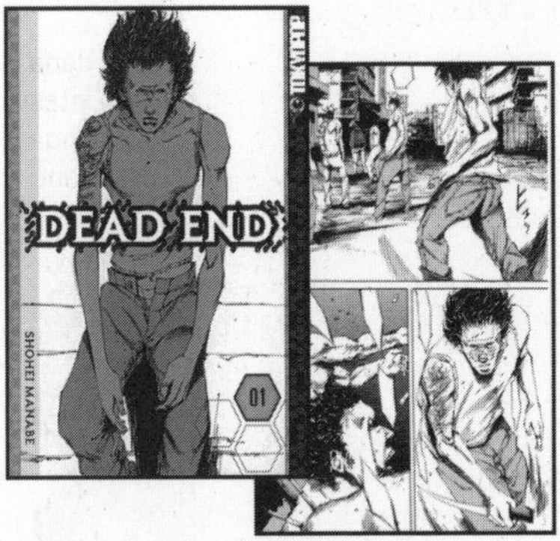
DEAD END
SHOHEI MANABE
01
TOKYOPOP

BY SHOHEI MANABE

DEAD END

Everyone I've met who has read *Dead End* admits to becoming immediately immersed and obsessed with Shohei Manabe's unforgettable manga. If David Lynch, Clive Barker and David Cronenberg had a love child that was forced to create a manga in the bowels of a torture chamber, then *Dead End* would be the fruit of its labor. The unpredictable story follows a grungy young man as he pieces together shattered fragments of his past. Think you know where it's going? Well, think again!

~Troy Lewter, Editor

SHOWCASE

© Granger/Henderson/Salvaggio and TOKYOPOP Inc.

PSY-COMM
BY JASON HENDERSON, TONY SALVAGGIO AND SHANE GRANGER

In the not-too-distant future, war is entertainment—it is scheduled, televised and rated. It's the new opiate of the masses and its stars are the elite Psychic Commandos—Psy-Comms. Mark Leit, possibly the greatest Psy-Comm of all time, will have to face a tragedy from his past...and abandon everything his life has stood for.

War: The Ultimate Reality Show!

T TEEN AGE 13+

© Yasutaka Tsutsui, Sayaka Yamazaki

TELEPATHIC WANDERERS
BY SAYAKA YAMAZAKI AND YASUTAKA TSUTSUI

When Nanase, a beautiful young telepath, returns to her hometown, her life soon becomes more than unsettling. Using her telepathic powers, Nanase stumbles across others who possess similar abilities. On a train she meets Tsuneo, a man with psychic powers who predicts a dire future for the passengers! Will Nanase find her way to safety in time?

OT OLDER TEEN AGE 16+

A sophisticated and sexy thriller from the guru of Japanese science fiction.

© Koge-Donbo

PITA-TEN OFFICIAL FAN BOOK
BY KOGE-DONBO

Koge-Donbo's lovable characters—Kotarou, Misha and Shia—are all here, illustrated in a unique, fresh style by the some of the biggest fans of the bestselling manga! Different manga-ka from Japan have added their personal touch to the romantic series. And, of course, there's a cool, original tale from Koge-Donbo, too!

Pita-Ten as you've never seen it before!

T TEEN AGE 13+